SCATTERED MOONLIGHT

Also by K.C. Harper

Shadowed Moonlight
Shattered Moonlight

Scattered Moonlight

K. C.
HARPER

HODDERSCAPE

First published in Great Britain in 2025 by Hodderscape
An imprint of Hodder & Stoughton Limited
An Hachette UK company

The authorised representative in the EEA is Hachette Ireland,
8 Castlecourt Centre, Dublin 15, D15 XTP3, Ireland (email: info@hbgi.ie)

1

A CIP catalogue record for this title is available from the British Library

Paperback ISBN 978 1 399 72674 0
ebook ISBN 978 1 399 72675 7

Typeset in Plantin Light by Manipal Technologies Limited

Printed and bound in Great Britain by Clays Ltd, Elcograf S.p.A.

Hodder & Stoughton policy is to use papers that are natural, renewable and recyclable products and made from wood grown in sustainable forests. The logging and manufacturing processes are expected to conform to the environmental regulations of the country of origin.

Hodder & Stoughton Limited
Carmelite House
50 Victoria Embankment
London EC4Y 0DZ

www.hodderscape.co.uk

To those who love to love. Who seek it in the light and the dark, and who seek it in the pages of books.

Trigger warnings

Sexual content, profanity, violence, gore, death, protests, terrorist events, war, discussion of pregnancy loss, discussion of death of a parent.

Chapter One

Sweat slicked my spine, running in fine rivulets down the back of my neck. My skin stung, an erratic heat rolling through my body as several small sparks sputtered from my palms. I pulled my power more, practicing my illusions—a power I had developed after taking one of the serums made by my former Coven Leader, Sierra. Secret serums that offered alternate magi abilities. Ones intended to counter the black-market equivalent designed for humans. Ones she'd sold to Zahara, a shady Ithican industrialist on the eastern side of that sealed-tight border between us.

"Sweet sage," I said through my teeth, fighting with everything I had to hold my concentration while my wolfy lover—and newly minted fiancé—Kane, his former Beta, Joaquin, and *my* former ex, Mason, watched me. All cozy-like.

The weight of their attention was too much, so I fixed my gaze on the sterile white wall inside the were's wing of the Recovery Center. The place was a Conclave-run human health facility offering preternatural treatments at the heart of Cambria. And it was also the source of said Conclave's endless income. "Unity for a common cause," as the slogan went . . . as long as you were uber wealthy. A sickening notion that grated on me. A notion that required handling, but we were in a "one problem at a time" kinda triage. And we had a lotta problems.

Mason and I had opted to practice here, seeing as Kane had needed to meet with Joaquin to sort some wolfy things, and hadn't been willing to leave my side. He was hardly ever more than a few steps away since everything had gone down three weeks before. Not that I complained. When we were home, he used his wolves to keep the place protected, but I still needed to practice, and killing three birds with one stone was the best option. Either way, after what Isaac had put us—put *everyone*—through, I couldn't blame him. Isaac had taken enough: our child, my mother, Naomi . . . and time. So much goddamn time. Things we couldn't get back, but we'd been working hard to make up for it.

Forehead creasing, I held my breath, the embers fading.

"Hold it," instructed Mason, my Coven Leader and de facto trainer, adjusting his newly replaced black-rim glasses.

We'd been together for a time after he'd stepped in, helping to pull me from the dark that'd crowded my life when Kane was forced from it. Things between Mason and I had been good … for a time. And I'd tried with him; I really, *really* had. But then my Alpha had exploded his way back into my life, and fight loving him though I'd tried, he'd burrowed himself into my soul. I'd belonged to that wolf way before he'd ever claimed me. It had always been him.

"I don't know how," I whined. Closing my eyes, I drew on my obsidian—a newer one, given when I accepted the place as Mason's Second. A position I hadn't exactly wanted, but one I'd needed in order to counter my changeling stepfather, Isaac. It'd worked. Kinda. I'd thrown up enough red flags about being controlled by him to get my Alpha's attention. But not before Isaac had brokered a deal with the humans. Well, more like one overly problematic and uber-calculating human, Zahara, who had plans of her own. Plans she'd kept exceedingly tight-lipped about. And I couldn't help the knot that formed in my chest at the thought of it.

Why she'd wanted those serums …

My strength waned, then dropped. I frowned. I'd used my new power *successfully* all of exactly once. But since then, nada. I didn't even know how I'd done it, which meant I had *not one clue* how to do it again.

"What am I doing wrong?"

Mason's mouth twisted and he shook his head. "Hells if I know."

Stood to reason, seeing he was an Empath. His forte was reading emotions, definitely not forging illusions. We'd been practicing for days, with less than zero progress. Asking for help might've been an option, if anyone outside of our little magi cluster of two knew what we'd done.

Like he'd plucked the thought from my mind, he said, "We could tell them."

Them … the Coven. I worried my cheek between my teeth.

He shrugged. "We've got at least sixty Illusionists, Briar. They'd be better equipped to help."

The torque of my stomach had bile kissing the back of my throat. That path was bound to breed questions—questions I wasn't sure we could answer. Not truthfully, anyway.

"Not yet."

His gaze pinched at the corners, but he nodded. "Maybe try picturing something in your mind to project."

My chin dipped. "Like what?"

"Whatever you want. Maybe just start small." His disheveled blond hair had gotten long enough for him to pull it into a top knot at the back of his head. It suited him.

That familiar magi strength stirred deep in my chest, quickly joined by another, the very wolfy one that tethered me to Kane. A link that shared healing and life and, as it turned out, a power I could reach out and grab.

I brushed it with my senses.

Kane tensed, then arched a lone brow. "*Easy, Bry,*" he said, his words a low rumble as they rolled across our connection.

I fidgeted with the hem of my knee-length navy wool dress. Warm. Practical. And easy access for Kane to reach up there and—

Mason scrubbed the back of his neck and glanced away. "You've gotta focus, Briar."

Iron fires. I really, really did. It came in spurts, that focus. Something I blamed on the miniature wolf-ling growing inside my womb. That pup had been messing with my head and body ever since they'd taken up residence. Sleep was intermittent, my emotions a chaotic storm.

I loved it and was so damn grateful. But still, a pang of sadness punched my chest. I was excited, so, so excited, seeing as I'd dreamed of having a child with my Alpha for an age. But being forced to hide it, to shove that happiness down and pretend it wasn't real because my ruthless stepfather used anything and any*one* to his advantage, it hurt. A lot. But hurt or no, sharing it was a risk we couldn't take.

My blood ran cold. Seven Iron Hells, we needed to find Isaac, because if we didn't find him fast enough, time *would* reveal us. I couldn't hide my bump forever. Not that I had one, yet. Sometimes I thought I could see one, and this overwhelming jumble of absolute elation and sheer and utter goddamn terror would take me.

I just wanted it over. Wanted to breathe again. Wanted Isaac dead. Wanted to watch the light bleed from his eyes, slowly. My mouth ran dry. I needed him to suffer the way Naomi had, the way my mother and everyone else under his thrall had.

Mason shifted into my sight, but the image of Mom reaching for me in those final moments drowned him out as they seared a painful path across my mind. She'd been a prisoner like the rest of us. But somewhere along the way, she'd given up. Stopped fighting for me. For Lucas. For herself. Not a surprise after everything she'd been through, but I'd never let myself get there. I couldn't do that. *Wouldn't.*

My palm itched to cradle my womb, that protective need and a gut-clenching urge for violence taking me over.

The death and chaos and sheer fucking terror left in my stepfather's wake needed to end decisively … with his goddamn head on a spike.

Mason's brow furrowed questioningly, and I shook myself, trying to control my ragged breaths as I came back to the moment. My mouth tugged to the side, and I took Mason's advice, peering around to get an idea. My gaze settled on the heart tattoo over my right wrist. The one my Alpha had put there.

I pulled on our combined power. It welled in my chest, then stalled, butting up against some invisible wall. A block. A weird one that only showed when I tried directing my strength toward manifesting. Breathing deep, I rolled my shoulders and tried again. But nothing.

Expression twisting, I ran a hand through my long, chestnut-colored hair, pulling it back from my face. "Why is this so hard?"

Joaquin shifted on his chair, hazel eyes flat as he raised his coffee mug, took a long drink, then deadpanned, "Because you're not good at it."

I lobbed a scowl his way. I had not one clue what advantage an Illusionist ability might give, but when it came to Isaac, I'd take every leg-up I could get.

Joaquin had … changed. He took up more space—not physically, but his presence had grown. Having him and my Alpha in the same room was heavy, the air charged with power. It crackled along my skin, making me glad they were friends. After Isaac had used the previous Southern Alpha, Victor, to sick his Pack on Kane, Joaquin had stepped in and ended Victor, which meant taking that Alpha seat. A move he'd made to save Kane, and me. And I thanked the wraith herself for it every day.

It was the best-case scenario having someone we trusted at the top of the Cambrian food chain, but good or not, I missed Joaquin's sullen ass. And with what he'd done, with how it had protected Lucas …

Cambrian law meant being a changeling put a "kill on sight" bounty on my brother's head too. But, thank sage, only a handful knew what blood coursed through his veins, including everyone in that room. He wasn't his father, one of the originals, an escaped torturer from the Deep of the Iron Hells. Not of this world. His kind were known instigators, twisted, with a history of wreaking havoc. Their ability to take on the shape of any sentient thing by simply taking a piece of them made them more dangerous than anything in our world.

I eyed Joaquin. "Have your wolves said anything?"

He shook his head, several strands of that perfectly styled, jet-black hair falling over his temples. "The Pack knew Isaac's house was a V den and that Victor hadn't done shit to handle it. He and Isaac spent enough time together, they figured something was off."

After my mother had been ousted from the Southern Coven, which was Isaac's doing, my stepfather had taken refuge in Victor's territory, which meant his Pack—*Joaquin's* Pack—knew Lucas. Had watched him grow. And *that*, thank the wraith, meant he mattered to them.

Lucky for us, the ones under Isaac's thrall saw first-hand what he'd put Lucas through. They'd seen my brother spiral down that V addiction, his vampire venom drug of choice. One he'd used to escape his father—an addiction he'd only beaten because of my Alpha.

Still, after so long spent hiding it, the idea of anyone knowing what my brother was set my teeth on edge.

"How's Ezra?" I asked, because the way Joaquin's recently minted partner had caught his eye tickled my withered soul. Him being a wicked tattoo artist and our latest Immortal Inc hire was just the cherry on top.

Joaquin cleared his throat and tugged the lapels of his button-down olive-green sweater. "Good."

I smirked.

His stare narrowed in a "shut your banshee mouth" kinda way.

We'd sent word to the rest of the Conclave about Isaac, forgoing the inconvenient details about his changeling blood line and Ivy being the source of his venom. Danika, the Southern Dowager, had already been on edge about losing her sisters. We figured her learning that Ivy, one of said sisters, had been alive the whole time before Cassandra Ryton, Danika's Northern counterpart, had ultimately killed her to free us all, wasn't likely to go down well.

"You can do this, Bry," Kane encouraged, dragging a hand through his hair. It was freshly cut with gunmetal gray along its shorter sides, fading to silver and white in its longer top lengths.

I itched to run my fingers through it. My touch brushed that claiming mark along the length of my throat, gaze sliding to his as he watched from across the room. His slate hoodie fit his broad shoulders as he leaned against the doorframe like he was holding it up. His thick, corded arms were folded over his chest, that silver topaz stare locked on me, because my Alpha needed me in sight. The feeling was mutual: I needed that wolf more than I needed air. He was a part of me, a part I couldn't function without. And planning our wedding, to tie myself to him in that final way, had been the light in the dismal dark.

He must've read that thought from my expression because those eyes flashed, going voltaic.

My body heated and I trailed my tongue along the back of my teeth.

Joaquin cleared his throat.

I blinked, trying to quell that wanton need, and succeeding. Mostly.

"Have you heard anything about Isaac?" Mason asked, the question a hard smack back to reality.

Kane's expression darkened as he shook his head. "Nothing." He chucked his chin Mason's way. "You?"

Mason frowned. "Nothing."

I didn't know what was worse, the shit Isaac had stirred, or the silence left in his wake. It made us all paranoid, looking over our shoulders, like he might be there, lurking, hidden behind someone else's face, just out of sight. We'd looked for that bite-shaped scar I'd given him years before on everyone we met, with no damn luck.

Kane and Mason had formed a truce, of sorts. My Alpha had been grateful for my ex sticking by my side after my stepfather had compelled me to leave him, but—though he'd not voiced it since—there would always be a part of him, the wolf inside, that couldn't settle in Mason's presence. And I got it, because Kane's own former fling, Whitney, had helped him in my absence. A lot had happened in the time since, and while she and Theo seemed entirely smitten with each other, it didn't mean I wanted her and my Alpha turning besties.

I trusted him with my entire being, but I was a greedy wench who refused to share.

Kane's low growl rolled through my mind. "*You're making it real hard not to throw you against that wall and fuck you senseless right now, Bry.*"

I offered him a lascivious smile before I trailed my tongue along my bottom lip. "*Promises, promises.*"

He cocked a lone, challenging brow. And, sage, I loved that side of him. Loved the trial of wills—a trial my big bad *always* won. But I lived to poke his wolf. To play. And he loved to let me. *Only* me.

"*Test me, Bry.*"

It might've been everything we'd been through or my wildly rampant hormones, but I couldn't shut down the need for him. It consumed me. All the time. There was no beginning or end. I was in-fucking-satiable, which was a problem, 'cause so was he.

Something tightened low in my belly, and heat pooled between my thighs.

Kane's stare dipped there. He pushed off that wall.

A heavy *thump, thump, thump* sounded at the door. My adrenaline spiked, head whipping that way—muscle memory kicking in because my Isaac-based fear was on point.

Stepping back, my hand shot to my abdomen.

Kane's eyes flashed. "It's Theo." He stalked to the door, his solid, broad, densely muscled shoulders and that I'm-the-biggest-of-the-badasses gait on full display as he moved. Stretching his neck, he pulled the door wide.

My Alpha's cousin sauntered in, but there was a hitch in his typically playful stride. It had been there ever since he'd lost his sister, Naomi, to Isaac. My stepfather had killed her to thieve her genetic makeup, to build a serum that gave humans the ability to become weres … for a time. A serum he'd given to Zahara. Fucking Isaac. Always fucking Isaac.

Theo gestured Mason's way. "You ask her yet?"

My gaze narrowed and roved between them. "Has he asked who what?"

Mason linked his hands before him and pivoted to face me, expression flat. Serious. Pure Coven Leader. "I've received a formal request. Whitney's asked for a transfer."

My gaze flicked to my Alpha, whose stare stayed locked on mine. There was no response. No feelings there. Every part of him belonged to me.

"*Your call, Bry,*" he silently said.

Theo set his hip against a table along the far wall, a desperate, almost pleading look in his eyes that stopped my heart in its tracks, because he needed this. It was written in the pulse at his neck. The anxious bounce of his foot. He needed something to look forward to. Some*one*. He needed not to feel alone.

And on that, I'd never make him wait. "I'm good with it."

Theo's chest sagged on his exhale.

Mason inclined his head. "We'll have to make it official with the Coven."

"I'm ready when she is," I said, body sagging as a wave of exhaustion took me over. I yawned, eyes drooping. Iron fires, I was tired. Turned out growing my mate's babe took a lotta energy … like, pretty much all of it.

Perceptive as ever, Kane closed in, his warm, calloused hand landing on my waist while his musk and wilderness scent filled my senses. His eyes tracked between my own. "We done for now?"

My Coven Leader nodded, then said to me, "I'll text you with a day."

Light caught on my engagement ring: the three-carat princess-cut one I was utterly obsessed with. Life being haywire meant Kane and I hadn't sorted the details yet, but we *had* settled a few things.

"Mason, wait," I said, movements jerky as I smoothed my dress. "There's something I wanted to ask you." My gaze flicked to my Alpha.

Kane stretched his neck and inclined his head. Stalking to the door, he and Joaquin stepped into the hall, still in sight, but giving us the semblance of privacy. Not that they wouldn't hear, with those preternatural ears of theirs. But really, it was the thought that counted.

Clasping my hands before me, I turned to Mason, decidedly nervous. Yeah, we'd worked things out between us. To me, he'd become a friend, but I had a suspicion where his feelings for me still fell. Regardless, he'd been a part of my life—an integral part—for far too long. I wouldn't turn my back on him.

"You probably figured out Kane and I are, um"—I raised that engagement ring—"getting married." I swallowed around the dryness in my throat. "We don't have a date yet. Still just planning, but … I wanted to let you know. Tell you you're invited."

His eyes widened, then creased at the corners as he pushed his glasses up his nose.

"You don't need to answer now," I fumbled. "I just wanted to put it out there. Let you know you're wanted."

Kane shifted in the hall.

"Yeah." Mason ducked his head and smiled, and while it was tight, it still touched his copper eyes. "Of course I'll go." He scrubbed a hand over his hair. "I'm happy for you, Briar."

He'd said it before, but this time, I truly believed it—and the warmth in his tone told me that so did he.

My chest fell as I let go of the breath I'd been holding. Easy. Relieved. "Thank you."

His laugh was rich and genuine. "Who knows? Maybe by then I'll have someone."

My smile was full. Sage, I hoped he would, because Mason Beckett *was* a great guy. Just not the right one for me.

We aimed for the door, joining Kane and Joaquin as we cleared out to leave. The RC was shaped like its logo, a cross, with the lobby at its heart, which is exactly where we were headed.

Joaquin moved in, flanking my side, his stride easy. Lithe.

Nudging him with my elbow, I said, "Alpha-dom suits you."

He side-eyed me.

"And it's a relief problem-solving stuff without all that"—I flicked my hand in his general direction—"Victor-induced wolfy bullshit."

"Wolfy bullshit?" he drawled.

I plunked my hands on my hips. "Yeah. You heard me."

Rounding the corner, the sunproof glass doors of the exit came into view. The place was wildly sterile, the orange lounger chairs that lined the waiting room the only pops of color. Well, that and the backlit cross that hung behind the front desk. Each one of its ends representing a group: magi, shadow walkers, wolves, and humans.

Kane stiffened and my chest constricted as I caught a head of white-blonde hair in the periphery of my vision.

Cassandra stood at the head of the shadow-walker wing. Her pale and semi-translucent skin was beautiful against the slim-fitting jade-green dress she wore, which was far more modern than her usual style. Her long, delicate fingers were linked together as she spoke to one of her people.

I stopped dead, blood running cold.

The walker with her turned, offering us a nod, but she didn't look. She would've known I was there, 'cause sure as the Iron Hells, she'd scented me. But still, those crimson eyes stayed averted.

Because I'd lied.

But she'd been there, had fought to break me free of my stepfather's hold. Had killed Ivy to do it. She'd become a friend, one I'd been forced to betray to keep Lucas's forbidden bloodline a secret. I'd done what I'd needed to do to protect him, and would do it again if I had to. But it didn't mean there hadn't been fallout. A painful one.

She hadn't come for my brother. But whether it was caution or because she'd readied a horde for an ambush to take us all down, I didn't know.

My heart twisted and I flinched.

Mason gripped his obsidian, throwing a cocoon around our conversation to shield it. "Has she talked to you yet?"

I shook my head. I'd tried. Sage knew I'd tried, but she hadn't returned a single one of my calls. I'd considered driving to her territory, pounding down that penthouse door, had climbed into the truck to do just that any number of times, but my Alpha had hauled me back out, 'cause crossing without invitation was a good way to have my throat violently removed.

Pressure built in my chest. I needed to do something. Try again. Running a hand along my upper arm, I advanced a step toward her.

Pivoting, she dismissed me, giving me her back as she glided away.

My throat tightened, and my heart sank. Tears pricked my eyes, because I wanted her back. Actually missed her. I needed to find a way to bridge the cavern I'd dug between us, but hells if I knew how.

Chapter Two

The buzz of Ezra's tattoo gun carried through Immortal Inc early the next evening as he finished up with his last client of the day.

Mason had texted a few hours before to let me know Whitney's joining was scheduled for Friday, in two days' time.

Light from the black chandelier overhead cast a surprisingly warm glow across the space. Sample sketches lined the teal back wall, and dark-stained hardwood and black crown molding set a warm vibe. It wasn't the perfect mirror of Kane's mother's former shop, but it was close. And I loved it.

Ezra tucked a strand of his bone-straight, coal-black hair behind his ear. He was an Omega, lower in Joaquin's Pack, less inclined to temper, and endlessly patient—which was an A-plus package, seeing as he was also the wolf my brother apprenticed under.

"See this," Ezra said, his angular chestnut eyes narrowing as he pushed his thin silver-rimmed glasses on top of his head and pointed to the edge of the design he'd inked on the shadow walker, some kind of crest.

Not just any crest. Cassandra's. I swallowed hard, then cut into the box of supplies I'd lugged over from the Recovery Center and started restocking the shelves.

Lucas inclined his head at Ezra, violet eyes locked.

I swore my brother had gained another inch in the weeks since everything had gone down. If I hadn't known better, I'd have pegged him for a wolf. He'd outgrown his wardrobe, all of it. Shirts fitting too tight. Pants running too short. Which was exactly why we'd started finishing that unfinished basement for him to take over. To give him room to grow.

He was still gangly, but he'd been slowly filling in, 'cause the kid always had food in his mouth.

No, not a kid. After everything he'd seen, everything he'd lived through, he'd lost that innocence. And thank sage it hadn't tainted him.

"We'll go over it again in the next sitting to give it more definition." Ezra hovered his gun over the curve of that crest. "Then we'll shade this section so it's got some depth."

He was a walking advertisement, tattoos covering his neck, and arms—well, what I could see of them below his crisp black dress shirt, the sleeves of which he'd tugged up to the elbows.

Tapping the pedal for the hydraulic chair, he lowered it.

The walker stood, her crimson stare inspecting his work. "This is impressive, wolf."

It wasn't an insult, more a begrudging acceptance.

Lucas grabbed the cleaning cloth and sprayed down the red leather of the seat, readying Ezra's station for the next day. That done, he lined several vials of ground were claws on a three-tiered metal tray. Preternaturals healed too fast for human tattoos, but claws scarred us all, so mixing this powder with the ink made it the permanent sort of artwork.

The front door swung wide, and Joaquin sauntered in, his hazel stare flashing when it fixed on Ezra, then holding. And holding.

I cleared my throat.

Joaquin blinked, snapping from his trance before his attention tracked to me. "Briar."

"Alpha," I said with a gallant bow and a flourished hand. "How fare thee?"

He stared at the ceiling like it would give him patience.

Ezra's mouth lifted at the corners. "I'll be ready in five."

The Southern Alpha adjusted his fitted vest, then linked his hands before him, a soft blush staining his cheeks. "Take your time."

I grinned.

The shadow walker sauntered my way and pulled out a wallet. Her crimson eyes were impersonal, her expression flat. Nothing about her screamed hostile. Either Cassandra had kept Lucas's dangerously illegal bloodline quiet, or her people were super good at keeping their mouths shut.

My phone buzzed and I plucked it up, heart fluttering at the name that flashed across the screen. Lisa Xing, the owner of No Man's Land, my old workplace, and also the bestest friend a girl could have.

"Lucas," I said, gesturing between the cash and the vamp. "Would you mind? I've gotta take this."

His nod was eager, that mahogany-colored hair falling around his handsome, lean face as he bounded his way over. "Got it."

Heading for the back office, I sealed myself in and answered. "Hey, you."

"Ugh. I miss your stupid face, chickie," Lisa said, voice carrying over my phone's speaker as I set it at the edge of the desk. Well, Kane's desk that I'd confiscated. Not that he'd minded, 'cause he wanted my things, my *touch*, everywhere. Our business. Our home. Anyone else taking over an Alpha's territory was the equivalent of pissing over their piss, a call for war. But I wasn't just anyone.

Popping open the top drawer, I tugged a catalog free—one with the baby supplies I'd spent weeks combing through, drawing heart shapes around all the things I loved. Entire collections of furniture and blankets, mobiles and toys. Things I couldn't have ... not yet.

The air in the room was warm. Maybe. Or it could've just been my pregnant ass not regulating my temperature *again*. I tugged at the collage of my pale yellow dress to cool myself. Sage, it was never-ending. Too hot, too cold. Hungry, or full. Bouncing or exhausted. I blamed my wolf and his big bad genetics, something I reminded him of. Often.

"I miss you, too," I said, slipping off my restrictive shoes and wiggling my toes into the new, plush, indigo-colored rug I'd ordered. Sweat slicked my skin as I unzipped the front of my dress, exposing my lacy white thong and bra. "How're things on your side?"

She huffed. "Lots of infighting."

My brow furrowed as I side-eyed the phone. "Infighting?"

"Yeah. Some anti-government faction causing trouble."

I sat straighter in my chair. *Ithican* anti-government? That was new. "What kinda trouble?"

"Protests."

Maybe we had different definitions, but… "That doesn't sound like trouble—"

"Protests where they burn cars, attack anyone with an opposing view, and call for bombing Cambria."

But of course. 'Cause that wouldn't stir up the shittiest of shitstorms. There were a thousand reasons to want Cambria's beasties dead, but with our borders the vacuum-sealed kinda shut and neither side having access to the other, that logic wasn't exactly tracking. "What triggered it?"

"They think Ithica should've acted when the mess with the Phantom started. That our own people were killed because our government did nothing to counter preternaturals. They say our leadership looks weak because of the inaction, and that it'll happen again. That we should have—"

"Bombed us into oblivion?"

"Yes," she said, tone dry. "That."

"Wonderful. They sound lovely." Not that I blamed them for that anger; Cambria's beasties meant we *were* dangerous. And our Conclave not getting their egos together had cost many lives, including human ones. But with Ithica's iron-wielding military, they weren't exactly helpless.

"Indeed." She sighed. "They're a small group for now, but they're gaining traction."

"What're the politicians saying?"

There was a clank as if she were moving a pot. "They're disagreeing on how to handle things. It's a mess. But most think after the Conclave's willingness to open a line of communication with us, and actively assisting our people in getting out of Cambria when things went down with Isaac, it would be 'imprudent to sever ties', and that maintaining a relationship with Cambria is 'necessary for Ithican security'.

'Cause if they cut us off, the chances we'd help again were less than zero. "And how, exactly, do you know all of this?"

Her laugh was sharp. "Bower's been keeping me in the loop."

Bower Caddel, the Ithican Ambassador to Cambria. The same human we'd brought in to give a peek behind the big, supernaturally thick curtain. Because the more looped in to our world they were, the less likely they'd be to take the lethal kind of issue with it. So far, anyway.

I flicked the end of my pink and fuzzy pen, spinning it in a circle. "And why would he do that?"

"Because I'm useful to him." There was a grin in her voice—the proud and toothy kind.

I barked a laugh. "You mean you and No Man's Land are a direct link to an endless tap of information?"

The hiss of something boiling over. "Sure am."

My smile was genuine and reached my eyes. Sage, I couldn't wait till she was allowed to leave Ithica, cross the border between our worlds. I loved my Alpha, but Lis was different. She'd been there when my life was the heart-crushing sort of dark. She'd given me a job, helped pull me out from those shadows. I wanted her back in Cambria.

Her tone gentled. It wasn't soft, 'cause Lisa Xing didn't do soft. But easy. "How're you doing?"

I breathed slow and deep. I flicked the pen again and it veered toward the desk's edge. Lunging, I caught it before it could fall. "Better. Feel like I can breathe again. You?"

"Same." Another clank. "How's Kane?"

Wolfish. Menacing. Out for Isaac's fucking head. "Protective."

"You complaining?"

"Not even a little." My Alpha's presence was a balm. It healed the frayed corners of my soul.

"Any leads on Isaac?"

My hands curled into fists, nails digging into my palms. “Nothing.” Not a sighting, a word, or a clue. And I wouldn’t find peace until he was the permanent kind of dead. I itched to be the one who fed his corpse to the earth. Hate wasn’t a strong enough word for the way I felt toward my stepfather. I needed his death for me. For everyone he’d touched. My gaze dropped to my stomach. For my child.

My throat tightened, because, wraith take me, I wanted to tell her. She’d held me and cried with me through the night when I’d shared about losing my first baby. But this time, I had something good, something beautiful, and something that’d shine a light in our dim circumstance.

But like Isaac was wont to do, he stole that too, because like it or not, he *was* a threat to this child.

I needed to find him, but how in the Iron Hells I’d ever do that without a big-ass amount of help was beyond me. Isaac aside, Zahara was still out there with those serums, ready to do obsidian only knew what with them. But without her real name, finding her was like finding Isaac. Damn near impossible.

A thought twigged as I worried my lip. It might be a shot in the dark, but it was better than sitting idle. “Hey, what’re your news outlets called there?”

A long, drawn-out pause like she was waiting for something—but when that something didn’t come, she said, “Whyyyyyy?”

I snickered softly. “It’s just … the way Zahara carried herself. She had this air about her, kinda like the Conclave.” Or the human equivalent, anyway. “Like she knew she was important.”

Or powerful. Or at the very least, like she’d been *linked* to power.

“You wanna try and find her.”

Her or one of those henchmen she’d had in tow, yeah. “It’s worth a shot.”

’Cause if I spotted her, or them, figured out exactly who they were, that’d be one less problem on everyone’s plate.

Lis bit into something, then chewed around her next words. "You're not the only one. Bower's been asking around. Whoever she is, she's good at keeping her mouth shut."

I grumbled under my breath.

"Only one problem," Lis went on. "Ithica's got you guys blocked from access."

My head drew back. "They … what?" Ithican news wasn't exactly high gossip for the preternaturals, seeing as we were—evolutionarily—the biggest and baddest around. And the lion never concerned itself with the snake, until the snake showed its fangs. But with those were, magi, and shadow-walker serums on the loose after Isaac and Zahara's buddy-buddy trade deal, that balance had shifted. Uncomfortably.

She snorted. "It's fine. I'll just take screenshots."

I was always fond of a workaround. And Lis. "You're the literal bestest."

"Don't forget it."

Pushing to stand, I strode toward the back window and stared out into the overcast, waning day. Dark clouds held at the horizon, threatening rain. Cold moved in, the kind that seeped through your flesh and into the bones. "Any idea when I'll see your smarmy ass again?"

"I don't know." Another clank before she grumbled, "I'm pressuring Bower, but he's more interested in 'public safety'."

"Rude of him."

"So rude." She sighed. "I'm hoping it's soon. Don't want you cretins finding somewhere else to go."

"Ha! You mean somewhere reputable?"

"Wow, chickie! It might be true, but you don't gotta say it."

I laughed.

"Iron Hells, I miss the bar. Things here are just … boring. Plus"—she pitched her voice low—"I think Rosa wants me outta here, too."

"Of course she does," I said, trailing a finger along the cool windowsill. "You're an even bigger pain in the butt than I am."

"Hashtag terrible friend."

My grin was saucy and all teeth. “And you love me for it.”

“I do.” She sighed. “I think there’s something wrong with me.” There was a shuffle on her end, then, “My lady’s home for me to harass. I gotta go. I’ll send you those articles later. Love ya, chickie.”

“Love you too.” The call ended.

Movement in the back lot pulled my focus, and my gaze held on Kane. His black hooded shirt and dark, low-slung jeans fit his dense frame in that mouthwatering kinda way. Wind snapped at his hair, and he dragged it back as he spoke, looming beside an ebony-skinned were named Cassian—his new Beta. The same were he’d had guarding me during Sierra’s dirge before Isaac had moved in, and, as usual, everything had gone to pot.

True to his protective form, my Alpha had the place surrounded by wolves. Ones he trusted.

As if he’d felt me looking, his stare tracked my direction. I grazed my touch along my breasts and the very exposed flesh of my body. His eyes flashed, and he tipped his chin, ordering Cassian away.

Heading across the room, my attention was fixed on the mirror through the open washroom door, and the not-yet-there bump of my lower abdomen. My hand trailed over it, gentle and warm.

The office door opened, then closed, the chilled air kissing my skin, followed a breath later by Kane. The steady thump of his heavy footfalls sounded as he sealed in behind me. His wilderness and musk scent coupled with something savory grazed my senses as his chest found my back.

He dropped a paper bag onto the desk before those calloused palms skimmed my waist, then tracked forward until they covered my own. “I’d prefer not to slaughter my new Beta for the misfortune of seeing you unclothed,” he taunted, voice a low rumble at my ear. “My wolves are of better use alive.”

I shimmied my shoulders. “Lookie but don’t touchie. Them’s the rules, right?” I bit my lip to hold back my smile. “Or is it the other way around?”

He angled forward, mouth finding my throat before his teeth raked that claiming mark and he growled. "Don't test me, Bry."

Did I think he'd slaughter his spanking new Beta for seeing my lady bits by accident? Probably not. Did I live for getting under his wolfish hide? Abso-goddamn-lutely. Dropping my head against his shoulder, I settled into him.

He nudged my temple with his jaw. "You good?"

My nod was soft, and I dragged his hand across my belly in a slow circle. "I love them, Kane."

A deep rumble vibrated through his chest, his grip flexing over mine as it pressed into me. Tender. "I do too, Bry. So damn much."

And he did; with every fiber of his being, he did. It permeated off him like a wave of power, palpable and warm. So unendingly warm.

As Kane Slade was wont to do, he pushed. "What else?"

I shook my head.

"Bry?"

My exhale was slow. "I'm just tired," I lied. Well, kinda lied, because making his baby *was* the tiring sort of work.

His silver topaz stare met mine in the mirror, hair falling over his brow. "What's going on?"

Leave it to him to notice everything. "I'm just … excited, Kane."

He cocked a lone brow. "But?"

My shoulders sagged and I looked away, trying with everything I had to keep the pain from my voice. "But I'm not allowed to be."

We'd lost the chance before, and now we'd finally gotten it again and I wanted to tell people—tell *everyone.* Lucas and Joaquin and Theo, Lisa and Cassandra. My heart tensed because I wanted to scream it for our entire batshit world to hear. I wanted to buy everything I'd circled in that damn magazine. To hold those baby clothes and toys and to stand in their room. To pick colors and names and all the fun things. I wanted to go to the Recovery Center, get an ultrasound, and stare at those images until my heart burst. But while we'd broken Isaac's control, the wraith only knew where he was or what he'd do next. We couldn't take the chance. And I got it … logically, at least.

Kane inclined his head and pressed a kiss to my hair. "I know." Taking my hips, he turned me to face him. His square knuckle tipped my chin up, forcing my gaze to his. "We'll have that, Bry. I fucking promise."

When he said it like that, so vehement and from the depths of his soul, it was hard not to believe him. But then … "When?"

Those eyes were strained with an archaic rage, one that promised a painful vengeance after he'd hunted down my stepfather. And he wanted that badly. It was written in every corded line of sinew along his arms and neck. But his silence said more than words ever could when his chest fell on a steady exhale.

I leaned into that touch. "Lie to me, Kane."

He cleared his throat and set his forehead to mine. "Soon. We'll get him soon."

I'd wanted the words to help, but somehow, they'd only dug that hole in my chest deeper. My nod was tight. Swallowing hard, I stepped away.

His hands flexed by his sides as those eyes followed me. He rolled his shoulders, then exploded my way until he backed me against the wall, that broad frame caging me in. One hand gripped my side, the other my hair. His mouth crashed against mine. I opened to him and his tongue plunged deep, sweeping in as he took and tasted. His knee pushed between my thighs, body eclipsing mine. And, sage, it felt so damn good.

A soft mewling sound escaped me as my fingers curled into his shirt and I melted against him. *Into* him.

He pulled back, chest heaving, his next words a guttural fucking vow. "Soon." Releasing me, his stare narrowed, going distant, like it did anytime he talked to his Pack. "Cassian says Hannah's wolf just dropped her here."

My Alpha had assigned a string of wolves to protect my brother's girlfriend, because Isaac was who he was, and we weren't willing to take that chance. And neither was Lucas.

Heading for the desk, he took a seat, then jerked his chin my way and patted his lap. "Now cart that ass over here. I got you something."

The tips of my fingers traced my swollen lips, and I smiled because that wolf did things to me. I finger-combed the mess he'd made of my hair, then scurried closer and plunked myself down. He opened the paper bag and got to work, dishing the takeout spaghetti and meatballs onto paper plates. The scent of garlic and tomato filled the room, making my mouth water.

Setting a heaping helping in front of me, he ever-so-Alphaly ordered, "Eat."

My gaze narrowed in feeble challenge. Regardless, I swirled the noodles around my fork and stuffed them into my mouth, 'cause this momma-to-be was a hungry minx. Those sharp and salty flavors coated my tongue, so damn good. Happiness had me wiggling my hips and I moaned, then shoved in another mouthful.

My Alpha's thick, calloused hand kneaded my hip as he hardened beneath me.

I peered at him over my shoulder, brow arching high. "Me eating turns you on now, does it?"

He ground my ass against him, lip arcing up at the corner. "You fucking *breathing* turns me on."

Heat pooled between my thighs. It was like the pregnancy, like me carrying our child—*his* child—had been a tap straight into the well of his virility. And I loved it. Loved the way he hungered for me. The way he watched me. Breathed me … and tasted me.

His fingers latched over my skirt, dragging up the material, inch by torturous inch. Cool air kissed my exposed skin, sending gooseflesh rising. His hand grazed down my leg, skimming my inner thigh. Those rough fingers trekked higher, trailing the lace of my flimsy thong.

Gripping my obsidian, I cocooned our sound as I sighed, soft and easy, giving him better access as I spread my legs wider.

Kane stopped, turning to stone. A heavy thump pounded at the office door. My bottom lip stuck out.

My Alpha's head dropped forward as he shifted my dress back into place, then zipped up the front. "It's Luke."

I swallowed hard, trying to cool my too-hot body and released my ring. "Come in."

That door swept wide, thumps carrying when Lucas's boney feet clambered into the office. His expression was intent, the lines creasing his eyes deep and infinitely older than his sixteen years. He stopped in front of the desk like he had something to say.

Hannah peered around the corner, her chestnut eyes cautious. "Lucas," she said, voice soft.

He half-turned, extending a hand her way, inviting her to him.

My gaze volleyed between them as she sealed the door over, and shuffled across the floor. Closing in, she took that hand, lingering a step behind him. She stood several inches shorter, her sepia-toned skin rich, body tight like she was braced for a storm. Which seemed fair, because with the set expression painting my brother's face, I sensed one coming.

"I wanna help hunt Isaac," Lucas said.

My gaze flicked to Hannah and back as I screamed my silent message. "*Careful, Lucas.*" Because the last thing we needed was—

"She knows."

Kane stiffened.

Lucas couldn't have said what I thought he'd said. *He better not have!* I blinked hard. "What?"

"I told her." His tone was unyielding. Not angry, but determined. Steadfast. And stronger than I'd ever heard.

My brow furrowed, a knot swirling in the depths of my stomach as that panic rose, moving like a slow tide that threatened to pull me under. "Told her *what*, Lucas?"

He drew back his shoulders, lifted his chin, and knocked the breath from my lungs when he said, "I told Hannah what I am."

Chapter Three

My lungs seized, stealing my air. My muscles burned; my mind raced. "Lucas," I uttered, his name a plea, like he could take it back. *Please, sage, just take it back!*

Kane's calloused palm flexed over me. A comfort or a restraint, I didn't know.

My brother inhaled, good and slow. "It's not like it's a secret. Not anymore. Cassandra already knows. And so do Joaquin's people, and everyone else who was under Isaac's thrall. It's gonna get out, Briar."

Bile seared the back of my throat, and my fingers curled over the chair's armrests as I gave them my weight. Learning I was pregnant had awoken something inside me. Something primal and protective, and absolute beast. The fear was still there but it was secondary, led by an instinct so powerful, it warred my Alpha for dominance. Maybe it was the baby, or accessing Kane's endless well of strength, or the fact I'd lost everything I loved until I'd fought and bit and clawed my way back, but that didn't mean I was about to start the deadly kind of trouble where that trouble wasn't needed.

"I know you two care about each other," I said, "but this is serious, Lucas."

Hannah tucked herself further behind my brother.

His grip tightened over hers while his head sliced to the side. "I love her, Briar. And I won't lie. She's got a right to know what she's signing up for."

Love? Power of obsidian, he was only sixteen!

My Alpha's voice rumbled across that bond like he'd read my thoughts. "*We weren't much older, Bry.*"

We weren't. And we'd had so many things taken from us. Top on that list was choice. I wanted choice for my brother, I did. But his *choice* had just ratcheted his already precarious circumstance into that "mortal peril" kinda realm.

My mind was a torrent of thoughts and fears and a thousand other emotions I couldn't pin down. None of them good. Rocketing to my feet, I stalked the office, back and forth. Back and forth.

Lucas peered over his shoulder at a trembling Hannah. Leaning back, he pressed a reassuring kiss to her hair, then straightened to his full height, and found me again. "I wanna go public."

My laugh straddled the borderlands between deranged and terrified. "That's a hard no."

Slowly, Kane rose, then strode my way. My glare locked on him, imploring, because his Alpha butt *needed* to say something, the super kind of fast.

He propped his shoulder against the wall like he was holding it up, then crossed his arms over that broad, tight chest. His body was coiled. Ready. Always so goddamn ready. But his silence pressed like an iron weight on my chest, 'cause when my Alpha disagreed, he had not one issue voicing it.

My brother's mouth was set in grim determination. "It's only a matter of time before someone says something."

"I said *no*!" I snapped. Tearing my hands through my hair, I inhaled long and deep, pulling in air. Outside, the wind kicked up, red and yellow fallen leaves smacking against the soaked window.

My shaking legs threatened to buckle as I gripped the sill. Hard.

The gentle padding of footsteps carried toward me as Hannah edged to my side. Her shoulders were rounded, hands tucked into the sleeves of her navy top.

I stared at my breath as it steamed the glass. Fogging and fading. Fogging and fading.

"I love him too," she said, voice gentle and meek, but there was something else. A strength. Maybe.

Twisting my engagement ring, I traced a finger over its diamond facets. My gaze met hers, and I looked. *Really* looked. There was a sincerity in that expression. She meant it. She loved him, and if the pink of her cheeks and warmth in her eyes was any indication, she loved him deeply. Yes, they were kids, and obsidian only knew if it would last, but to them, what they had was real.

The same as what Kane and I'd had. But real or not …

"I'd never hurt him," she said.

"I believe you wouldn't, not on purpose. Not now." I swallowed. "But what if you *stop* loving him? What if things between you end? And what if they end badly?" What if. What if. *What if.* "I've been shielding my brother a long time. He's mad, and he's got every right to be. But—"

"But you're afraid."

"No." I shook my head. "I'm fucking terrified. I know what comes for him if he's outed." And that bloodthirsty mob that would call for his head wasn't my only fear. Bigger than that was the unknown. If he was killed, what the obsidian waited for him in the Iron Hells? "And if that happens, how do we protect him?"

Hannah and my brother exchanged a look. "Lucas and I were talking, and we had an idea."

Kane's head canted while my gaze narrowed.

Lucas edged forward. "I get a tattoo."

My frown was soul-deep. A tattoo? A fucking *tattoo*? That was his solution?

He raised his hands, palm out. "Changelings hold scars. You saw it with Isaac. We carry them through every form. A tattoo makes me recognizable in *any* form."

"Exactly"—I threw my arms up—"so why, then, would you need a *tattoo*?" Why would that help?

Kane's brow arched, impressed. "Because preternatural tattoos are permanent and distinctive, Bry. It'll stand out. A clear mark of who *Luke* is. It's not a bad plan."

"No. It's not a bad *theory*," I said, because it was a distinction with a giant-ass difference. My panic rose, my breaths short and shallow. They couldn't be serious. "We don't know if it'll work. And even if it does, we don't know if anyone will accept it."

My Alpha pushed off that wall, towering over me as he rose to his full height. He tipped his head toward the back door. "Walk with me?"

Obsidian, I didn't want to. I wanted to yell and bite and scream until my brother relented. Until they understood. But Kane Slade did nothing without purpose. Which meant I bit my trembling lip and inclined my head.

His hand rested over my elbow and his eyes found my brother. "Cassian'll take you two back to our place and wait with you there." His stride was easy as he steered me away, then popped open the back door and held it. "I'll find you when I get back."

Lucas's nod was sharp.

I stepped out as the night slowly crept in, those dark clouds crawling closer as they blanketed the dying sun. Kane veered us toward the tree line at the edge of the back lot.

I jerked my arm from his grasp, aware I could only do so because he let me, then moved away, putting distance between us. "You could've said something back there."

His jaw worked, fist flexing at his side like he wanted to reach for me. Or like he was braced. "Luke's right, Bry. We should get ahead of this. Keep some trust."

Some trust—because we'd held that secret entirely too long to keep it all. My heart hammered in my chest while I rubbed my forehead like I could shove back the headache that crept in.

He advanced, and I backpedaled until my spine found a tree. He penned me in as those thick, rough hands came up, landing on my cheeks and engulfing my face. His silver topaz eyes locked on mine, and his voice was low and easy as he said, "What other option do we have?"

None, but I'd rot before I'd ever concede that to him. So instead, I folded my arms over my chest and looked away.

Leaning forward, he nudged my jaw with his own, that stubble grazing my skin as he brought me back to *him*. "I'm not trying to hurt you, Bry." He tipped his head toward the shop. "I'm trying to save him."

My shoulders sagged. I knew it—I did—but the walls I'd built to shield my brother were so high, even I could barely climb them. "I know," I breathed. Scared or not, their less-than-stellar plan was the only one we had.

Kane pressed a kiss to my temple.

I batted his chest, pouting. "Stop being nice to me."

His mouth tugged at the corners, all wolfish and teeth. "Say the word and I can play it not nice."

I batted him again, trying to ignore the heat that simmered low in my belly. Sage, the way he affected me. Turned my fire to heat and my heat to flame.

He nipped my bottom lip, and, like he had all the time in the world, dropped to a knee.

My brow furrowed so deep it was a wonder I could see. "Not sure if you remember," I said, waggling my engagement ring in his ridiculously sexy face, "but you already asked, Big Bad."

He huffed a laugh, then pivoted, giving me his broad back. "Hop on."

I excitedly wiggled my ass, bouncing in place before I launched myself forward and threw my arms around his neck.

He grinned, hooking his grip around my knees as he rose. "I love you, Bry."

His smile touched my withered soul, and I grumbled, "You'd better."

His footfalls crunched over the fallen leaves as he took us deeper into that forest. "I've loved you from the first second I saw you."

My heart fluttered a wild beat. Tucking my face into the curve of his neck, I let his words roll through me with the rumble of his voice.

"I'll do everything in my fucking power to protect our family and finish this."

"I know you will," I murmured against him, and gooseflesh rose along his skin. If there was anything I'd never, not for a single second, doubted about Kane Slade, it was the depths he'd go to in order to protect what was his.

"But things are different now. Which is gonna mean making tough calls."

I sagged against him. "Lucas."

He inclined his head.

My Alpha was practical. Never acted without thought—a lot of it. His moves were careful and strategic. He took risks with himself, but not with me. And not with my brother. So the fact he thought Lucas's plan was viable …

I thunked my chin onto his shoulder.

The autumn breeze rustled the leaves as a cluster of them fell, drifting on the wind like snow. The cool bit at my exposed skin, but his heat kept me plenty warm.

The first rays of the moon broke through the forest ceiling, the smell of soil and ozone filling the night.

Kane stopped dead, body turning to stone. He snapped to the right, brows furrowed deep, head angled back as he scented the air, those eyes going molten.

I followed his line of sight and pushed my gaze into the dimness, but there was nothing there. "What's wrong?"

He crouched, settling my feet to the ground, voice guttural when he said, "Try scenting it."

What the hells?

"Kane?"

"It's fine, Bry." He stretched his neck and pointed a loose hand at my obsidian. "Just try."

I frowned, 'cause nothing in his reaction had screamed "fine", but okay. Pulling on my ring, I reached for his power, then inhaled long and deep. There was a smell there, one I wasn't familiar with. But the hard set of my Alpha's expression told me he sure as shit was. It was almost sharp and … bitter. Like something rotten or tainted—but still very much alive. "What is that?"

He rolled his shoulders. "Wolf."

Not exactly helpful, seeing as we had lots of those around. Still, I swallowed hard. "Which wolf?"

He squared himself to me. "Amber."

My hair caught on the breeze, blowing across my lips. I brushed it aside to give him the full force of my glare. "What the actual shit, Kane?"

"She's not here." He shook his head. "The scent's a day old and far off."

After Joaquin took Victor's Pack, he'd not been overly keen on Amber's presence, so he'd ousted her. She was a lone wolf, and wolves separated from said Pack were a problem with a capital P. It wasn't like Amber had been well adjusted from Jump Street, considering everything she'd done.

I put my hands to my hips. "*How* far off?"

"A few blocks." He indicated the trees. "I didn't catch it until the wind shifted this way."

A few blocks? Iron fires take me. "What's she doing this goddamn close?"

He tugged a leaf from the branch to his left, then rolled it between his fingers. Pieces crumbled away, drifting on the breeze before they faded into the night. "Testing."

Nothing about that sounded good. "Testing what?"

"Us."

My chest tightened. "Why?"

His silence reigned.

There were only a handful of reasons I could conjure for that. Either she wanted to get close to my Alpha, or …

"She's working with him again, isn't she?" I swallowed. She was definitely cunning enough—and desperate. "Isaac?"

Having drawn the same conclusion, he inclined his head. Amber was isolated, her mind fraying, and Isaac had somehow grabbed one of those threads to pull her back in, which meant nothing Amber did was a shock anymore.

Still, her even testing was bold. And bold moves from any preternatural were dangerous. Least of all from one whose tether to sanity was slim at best.

He gripped my chin and angled my gaze to his. Those eyes roved between mine. "Remember that scent."

Remember it, because I needed to know. And if he thought I needed to know, it meant only one thing. "You don't think she'll stop?"

He shook his head. "She's isolated. She's lost her ground and will do anything to regain it."

After Joaquin had ousted her, we'd let her go. But if she was a threat …

"She'll need supplies, Kane. There's nowhere in Cambria she won't be recognized. And no one's the hundred shades of stupid enough to help her."

"No, but help's not her only option."

Right, 'cause she could kill or steal or utilize any number of nefarious methods to get what she needed.

My laugh was bitter. "What do we think Isaac's using her for? To spy?"

"Possibly."

"You're not sure?"

His mouth thinned. "With Isaac"—he shook his head—"I don't fucking know."

My stepfather's moves were nothing if not tactical. Still, she was on the dangerous kind of decline, so if he'd hitched his wagon to her, he had a reason.

Sweet sage. "What if she catches my scent?" My hands rose to cover my mouth, muffling my voice as I spoke. "What if she smells the baby?" Hells only knew what she'd do—

"She can't." There was a vehemence there, one shrouded in complete and utter confidence. "That's not a thing. *You* mask that scent." Taking my wrists, he drew down my arms, lip arcing brashly at the corner. "Because you smell like me."

I exhaled, then rolled my eyes, 'cause he was entirely too proud.

He advanced, closing the distance between us. His chest pressed flush against mine, crowding me before his knuckles grazed my cheek. "She's long gone now. It's just us."

I sank into him, letting those words wash over me. *Just us.*

His hands tracked along my forearms to my elbows, then the caps of my shoulders. That touch skimmed my throat before he cradled my jaw. His eyes were fixed on mine.

Pushing up to my toes, I set my mouth to his throat and licked, trailing my tongue along the corded muscles there.

He growled, his molten stare lighting the night when it landed on me. He cocked a lone brow.

I nipped his throat again.

Faster than I could track, he hooked his arms under my thighs and lifted, crushing me against the tree. The bark pressed into my flesh, a sharp bite that drove me fucking wild.

Stepping between my legs, he spread me wider.

My breaths broke from me in staccato pants as he crushed my breasts against his torso. I reached for the branch with one hand, while the other plunged into his hair.

His fingers dove inside my thong, then between my slick folds. He found my clit, thumb circling it, setting my body aflame while his mouth tasted the curve of my ear. "So fucking perfect."

My moan was loud, untempered, and nearly as feral as him.

Those fingers roved deeper, slipping into my core. I arched against him, grinding into the hard length of his cock. Sage, it felt good. It felt like more.

His voice was a harsh rasp when he ordered, "Tell me what you want, Bry."

I smiled, raking my tongue along the back of my teeth as I settled my palms over his shoulders, then guided him down. He followed, holding me steady as he took a knee before me. And the sight of the most powerful man in Cambria like that … it did dangerous things to me.

"Taste me, Kane."

He grunted, all primal and hunger, then hiked up my dress until it was gathered around my waist. Those eyes turned molten as he took me in. "You're perfect, Bry. So. Damn. Perfect."

His touch trailed along my ankle, then latched around my thigh before he lifted it, hiking it over his shoulder. He grazed his rough stubble along my inner thigh and peered up, eyes locked on mine as he set his canines against the flesh there and bit down. Not enough to pierce, but the sting had my body bucking as he rode that line between pleasure and pain, electrifying my nerves and charging me closer to bliss.

"Open wide for me," he rumbled.

Shadow and sage, I loved the command in that voice. The way he owned me. Claimed me. My arm looped around the back of his neck, legs parting further. Grasping my thong, he tore. I sucked in a sharp breath. Not sure why I bothered wearing any underwear.

He trailed his thumb along my center. "So wet for me." His tongue found my core, tracing a languid line up that made my nipples harden. He sucked and flicked, working my clit as he rolled and tasted.

I cried out, one hand clutching his hair as the other clung for dear life to that branch.

He slipped in one thick-knuckled finger, then another. Curling them forward, he hit my g-spot. Iron fires, it felt so good.

His stare was on mine as I rocked my hips, grinding against his tongue. I moaned, then opened my legs wider.

His hands dug into my ass, dragging me closer.

My orgasm climbed, hot and fast, throwing me over the edge until it burned me within. I gasped, calling his name again and again as the heat shot through me.

Gripping my hips, he rose, preternaturally fast. Eager. I pawed at his jeans, desperate for him as I unfastened them, then freed his thick and ready cock. He groaned and rocked into my hold, pumping into me. I set his head at my center, shaft pressing against my needy core.

My palms glided up his chest as I purred, and the smile I offered was sheer vixen.

He growled, a gruff, resonant sound, before he pushed inside. My spine arched, breasts straining against my bra. He palmed them, dragging the material aside. One hand grasped the hair at the base of my neck, angling my head back. His canines raked my throat, over that claiming mark, before he descended to my collarbone, then my nipple. Taking it between his teeth, he closed over it. I cried out.

He thrust again, burying himself to the hilt, filling every inch of me to completion.

"Oh, sage. Faster."

He cursed and thrust harder, the force slamming me against that tree. He cursed again before his hands latched over my ass, lifting. My arms looped languidly around his neck as he drove inside, using that resistance to set a brutal pace.

The crack of our bodies colliding had my core tightening around him as that riotous bundle of nerves surged higher, seeking euphoria.

"Kane," I begged. "I'm close."

"Iron Hells." His jaw clenched, muscles along his neck and chest cording like he could barely hold back. "Come for me, Bry. *Now.*"

I moaned, my sultry gaze holding his. "And what if I don't?"

His lip arced up at the corner. "Try it."

And power of obsidian, the carnal, sex-charged challenge in those words made me wild.

My walls seized around him, nails digging into his back as I came.

"*Fuck!*" he snarled, plunging into me over and over. He set a ruthless pace, grunting as he rutted me harder. Deeper. He crashed into me one final time, then groaned as he spilled inside me.

That familiar wave of Kane-induced heat flooded me, and I sighed, a completely sated sound.

He collapsed forward, one hand holding me in place, the other braced against the tree while he caught his breath.

I loved us like this. Desperate. Sated. Together. But the longer we stayed there, the more our reality crept back in. Because no matter how much I tried to shut it all out, convince myself Isaac and Amber and Zahara weren't coming, that Lucas's secret was safe, the more that knot in the depths of my chest tightened—a noose drawing closed, making it harder and harder to breathe.

Making it harder and harder to be.

Chapter Four

The truck tires hummed over the pavement as Kane wove us through Cambria, heading to the Coven gathering for Whitney's joining. A musky, sweet scent carried from the wisteria that grew in the medians and clung to the sides of the buildings, overgrown, just the way us beasties liked it. The midday sun was high, the sky cloudless and bright, a deceptive contrast to the nip in the air.

Dragging a finger up my phone's screen, I scanned the images of articles Lisa had sent. An ad popped up and I lingered on the picture there, one of a cottage at the base of the Ithican side of the Cortez Mountain range. The place was two stories with a log exterior, situated beside a striking, aqua-colored glacial lake. My heart ached, longing to go.

I sighed wistfully as I moved on, flicking through those headlines and pictures. Society pages, obituaries. No faces jumped out, but there was one bizarre story about two deaths near the border that were "still under investigation", and another about a sunglasses-clad woman who'd run around the theater district, biting people.

After I'd perused everything, I scrolled back to that opening page and the lead article. "Anti-Government Protests Persist Outside Capital". Lis forwarded a corresponding screen-recorded video that opened with a warning of "disturbing content".

A masked horde crowded the camera, several men gripping torches while six others shook signs that read "Flesh Traitors" and "Cambrians Can't Be Trusted".

"They don't give a shit about us," one guy yelled.

"Fuck the beasts!" another added. "If Ithica won't deal with them"—he stabbed a finger to his chest—"we will!"

The camera panned to the Ithican police force who stood opposite them, riot gear on, clear shields raised and batons at the ready.

I frowned down at it, 'cause the last thing anyone needed was a repeat of our border tensions. And I thanked sage that their previous trigger-happy General had been let go.

Kane's hand flexed over my thigh, thumb tracking a slow line along my bare skin there. It grazed back and forth, back and forth, a balm to my nerves.

He tipped his chin toward my screen. "Find anything?"

"Nothing helpful," I said, exiting the video before I stuffed my phone away. Sighing, my gaze dropped to the small, heart-shaped tattoo on my wrist. I traced it with the tip of my nail, letting out a frustrated breath as I set my head on his shoulder.

All I wanted was to protect the ones I loved. To be done with Isaac and Zahara and everything. Done with all of this.

Staring down at my hand, I held it in front of me. Gripping my ring, I pulled my power, doing what Mason had said: picturing something in my mind to project and starting small.

I inhaled deep and shook myself out, then settled that image to the forefront of my thoughts. I pushed, skin prickling, against that strange wall that was still there, blocking me. But slowly, a stream of particles slipped through, lifting from my palm before they hovered several inches above it. Bit by bit, the hollow outline of a howling wolf slowly took form.

"Shit, Bry," my Alpha said, impressed.

It held for one second. Two. Three. Then the particles vanished, the illusion fluttering away.

I hmphed. "I still lost it."

His touch kneaded my thigh. "It was progress."

I repeated it again and again until, ten minutes later, we pulled into the markedly empty lot of the old church that functioned as the Northern Coven meeting place. As a surprise to no one, my Alpha had brought us early to scope out the location—and every magi that crossed its threshold.

Checking my watch, my mouth thinned, because Mason wasn't there and he'd been supposed to meet us to do a last run-through of the plan. Not that I hadn't already memorized it, but still …

We climbed out as Theo veered in, a handful of the Pack in tow. They parked, and Theo aimed our way while the others took up posts around the perimeter.

Unlocking the entrance, I swung open the creaking door and advanced—or, at least, I tried to, but my Alpha's grip locked over my wrist, stopping me.

Right. Cardinal rule number one. Big Bad first, lest trouble lie in wait.

He stepped in, filling the doorframe for several steady heartbeats. Then he advanced and I followed, his cousin nipping at our heels.

The sun's rays pierced the stained-glass windows, painting the floors and wooden pews in a wicked rainbow of scarlets, indigos, and golds. The Motherstone, the primary obsidian each magi linked with, a stone unique to its individual Coven, sat at the head of the church, a wall of black full of smooth curves and jagged edges. It lined the majority of that backdrop from floor to ceiling. Immediately before it sat a small dais covered by a pristine white sheet, a black dagger laid upon an elevated holder at its center.

The place might've been pretty, but it was old as dirt, and the insulation was crap. My breath puffed on the air as a shiver rolled over my skin. Gooseflesh rose in its wake, and I tugged my cardigan tighter.

Kane side-eyed me, then grabbed his hoodie at the shoulder and pulled it over his head. Closing in, he held it high. "Arms up."

"I'm fine, Kane."

"Wasn't a question, Bry."

I glowered, sheer petulance making me want to turn him down. But I was cold, not daft. I lifted my arms and he tugged it over me, the thing falling just above my knees while that wolfy warmth enveloped me. I snuggled deeper.

He huffed, then said to Theo, "Check everyone that crosses." He meant, check them for that scar. The tooth-shaped one I'd left on my stepfather's right hand all those years ago.

With that, Kane stalked away, molten stare raking every corner and shadow as he went.

The front entrance opened, and Whitney filed in. Her russet-colored gaze landed on Theo. She smiled, warm and inviting. He inclined his head, posture stiff as she sidled our way, moving with a fluid grace that would put any shadow walker to shame. Her black heels clicked over the floor, her form-fitting white dress stunning against her ebony skin.

Theo's stare flashed and he swallowed hard.

"Hi," Whitney said.

Theo smiled, but again, like everything else with him of late, it was off. He tucked his hands in his pockets as if holding back from touching her, and sidestepped. "I gotta keep eyes on the door," he said, then left.

My head drew back, 'cause *that* behavior wasn't the concerning kind of weird.

Whitney watched his back as he went.

Scratching the line of my jaw, I made the air of awkwardness infinitely more awkward by asking, "So, how're things with you two?"

A small blush stained her cheeks. "Good?"

I side-eyed her. "You don't know?" Frankly, neither did I, which is why I'd chosen the probing approach.

She lifted a shoulder, her long, fine braids falling forward. "He's not … *doing* anything."

My face twisted, because Theo wasn't of the "do nothing" variety. "What do you mean?"

She shook her head and threw her arms up. "I know he likes me—he's giving all the signs—but he still hasn't made a move."

My gaze drifted Theo's way. There was a strain in his eyes, different from the one Isaac's compulsion had put there before.

There were a thousand things that could've been behind it, but which one it was, obsidian only knew.

His attention shifted to mine, and my brows sank low with my silent question. "*You good?*"

A pause. The shake of his head was subtle, but it was there. Still, I couldn't tell if it was of the "We'll talk later" or "Leave it alone" variety.

My Alpha strode past, grazing my hip before he prowled row after row of pews to my left. Straightening, I turned back to Whitney. "So, you ready for this?"

Her gaze fell to her feet. "I think so."

I edged closer and nudged her elbow. "You don't have to do this, you know."

The weight of Theo's glare was crushing while his facial expression screamed, "*You shut your witchy mouth!*"

I frowned deeper because, mixed signals much?

He crossed his arms over his chest, petulant and confusing as all get out.

Whitney followed my line of sight, that smile cresting her lips again. "I kinda do. Alistair already smashed my obsidian."

Sure, my own mother had been ousted from the Southern Coven, but I'd been too young to witness it. "That feels excessive."

"It's symbolic more than anything. Severing my connection to the Coven, though …" She rubbed her chest like it ached. "*That* was very real." Straightening, she angled her chin up. Proud. Eager. "But I want this. I love Alistair, it's just that his Coven's so …"

Cantankerous? Cruel? Judgmental?

"*Stuck*. I feel like I'll have more room to breathe here, you know?"

I offered a single nod. I hadn't served under Alistair directly, as I'd opted to start my Coven life North. And while things under Sierra hadn't been perfect, they'd definitely been better than the disdain my mother had faced in the South.

Pushing up her sleeve, Whitney checked her very sparkly watch. "When's Mason supposed to be here?"

I blew several strands of hair from my face. "Now."

Time ticked by, more and more magi filing in as I fired off text after text to Mason, my messages ranging from chill to borderline panicky as they progressed. I wasn't mad, not anymore—because the more time that passed without him showing up, the more the knot in the depth of my gut twisted.

By the time Kane had finished his multiple sweeps, the meeting was half an hour late. The place was packed, with every member of the Coven there. Every member *except* Mason.

"Where the shadow and sage is he?" I grumbled, eyeing my phone like it had answers— which, of course, it might, if my goddamn Coven Leader *would just respond.*

Voices hummed and complained, and people shuffled around, restless and annoyed.

I scanned the room, praying to the wraith that he was there and I'd just missed him. "Something's not right, Kane."

Mason no-showing was as out of character as it got. He'd coveted that Coven Leader position since I'd known him, so him going M.I.A. just wasn't a thing.

My Alpha's palm skimmed the small of my back. "I'll send a few Pack by his place, get them to have a look."

I nodded. I wouldn't take chances, not anymore.

Kane shifted, looming over me as he grasped his opposite wrist. "You just gonna call it?"

My mouth thinned. "They didn't come to have their time wasted."

Whitney's gaze slid from my Alpha to me, concern creasing her expression. "Can you bring me in without Mason?"

I lifted a shoulder in a half-shrug. "Law dictates only one of us is required to be present."

She exhaled, some of the tightness in her body easing. Kane, on the other hand …

I peered around one last time, to no avail. Looked like that call was gonna be mine, and I needed to make it. Me taking over in Mason's stead, doing what needed to be done, that was priority one. I'd studied enough to swear in Whitney on my own. It wasn't ideal, but it was what it was.

Sighing, I gave Kane a small shove. "Alright," I said, shooing him with a flick of my wrists. "Out."

His scowl burrowed good and deep. "Not happening, Bry."

My hands slammed onto my hips. "This is Coven business, not yours, Big Bad."

He angled close, mouth skimming my ear as he snarled, "Last time I left your ass for Coven business, *Isaac* happened."

Fair, but still ... "Everyone here's been checked. I'm not gonna shield us, so you'll hear every word that's said." I pointed to the exit. "Just watch through the glass and spy from outside."

He cursed and bared his teeth, looking ready for a fight.

Of all the things I wanted in that moment, fighting with him was bottom on the list, so I settled my palm over his chest to quell that rising ire. "There are rules, Kane, and they apply to me too. If I want the Coven's respect, I need to abide by them."

His shoulders heaved, a wildness in his eyes I'd only ever witnessed a handful of times. Fear. "I don't like leaving you."

My irritation ebbed, because I got it. I really, really did. "I'll be at the head of the room. Right where you can see me." I slipped my arms around his neck. "Isaac's not here."

The muscles of his jaw worked as he ground his teeth. "He'd better not be, woman."

Iron fires, the way that wolf loved me ...

The curve of my mouth was slow and easy. "Go. I'll call if I need you."

He let loose a low growl, then pressed a hot kiss to my forehead. Stabbing a hand toward the door, he reiterated, "I'm right fucking there." Then, to his cousin: "Let's go."

Theo offered a tight salute and flanked his Alpha as he left. The clunk of the door closing behind them echoed through the room.

Whitney tucked several braids behind her ear. "Kane seems a little—"

"On edge?"

"Yes," she said with a nod. "That."

"He's been through a lot."

Her hand landed on my elbow. "He's not the only one."

No, but I could tuck my pain aside. With his, it wasn't so easy. He buried it well, but losing me and Lucas twice over, along with his mother, and our child, and being commanded by Ronin—I swallowed the bile cresting my throat—and violated by Amber: they had all left their marks. And those scars had only grown broader. Delved deeper.

When it came to my Alpha, my protectiveness had no limits. And while he wore his on his own on that sexy, snarly face and those broad, ready-to-do-slaughter shoulders, inside, our need for violent retribution was the same.

I glanced around the church, at the sea of unsure faces.

Mason, Kane, Joaquin, Cassandra—they were built for this stuff. Not that I wasn't capable, it just wasn't something I'd ever wanted. I sighed, because what the Coven needed mattered more.

"Let's do this," I told Whitney. Clearing my throat, I aimed for the front of the church, taking my position by the cauldron as I squared myself to the room. "Everyone, please take your seats."

There was a shuffle as they did just that, and a younger magi, one of our newer members not much over eighteen, raised her hand. "Is Coven Leader Beckett coming?"

Seeing as I had not one clue what'd kept him, I didn't actually have an answer. But they needed reassurance. Stability. Someone to take control. They needed me. I shook my head. "No. I'll be leading tonight in his stead."

A younger guy with electric-blue hair asked, "Why are the wolves here?"

I swallowed around the lump in my throat. "For protection against Isaac."

An older woman stepped forward. Her face was familiar, and it took me a moment to place it out of context. Marisol, the owner of the Illusionist restaurant in the neutral grounds—the same one my Alpha had stood me up in, because of Isaac. "Why are there so many?" she asked.

"Yeah," the younger girl added. "Wouldn't your Alpha be enough?"

My chest tightened. "We're not certain Isaac's working alone."

Everyone exchanged glances.

It wasn't a lie. Not exactly, seeing as we did suspect Amber was in his pocket, but still, the guilt swelled in my soul. I was so sick of secrets. I hated the weight they bore on my shoulders. All they'd done was cost me. Losing Cassandra was a testament to that fact.

When no more questions came, I waved Whitney forward. Linking my hands before me, I drew back my shoulders and faced the crowd. "Joining a Coven is a life-altering choice. And accepting a member, growing our numbers, is a privilege we welcome.

"Whitney Harris, do you come to us freely? Of your own want and will?"

Her head dipped in a bow. "I do."

"And do you agree to uphold our laws as decreed? To come when your Coven needs you? To shield our reputation and represent us in good faith to the best of your ability?"

Another dip of the head. "I do."

"Each Coven gathers their obsidians from their Motherstone—one unique to them and separate from all others. It is this stone that tethers us. And now, it must tether with you."

Turning to the dais, I took up the dagger, the end of the hilt in one palm, the pointed tip against the other. Facing Whitney, I extended it her way. "Our Motherstone calls for your blood."

She took the dagger, trembling as she set its razored edge to her palm, and cut. Her blood welled, spilling free as it trickled across her flesh. Stepping forward, she set her hand on the obsidian.

"The power of the Coven is a collective, and today, we offer it to you." Nods of ascent rolled around the room as I raised my arm, ring held high. There was a shuffle of movement as the others followed suit.

Reaching for my strength, I pulled. Heat spread through me, crawling from my heart across my torso and limbs, up to my ring. The metal grew warm against my skin.

The Motherstone pulsed, a wave of energy rolling through the room. Whitney's blood spilled down its front. Her fingers curled, breaths coming in rapid bursts. My ring heated further, vibrating as it took her in.

Her body snapped back, then jerked forward as her blood vanished, absorbed into the Motherstone's surface. Soft smoke rose from her flesh, power coursing through her and embedding itself deep. Sweat beaded along her brow before her arm slipped to her side.

"Take your obsidian," I said.

Gripping the dagger tight, she plunged it into the Motherstone. A sharp crack sounded out, ricocheting around the church. A small chunk broke free, collapsing to the floor with a thunk.

She bent and retrieved it, eyes wide.

I smiled. "Welcome to the Northern Coven."

A chorus of claps and cheers rang out, followed by a piercing whistle.

We'd have the stone shaped and set for her in the coming days. But the hard part was done.

Everyone rose. Shoes clicked and bodies shuffled as the Coven formed a single line and approached, offering Whitney their welcome. With the pomp and circumstance complete, they gathered their things.

Marisol, the older Illusionist, found me, her withered voice kind. "Is that everything, Second?"

The guilt crested again, the pressure in my chest getting tighter. Keeping all these secrets, holding back the truth about Isaac and Zahara, and what Sierra had done—it was crushing me, squeezing my lungs until I could scarcely breathe.

My conversation with Kane echoed across my mind. Tough choices, he'd said. We'd need to make tough choices. Yeah, I needed help with my new ability. But more than anything, they needed to know.

Mason had mentioned telling the Coven, giving them what truths we could. I'd gotten so used to holding my tongue, it was a wonder I knew how to use it anymore. That pressure grew crushing. My hands made fists by my sides. I stared down at the floor.

I would share what I could.

I exhaled long and slow to steady myself.

"No," I said. The word echoed through the church, rising higher and higher toward the vaulted ceiling. *No. No. No.* "That's not all."

Every head angled my way. Brows furrowed, likely at the bizarre vehemence in my tone—which, fair.

"There is something else." I smoothed the front of my dress, forcing that fear down, 'cause this was about more than me. More than Mason. This was about all of them. And all of them deserved to know.

"You asked about the wolves." I gestured to the window and my Alpha beyond. His stare was on mine. I looked away. "In light of the circumstances in which we find ourselves, there's more you need to hear."

Bodies stiffened, the rising tension making the air thick with a cloying, bitter scent. Those before me exchanged glances, some confused, others concerned or annoyed. Regardless, they took their seats once more.

Pain stung the back of my throat, guilt coating my tongue. It wasn't right to keep everything to ourselves, not when we weren't the only ones affected. Still, I wasn't ready to talk about my brother, to share his identity.

"After Mason took the seat as Coven Leader, he discovered Sierra had been working on something."

"Working on what?" a dark-haired woman named Aster demanded, mouth thinning as she folded her arms across her chest.

I worried my lip between my teeth, biting down hard. But I'd opened this door, so it was time to walk my ass through it.

"Brokering a relationship with an Ithican partner."

Heads cocked. Some leaned forward.

Marisol's forehead creased. "What exactly did she broker?"

My throat ran dry, because my next words would destroy their illusion of who Sierra had been—and, power of obsidian, I didn't want to do that. But want to or not, it needed to be done.

"Preternatural abilities."

A sea of lost faces stared back at me, expressions contorted. So, I told them. I told them everything. About the serums, about Isaac and Zahara. About Mason and me and the counter-serums we'd tested. All of it. Ugly and raw and so goddamn terrifying.

Curses sounded. Eyes widened, jaws dropped—in disbelief or hurt, I couldn't tell.

My Alpha shifted, his stare voltaic.

I raised a hand, staying him. "*Let me handle this, Kane*," I ordered across our wolfy bond.

He growled, uttering a string of highly unimpressed epithets as he stretched his neck, but held where he was.

"So Isaac—he's armed Ithica?" a lanky man in the back called.

"He's armed *one* Ithican." I scrubbed a palm across the back of my neck, tired. So goddamn tired. "Zahara wants power, but over whom, ultimately, I do not know."

"So Sierra sold us out then?" Aster cried. "She just ... handed over Cambria's advantage. To the *humans*."

I wanted to say no, but in the end, it was what it was. "She thought she'd *gain* us an advantage, and built the counter-serums specifically to try and *hold* it."

Marisol raised a wrinkled hand. "What are they? These counter-serums?"

"They're specifically for us. To offer additional abilities," I replied. "The one I took was Illusionist."

"And it worked?"

I nodded. "It worked. Though I'm still figuring out how to use it."

"And Isaac has forged a relationship with this Zahara." A statement, yet very much not.

"I don't know where that relationship sits. And while he might be cruel, he's not stupid. The powers he sold had limits. They fade after a few hours."

"Who is she, this Zahara?"

I shook my head. "I'm still trying to figure that out."

"Why weren't we told before?" Aster pushed.

"Mason and I weren't in a position to share anything at the time." I propped a hip against the dais. "Even if we'd *wanted* to say something, we couldn't. Isaac's compulsion was too strong. But now circumstances have changed."

"Our Coven Leader should've said something himself."

"He wanted to." I folded my arms over my chest. "I don't know what's kept him tonight, but if he could have done this himself, he would have."

"Either way," Aster said, "the border's shut. At this point, if Zahara tries to use anything, it'll be against her own people. It's Ithica's problem now."

My brow dropped low, and I opened my mouth to reply, but movement in my periphery had my attention snapping to the door. Kane's back was to me, his body coiled, one hand making a fist, the other gripping his phone.

A knot twisted deep in the depths of my chest, my heart kicking up a staccato beat. "*Kane?*"

The faint scent of smoke cut through the church. It was like being downwind from a distant bonfire.

He pivoted my way, his stare locking with mine for one heartbeat. Two. His jaw was tight, sinewed fibers of his forearm rolling when he said something to whoever was on the other end of the phone.

"What's going on?" I questioned, the words low and tight. My stomach clenched, bracing, because every inch of my wretched soul knew I wasn't about to like the answer.

The entrance boomed open, and Theo exploded in. His eyes were wild and fixed on me as he said, "The Recovery Center's burning."

Chapter Five

Theo's chest heaved, his stare snapping to Whitney, whose hands covered her mouth.

Sweet sage, all those people. I stood frozen for less than a breath as the words sank in. Then: "Everyone, go!" I ordered. "Get there, now!" Barreling for the exit, I burst outside, the cool mid-afternoon air kissing my skin, the scent of smoke heavy.

Kane's wolves were on the move, already in their vehicles and careening out of the lot as I beelined for the truck.

"Bry!" my Alpha snarled.

I rounded on him, ready to let my fury loose.

His silver topaz stare locked on mine, searing me through. "You're not fucking going." He stalked to the driver's door and whipped it open, the vehicle dipping as he climbed inside. "You stay with Theo."

Oh no, he goddamn well didn't! I offered him a glare of my own, because like the iron fires I'd be hanging back when people needed help. Stabbing a finger to my chest, I said, "I'm Conclave, Kane. I *have* to go."

He stretched his neck and rolled his shoulders, looking very much as if he was about to strap my ass to the façade of the church. His jaw clenched as he bared his teeth. "I'm not taking you there." He slammed his door.

My blood turned hot. I crushed my obsidian, shielding my words as I stormed around to the passenger side and tore it open. "I'm. Going. Kane."

His glare was molten. And I got it, I did, 'cause the idea of putting me at risk went against every preternatural bone in his protective wolfy body. But that didn't change the facts.

"I'm Second in my Coven. If stuff's happening at the RC, I need to be there." I clambered into the truck and sealed myself in.

"Get out, Bry, or I'll drag your ass out."

Ha! He was gonna have to. Crossing my arms over my chest, I cocked my head and offered him a try-it expression. Because my Alpha and I, we were cut from the same damn cloth.

His knuckles went white, his grip making the steering wheel groan as he stared straight ahead through the windshield.

"It's Isaac, Kane. We both fucking know it."

He inclined his head. "And what if he's using it to lure you in?"

I exhaled to calm my fiery emotions, because logic was the only weapon with which I could face my Alpha if I wanted to win. "And what if he's using it to lure *you* out?"

To separate us.

He must've read between the lines, because those silver topaz eyes narrowed, and he cursed.

"I know you want me safe, Kane." I set my hand over my abdomen. "I want that too. But this is bigger than us. I need to be there, and you damn well know it, so stop being a stubborn mutt and drive."

That stare held. He took a slow inhale that hiked his shoulders, then shoved the truck into gear. "You're a pain in my ass, you know that?"

I raised my hand and tapped my engagement ring. "Forever."

Grumbling under his breath, he grabbed my skirt and dragged me to his side. When he punched the gas, we shot forward, random chunks of gravel clunking against the wheel well before they went airborne. The tires chirped as we hit the road and made for the neutral grounds.

The drive was long, time crawling as we wove our way through the city. My feet bounced as high-rises ticked by, like the lines on the road, too slowly. A sinister orange glow stained the horizon and the underside of those black low-lying clouds. Clouds so dense, they blotted out the sun, creating a dark, bloody sky that turned day to night. It churned my stomach and slicked sweat down my spine.

The closer we got, the heavier and more cloying that smoke grew. Iron Hells, it burned my lungs, making it hard to breathe.

Kane was silent. Deathly so. His body was tense, the tendons along his forearms straining under his skin like they were trying to tear free. I shifted beside him, fingers twisting the waist of my skirt.

We rounded the corner, and I gasped. Flames burst from the windows, engulfing the front of the RC, swallowing the west wing—the *human* wing. Embers flooded the sky, sparking against the inky night like burning stars. The fire painted the buildings and surrounding faces in its eerie glow.

I dialed Mason. The phone rang and rang before his voicemail kicked in.

"Hey. I don't know if you've heard what's happening, but call me when you get this." I hung up. Sage on a stick. Of all the times for him to be absent …

Kane veered down a street to our left, cutting through the hectic crowds. The closer we got, the more the chaos thickened. People blocked the roads, trying for a better view. Voyeurs to the mayhem. Kane kept advancing. When they spotted his imposing form and blazing eyes behind the wheel, everyone ducked their heads and moved from our path. Several painfully long minutes later, we pulled up to the building. Well, as close as we could get without the heat it kicked off melting the tires, or the metal.

My Alpha jumped free, stance wide, as he surveyed the scene. I slid out behind him, the white noise of the fire's roar blaring in my ears. Wraith take me, it was so loud, I could hardly hear myself think.

The blaze stung my skin and dried my eyes. Soot coated my tongue and filled my airways.

People ran: weres, magi, shadow walkers. Some headed toward the inferno, others away.

Wood snapped and images flashed across my mind. Memories from another day. Another fire after Isaac set his lab ablaze. Jared, screaming for help. Mason, saving my life. I shook myself to break from the flashback.

"Bry?" Kane said, his tone thick. His brow was furrowed, the concern there deep. "You good?"

I nodded 'cause I didn't trust myself to answer, or that he wouldn't scent the lie in it if I did—if he could scent anything over that barrage.

"Holy shit," Theo said, appearing at my left, Whitney several steps behind.

Joaquin's G-Class sped toward us, Ezra in the passenger seat. The Southern Alpha slammed to a stop before they both tore free, attention locked on the flames.

"Shadowed fucking moon," Joaquin said.

The white river-stone façade and walkway, gold window trim and hedges that had previously stood out in our overgrown city, were all scorched or melting. Burnt vehicles in the visitor lot formed a veritable graveyard near the perimeter of the building. My stomach dropped, bile searing the back of my throat, because those cars belonged to …

"How many are people in there?"

A BOOM rocked the area, glass and wood and all manner of debris tearing through the air. Kane dove in front of me, his body crushing mine against the truck, heavy and hulking. A pair of grunts followed when Theo did the same for Whitney, and Joaquin to Ezra.

The debris landed, clacking and clanking.

My Alpha drew back, his stare snapping up and down my body as he took me in. "You hurt?"

I managed a tight shake of my head as my trembling hands roved his back, checking him over. Theo and Whitney did the same for each other, as Joaquin released Ezra, who stood wide-eyed and stiff, but unharmed.

Screams carried. Loud, and terrified: the things nightmares were made of.

Kane gripped my hip, pulled me to him, and pressed a rough kiss to my forehead. He eyed Theo and chucked his chin my way. "Don't leave her fucking side." Then he was gone, advancing on the carnage. His voice roared across the night as he called orders to his wolves on positioning.

Joaquin eyed Ezra, expression strained.

"What can I do?" Whitney asked.

I scanned the place, looking for something. *Anything*. Without the uber-convenient healing enjoyed by the wolves, my magi getting near those flames would be a bad kind of idea. Sure, *I* could tap into my Alpha, but being pregnant meant I wasn't taking that chance. Still, there had to be something.

My gaze lit on a human man who crawled across the ground, hacking as he tried to catch air.

Theo must've seen the second my brain cells connected, 'cause he edged closer. "Kane said—"

I grabbed Joaquin's wrist. "I need Ezra. Leave him with me."

His shoulders sagged, relieved. So goddamn relieved. He inclined his head, and I released him. He ran.

"NORTHERN COVEN!" I bellowed. Theo hung his head and cursed as all eyes landed on me. "HELP THE WOUNDED!" To Whitney, I said, "You organize them." Then, to Ezra: "Give them your blood." At that, I was gone, taking up the lead as I aimed for the fray, Theo nipping at my heels.

A male were dragged a limping, blood-soaked woman away. Closing in, I threw her arm around my shoulder.

"Go, I've got her," I told him, because the more hands at work, the more people we could save. I hoped.

Theo beelined for the human man, hefting the guy over his shoulder.

The wind shifted as the acrid scent of cooked flesh filled my lungs, and my stomach rolled. The bile climbed higher, searing my tongue with its bitter tang. I covered my mouth and nose, trying to staunch the smell, to no avail.

Whitney called directions, assembling the injured into lines—bad and worse—while Ezra moved from person to person, using his canines to tear into his flesh and give them that near-priceless, all-healing were blood. It was what they needed.

Marisol sat with a cluster of small children, using her Illusionist ability to paint a picture of puppies and bunnies playing, keeping their little eyes from the terrors that played out around them.

My Alpha's powerful legs worked as he lugged two coughing and soot-coated children in each arm. Several magi closed in, snatching them from his hold. His stare fixed on mine and flashed, then he was gone.

Hoses were brought in, buckets of water thrown.

On and on we went until the last person was pulled out—the last *living* one, anyway. Efforts shifted, the wolves' stamina endless as they worked to beat back the flames, while the rest of us could only watch.

Theo pivoted as the pound of fast-moving footsteps closed in.

Bower, the Ithican Ambassador, skidded to a stop at my side, chest heaving. "Iron fucking Hells." He stared around. "Where's your Coven Leader?"

The pit in my gut burrowed deeper. I shook my head, because the words refused to come.

He swallowed hard, then was gone a second later, diving in to help.

There was a buzzing at my hip, and it took me several seconds to realize it was my phone. Reaching for it, I pulled it out and squinted past the soot in my eyes to see the screen. When my focus locked on it, I blinked, then blinked again.

A text … from Mason.

"Thank sage," I murmured, then clicked to open it.

I froze, sweat tracking along my forehead and down my spine as I stared at the picture on the screen. It was Mason. His glasses sat broken and crooked over his nose. Blood matted his hair and streaked his face, and his arms and legs were tied. I hyperventilated at the sight of him strapped to a chair—an ergonomic one beside a familiar sit/stand desk that held a state-of-the-art computer with multiple screens, and a sleek, wireless keyboard.

A set-up I'd seen before inside the magi labs.

My head snapped up, sheer and utter panic gripping my soul as my gaze locked onto the RC. "No!"

Theo's voice was thick when he peered my way. "What's wrong?"

Another BOOM exploded across the night, stone and metal and glass slicing through the air. Theo moved in front of me, taking the brunt of the debris that sailed our way. His head snapped back. He dropped.

"*Bry!*" Kane screamed across our bond.

I took myself in. "*I'm alright,*" I replied, my attention shifting to Theo. My eyes grew wide at the sight of his unconscious form. He was collapsed on the ground, his lower leg bent at an impossible angle.

My stomach rolled. That bone needed to be set, otherwise it risked getting stuck that way. Scrambling around, I grabbed his ankle, then winced, sending out a silent apology.

Counting down from three, I jerked it straight.

I hated to leave him, especially like that, but he'd come around, and that leg would heal—it was already halfway there. Mason didn't have that privilege, and I didn't have the time. Still, I wasn't about to abandon Theo completely.

I searched the magi. "WHITNEY!"

Her gaze snapped in our direction, then landed on Theo. She ran, closing in on him fast.

"Stay with him," I ordered as I rushed away.

Sweat streaked Theo's brow, his head lolling as he slowly came to.

"*Kane!*" I cried across our bond, because I needed him to know. "*Mason. He's in trouble.*"

He cursed. "*I gotta get this fire first, Bry. I'll order Theo—*"

"*Theo's hurt,*" I cut in. "*I'm the only one, Kane.*"

It was the only answer I could give, because Mason's clock was ticking. The last thing I wanted was to run headlong into the danger in front of me, but I was his one chance. And he'd come for me before. I wouldn't let him down.

My Alpha cursed, then cursed again. "*I'll find you.*"

I bolted, my legs burning as they pumped, driving me forward. Veering around the carnage, I aimed east for the magi wing, skirting the embers and ash that filled the air. Before long, the emergency exit became visible through the smoke, looming thirty feet away. Twenty. Ten. I slowed, my arm extending when I hit the push bar to open the door.

And came up short.

I crashed against it with a thunk, breath whooshing from my lungs. Pulling back, I shoved again, but it didn't budge. I cursed.

Gripping my obsidian, I scurried back several steps and reached for my Alpha's power. I breathed deep, then charged, kicking out, foot planted in the center of the door. A deafening bang sounded as the metal buckled. Rearing back, I kicked again. The door exploded inward as tufts of soot billowed out, rising on the air.

Clambering inside, I tripped over something on the ground, landing hard on my knees against the slick slate floor.

Two eviscerated husks sat on either side of the entrance, their formerly white lab coats soaked in red.

I gagged, fighting to keep down the contents of my stomach. I scrambled back. Away. Clambering to my feet, I fled, the lights flickering overhead as I careened down the hall. The white stained walls seemed to go on forever as I made for the lab. "Be okay. Be okay. Be okay," I chanted, gripping my obsidian tighter as I scented the air. There—I'd caught it. Something familiar.

Something distinctly Amber.

It was faint, smothered in char and half burnt away as it was, but it was there. There hadn't been a fire in this wing, but it was like she'd brought the stench of it with her.

I prayed to the wraith and the Iron Hells themselves. *Be alive, Mason. Please, sage, just be alive!*

Red claw marks gouged the sterile walls. Broken chunks of wood and plaster littered the ground, splinters and debris crunching under my feet as I moved.

A chrome, half-shredded sign that read "Magi Observation and Assessment Facility" came into view. The keycard pad was torn and tattered, the door buckled and wide. I flew inside, then came up short, feet rooting to the spot. Because everything, *everything*, was coated in blood. It dripped from the ceiling and the walls; it rolled from desks and tablets. It soaked the Castor stones and the frosted glass of the labs across the way.

My heart stopped, limbs going cold when my gaze landed on the body in the corner.

The very dead, and headless body—in an ergonomic chair.

Chapter Six

Blood dripped from the body—at least, what was left of it. The ribcage, spine, and limbs sat in that chair like they'd been left on display. This person hadn't just been killed. They'd been butchered.

My legs grew weak, and I gripped the doorframe to hold myself upright, *refusing* to believe. I swallowed and glanced around, trying to scent it, but there was not a damn thing, save the smoke, and Amber.

It's not Mason. I can't scent it. It's. Not. Mason.

I might've been able to hedge a guess who it was from the clothes, but like everything else in the room, they were soaked in red.

Feet pounded with an uneven thump from out in the hall. "Briar?" Theo called, voice strained. He burst inside, then hobbled to a halt. He paled, and slowly pushed in beside me, his eyes raking over the carnage. He swallowed hard before he said, "Wolfsbane."

Wolfsbane. Tears seared my sight, stinging the backs of my grit-filled eyes, but I pushed them back.

He advanced a step. "Where's the head?"

That sinking feeling dropped my stomach, and I swayed like the ground wasn't stable. Like the world had stopped turning—because I couldn't shake the feeling that had burrowed a hollow pit in my gut. One I refused to acknowledge.

It's not Mason, I told myself. *It's not Mason!*

I shook my head. "There isn't one."

Seven Iron Hells.

Gripping my obsidian, I let my eyes become unfocused.

The body's aura shimmered with a swaying blue sheen. A magi.

It's not Mason. It's not Mason. It's not fucking Mason!

Iron dread locked around my spine, making it hard to move. To breathe. To think. But the scent of ether mixed heavy with that smoke. The wraith hadn't come, not yet. But she wouldn't be long.

Shadows below, I didn't want to do it. Didn't want those answers. That finality. But nor did I have time to waste.

Steeling myself, I closed in. The floor was slick, and I slid, my foot jerking to the side again and again until I was forced to my knees, crawling the rest of the distance.

My hands trembled wildly, and my hair vibrated in the periphery of my vision as I reached out and set my palm over the still warm, still wet and dripping hand of that body.

Holding my breath, I dove in.

"Where is it?" Isaac crooned, inside the memory, his violet eyes staring straight into the aura. He stood there, in that lab, one grim reality superimposed over the other. Except in his reality, the room was free of that macabre smear of crimson blood.

I stared through a set of black-rimmed glasses. The glass was cracked, fracturing my stepfather where he stood, several steps away, hands linked before him while he surveyed Mason with a frown.

Mason.

A howl of agony filled the night. Mine. It was horror and guilt and sheer goddamn pain as it grated through my lungs and up my throat. It curdled as my tears broke free, stealing my vision. I collapsed forward, face pressing to the damp ground, blood smearing across my cheek. My breaths rasped from me, short and shallow, as I fought to pull in air.

Theo tore a hand through his hair, staring at me. "What's going on?"

"It's …" Words failed me. I blinked, and warm rivulets of tears slithered free.

"It's who?" Theo said, tone easy, gentle. But the words were knowing, like he might already have the answer.

And I'd already had it too; I'd just refused to accept it.

A sob broke from my chest, and the years since Mason had come into my life flashed before my eyes, a tickertape of memories. Finding me in the Coven. Helping me through Isaac. Saving me.

Guilt. So much guilt.

"You gotta talk to me," Theo coaxed.

The words burst from my lips in a ragged flurry. "It's Mason."

"BRY!" Kane roared, voice distant.

I blinked, then scrubbed my vision clear. "Kane?" I uttered hoarsely, my voice scarcely above a whisper.

"BRY!" he said, closer now. Closer. I needed him.

"She's here!" Theo called back.

Kane exploded into the room, his stare voltaic as it tracked across Mason's torso, then fixed on me. His footfalls were heavy and sure as he closed the distance between us in three easy strides. His hand landed on my shoulder. Heavy. Calloused. Familiar.

He was there.

My Alpha dropped to his knees, his hand latching over my wrist before he dragged me to him, cradling me against his chest. His touch roved up and down my waist, his thumbs grazing my abdomen like he needed to feel me—to feel us.

With my strength waning, I collapsed into him and gave him my weight.

Kane's stare went unfocused, one of those silent Pack conversations passing between him and Theo. My Alpha cursed, grip cinching tighter around me as he said, "I'm so damn sorry, Bry."

Mason. Dead.

No, not dead—slaughtered. Torn apart. Mason and I, we'd faced the worst, and had come out the other side stronger, as friends. I'd known he still cared, but he'd set that aside for what was right … for me.

I drowned in that guilt.

Kane trailed a hand over my blood-soaked hair. Mason's blood.

I swiped my eyes again, blinking my tears away. Joaquin stood in the door, hands linked before him, Bower at his side, his soot-covered face pale as he took in the massacre.

"Come on," my Alpha said. "Let's get you outta here."

I shook my head and gripped his shoulder, the movement feeble. "Don't."

"You don't need to see that."

"Yes, I do." Because I needed to finish. I couldn't walk away. Not yet. I owed it to Mason to figure out what Isaac had been after.

"No," my Alpha said, his voice firm. "You don't."

Joaquin shook his head. "No good's gonna come from this, banshee."

I leaned back, disentangling myself from Kane as I straightened my spine, because cowering in a crumpled mess wasn't about to convince them I could do what needed to be done. Clearing my throat, I said, "Answers might."

Silence reigned.

Sliding to the side, I unfocused my eyes, and slipped back in.

Amber paced around Mason. His breathing was frantic and staccato. Broken. Her hair stuck off in all directions, several matts knotting the tufts at the crown of her head and above her ears. Her skin was dirty, like she hadn't showered in weeks. Her jeans had grass and blood stains, small holes pockmarking their front, while her formerly white shirt had yellowed around the neck and hems.

She loped to the side, her movements decidedly canine as her honeyed eyes darted from Isaac to Mason, frantic and wild. There was a disconnect in that stare, like a circuit had snapped, the signals not bridging the gap. Like she'd been severed from reality. She was there, and yet very much not. Not fully feral. Not yet. But she'd stepped dangerously close to that path.

It reminded me of Ivy. Of the loss of anything sane or safe.

I sniffed, frantic. Why wasn't soul-Mason coming? I'd talked to Naomi and Cassandra's shadow walker, Frances, after they'd died. Where the hells was he?

Isaac eyed Amber, his posture stiff, as if he recognized the danger she posed as he prowled closer to Mason. Clearing his throat, Isaac cut in. "It's imperative you work with me, Mason. You will regret it if you don't."

Work with him? What the shadow and sage?

The aura started to fade, particles slowly scattering like dust.

"I'm not giving you anything," Mason said, his fear cresting, pressing in on my chest. Its tang coated my tongue.

"Zahara would like to offer you great wealth and protections if you assist to our end."

Mason stilled. "You told her what you are?"

"I did." His chin lifted, a malevolent smile taking over his face.

And from his position, it made sense, considering that—whether anyone had gone public with it or not—his secret wasn't exactly a secret anymore.

"You'll give me what I need, or Amber will *make you." My stepfather edged into Mason's line of sight. His violet eyes might've matched his son's in color, but the cold, dead, watch-the-world-burn look they contained was a savagery all its own as he added, "Limb by limb."*

What do you want, Isaac? Just say what you fucking want.

The scent of ether grew thicker.

Amber's boned claws extended as she bared her canines in an empty smile and set her claws to Mason's throat. "Tell me where it is, witch boy."

He shook his head.

"Tell us and we won't hurt her,*" Isaac said, raising Mason's phone, showing the screensaver of my smiling face.*

My heart shattered.

Mason's laugh was a ragged half-sob. "You can't *hurt her." His stare tracked to Amber. "Kane won't allow it."*

Amber's nostrils flared, her boned claws vibrating at his neck. "He will."

"She's his mate," Mason spat.

What the hells was Mason doing, goading her?

She rocked on her feet, restless. "She can be replaced." Spittle flew from her lips, landing on her chest. The floor.

Replaced? She'd said something similar before, the day I'd run with Lucas. Something about my Alpha claiming her, too, so I wouldn't be needed anymore.

Mason met her unhinged glare. "You think he'd ever replace her *with* you*?"*

Amber shrieked, then exploded forward, claws extended. She plunged them deep into Mason's neck. He bucked, a loud, gurgling hiss breaking from him as he struggled to breathe.

I flinched. Isaac's face went red, and he tore his hands through his hair and cursed. "What have you done?"

"He wasn't talking." Amber smiled, all hunger and teeth—then she twisted her wrist, tearing Mason wide.

He jerked, convulsing.

Isaac's attention snapped around like he was hunting for a solution. He tugged the wolfsbane from his pocket, then shoved it her way. "Douse the place." His stare darkened, a malevolence taking root in that expression, like another solution had just presented itself. "Make a mess. Have fun." He aimed for the door. "Use it to send a message. Show them we're serious."

I looked away, but held Mason's hand tight. I couldn't let go. I wouldn't. "*Talk to me, Mason,*" I silently begged. "*Please!*"

"I'm here, Briar," he said, words echoing through my mind. Faint. Drifting. *"I just needed you to see."*

"*Mason,*" I uttered, replying in kind through a sob. "*I'm sorry. I'm so sorry.*"

"*Don't blame yourself.*" A sigh. "*I couldn't be his prisoner again. I'd rather be dead.*"

He faded out more.

The ether grew thicker. So thick, I could barely find air.

My grip locked over my obsidian as if I could hold him there by sheer strength alone. The pound of my heart filled my ears and drowned out all other sound. I coughed, my voice a croak as I begged the wraith, "Not yet. Don't take him yet."

"*Listen to me, Briar,*" Mason said, his words desperate. "*You need to be ready. He's going to come for—*"

The aura vanished.

My heart stopped. "NO!" I screamed, my hands balling into fists as I collapsed forward.

Kane lunged, arms shooting out to catch me.

Bower swiped a hand over his forehead, streaking it with a line of soot. "We should call in the others," he said: a suggestion, not an order, because the predators were already on edge, and tipping them over it was the worst of ideas.

"The sun's still up. We'll figure out a time," my Alpha cut in, then gestured at me like it explained everything.

And it must've, because Bower inclined his head.

"We'll let you know when," Joaquin added.

The sun. It was still up. Not for much longer, but in the moment, that was all that mattered. Sluggishly, my mind caught on a thought.

"The tunnels," I uttered. The ones the shadow walkers used for daytime passage into the RC. "We need to check the tunnels." Because sage knew who might be down there, trapped or otherwise.

Joaquin inclined his head and his eyes drifted out of focus as he talked to his Pack. "On it."

Kane's hard body was strung taut. I burrowed my head into the crook of his neck, trembling as he carried me away. The steady rock of his gait lulled me as we moved—to where, I had no clue, until the creak of the truck door sounded. The vehicle groaned when he set his ass down, slid into the driver's seat, then settled me in beside him.

My gaze slid forward. Smoke rolled from the charred remains of the RC's human wing. Wolves and magi sifted through the damage. To the right, bodies. Dozens of them. All patients—all human. All fuel for those anti-government sentiments in Ithica.

Kane's square knuckle hooked under my chin, pulling me back to him while his other arm gripped me tight as if he tried to offer me something. Reassurance. Love. Anything he could.

I reached for my phone. "I'll make the calls."

"It can wait," he said against my hair, voice hoarse.

"The Coven, Kane." I sniffed, and leaned back so I could see him better. "They need to know." I had to think about the dirge … About everything.

His eyes moved between mine, the rough pad of his thumb tracking a line across my cheek as he swiped away my tears. So many tears. "It can wait," he repeated.

I inclined my head. It wasn't like I had the words to tell them anyway. Not yet. So instead, I sagged against him again.

He turned the truck over, and the rumble of the engine filled the world as Kane put it in drive and steered us away, but it couldn't drown out the memory of Mason's gurgling gasps.

Chapter Seven

My eyes were heavy, the sun falling, that day painfully long by the time Kane steered us up to our home. He'd been silent on the drive, left hand on the wheel while the other gripped me, thoughts I couldn't discern writhing behind his gaze.

I'd quietly sobbed the whole way as I stared down at my blood-soaked palms, the sharp, copper scent of it searing my airways. My Alpha slowed the truck to a stop, the gearshift clunking as it slid into place when we parked.

My phone buzzed. Sighing, I pulled it free, a hint of my sadness ebbing at the text on that screen.

Lisa: *Back in Cambria in the morning. Bower got me clearance to assess the bar.*

I frowned at those words.

Me: *Damage?*

Lisa: *Water from the run-off of the fire. You better cart your ass over to see me, chickie.*

My thumbs moved slowly, and I had to force them to work as I replied.

Me: *I will.*

The leather seat groaned, the truck lifting as Kane exited. I slipped away my device and stepped into the cool evening air as I followed my Alpha, his stare fixed on me. That big hand engulfed mine and he led me inside.

We passed the mirror, and I turned to take myself in.

He guided my face away. "No, Bry. Don't look."

Kicking off his boots, he took a knee, then gingerly, like he feared I'd break, took off mine too. Rising, he aimed us upstairs, through our room, and into the shower. His warm hands brushed my hair back, his words a low, easy rumble when he instructed, "Arms up."

I moved, rigid and robotic, and did what he said.

Taking the hem of my dress, he tracked it north over my hips and waist, then tugged it free. Next, he drew down my thong and unlatched my bra. Grabbing his shirt at the shoulder, he pulled it off, baring his cut abs and broad chest before he stripped the rest of the way.

His stare was distant, like he was lost in some thought, or idea. And if the tensing of his body was any indication, it was one he didn't like.

Turning the tap, he tested the water, then maneuvered me under the warm stream. His thick, powerful legs carried him into the shower and his torso pressed against my back. Taking the soap, he lathered it over my skin, working it slowly. Methodically. He covered every inch of me, his coarse palms washing me clean. Blood and soot slithered down my body, then swirled away and vanished into the drain.

"Eyes closed," he said, as the fruity scent of my shampoo filled the void and his fingers dove into my hair, working my scalp.

I fell into his touch, desperate for everything it offered. Safety, warmth, and that timeless, unyielding love that sated my soul.

Bubbles trailed down my flesh until he'd rinsed me clean. Taking my waist, he turned me and braced my palms against the cool tile of the wall. He kneaded my weary muscles, and I moaned, spine arching as I pressed my backside into him.

He hardened against me, but shifted back, putting space between us. He kept kneading, but made no move to act on it.

I reopened my eyes and pivoted to face him.

He must've read my intention, 'cause his expression creased. "No, Bry. It's not—"

I flattened my palms over the rigid lines of his stomach. "Please, Kane."

His shoulders bunched and rose with a ragged inhale, his eyes meeting my own. "I don't wanna hurt you."

"You won't." He couldn't. Wasn't capable.

Pressing up on my toes, I kissed him slowly. His arms bracketed my back, engulfing me as his body eclipsed mine. And it felt good to be surrounded by him. So, so good.

One of those broad hands tracked along my jaw, fingers grazing the base of my neck.

I moaned, soft and desperate. I needed to feel him. To know he was real. That we were still there, and everything was alright. For now.

His tongue swept over mine, the kiss slow and ardent and everything I needed. He pulled back, his stare spearing mine as he shut off the shower then reached for a towel, drying me slowly, as if one wrong move would cause me to crumble. And really, maybe it would.

He moved on, drying himself as droplets rolled down his hair, slipping from his brow and chin. They struck my chest and trickled low, slithering between my breasts. But his molten gaze never left mine.

Edging close, he set his palm over my heart, then leaned in and rested his forehead against mine.

My fingers traced a delicate line along that V of muscle in his abs, before brushing his hard and oh-so-ready cock. I gripped him and his length pulsed against my hand. But still, he didn't move.

"Take me to bed, Kane," I murmured, because I needed more. Needed to loosen the knot that twisted inside my chest. To chase the dark thoughts shadowing my mind. To forget … for a while.

That voltaic stare took me in, every line and crease and movement, as if he wasn't sure, and desperately needed to be.

But I was. "Now."

Bending, he gripped my thighs and lifted, wrapping my legs around him as he maneuvered us out. Crossing to the bedroom, he slowly lay me back on the bed, then moved up my body, his powerful form ranging over me, his touch tracking my cheek.

Peering at him through my lashes, I opened for him.

His throat dipped as he swallowed hard, like it took a solid amount of effort to hold himself back. "If you're doing this for me—"

"No. This is for me." I insisted. "*I* need this, Kane."

He inclined his head and shifted, his movements steady as he lined up his tip with my entrance. Gradually, like he was giving me the chance to change my mind, he rocked forward, one thick inch. Two. He kept going until I'd taken him all, and his entire length was inside me. He groaned, his right arm bracketed my waist, his left holding him up. His movements were tentative as he arched forward and retreated.

It felt good to be held by him. Loved by him. So damn good.

My palms dug into his back, holding him close, and urging him on.

"I'm here, Bry."

I pressed my face into the hollow of his neck, wrapping myself around him as I breathed him in.

"I've got you." His deep voice rumbled through me.

My nails dug into his shoulders, using them as leverage while he moved. Craving contact, I arched my spine and rolled my hips, taking him deeper and deeper.

His hold cinched tight, and I fell into it—into *him*. He was all I needed. His warmth. His love. He held my broken shards together.

My body heated, my core tightening around him as I crested closer to the edge. His expression changed, his breaths coming in rough, jagged grunts. Close. He was close.

"Come, Kane. Please," I uttered, my words a desperate command.

He grunted, then bared his teeth as he locked me in place and rocked into me harder, grinding against me again and again and again.

My orgasm seared through me. It raced out, a current of pleasure so intense, my vision flashed white. I gasped, that friction burning me whole as he ground into me and loosed a low snarl, coming hard. His hot seed flooded me. Marking me. Consuming my scent with his own.

I kept going until I had rung out the last drops of our need and every muscle in my body fell limp and languid. I sagged, and he withdrew, then rolled onto his back, taking me with him so I could collapse onto his chest.

We lay that way, my Alpha's broad hand resting over my knee until our breathing slowed. I leaned in, set my head against his arm and gave him my weight.

The more time that passed, though, the more those macabre-tinted thoughts crept back in. *Mason. Blood. Amber. Blood. Isaac. Blood.*

Kane shifted, propping up his head on one arm to better see me. Deep lines creased his forehead. He looked pained. Not for himself. Sure, he and Mason had mended fences, as much as they could, but Mason had been a critical part of my life for a long time. Including a time when my Alpha couldn't be there.

It was just another loss I carried. Another loss to take.

Taking my chin, Kane trailed the pad of his thumb over my bottom lip.

"Isaac was after something," I muttered, because I had not one doubt that he wanted to know what I'd found out. But my Alpha was who he was, and when it came to hurting me, he'd never push.

He watched me. Waited.

My stomach sank. "I don't know what it was."

I'd naively hoped that losing his puppets would send Isaac slinking into the shadows where he'd wither, rot, and die. Unsurprisingly, that hope had been wholly misplaced. He'd never go away. Not until we stopped him. Not until we separated his head from his fucking body and handed it to the wraith herself.

"You and Lucas are right." I traced a finger down his chest. "The Conclave need to know about Isaac."

Everyone needed to know.

He inclined his head.

We needed every eye we could get hunting him down. Looking for that scar. Stopping him. Me keeping his secret had only ever protected him. And I'd rot before I helped that man for one more goddamn second.

"I wanna do it in stages." Because moving too fast could mean devastating consequences. "We'll test Lucas's theory first. Get the tattoo, make sure he's shielded, then tell the Coven, and see how they react before we go to your Pack. After that, we'll tell Danika and the others." Our people deserved to see we'd put them first. Besides, we'd be needing to get our shit together fast, 'cause obsidian only knew how things would shake out once the Conclave found out.

He pressed a kiss to my forehead, those silver topaz eyes filling my sight. "You sure?"

I dragged a deep breath through my lungs to slow my pounding heart. It didn't work. "It's time." I forced my tongue to work around the lead weight trying to pin it down. "We gotta do this. If we don't, he's never gonna stop."

His chin dipped in a nod, his fingers stroking my cheek before he brushed several fallen hairs away from my face. "Once we start, there's no looking back until he's fucking dead." He set his mouth to mine, and I closed my eyes, taking everything he offered, because the wraith knew, I needed it.

Those muscled arms encased me; it felt like he could shield me from everything. From Isaac. My Alpha would inflict any violence necessary. Problem was, we were a trio now, locked in a life-sharing bond. Our baby's fate depended on me, while my Alpha and I depended on each other. It was a wholly powerful and yet wildly delicate scenario.

Victor outing the life-tether my claiming mark offered between me and my Alpha to Isaac had ratcheted that fear to a new precipice. And while Amber'd protected my Alpha through me before, she *was* working with my stepfather now. That aside, it wasn't exactly like she'd been operating at peak capacity.

Worrying my cheek between my teeth, I asked, "Can a were claim more than one mate?"

His head drew back and his eyes darkened. "You trying to tell me something?"

I shook my head. "It was just something Amber said." Clearing my throat, I repeated, "Can they?"

His stare was distant while he considered. "I don't know." His warm knuckle hooked under my jaw and forced my gaze to his. "You're the only one, Bry."

My mouth tugged to the side, 'cause I had no doubt on that front, but my distrust of Amber was on point. Yeah, she loved my Alpha—or whatever her tainted version of love was. But she'd made a crap ton of less-than-stellar decisions in the name of that love before, when she wasn't a lone wolf losing her mind, so I wasn't holding my breath for any rational plays from her.

Pressing my face into him, I sniffed and muttered, "I love you, Kane."

His grip flexed against me. "I love you, too." He stilled then, going silent. The questionable kind of silence that set my alarm bells pinging. His eyes narrowed, that thought from before our shower seething in their depths. But whatever it was …

"What's going on, Big Bad?"

"I've got an idea, Bry." His deep voice rumbled, but there was something in the way he'd said it, a strain in those words, that made my heart clench and told me I wasn't going to like what he was about to say.

Settling my chin on my hand, I took my lip between my teeth. "What kind of idea?"

"The solving-a-problem kind."

I pushed up onto my elbows, eyes narrowing. "What *kind* of problem?"

"The Isaac kind."

It shouldn't have sounded bad, but …

"Why do I get the feeling I'm not gonna like this?"

"Because you won't."

My stomach roiled and my chest tightened. "Gonna need more than that, Kane."

He rolled his shoulders, his fingers flexing over the small of my back as he crushed me to him like he feared I'd vanish. Or run.

"Last time I did things behind your back, I fucking hurt you." He tilted his head to the side, and his voice was thick as he said, "I won't make that mistake again."

The last time, he'd gone to Whitney—his ex—asking for help. He'd been trying to learn about how carrying his Alpha-baby might affect me before we'd known I was pregnant. He'd been trying to protect me, but it had backfired hard and become just another weapon Isaac had used against us.

The arch of my brow was high and sharp, and a bitter tang coated my tongue. "Does this involve Whitney?"

I trusted him and could handle a lot, but the searing jealousy that stole through my veins—

"No." The answer was hard. Vehement.

I exhaled a wholly petty and utterly relieved breath. "But I still won't like this plan?"

His lip tugged at the corners, but the smile was stiff, and it didn't reach his eyes. "No, you won't."

My mouth ran dry, my pulse kicking up.

He took my face, his hands wrapping into my hair. "If this is gonna work, I'm gonna have to do some things, Bry."

Iron fires, take me. What the shadow and sage did he have in mind?

I dragged in a steadying breath, because his level, no-bullshit tone told me he meant it. There was a fire in those eyes, one that said he thought whatever this was could work. And if my Alpha thought that …

Isaac was endgame. We needed to get him. And we needed to end this. Decisively. With blood.

I shoved my nerves and desperation down to the hollow pit that had opened inside my chest. Because, at the end of the day, too much rode on us winning, and my fears weren't reason enough to hold back. That didn't stop the cold terror chasing down my spine, which meant my nod was weak. Obsidian only knew what I was about to sign myself up for, but I trusted Kane with my life. "Okay."

He swallowed hard, his throat dipping as he inclined his head, then told me.

And he was right. I really, *really* hated his plan.

Chapter Eight

The sky the next morning was bright and full of life, a stark contrast to the soot and carnage staining the better part of the neutral grounds. I stared at No Man's Land as Kane rolled up to the lot, thumb trailing the pages of *Ancient Histories*, the journal Mason had grabbed from the RC's restricted library—the only book he'd found with any talk of changelings. I'd read it again and again, trying to understand, and had already memorized the only passage that seemed to carry weight.

Changelings are made of the Deep. Of the Dark. Fear is what they know. It is why and what they are. Broken things that seek the chaos. When the call to the wraith comes, they die in the light and return.

But whatever the hells it meant, I still had no clue. Sighing, I tucked the book inside my purse.

I'd put out the call just an hour before, notifying the Coven about Mason's death. My heart was still weak and broken, but seeing Lisa … I needed it. Needed something normal, and someone warm. The list of people I could turn to had rapidly been dwindling. And, chances were, after everything went down, it'd be shorter still. But Lisa? Her, I could count on.

The glass entrance stood open, my human bestie hovering in its frame, arms wide and ready for me.

My Alpha had barely slowed the truck before I flung the door wide open and bolted, beelining for the bar.

"*Bry!*" he roared, vehicle clunking as he shoved it into park. But I was already gone.

The place looked exactly the same, and yet wildly not. The leaves coating the tall vines that climbed its red-brick façade and the nearby lamppost were a colorful collection of fading greens, burnt oranges and reds. Graying Spanish moss covered the trees that towered toward the back of the building, putting a floral scent on the air.

And Lisa, she looked good. Her sleek, midnight-colored hair fell over her shoulders, impeccably straight. Those angular umber eyes had an edge of weariness—the same one we all wore—but they were bright. Free. Her own.

Her face softened. "How are you?" she asked as I closed in. Fast.

I shook my head, wide eyes begging "*Not now*." I just needed that breath. A moment of normalcy. I needed her.

Launching forward, I flew past the Castor stones and threw myself at her, our bodies colliding in a violent crash. She stumbled back, legs buckling under my attack. We slow-motion tumbled, landing lightly on the ground.

"Ow!" Lisa grumbled.

"Shush!" I squished her in my embrace. "You're ruining the moment."

My Alpha's heavy-booted feet pounded behind me, that pissed-off, wolfy glare locking on mine as he reached down and lifted me like a suitcase. I disentangled myself from my best friend, offering him the scowliest of scowls before he righted me and aimed a loose fist Lisa's way. "Gotta see your hand."

"Of course." She eyed me askance and tsked. "Very irresponsible not to ask first, chickie."

Kane chucked his chin her way in a "what she fucking said" gesture.

I rolled my eyes, a gift specifically for her. "Traitor."

Brushing away the clumps of gravel she'd accumulated, Lisa tugged up her right sleeve and showed him.

He scanned her scarless hand, inclined his head and stretched his neck.

Had I gotten ahead of myself? Sure. But like the Iron Hells I'd ever concede that to either of them.

Plastering on a grin, I wiggled in front of my temperamental wolf, giving him my back.

His palm clamped down over my ass when he said across our bond. "*Don't make me punish you, Bry.*"

That sounded more like a challenge—one I was unequivocally up for. Peering at him over my shoulder, I waggled my brows.

He grunted; it might've been eagerness or irritation. Who could say?

Lisa's head was cocked. "Are you two finished?"

Clearing my throat, I turned to her, face beaming bright at the sight of her. "I can't believe you're here!"

She dropped her hands to her hips. "Who else is gonna spy on all your preternatural behinds?"

Kane's mouth ticked up and I barked a laugh. "Thought you were sent back to clean up a mess?"

She winked. "I'm multipurpose. Now, cart your ass in here," she said, waving an arm for us to follow as she strode inside.

As we entered, the sun cut hard lines through the windows. Soot coated the walls and the wooden beams along the ceiling, while water stained the hardwood floors, buckling them in places where it had soaked in. The air was damp and musty, smoke coating the bar top, stools, tables, and floor, while chairs sat flipped on their sides. Sage, it hadn't even burned, but the damage had been brutal.

My nose crinkled. "I like what you've done with the place."

Her mouth pulled to the side. "Should've smelled it an hour ago."

Kane huffed. "Still can."

I batted his arm, my booted heels clicking on the floor as I walked around, gathering the detritus and piling it onto tray after tray. My Alpha righted the downed furniture.

"You look great, chickie." Lisa's expression softened as she combed her fingers through my hair. "Glowing, even."

I fought the widening of my eyes and swallowed hard. "Any changes in Ithica?"

Sauntering to the bar, she grabbed a stack of papers and aimed for a nearby booth.

My Alpha gestured for me to sit first, but I lived for rankling Kane Slade, so I did what I did best and rooted my feet to the floor while offering him an obnoxious, toothy grin.

He arched a slow, singular brow in challenge.

Lisa sighed. "We all know who's gonna win here, Briar."

"Pfft!" I folded my arms over my chest. "Yeah, we *do* know exactly who—"

Kane hefted me off the ground, took his seat, then dropped me into his lap. His expression was a brash "test me" challenge with a side of "wanna play?".

My jaw dropped. "Rude. Just rude."

He offered a devastating wink before that rough hand settled between my thighs.

The touch had my core burning up, 'cause push my buttons though he might, he still managed to hit all the right ones. Straightening, I tossed my hair over one shoulder, then leaned respectably onto my elbows, giving Lisa the full weight of my attention.

Her chest rose with a heavy inhale when she shoved the papers my way. "There've been more deaths along our western edge. Things are getting tense. Talks of what happened last night. Debates on how to handle things."

"Handle what kind of things?" I prompted, the pages crinkling as I sorted through them, looking for Zahara. A front-page headline jumped out: "*Citizens Demand Government Does More in the Face of Cambrian Chaos*".

"The situation with you." She tucked several strands of hair behind an ear. "The public sentiment is shifting. When news of the RC burning hit, people took to the streets to celebrate."

My brows cinched together hard. "People *died* at the RC."

"Rich people," she said, then raised her hands, palms out, to stay my rage. "Not saying I think it's right, but you've gotta understand what they see. Most Ithicans don't have connections or deep pockets, which means the RC is out of reach. So they see the uber wealthy help their friends and families to get whatever they need while their own children suffer." She shook her head. "This faction is just stoking the fire. Things are a mess."

Wraith take me. My gaze slid to Kane's; his own eyes were narrowed.

"The Conclave can do something about this," I said. Do something about that inequality.

He inclined his head. "We'll broach it," he said, then dragged the pages his way, scanning them one by one.

My phone buzzed and I swallowed hard. A number I didn't know flashed across the screen. I had no desire to answer, but what with me being de facto head of the Coven, along with everything that'd gone down the night before …

I reached for it.

"Hello?" I said, fidgeting with the hem of my dress as I tugged it down.

"Briaaaaaar."

My lungs seized.

Isaac. It was fucking *Isaac*!

The warmth drained from my body. My eyes flew wide as I rose, heart stuttering in my chest. I edged away from the booth.

My Alpha must've heard who it was, because a wave of power rolled through the room, rocking me hard. He exploded toward me, heat pulsing off him in waves. He stopped less than a breath away and his stare blazed as it pinned mine, his canines extended, looking ready to tear out an Isaac-shaped throat. Speaking through his tightly clenched jaw, he muttered, "Gimme the phone, Bry."

Lisa's gaze snapped between us. She clearly pieced together that puzzle quick, 'cause she paled, body trembling wildly.

Was denying my Alpha an option? No. Did I want to talk to Isaac? Also no. But nor was I about to cut myself off from that conversation.

Putting the device on speaker, I passed it over.

Kane's grip flexed like he was fighting not to crush the thing in his grasp. He tossed the phone onto the table, and his hands made fists as he dropped them down on either side of it, angling forward as if he itched to pounce through the screen. "What do you want?"

"Oh, Kane. How could I have guessed?" Isaac taunted. "How's my son?"

My Alpha's eyes blazed electric, charged with a violence that lit up the bar like a second moon. "He's not your fucking son."

"Spout your whims all you like; it doesn't change what's true. My blood runs through his veins. It won't be your footsteps he follows in; it *will* be mine."

I'd never loathed anyone the way I loathed that man. Lucas was a possession to him. A pawn. Isaac had played this game again and again. Only this time, the game wasn't his.

Kane's voice was so guttural, he sounded more wolf than man as he said, "Never."

Isaac's answering laugh burned across my already-frayed nerves and set my blood aflame. My stomach hardened. "You burned the RC, Isaac."

"Oh, no, Briar dear," he said, all innocence and lies. "Amber did that."

"Because you *unleashed* her," I snarled. "She's a lone wolf for—"

Kane cut his hand through the air, silencing me. My head snapped back, the power of my glower on goddamn point.

"*Leave it, Bry,*" he warned across our bond.

"*She's losing herself, Kane,*" I reminded him. If Amber had just been a danger to Isaac, I'd have stepped back to let that train wreck itself—but she wasn't. Not even close.

"Briar?" Isaac said, tone entirely too calm. "Are you there?"

My Alpha's stare met mine. "*Trust me.*"

My brow furrowed so low, it was a wonder I could see him. "I'm here," I replied.

Lisa appeared at my side, chin resting on my shoulder as her arm looped through mine as if she needed the support.

"Ah, good," my stepfather crooned. "While Amber took some … liberties, she was still helping to show you how far I'll go to get what I want."

I rolled my eyes. "Like I didn't already fucking know that."

"Tsk, tsk. No need to be rude." A rustling cut through the line, like trees on the wind. "I merely require a barter, Briar."

The muscles of Kane's forearms flexed, sinew and tendons rolling as he moved. "Stop wasting our time, Isaac." He edged closer to the screen. "Now, what the fuck do you want?"

"I want more serum supplies."

My eyes crushed closed. *That's* what Isaac had wanted from Mason? I steadied the frenetic beat of my heart as I exhaled slowly and let the rage rush in. "Hard pass."

"You will give them to me, Briar."

"Why?" I pushed.

"Because I said so."

Ha! That was bullshit on bullshit. Still, it didn't take much to ferret out what he wanted, 'cause Isaac had already given Zahara those magi, were, and shadow-walker serums—ones he'd saddled with time constraints, making them useful for just hours. The only thing she'd wanted, the only thing he could barter, were the limitless ones.

My heart stopped when realization hit. "*He told Zahara what he is, Kane.*"

He stiffened as his mind caught up. "*He promised her his ability.*"

It only stood to reason—why else would he give her his absolute, most deadly secret? That gift from Isaac, it was a massive goddamn boon. One that would give her the ability to slip from skin to skin, making her just as dangerous as him. And one that would get him whatever the hells he'd wanted.

The man had gotten so used to having power, he'd actually lost it. Steadying myself, I told him, "You've got no leverage here."

"There are always deals to be made. Everyone wants something. And I know what it is you want."

"Your head," my Alpha answered, his voice so rough it grated over my skin.

Isaac let loose a dark laugh. "Let's be reasonable now. We both know that's an unattainable request. However"—a pause—"I can offer the next best thing."

His heart, if he even had one of those.

"Then what?" I said.

The smile in his voice was poison. "Then I'll leave you alone."

My lips pulled into a sneer, I didn't have to be a wolf to scent the lie in those words. Isaac was a trickster from the Deep. Carnage was what he was. But the fact that he wanted his supplies bad enough to even lay that offer on the table …

"Tell us why you need them," Kane demanded, since our minds were on the same track. Get him to confirm so we'd understand, have the full scope of what we faced.

The answer didn't matter, 'cause there wasn't a chance in the hells he'd be getting his hands on anything, seeing as we weren't the ten shades of stupid it took to give him any kind of access.

"I've encountered some … problems."

Problems? The hairs on the back of my neck stood on end. Anything Isaac deemed a problem was the cataclysmic kind of bad. My gaze sought Kane's, but my Alpha's seething glare was still fixed on the phone.

Kane's boned claws pushed against his flesh, begging to tear free. To sink deep into my stepfather's throat. To repay him for everything he'd done. He snarled, "What kind of fucking problems?"

Silence, long and drawn out.

"Start talking or we're done," Kane said.

A heavy, disappointed sigh. "Zahara has plans I am unaligned with."

At that, Kane's blazing gaze tracked to mine.

Lisa's grip locked down around me as I swallowed hard, then demanded, "Gonna need more than that, Isaac."

"I can't just *tell* you, Briar. I'm in need of that advantage for the time being." The words were a taunt. A game. But there was a cold ice in his voice, one that set my teeth on edge, because it told me he wasn't bluffing.

Isaac's morals were on the level with pond scum, so if he was against something, that meant whatever it was went against him. Specifically, that it took something from him he sure as sage didn't wanna lose. Seeing as we'd whittled down his world to a fine-ass point, the list of what could be taken from him was ultra-goddamn limited, so it didn't take much to deduce.

Power, safety, or Lucas.

Bad. All of it was the super kind of bad. And the fact he'd be willing to loop us in and make a deal …

Still, in his current position, what in the iron fires would he consider *power*? I wanted answers, but I was sure as the shadowed moon that my Alpha wasn't about to negotiate—

"What do you need?" Kane offered.

My mouth dropped, my spine snapping straight, 'cause what the actual hells? The scowl I lobbed my wolf's way would've been a challenge if our lives weren't the permanent kind of tethered. Since when did he do *anything* to help Isaac?

"I will send you a list."

My Alpha's jaw ground, lips drawing up in a snarl. "When do you need it?"

Isaac's answer came fast. "Now."

Now. My mind tripped and stumbled before righting as I caught my Alpha's game. Information. He was sniffing out information, trying to gauge the urgency, to determine the stock and scale of Isaac's need. And lure him out.

"Where do we meet?"

Isaac's laugh was harsh and knowing. "Come now, Kane. I'm not simple enough to fall for that." There was a clank of glass through the line, then he added, "We both know what you'll do if you see me again."

If. Not when. My shoulders fell. It wasn't like I'd expected any different, but a girl could hope.

But then a truth hit. One more terrifying than anything else he'd said. I took a steadying breath and uttered through our connection, "*He wants them* now, *Kane*."

His chin dipped in a nod, 'cause he'd picked up what I put down. "*If he's in that much of a rush, it means—*"

Kane stretched his neck. "*It means there's a clock ticking*."

A clock that counted down to big-ass trouble. It meant Zahara had a plan, one that was already in motion. One that made Isaac think he didn't have time to waste.

The question was, who was that trouble for?

I cursed internally and turned away. Lisa's face was ghostly.

I mouthed, "Call Bower."

She nodded, slipped from my hold, and quietly padded toward her office at the back of the bar.

Zahara had a plan. My mind spun, limbs going weak as the conversation we'd had the first time I met her flashed across my memory.

"Why do you want this?" I asked her.

A cool wind cut down from the mountains, sending a chill across my skin and ruffling the strands of Zahara's strategically spiked, pixie-cut gray wig. She looked somewhere in her forties, her dark shades shielding her eyes.

There was an air about her: the way her chin angled just a tad too high, spine a bit too straight. She stood like she owned the place. Like she'd never faced a problem her status couldn't fix. Like she had zero comprehension of the word no.

She smoothed the lapels of her crisp white pantsuit. "Because I don't like being weak."

I rubbed my temples. "You're anything but, Zahara. Ithica has *weapons."*

"That they do." She leaned closer. "But I'd much prefer to be *one."*

My head was spinning, my limbs going weak. Wraith take me.

She tugged her shades free, those onyx-colored eyes sharp. "You think our government is strong, but they fear you as much as you fear our iron. And what happens to us if our stores deplete, and the bullets run out?"

I raised my hands. "Okay, but what if—and hear me out on this—we just didn't fucking fight?"

She smiled, but nothing about it was pleasant. "You're born predators, Briar. And I no longer want to be prey."

Sweet sage.

The shake of her head was slow. "Don't worry. For the time being, this is merely a … precaution."

I swallowed hard. She wanted to be a weapon—but against whom? At the time, she'd implied it was against the beasties of our world, but the border between us was locked tight, which meant she had nothing to defend against.

My chest cinched over my lungs, making it hard to breathe. It didn't make sense, and I needed to figure it out fast, but first things first.

"*We need to find Zahara, Kane.*"

My Alpha's stare turned inward as he considered those words. "Tell us where Zahara is, and we'll make the trade," he instructed my stepfather.

"If I tell you where she is," Isaac drawled, "you won't give me what I want."

My mouth thinned to a hard line. "If you tell us how to find her, we can handle her from there."

His response was hard. Unequivocal. "No."

Power of obsidian! If Isaac was desperate, why hold back? I stiffened, realization hitting like a brick to the face. She wasn't his problem; she was his damn *solution.* "She's promised you safety."

His laugh was ominous. "Get me what I need, Briar. I'll be in touch." He hung up.

Kane slammed a fist onto the table and roared.

Reaching forward, I snapped up my phone. Enough was enough. I was done talking. I needed to make plans. It'd taken Cassandra an age to find the changeling who'd killed her father. My Alpha might've shared some of his longer lifespan with me, but it wasn't the immortal shadow-walker kinda time. Nor was I gonna give Isaac that long. He'd breathed enough free air. We'd still hunt Zahara, but giving him any more power was a hard fucking no.

I needed to move fast, as we'd only be able to stall that Conclave meeting for so long.

My Alpha rose to his towering height, then eyed me. "What's going on, Bry?"

"Doing what needs to be done." Punching in my brother's name, I fired off a message.

Me: *You got a tattoo idea?*

His response was instant.

Lucas: *What?*

Me: *Figure one out fast and get ready. Your ass is going to the shop in the morning.*

***

Later that night, I sat in the kitchen, stuffing my face with my hastily made sandwich, because momma was hungry, and my little wolf pup needed to eat.

Crumbs sloughed over my tummy as I took an obnoxious bite. The bacon and tomatoes offered a savory, acidic sweetness—so, so good.

The scent of lumber filled the air. Wood was stacked here and there, waiting to be carted to the basement for Lucas's room.

Kane's hip was propped against the counter as he watched me, a possessive pride in his silver eyes.

After Lisa had filled in Bower, he'd called, pushing for that Conclave meeting, and we'd set it for the next night. For a thousand reasons, I'd wanted to hold it off, my guilt over facing Cassandra among them. But regardless of what she might do, I missed her. A lot.

We'd tell them about Isaac and what he was after with Zahara; we'd talk about the Ithican riots and the RC. We'd see what happened, and—*hopefully*—what we could figure out.

A phone pinged, the sound piercing through the room. Kane's phone. He turned to stone.

My gaze narrowed.

Reaching into his pocket, he pulled it out, then cleared his throat. "I gotta take this, Bry."

"Oooookay …" My gaze narrowed further, and I set my sandwich aside. "Then take it."

"Not here." He aimed to leave.

Not here?

The phone pinged again, and my lungs seized.

His hand flexed over it, his stare a molten torrent of emotions I couldn't read, because he was shielding them. He cursed, then winced. His voice was low and gentle as he repeated, "I gotta take this." He stepped toward me and closed his hand over my shoulder, holding for one second. Two. Then he released it, pivoted on his heel, and left, his heavy footfalls drumming a steady beat as he cut through the living room toward the front of the house.

My inhale was slow and steady as I rose and closed in on the foyer, but he was already gone.

Pulling the front door wide, I stepped onto the porch. Cassian hovered to the side, hands linked before him, a grim expression on his face.

I stared past him to where my wolf stood about forty feet away, at the end of our drive. His back was to me, his voice a low rumble, words too muffled for me to parse. But I could tell he was speaking softly. Gently. Like he cared about whoever it was. My hand rose to my chest.

His movements were stiff, his body taut when he looked my way. My throat dipped as I gripped my obsidian and sent out my power, hunting that wolfy connection between us. I brushed it. His fists unclenched, his shoulders lowering. He exhaled, then stalked away.

I stared at his broad, powerful back as he faded into the distance, my heart aching inside its bony prison. I wanted to run, wanted to hear what was being said. To tear that phone from Kane's hands and smash it to pieces. To make it stop.

Cassian shifted, pulling my attention his way.

Clearing my throat, I turned back to the house and sealed myself inside. Climbing the stairs, I set myself at the edge of the bed, curled onto my side, and tucked myself under the blanket. My emotions were a storm, and whether they were from the baby, or proportional or right, I couldn't gauge. But they were what they were.

Time slowed to a crawl. I stared out the window as the night waned and the waxing silver moon climbed high. An hour passed. Then two. The longer my Alpha was gone, the more those emotions festered, gouging their way deeper and deeper into my chest until it hurt.

My eyes grew heavy, then closed. Hugging my knees to my chest, I tried to sleep, but the chill brushing my flesh and the sluggish beat of my pulse meant sleep refused to come.

Time kept ticking, until eventually, the steady drum of footsteps closing in sounded. It was a cadence I'd know anywhere.

Kane's power rolled over me. There was a creak, followed by a thump. I opened my eyes, turning to face him as he undressed, clothes hitting the floor. He set himself onto the bed, one of those thick arms bracketing my body, crushing me to him as he lay back and pulled me to his chest. Nuzzling closer, I breathed in that wilderness scent, letting it wash over me. Calm my torrent.

His voltaic gaze tracked my face before he dragged a hand through his hair, his expression creased. Pained.

Sage, my emotions were a tempest of chaos, wild and twisting as they threatened to tear me away. My fingers curled into him, nails digging deep like I could hook myself under his skin, because I needed to tether myself. If it bothered him, he didn't say. Instead, his hold locked tighter.

I breathed him in as I grazed my lips over his throat. His groan vibrated against me and rumbled through his chest. My thighs clenched, because that sound did things to me. I flicked my tongue out, raking it up his neck, and power of obsidian, he tasted good.

"Easy, Bry." His cock hardened, digging into my side when he pulled back to better see me, peering down with that hungry, hooded gaze. "I don't wanna fuck you while you're sobbing, but I'm not above it."

The laugh that broke from me was strangled by the cacophony of emotions that roiled under my surface.

"What can I do?" Palm gliding down my spine, he kneaded my back. "To make you feel better?"

Good question. I eyed him up, considering his penance. Trailing my tongue along the back of my teeth, I smiled, all vixen and lust. "I wanna watch you, Big Bad," I said, fingers raking down his torso.

The arch of his lone brow was brash. "Watch me do what?"

I tipped my head down. "Touch yourself."

Those eyes flashed. "That so?"

I took the hem of his shirt between my fingers and tugged. "Take it off."

Gripping it at the shoulder, he pulled, dragging it over his head before he tossed it aside.

"So compliant." For me. Only for me. A playful grin tugged my expression as I peered down his body, giving myself a better line of sight. "Now, get to work."

His stare held mine, electric and charged, as he tracked his hand down his torso, then gripped his shaft at the tip and stroked, good and slow. The sinewed fibers along his forearms and chest tensed and corded. His stomach went rigid, the hills and valleys of those muscles flexing with his movements.

I sucked in a sharp breath, because the sight of it—of *him*—like that, all male and confident, totally self-possessed, like he owned the goddamn world, drove me wild. My mouth watered, thighs clenching. Sage, I was so turned on. A liquid heat pooled at my core, and I ground against his leg, needing that friction.

He stroked himself again, sucking a sharp breath through his teeth.

Impatient as ever, I couldn't take it anymore. Knocking his hand aside, I gripped his shaft. It pulsed as I took over, working him from root to tip.

I loved the control. The absolute power I had over him, the most dangerous beast in Cambria. My Alpha. Mine. It was a heady, intoxicating feeling. And I intended to drink my fill. Sliding south on the bed, I wrapped my mouth around him and took him deep.

"Fuck," he snarled, head leaning back. His hand latched around my hair, and he guided me down, encouraging. I let him set the rhythm. His hips rocked, and I sucked, tongue tracing unhurried lines.

I sucked him harder, his body growing tighter and tighter.

"Shadowed goddamn moon." He grunted, then shoved me back with a snap, jerking his chin as he ordered. "Turn around and get on your knees."

I wanted to be mad, seeing as it was my party he'd just crashed, but the challenge between us, our push/pull war for power, had always turned me on. So, like the malleable clay I was, I bent for him.

Moving with a seductive grace I'd never known I had, I glided into position. He watched, languorous attention trailing down my body. Pressing my chest into the mattress, I eyed him over my shoulder and through my lashes.

His savage attention speared mine before his eyes lowered to my wet and ready slit. His chest rose as he lined his cock against me. "This what you want?"

"Yes," I murmured.

He stroked the head down, trailing it along my clit again and again. "Say it louder, Bry." A brazen smirk. "Not sure I heard you."

I moaned. "I want it, Kane."

"You want *this*?" He bucked forward, sinking deep.

"Ah!" I gasped when he stretched me, purring as he hit every ravenous nerve in his path. "Hells, yes."

He stopped moving, expression brash when he threw my own words back at me. "Then get to work." His palm came down on my ass with a crack, and I tensed around that thrill before he kneaded my flesh, then smacked it again.

I cried out, desperate to please, then gripped the sheets and rocked forward, before driving myself back into him.

His growl was all hunger and teeth. "That's it, Bry," he said, proud. So damn proud.

And that praise only drove me harder. I rocked again, arcing my hips as I pushed into him, sliding him along my g-spot like the greedy minx I was.

He must've figured me out, because his mouth tugged high at the corners. "Take what you need."

His palm snaked around, the broad pads of his fingers pressing against my clit. He worked it in slow circles, and I rolled against him. Urging him with my body. *Begging*.

"Oh, sage, Kane. Yes."

I slammed back into him, harder and harder, fucking him like my life depended on it—because if I didn't find that release, I was pretty sure it did.

He cursed, and cursed again, then bucked, taking over as his hand latched around the headboard to give him leverage. He crashed into me, and the wood of the headboard groaned under his force before it splintered and buckled, then snapped in half. He plunged deeper and deeper, filling me to completion, propelling that need further. Higher. I was flying. Untethered.

"Harder, Kane. Fuck me harder."

Wraith take me, but I never wanted it to stop. My orgasm hit, and I clenched around him. He fell forward, one hand bracing himself while the other banded my waist. His sweat-slicked chest pressed against my spine as he came hard, roaring as he pistoned in and out, over and over, his come heating me from within. The warmth spread through me as the waves of my own climax slowed, then slowed some more, until they stopped altogether.

My limbs grew weak, body completely spent.

"Iron Hells," he said, breaths hoarse and heavy. He collapsed forward, taking me with him. Flipping me onto my back, his body engulfed me as his weight pressed me into the mattress. Reaching for my left hand, he pressed a kiss to my engagement ring. "I love you, Bry."

My exhale was soft and sated. "You'd better, Big Bad."

He huffed a laugh as he nudged me with his jaw before he set himself down at my side.

My heart fell into an easy tempo … until those earlier worries slithered back in, twining my stomach into knots.

But I trusted him. Full stop.

Because there wasn't any other choice.

Chapter Nine

I flipped through a cascade of documents behind the till at Immortal Inc the following morning, sorting what could stay or go. A sheen of sweat slicked my spine; my temperature was outta control. Five garbage bags sat to my left; I'd gutted the place in a frenzy, cleaning to keep my three brain cells otherwise occupied, 'cause if I thought too long on Isaac, or Zahara, or facing Cassandra at the Conclave meeting later that night …

No. I shook myself to clear my thoughts. I could only handle one big-ass problem at a time. And in that moment, Lucas was tops on the list.

Kane stood a few steps away, gunmetal gray hoodie hugging his broad shoulders, low-slung jeans fitted over those powerful thighs, one of his square-knuckled hands linked over the other wrist. He was talking to Joaquin. The former Beta's hazel eyes held on Ezra, a warmth there I'd never seen before. It wrapped around him, softened his edges. It looked good on him.

My brother sat in Ezra's tattoo chair, a goofy grin on his face. The red leather creaked as he leaned back, settling in. Sage, he was so damn confident. I just wished that confidence was catching.

Hannah sat at his side, a bright smile cresting her lips as the two talked quietly. He took her hand and pressed a kiss to it, and the blush that stained her cheeks was the adorable kind of cute.

Ezra worked off to the side, prepping his tools, organizing the were-claw powder, and sorting colors.

I worried at my lip, a bitter tang coating my tongue as the guilt swept in, because Ezra was taking a risk by helping us—the potentially problematic kind. One I never wanted him, as an Omega or our employee, to feel pressured into, because he was important to Joaquin, which meant he was important to me. I wouldn't force him into anything. Ezra deserved a choice—a *real* one. He had a right to make that call on his own.

If he said no, we'd find a work around. We'd get my Alpha to take over, do the work. But it had been a long time since he'd done anything like that, and seeing as tattoos were the super kind of permanent—sage, I didn't want him to.

Clearing my throat, I tipped my chin Ezra's way. "Hey." His attention slid to me. "You got a sec?"

"Of course." He set down the vial he'd been holding, and it tinked against his tray. He stood and headed my way.

Joaquin's stare found mine and held it for several seconds before his focus returned to my Alpha. I propped my hip against the counter as Ezra closed in. His expression was bright, but there was something else there I couldn't read.

He tugged back his hair from his face, looping it into a ponytail at the nape of his neck. "What's up?"

I flattened my palms over my thighs to smooth my frilly skirts. "Ezra, do you wanna do this?"

His gaze narrowed in question.

"I just ..." I dragged a hand through my hair. "Helping Lucas has the potential to bring heat down on you. If you're gonna do this, it needs to be because you want to. Not because you think you have to."

He nodded. "I want to."

My mouth hinged open, 'cause I unequivocally hadn't counted on such a decisive response. "It doesn't bother you?" I asked, the "what my brother is" part silent.

He lifted a shoulder in a shrug. "I've worked with Lucas enough to get a sense of him." His expression softened, a small smile tugging at his mouth. "But even if I hadn't, I trust Joaquin. If he says you're good people, you're good people. And, honestly, just knowing why Joaquin took Victor's Pack is enough."

My brow furrowed at those words. "*Why* he took the Pack?"

Ezra's eyes widened, hand hovering over his chest. "Shadowed moon. You don't know."

I didn't know what I didn't know, so I shook my head.

Reaching for his silver-rimmed glasses, he shifted them on his nose. "He took the Southern Pack to save you and Kane." His gaze flicked to Lucas, then back. "And to protect your brother."

My heart clenched tight in my chest, and I swallowed around the lump in my throat. He'd taken it to protect Lucas, because Joaquin was smart. He knew that him taking that seat was another shield. One we'd desperately need. He'd done it for us.

Tears stung my eyes, and my gaze found the former Beta. His stare met mine, and my tears spilled over. He swallowed hard.

"Excuse me," I said to Ezra, voice frail. Then I closed in on Joaquin fast, throwing my arms around him. Sniffing, I buried my face against his chest and whispered, "I love you."

His hold locked around my shoulders, his chin resting on my hair. His words were thick as he replied, "Love you too, banshee."

I stayed that way for several long moments before I pulled back and peered up at him. "Thank you."

He shook his head. "You don't need to thank me. Lucas is a good kid." His mouth tugged in a rare half-smirk. "And you're tolerable."

My laugh was a garbled snort; the smile that followed was soft and infused with every ounce of emotion that brimmed in my chest. "You're family, Joaquin. You know that, right?"

He cleared his throat. "I know."

I stepped back. My Alpha's touch sealed against my lower back, and he tugged me to him, crushing a kiss to my temple.

Ezra wheeled over his stool, then took a seat at my brother's side. "So." He grabbed a bottle. "Where are we doing this?"

Lucas dragged a finger along the back of his neck. "Here."

If we actually wanted the tattoo to protect him, it needed to be somewhere visible. Somewhere everyone could see it. An immediate identifier.

I worried at my lip again, pulse pounding in my ears. *Let it work. Let it work. Please, sage, just let it work.*

Because if it didn't—

Kane gripped my waist, lifting me and setting me on the counter. He stepped between my thighs, thick knuckles hooking under my jaw as he angled my gaze to meet his. "This'll work, Bry."

I held that stare, taking everything it offered, because wraith knew I needed it. Kane leaned in, his stubble-lined jaw brushing my cheek before he grazed my lips. Once. Twice. He pivoted between my legs, turning so his back was to my front. I leaned into him, chest pressing against him as I set my chin on his shoulder and gave him my weight. His warm hands rested on my thighs.

Lucas stripped off his shirt, then got into position on his stomach. Ezra adjusted the hydraulic chair's height, took several swabs, wiped the area to clean it, then used the stencil solution to wet Lucas's skin. That done, he lined up the stencil and pressed down, adhering it. He inspected it carefully, making sure it had contact with every dip or hollow before he slowly peeled it away.

Blue lines snaked across the back of my brother's neck, and up toward his hair. A map of Cambria, with the were territories to the right, the magi central and the shadow walkers left.

My brow furrowed, my gaze narrowing on a thicker line that tracked through the design, headed straight for … our house.

Lucas's lips tugged up at the corner. "It's the road to home."

The tightening of my chest stole my breath. A watery smile was the best I could manage, because words escaped me. Emotional. I was so damn emotional.

Kane's grip tightened over my knees. "*This kid's trying to kill me,*" he said across our bond, before he cleared his throat and spoke aloud. "I fucking love it, Luke."

Ezra peered my way, double-checking I was good to go. But Lucas's changeling ass *needed* a mark, and we were running low on time, so when no argument came, Ezra straightened, took up his tattoo gun and set it to my brother's skin. "You ready, Lucas?"

His nod was sharp and short. "I'm ready."

The Omega grinned. "Let's go, then."

The rhythmic buzz of the tattoo gun vibrated through the room, changing tempo as he moved, pushing harder and lighter, veering right and left.

My brother's eyes closed, and Hannah ran her fingers through his hair. His shoulders fell loose at her touch, and the way he looked at her … Power of obsidian, it was so deep. He really did love her—like, a lot.

The front entrance swung wide as Theo sauntered in. He saw my brother and a broad grin took over his face, but, like usual of late, it was tight—a show. "Didn't chicken out then, boss?"

Lucas's mule laugh echoed through the room.

Theo held the door open, and Whitney stepped in behind him.

"You filled her in?" I asked him.

He inclined his head as she moved to his side, close, but not touching. He shoved his hands into his pockets, body rigid.

My mouth twisted. What the Iron Hells kinda message was he trying to send? He'd brought the woman here, then what? Nothing? It was like he wanted her, yet didn't know how to have her. But if the wistful gazes she kept lobbing his way were any indication, he literally just needed to touch her and she'd melt.

As if Theo had felt her looking, the lines around his eyes deepened, as if the emotion he carried was a chain around his neck, leashing him down.

Kane shifted. "*Something's up,*" he rumbled over our bond, pure Alpha as he gauged his cousin.

Yeah, and it had been for too long. The grim energy rolling off Theo was palpable and thick with a cloying scent of rage, but it was deeper, too, like it had turned inward.

My Alpha advanced a step, but my palm shot out, landing over the densely muscled juncture of his upper back, staying him. "*Let me.*"

He half-turned as he eyed me over his decidedly tense shoulder.

"Please, Kane," I murmured.

He crossed his arms over his chest, then inclined his head, moving to the side so I could pass.

Pump the brakes. My brows rocketed up my forehead. Had he just … relented? Kane Slade—the most Alpha to have ever Alpha'd—was handing over the lead? I'd have patted myself on the back, but the fact that he'd done it spoke volumes, 'cause it meant only one thing: that I was better for the job.

Maneuvering around him, I slipped from the counter, then tapped his ass. "Such a good boy."

A low, gruff sound grumbled through his chest, and he flexed his hands by his sides like he was about to reach for me, so I scooted my sweet little behind outta there.

Making my way around the counter, I snapped up the stack of papers I'd been working through before.

"Theo."

He turned my way, and I nodded toward the garbage bags.

"Help with this mess, will you?"

He frowned, and side-eyed the hells outta me, the trash, then back to me. Then he slunk his wolfy ass over. "Of course," he deadpanned. "I'd love nothing more."

The bags rustled as he grabbed three in one hand and two in the other. He followed me through the office, where I chucked the papers I'd been holding onto the desk, and kept going toward the back of the shop. I held open the back door as he thumped his way down the steps to the bin. Flipping the lid, he chucked said bags inside, contents clanking as they crashed to the bottom.

He dusted his hands and aimed back my way. Taking a seat, I indicated the step beside me.

His mouth twisted. "You're being weird."

My frown was soul-deep. "That's rich, coming from you." I stabbed a finger down. "Now, sit."

He set a palm over his chest. "And mean." His tone aimed for playful, but hit somewhere south of distant. He dropped down heavily at my side.

Folding my hands over my knees, I asked, "What's going on, Theo?"

He shrugged. "Helping your lazy ass do chores."

I forced a smirk and nudged his shoulder with my own. "Come on. Seriously. You're off. You've *been* off. What's up?"

He bit the inside of his cheek, worrying it between his teeth. "Do I really gotta answer that?"

It was a question, but very much not. Still, when it came to his pain, there were entirely too many options on the table, so I wasn't about to assume.

"Yeah, you kinda do. Whatever this is, you're holding it in, and it's eating at you. So let it the hells out. All of it. Don't let it fester like some pus-filled wound that slowly eats you alive."

His expression twisted. "That was … graphic."

I offered him a toothy grin. "I can do better."

He rolled his eyes and lowered his head. His exhale was broken and deep, and his body sagged. His attention landed on me, then flicked to the back door.

Point taken. Gripping my obsidian, I threw a cocoon around us. "No one can hear."

Inclining his head, he thunked his elbows onto his knees and dragged a hand through his hair. "It's Whitney."

Yep. I'd half-ass pieced that much together myself, but still … "Why? I thought you wanted her?"

"I do. Shadowed moon, I do." Leaning to the side, he gave the wooden railing there his weight. "But I wanna be worth it. I never want her to doubt that I can keep her safe—and I never wanna doubt it myself. If I can't do that, I don't deserve her."

My stomach knotted, but his tight expression told me more words hovered there, at the tip of his tongue, so I waited for them to fall.

"The deeper things get, the more I just … pull back." His knee bounced rapidly. "I can't forget." At the tilt of my head, he went on: "The shit with Isaac. I thought I was good, and I was for a bit, but I keep running through everything in my head. Like I failed, like I was weak, and like I should've done more."

No. He. Didn't.

I shoved his temple, and when he gave me a what-the-actual-hells glower, I plunked a hand onto my hip. "No."

"No, what?" he asked.

"No. You're not doing that. You're not giving him that kind of goddamn power. You were Isaac's prisoner for long enough." I jabbed a bombastic finger into his cheek over and over, sinking it into the flesh and punctuating my words. "Don't turn your mind into his prison too."

He leaned away and rubbed his face. "It's not that easy."

"Yeah." I flailed my arms. "It is."

"No, it's fucking not." His voice broke. "I didn't save her, Briar. My own goddamn sister, and I didn't save her. I can't get it out of my brain." He rubbed his face so hard, it was a wonder it didn't bleed. Up down, up down. "I can't fucking protect Whitney. Shadowed moon, I couldn't even protect myself."

The way my heart ached, I had to fight not to clutch my chest. "There was noth—"

His head cut sharply to the side. "Don't."

My throat tightened. He'd lost a piece of his soul when he'd lost Naomi, some irrevocable bit that'd been ripped and clawed away then shredded to nothing. It had left a gaping hole that other pieces kept tumbling into, eroding who and what he was. Wraith knew he was entitled to that pain, but that didn't give him license to cruelty, even with himself.

"That's enough," I barked.

He side-eyed me again.

I hated Isaac for what he'd done. For stealing Naomi from us, for using her blood, her genetic link, to build those wolfish serums for Zahara. For everything he'd taken: things that left us with the irreparable kind of loss.

Isaac took pieces of your heart. Your soul. Your goddamn sanity. He rocked your foundation and the trust you had in the world ... in yourself. I got it, 'cause I felt it too. I'd blamed myself for everything. Hated how fucking weak I'd felt. I'd been alone back then, but I wasn't anymore. And neither was he.

"No one could've saved Naomi, Theo."

Her. Mason. Anthony. My mother. My father. None of them.

He kicked at a small rock. "Kane could have."

I shook my head. "Isaac didn't come for Kane."

"And why was that?" He stared into the distance as if hunting answers that weren't in sight.

My ribs constricted and my lungs seized. My tongue locked down, refusing to work.

"Exactly," he said. "Isaac didn't come for Kane because Kane was too strong." His Adam's apple dipped as he swallowed hard, then balled his fist and thumped it against his chest. "And what's that say about me?"

I fought a wince and failed miserably.

"Isaac targeted me because I'm weak," Theo said. "I've always been middle of the goddamn Pack. Didn't give a shit before, 'cause it never mattered. I've always just existed under the threshold of trouble. Never challenged for more. Just coasted." His sable gaze speared mine. "Isaac pulled me in because I was pathetic. My sister's dead because I was pathetic. And I'm terrified to fucking death that I'm not good enough for Whitney because *I'm fucking pathetic*." His eyes glassed over, going bloodshot, and his breath hitched.

The breeze that cut through the lot rustled the trees and whipped my hair across my face. I tucked it aside as tears stung my eyes and blurred my vision. "Do you think *I'm* pathetic?"

His head snapped my way.

"Do you think Lucas is? Or Ivy? Or Anthony? Lisa? My mother? Everyone Isaac killed?" I swiped away the tears. "'Cause Isaac came for all of us, too. So if that's your benchmark ..."

Deep in his sable eyes, that realization struck, and he flinched. "Shit." His body sagged.

It broke my damn soul to see. Leaning closer, I threw my arms around him and held him so goddamn tight, it hurt. "You weren't weak, Theo. You were vulnerable. *Isaac* is the weak one here." Pulling back, I took his face between my palms and forced his attention to mine. Yeah, he could scent the truth in my next words, but more than that, he needed to see it. "He's so weak, he has to hide in other people's skin. Has to steal their powers so he can steal their will, because even he knows he can't stand on his own."

A tear streaked his cheek. "I'm just so goddamn terrified—and I hate myself for it."

My breath left me in a rush. "We're all scared, Theo. Me. Lucas. Kane—"

He scoffed. "Kane's not scared."

My brows ticked up. "Really? Why do you think he won't leave my side? Why do you think our house is a veritable fortress, surrounded by Pack? Why do you think he doesn't sleep? Shadow and sage, he checks every fucking face and scar. Because he's just as terrified as you. Maybe more. You're not alone in that. But we can't let Isaac live in our heads. He doesn't get that space anymore. Only you can let him in now. And only you can throw him the hells out." I wrapped my hand over his and held it so tightly my skin blanched. "It's not being scared that matters. It's what you do in spite of it."

He stared at me, the strain at the corners of his eyes easing as if the weight he'd been carrying had lifted. Not totally. No doubt part of it would linger until my stepfather's rotting corpse fed the earth, but it was as if he'd needed those words to drop the burden that wasn't his to hold.

Theo's expression shifted, a sly smile stealing across his face. "Since when did you get smart?"

I settled a palm over my heart. "I've always been smart. You were just too dumb to understand until now."

"Wow," he said, then motioned between us. "So glad we did this."

I winked and leaned against him. "You deserve her, Theo."

A small smirk tugged at the corner of his mouth. "You sure you don't just want Kane's sexy-as-hells ex otherwise occupied?"

I offered a grin of my own. "It's not the *only* reason."

He laughed, head hanging and shoulders shaking. "You know you're a pain in the ass, right?"

Rolling my wrist, I flipped my hair, all sassy-like. "So I've been told."

He fell silent for several long seconds, his breaths coming easier. "You're as much a sister as Nay ever was, Briar. I've always thought that—and so did she."

My throat tightened. "Of course she did," I said, fighting not to hiccup a sob. "She had impeccable taste."

His next laugh was deeper, freer. "I wish I could've seen her one last time."

"Me too." And it was his turn to pull me in for a hug.

He squeezed hard for one moment. Two. He released. "I should get back in there before your wolf thinks I'm making a move on you and threatens to gut me. Again."

I gave him an easy shove, then, not one to quit while I was ahead, added, "Go and get your girl, *finally*, will ya?"

He pushed himself up, gave my head a brotherly shove, wiped his face one more time, then left. The second the back door cracked open, my Alpha appeared. I snickered at the sight. Theo offered me a "fucking told you so" expression before he slipped inside.

Kane stepped out, his booted feet thumping over the steps as he descended, jeans creaking as he crouched before me. "My cousin make a move on you?" he asked, but the question was easy. Teasing.

I snickered again.

His calloused fingers grazed a slow line along my cheek. "Everything alright?"

"Yeah. He's just finding his way."

"Anything I can do?"

I sighed. Seven Iron Hells, I loved that wolf. Totally. Completely. Irrevocably. An idea hit, one so perfect it warmed my soul. I held my obsidian tighter, then leaned into my Alpha's touch, brushing my cheek over his palm. "What if Theo was the baby's godfather?"

A lone brow arced up. "What about Luke?"

"He gets the uncle title."

He smirked and ticked his chin my way. "You know Theo's gonna be a problem, right?"

He was, but still …

"The good kind."

"See if you're still saying that when he's teaching our kid to bite."

I barked a laugh. "I'm having *your* baby, Big Bad. I expect they'll come outta the womb that way."

His growl was low and warm as he reached out, hooking his grip around my ass and dragging me closer. "You won't be laughing when it's your ankle getting nipped." His hands flexed against me. "Who were you thinking for godmother?"

A loud thump carried from the shop, followed by the screech of tires and a chorus of curses, then the staccato pound of fast-moving feet. Kane snapped up, grabbed my hand, and dragged me with him as we exploded inside.

I stumbled as I ran, barely keeping pace. When we reached them, everyone was hovering at the front entrance to the shop, save Joaquin and Theo, who loomed in the road, jaws clenched and chests heaving like they'd tried to give chase.

My Alpha scented the air and rolled his shoulders, his grasp crushing mine before he released me and joined them.

Whitney lingered at the threshold, her eyes wide. Hannah stood beside her, palms over her mouth. Lucas tugged his girlfriend back inside, pulling her face away.

"Amber," Kane snarled.

The Southern Alpha inclined his head. "She headed south."

"Didn't recognize the car," Theo cut in. "Guessing it's stolen." His attention snapped to a trembling Whitney, and he moved toward her, stepping close. So close, he blocked her sight and forced her attention onto him.

Something caught in the periphery of my gaze. The hairs on the back of my neck pricked, every instinct in my body begging me not to look, but it wasn't like I'd ever been good at listening.

My eyes moved to it.

Kane cursed. "Bry, don't!"

But it was too late, and an instant, all-consuming regret took me. Bile kissed the back of my throat, and my knees went weak. I gripped the door and crushed my eyes closed, but it didn't matter, 'cause the image had seared itself across my memory. An image of Mason's milky, lifeless gaze as it stared back at me from his rotten and savagely severed head.

Chapter Ten

A short while later, with my Alpha and several of his Pack keeping watch, I stood in the staff lot of the RC, kitty-corner to its charred remains. I'd picked it for the optics, in hopes of punctuating a point. One I prayed the Coven would hear.

The day was overcast, and the air cool. A nervous pulse thrummed in my chest, heating my body until sweat slicked my spine. I tugged the collar of my dress, my skin stinging as I practiced my illusions. Well, tried to. I'd managed to hold the partially formed wolf I'd conjured for all of fifteen seconds before that mental wall had slipped back and it had dissipated on the wind, the best I could get.

I exhaled slowly, arms dropping as the image of Mason's severed head flashed across my mind. As it turned out, Isaac's "list of supplies" had been strapped to it with a note that said: **"Zahara appreciates your cooperation. So you understand I'm serious."** As if his previous bullshit hadn't already made *that* abundantly clear.

I'd rot before he'd ever get anything else from me, because I was done helping him.

After what had happened, we'd tested Lucas's tattoo. My heart had been in my throat when he'd changed, taking on Theo's face. I'd forced myself to look, my pulse kicking a wild beat when I saw it had worked. And the relief that had offered … My shoulders had sagged, my chest practically caving. This didn't guarantee Lucas's acceptance, but it gave us a chance. Something we didn't have before.

Next, I'd called Marisol to put out the message. Mandatory Coven gathering. I wasn't willing to wait, and with the Conclave meeting set for that night, I needed to bump my people up, because I wasn't about to shield my stepfather. Not anymore. I wanted my people aware and vigilant. I wanted them looking.

I had not one doubt that by the end, I'd be hated, maybe even stripped of my obsidian and tossed. While the idea stung in any number of ways, if it meant stopping Isaac, I'd pay that price.

My Alpha loomed less than a foot away, those wolfy eyes scrutinizing my every expression. Grabbing the truck's tailgate, he lowered it with a thunk, then chucked his chin toward it. "Sit, Bry."

I shook my head. "I'm fine."

A lone brow arced high. Closing in, his hold cinched around my waist, and he hoisted me up and set my ass down.

My glower was strong.

His hands landed on either side of my hips. "Rest."

I folded my arms over my chest. "I don't need rest."

"We both know what's coming is gonna be shit. Give your body a second while you can."

It *was* gonna be shit. The worst kind.

Magi started arriving, clustering in groups as they watched the crews working, tearing down walls as they hauled charred debris from the emergency wing.

Kane's phone rang. He cursed, his eyes hunting mine.

My chest tightened and I frowned. "You need to take it, don't you?"

His eyes narrowed and he nodded his head. Pivoting, he stalked to the truck's driver's side and climbed in, then answered the phone.

Cassian sauntered closer, his hands in his pockets. He followed my line of sight. "He says the Pack is next."

My gaze darted to Cassian's, because it sounded dangerously like—

"I know about Lucas," he confirmed. "Saw Isaac during the fight."

Sweet sage. I sucked in a sharp breath, and bit my lip.

He raised his hands, palms out. "It's alright. I understand."

I wished like hells I knew how to scent a lie, because did he? I swallowed hard. Enough time had passed, and he hadn't challenged Kane, so maybe …

"*Cassian's good, Bry,*" my eavesdropping Alpha rumbled over our bond.

My breath left me in a rush. Clearing my throat, I turned Cassian's way. "How, um, how do you think they'll take it?"

He shrugged a shoulder. "They know Kane. Trust him. I suspect most should be okay."

My stomach clenched, because I was not a fan of *that* word. "Most?"

"A lot of the Pack lost something to Isaac. Some more than others."

There could be resistance from anyone linked to the wolves Isaac had killed. Naomi, or Priya, one of his earlier victims—the first were dead whose aura I'd read after Kane had clawed his way back into my life. Doubtless, she'd had a family who mourned her.

I rubbed my temples between my thumb and forefinger, the scent of lingering char cloying as it clung to my airways and coated my skin with grit.

Scanning the area, I counted as many heads as my little brain cells could manage, then turned to Cassian. "I should go."

His nod was steady, and he moved off to the side, giving himself a strategic view of the crowd.

I slipped off the tailgate and the ground crunched as I advanced, putting myself between the gathered crowd and the RC.

Whitney offered a smile from where she hovered at the side. Everyone fell quiet. Somber. Most stared at the building, or off into nothing. Fear: the air was rank with it. Not that I could blame them. Two Coven Leaders had been lost. Two Coven Leaders who'd faced gruesome ends. Two Coven Leaders killed by Isaac.

"First, I'd like to say how sorry I am for Mason's loss. My heart breaks with yours. He was a good Leader." My voice hitched, and I forced myself on. "He deserved more time."

Heads bobbed in assent.

"When will we hold his dirge?" Marisol asked.

"In two days, with the next full moon."

Eyes widened; brows rose.

"Why so soon?" Aster pushed.

Considering it was so close, I got it. Still …

"That leads into my next reason for calling you here." I inhaled deeply to steady myself, but no breathing would've ever been enough. My tongue was heavy, hard to lift and work, but I threw a cocoon around our group and forced myself on. "Isaac is a changeling."

Ohhhhhh—I'd said it. I'd actually fucking said it.

Gasps filled the world. Hands flew to mouths. Horrified looks were exchanged.

Then silence. Cold. Hard. Terrifying.

"Did you know?" asked Marisol.

A lie would've been easy, but I was so. Damn. Sick of them. "I knew."

"For how long?" Aster said, her words more an acidic accusation than a question.

My hands flexed by my sides. "Years."

Silence descended once more, heavy and true.

Kane brushed the connection between us, and my chest warmed.

Aster's eyes had turned wild. "You could've told us!"

"I could have," I admitted, 'cause she was right, and it wasn't like denying it would help.

Marisol stepped forward, black skirt flitting with her movement as she linked her weathered hands before her. Her voice was soft as she asked, "Why did you hold this information?"

The words were even. No judgment, not yet. It was more like she sought a reason. Like she'd had enough life experience to understand that big decisions were often made for big reasons. And, sure, I had one, but I doubted it was about to win me points. Either way, the truth was the truth, and terrified as I was to share it, they deserved to hear it.

I straightened my spine. "To protect my brother."

Sharp inhales carried as that realization struck. It wasn't like they wouldn't have pieced it together eventually; regardless, it was a lot.

"He's a changeling too," Marisol said, more a confirmation than a question.

"Two of them! There are *two* of them!" Aster shrieked.

Whitney stood still at the front, arms hugging herself as she stared at me, the whites of her eyes standing out starkly, presumably nervous about what was to come and … me too.

"I get it. You're entitled to feel how you feel. But he's my brother." I inhaled long and deep to calm the frenetic beat of my heart. It didn't work. "He's only sixteen. And he's a victim just as much as anyone."

"He's an abomination!" Aster cried.

A pressure built in my chest—a protectiveness, yeah. But the intensity and savagery behind it came from an untapped corner of my soul.

"He is *not* his father!" I snarled with a ferocity that would put my Alpha to shame.

Eyes widened.

Straightening my spine, I cleared my throat and said, "I did what I needed to do to protect him. If I had to do it again, I would." Full fucking stop.

Aster's tone lowered; her voice was still cutting, but she'd pulled back her horns. Kind of. "It doesn't change the facts. They're born of the Iron Hells."

The truck door thunked closed. From beside it, my Alpha's stare flashed.

"No. *Isaac* was," I corrected. "Lucas was born in Cambria, like all of you. He's not twisted like them."

"Wasn't he raised by Isaac?" It was a question, and yet very much not. The softening of her tone grated over my nerves like fine sandpaper. Her smile was a challenge I itched to wipe from her face. "And your *mother*?"

No. She. Didn't.

Sure, Mom's reputation as a drug runner had cost her her obsidian and gotten her thrown from the Southern Coven, but like everyone in my stepfather's sphere, it'd been a fate she'd never deserved. And they needed to know.

"My mother? The woman whose husband was murdered and replaced by an imposter?" I advanced a step. "The woman Isaac tricked into bearing his child?" I advanced another. "The woman who was compelled to do his bidding for *years*?" I closed the final gap between us, coming eye to eye with her stupid, cocky face. "The woman I watched him murder slowly. Painfully. *That* fucking mother?"

Hands lifted to mouths. Aster sank in on herself but held her ground.

Marisol's stare was intent. "Does the Conclave know?"

"No. Not yet." I tipped my head toward my Alpha. "We'll tell Kane's Pack first, *then* the Conclave."

Whitney shuffled nervously.

Marisol's gaze was creased, considering when she asked, "Why tell us now?"

"Because I have to."

"Because you *have* to?" Aster scoffed and threw her hands up. "What, is that supposed to make us trust you more?"

"No," Marisol interjected. "It's supposed to make you believe her."

My nod was tight. "Isaac's out there. He has allies. Zahara, Amber. They may be few, but they are dangerous," I said, then waited, giving them time to absorb it—because sage knew it was a lot to absorb.

They glanced around, aimless and unsure.

They needed guidance, and as Second, it was my job to steer them.

"We need to vote, sort a new Coven Leader. I'll need names put forward for nominations." I tilted my head to the side. "No appointing. No usurping. We do it right this time."

"Now?" Aster balked.

My voice grew hard, 'cause what the obsidian did she expect? "We don't have time to waste."

"We need to consider—"

"*We don't have time!*" I boomed.

Her head jerked back, a hand fluttering to her chest.

"Isaac is moving as we speak. Countless people are dead. Sierra. Mason." I gestured to the RC behind me. "He means to barter his ability with Zahara, to make a play for her protection. For allegiance with her and access to the *army she means to build*. So, no. We. Don't. Have. Time."

Aster gaped, her jaw practically unhinging, and I was pretty sure that if she could've sprouted fangs and bit, I'd have been missing some vital chunks.

"So." I stalked back to the front of the group and instructed, "Put forward your nominations."

Flicking her hair over her shoulder, Aster angled her nose high. "I'd like to nominate myself."

Shocking.

Turning, she faced the Coven, stretching her neck like that somehow gave her more presence. "Vote for me, and I'll deal with Isaac. I'll—"

"How?" Marisol inquired.

Aster's incredulous glare snapped to her. "Excuse me?"

"I said, how?" Marisol clasped her weathered hands before her. "If you intend to lead, I suggest it's only reasonable you share your plans. So, I ask again: how do you plan to deal with him?"

Nostrils flaring, Aster rolled a hand through the air. "We'll hunt him down."

"Wonderful." Marisol smiled, all dentured teeth and baiting. "Again—how?"

Eyes volleyed between the two.

"You can't ask me now. I'd need time to figure it out."

"But as our Second has already told us, we don't *have* time."

Aster's face turned so red it was a wonder she didn't steam.

I tilted my head. "Anyone else?"

The silence that followed was so heavy, I swore I heard crickets.

My chest tightened. Please, sage, anyone but Aster. If she took the helm, our ship would sink before it even left port. She'd go on a witch hunt, call for Lucas's head. Wraith take me, we needed another name. *Any goddamn name!*

Marisol's gaze met mine. "I'd like to nominate you."

My head jerked back, because pump the brakes!

A purple-haired magi two rows back frowned. "But her brother—"

Marisol wheeled on her. "Her brother is a *boy*. Changeling or not, I will take no part in the slaughter of children."

Aster huffed a derisive laugh, then folded her arms over her ample chest. "You can't be serious? She lied to us!"

"Mind your tongue, child," Marisol scolded her, like a mother talking to an errant toddler. "She did no more than any of you would have if the tables were turned."

"I would never—"

"You'd turn in *your* sister?" Marisol wheeled to face the group, pointing to another magi. "And you, you'd hand over your mother?" She shook her head. "You stand on your high ground and judge, but you lie. You lie to your Coven, and you lie to yourself." Her gray hair flitted around her mouth, and she brushed it back. "You may not have liked Briar's timing, or her answers, but we don't need to *like* her. We need to trust her."

Being liked would've been nice, but it wasn't exactly as if I had a say—so, really, I'd take what I could get.

"She's the only one of us with any experience against Isaac. The *only* one who knows what we're dealing with. She has the Northern and Southern Covens in her pocket. She's our best chance at finding or facing him, and we'd be fools not to use her."

The quiet that fell echoed against my soul.

My shoulders hiked as I inhaled deeply. "Alright, let's vote." My gut twisted, and I said, "A show of hands for Aster."

One lifted, then another. And another.

I bounced a foot, trying to chill the panic that threatened to well within me. When only a handful of votes appeared, I nodded my head.

"And a show of hands for Briar Stone," Marisol called. She raised her own.

Whitney's rose. There was a loud shuffle as more and more and more followed. Slow, but there. Iron fires, so many. My heart thumped heavily in my chest at the sight of it.

Marisol's head bowed in a decisive nod. "It's settled. Briar Stone takes the seat."

Wraith take me. Of all the outcomes I'd envisioned … The tide that'd been dragging me under slowed its pull. The surface came closer. Not in sight, not yet. But attainable.

Aster's glower bordered on a sneer.

"I would nominate Marisol as Second," I called.

Hands shot up across the gathered crowd. Everyone except Aster.

"Good." I dusted my hands and turned to the older woman. "Before"—I rubbed the center of my chest—"Mason was trying to train me on my Illusionist ability."

Marisol inclined her head. "I will help you."

We'd have to sort our rings, since our new positions called for upgrades, but that was the manageable kind of problem.

Something akin to hope bloomed in my chest as I told them about Isaac's scar, and Lucas's tattoo. About identifying them. About everything. When I was done, their expressions were hard. Intent. Because, like me, they wanted this to end. The fear and the deaths. The never goddamn knowing.

Marisol looked at me, her eyes sharp as she asked, "What do we do now, Coven Leader?"

The smile I offered her was a dark promise of my unequivocal intentions. "We start hunting."

Chapter Eleven

Kane and I closed in on the Atrium, the abandoned human mine that constituted the Conclave's neutral-territory meeting place. Our feet crunched over the ground as we advanced, waiting for the rest of our group to arrive. What was left of us, anyway.

Isaac had wanted dissention in our ranks. Turned out he'd succeeded, like, really goddamn well.

The night was dark, the cloud cover low and muting all light. I tugged my thin sweater tighter as the brisk wind blew my long skirt and brushed my skin. I breathed deep, trying to calm the frenetic beat of my heart. The sharp scents of earth and ozone were thick against my senses.

Things with the Coven had gone … not great, but better than I'd expected, considering being chosen as Coven Leader hadn't been on my list of potential outcomes. Ever. I could only pray my Alpha's wolves reacted in the same vein.

"I wanna be there, Kane, when you tell the Pack." We'd wanted to do it before the meeting with the Conclave, but sorting things with the Coven had cut our time short, which meant we'd be forced to tell them after.

He dragged a hand through his hair, raking it into a sexy, disheveled mess. "Let's get through this first, Bry."

It wasn't a no—which, with my Alpha, was a good start.

A sleek black car veered into the lot, Bower behind the wheel. He pulled to a stop beside us, then climbed free. He was dressed sharply in a crisp navy suit with a matching dress shirt underneath. His attention tracked our way. He inclined his head. "Kane." His stare moved to me. "Briar."

"Bower," my Alpha said as he rolled his shoulders, the muscles in his forearms flexing and his thick hands balling into fists, 'cause, well, Bower wasn't exactly his favoritest of people. Yeah, he'd worked with the guy, but with the "special interest" the Ambassador had taken in me, I was pretty sure Kane's tolerance hovered a smidge above gutting level.

Joaquin's G-class pulled in next. His new Beta, a stout woman with ebony skin looking somewhere in her mid-forties, sat in the passenger seat.

They came rapid-fire after that. Cassian, Alistair, and then …

A black sedan rolled toward us, the dust in its wake kicking high. Crimson eyes hovered in its dim interior when it drew to a halt.

My ribs cinched around my lungs, heart aching at the sight.

The shadow-walker driver exited, then opened the back door wide. Cassandra glided out with that inhuman, fluid grace. Her teal dress was from somewhere in the last fifty years, its skirts billowing from the waist and floating like a cloud as she advanced. Her spine was straight, rigid. Her white-blonde hair caught on the breeze, strands of it drifting around the semi-translucent skin of her cheeks. Her stare was fixed forward and very blatantly not on me as she drifted past us and inside.

I swallowed around the dry lump in my throat, wanting to chase her down. To say something, apologize again. But her utter, echoing silence to my previous efforts had been a message of its own.

She was done with me.

And that loss kept growing inside my chest, because I missed her. So damn much.

Kane followed my line of sight, voice rumbling inside the din of my mind as he said, "*You did what you had to do, Bry.*"

My nod was weak. It was true, but it didn't mean it hadn't cost me, or that I hadn't betrayed her in the process.

A frenzy of emotions snaked inside my chest and slithered around my ribs, making it harder to breathe. I muttered, "Let's go."

His hand engulfed mine and he advanced toward the entrance, where the ever-present guards dressed in black suits loomed. Their hands were linked before them, iron daggers at their hips on full display.

The place was objectively opulent. Massive, hand-carved salt chandeliers hung from the ceiling, dotting the way every twenty paces, while the garnet-faceted walls reflected their muted light. I hated it. I'd never been a fan, and that loathing had only gone downhill since being dragged into the mayhem that was Cambria's circumstance.

When we crossed into the meeting hall, everyone took to their places. It was quiet. So unendingly quiet.

Danika's people entered last, her shock of fire-kissed auburn hair pulling my gaze, and I fought a wince, because iron fires, all I could see was Ivy.

Kane lowered himself into the designated Northern Alpha's seat, his broad shoulders wider than the chair's back. Reaching over, he pulled out my chair. My gaze flicked to Cassandra, who sat stiller than death on my other side as I sat myself down. Alistair, Joaquin, and Danika occupied the southern counterpart. Lining the walls behind us, our people lingered, while Bower took position in a newly placed seat at the foot of the room.

Three long, live-edge tables formed a loose "U" shape, with a circular, stone-carved map of Cambria in the middle. It looked like a poorly cut six-piece pie, with the were territories to the east, magi in the middle, and shadow walkers to the west.

The silence continued and I sighed, 'cause it wasn't like the shit show was gonna start itself.

Swallowing, I said, "As you were all made aware, Mason has been killed."

"Indeed. By your stepfather." Danika lifted a brow. "Your family."

It didn't take much to read between the lines of what she was saying. My family. My fuck-up. My fault.

Kane shifted, then huffed a warning.

"Yes," I said, attempting to keep my cool, because I didn't need things going off the rails before the train had even left the damn station. Besides, it wasn't like pointing out that Isaac and I weren't blood was about to help Lucas when they eventually learned what Isaac and, by default, he were. "Isaac."

Her stare raked me up and down. "Do you even have the right to be here anymore?"

Kane stretched his neck.

"She was Second in her Coven, Danika," Alistair cut in.

My pulse thrashed in my ears, almost drowning out my thoughts. But we needed them. Needed every last preternatural in Cambria if we wanted this to work. We couldn't be scattered, our moonlight broken. We need unity.

Inhaling good and deep, I said, "I was voted Coven Leader earlier today."

Danika's stare narrowed to slits. "Yes, and this fact is *Coven* business."

"*I* called the meeting," Bower cut in.

"Yes, and wasting our time with this meeting was not required." Danika's crimson glare tracked to me. "You could have simply sent word."

The hairs on the back of my neck stood on end.

"That's what you do now, is it not?" she accused. "*Send word?*"

Soooooo, the gentle approach wasn't about to fly. Time for a different tack. Straightening my spine, I rolled up my very short mental sleeves. "If you've got something to say, Danika, for sage's sake, just say it."

Her mouth thinned to a line so hard, it was a slash across her face. "You didn't inform us about Isaac until afterward. Did not invite us to the war."

A pissing contest? She was turning it into a goddamn *pissing* contest? 'Cause she didn't get picked for the team?

My Alpha leaned forward, resting his elbows on the table. "She couldn't tell you shit, Danika. She was compelled."

Her glare raked from him to Cassandra and back. "And what of the both of you? Were you also compelled?"

His stare flashed and, across our bond, I felt his power surge. He held it at bay, but barely. "We were strategic."

A sardonic laugh slipped from her lips. "Strategic with whom you trusted. And you expect me not to read this as an insult?" She rolled her wrist, displaying her black, talon-like nails. "If my people had been there—"

"Even my own people were not called upon, Danika Trevino," Cassandra said. And the lilting sound of her voice, luring and deadly or not, was so damn good to hear.

"You did not trust them, either?" Danika hissed.

"Compulsion overpowers loyalty; you know this. Isaac's network was too vast to call upon everyone. We did not have time to sort his ranks."

Bower crossed an ankle over his knee, his arms held loose in his lap. He frowned at the conversation as if he were studying it.

Alistair flicked a hand to pull the room's attention. "What exactly happened that night?"

The incline of Danika's head was sharp, an accusation of its own. "Excellent question."

"You were given that information," Kane countered.

"Of course." Those talons rolled along the back of her opposite hand. "But your missive didn't provide the opportunity for follow-up questions."

My jaw worked, teeth grinding hard. "Then ask."

Her upper lip twitched. "Isaac—the *Phantom*—was under your nose the whole time. How is it you missed this?"

Well, shittiest of shits.

Kane rolled his shoulders, mouth open as he readied himself to answer. But I spoke first.

"I didn't miss it," I said.

Danika's smile was so acidic, it was a wonder it didn't burn. "You admit you knew."

Joaquin stared at the ceiling like he was praying for strength. Then he spoke, enunciating each syllable: "She was *compelled*, Danika."

Cassandra's palms flattened against her lap.

The crimson in the Southern Dowager's gaze darkened. "You say he used venom to achieve this."

Seeing as it was compulsion, venom was kinda the *only* way to achieve it—a fact that wouldn't have been lost on her, which meant her question was baiting, and it set my teeth on edge.

"He did."

She tilted her head, a tinge of inhuman predator in the sharpness of that movement. "Exactly whose venom was it?"

My attention flicked to Cassandra, my mouth clamping shut, 'cause there wasn't a chance in hells I'd be laying down the gauntlet *that* answer would bring—

"It was Ivy's," Cassandra said.

Wraith below.

The Southern Dowager froze, going stiller than death before she hissed "Ivy? My sister?" Her voice fell, becoming almost guttural. "He stole power from my *sister*?"

Chest constricting, I linked my hands before me to hide their shake. I might've felt like prey, but I didn't need to look it.

Something sparked in Danika's gaze. A dangerous realization, because if Ivy's venom had worked, that meant …

"My sister was *there*?" Her palms flattened over the table as she leaned forward. "Alive?" Her crimson glare snapped from Kane to me before spearing Cassandra, her voice steadily rising when she said, "And you did not think to *tell me*?"

Kane squared his shoulders, holding his arms loose by his sides. "There was no point in telling you."

"Why the fuck not?"

Cassandra fixed her gaze on Danika's. "Because she is dead now."

Her words hit like a blow that resounded through the room. The flicker of hope that had burned in Danika's eyes guttered, replaced by an archaic rage that cried out for revenge—something I needed to head off at the pass.

"By the time everything was over, she was gone," I said, softening my tone. "You already thought you'd lost her. We didn't think hurting you more would help."

The tips of Danika's nails gouged the wood of the table, leaving clawed trails in their wake. "You mean you didn't think the truth would serve you." Her fangs extended, and black filled the whites around her crimson eyes.

Kane's power broke across the room and rocked me to the side. Leaning forward, he glared at her through his brow with a back-the-fuck-down-or-I-will-make-you air.

Bower's attention drifted from one to the other. The guy was either super calm or great at feigning it. That made one of us.

Danika's lips slid over her incisors, then twitched like they begged to release again. "What. Happened?"

I set a palm on my Alpha's arm, staying him, then scratched my throat and said, "Ivy was under Isaac's thrall. He had her caged. Starved. The Madness had already taken her."

Cassandra's voice was a soft caress filled with a hypnotic lilt—velvet overlying a blade. "She was lost to the night," she explained.

The Southern Dowager's head sliced to the side, her movements jerky and distressed. Delirious. A bad combination for one of the most apex of predators.

Super bad.

"That did not require her death. Something could've been done!"

"It could not. Compulsion is tethered to the walker of origin. You know this," Cassandra said, as if trying to pull Danika from the spiral she'd descended into.

"NO!" Danika shrieked, latching onto the table before she launched it across the room. It whipped past a paling Bower before it crashed against the wall and exploded. Splinters and garnet flew in every direction, clacking and clanking as they hit the floor.

I tensed.

Kane rose slowly, chair raking over the floor as he made a show of pushing it back. His broad form towered over me, seeming to make the place smaller with his presence. That feeling only grew when Joaquin joined him.

"*Get ready to run*," my Alpha said across our bond.

Run? From a predator? The biggest of bad ideas.

Wait—if he wanted me to run, that meant …

"*You're not fighting her, Kane.*"

He stretched his neck, but made no promises.

Cassandra stood next, floating from her chair as she stared straight ahead. My hand locked over my obsidian as I forced every ounce of will I had into *not fucking panicking*.

Alistair's gaze was wide, and he looked very much like he regretted his proximity to the Southern Dowager. Which, fair.

"Who—" Danika's stare darted around the room, the bloodlust in her eyes the thing fear was made of. "Who killed her?"

Nothing.

"If my *sister* was the crux of Isaac's power, then I doubt it was *him* who wanted her dead." Her glare sharpened, honing as it tore across the room. "So who?"

Oh, crap. Super goddamn crap. Because the answer to that question was the deadliest sort of trouble. If she learned it had been Cassandra, it could mean war. I couldn't let that happen. We needed to stop Isaac, but the dissent he'd sown in the Conclave was diverting our attention. Stopping Isaac and whatever the Iron Hells Zahara had planned wasn't about to happen if we didn't have the Cambrian elite onside.

There wasn't any defusing the bomb that was readied to blow, but *if* I played my cards right, I might be able to deflect it.

I hoped.

It was a crap-ass plan, but I was plum outta good ones, and I needed to act. And I needed to warn my Alpha, because if this worked, I was about to lob a big-ass problem at his feet.

Swallowing hard, I said across our wolfy bond, "*So, remember how you had that plan I didn't like?*"

Kane's stare slid to mine before he gave a single, slow nod in answer.

I internally winced. "*My turn.*"

"*Do it.*"

My head snapped back. "*It's gonna be a—*"

"*I trust you, Bry. Whatever it is, do it.*"

That wolf was everything I needed. I loved him more than life itself.

"WHO WAS IT?" Danika roared. The sound tore around the room, reverberating off the walls.

Cassandra's chin was lifted. She was readying herself.

Playing my cards right was key. My response was key. Every goddamn word was key, because if I messed this up, I was well and done. Might be anyway, but that was a later problem. Not much later, but later, nonetheless.

Exhaling good and slow, I pushed myself to my feet and raised my hand.

Chapter Twelve

The silence in the room rang hollow in my ears, reverberating painfully around my skull.

Cassandra's head whipped my way inhumanly fast, her crimson eyes wide. Disbelieving.

Trust me, I silently begged. *Iron Hells, please, just trust me.*

She had not one reason to, not after what I'd done, but it didn't stop me from asking. And if it curried me a bit of good grace in the interim, I'd take it.

My Alpha rolled his shoulders, the sinewed muscles of his neck and arms cording so taut, I worried they'd tear through his skin.

Because me taking the heat meant I'd also dumped this problem square in his lap. "*I'm sorry, Kane. It's the only way.*"

I hoped.

He cut his head to the side, shoulder pressing into mine. "*I've got you, Bry. Always.*"

Joaquin's stare narrowed on me like I'd lost my damn mind—which, who knew? Maybe I had.

"*You* killed my sister?" Danika said through her tightly ground, extra-bitey teeth. It was less a question, more an accusation. "You expect me to believe you faced her, a shadow walker, and won?"

In the scheme of my life's questionable decisions, convincing one of Cambria's preternatural elite that I'd slaughtered her sister landed well below stupid. But it wasn't like backtracking was an option.

I'd needed to pull her fury from Cassandra and pin it on me, because, like Marisol had said, at my back stood Kane's Pack, and Joaquin's. Danika couldn't contend with all of us. It didn't mean she wouldn't try, but I'd counted on her logic being bigger than her rage.

Fingers crossed.

Either way, answering that question in the right way was a problem with a capital P. If I didn't want her scenting the lie, my wording needed to be super-goddamn precise, so a misdirection it was.

"You can't think I'm the ten shades of dumb I'd need to be to take responsibility for it if it wasn't me?" I shrugged. "You were told before, she needed to die." This was true, because Ivy being the origin of the venom Isaac had used meant she was its master, so her death, and her death alone, was the only thing that could sever my stepfather's hold.

The Southern Dowager stood frozen for several agonizingly tense seconds until, slowly, her face contorted and she let loose an ungodly shriek that pierced my ears and rattled my bones. Her stare hunted me. "And for that, you *will pay*!"

She advanced.

Time slowed as Kane's arm shot out, shoving me behind him. He exploded forward, his movements a preternatural blur as he vaulted himself over the table toward Danika. She snarled and swung those talons straight for his eyes. He ducked, his right hand latching around her throat. He lifted and kept advancing as her feet became airborne. They careened back, Kane slamming her into the garnet wall with a sickening crack that would've killed a lesser beast … or me.

A crack fissured across the ceiling and the Atrium shook, a deafening snap echoing through the space.

My stomach torqued.

Cassandra lunged in front of me. Whether she meant to shield me or find a more strategic position, I didn't know.

Joaquin closed in, hazel eyes igniting as he flanked Kane. Cassian and the Southern Beta followed, a veritable wall of violence engulfing Danika.

She fell still, and her lips peeled back from her fangs. "Give her to me!"

My Alpha held her tighter, his savage face less than a breath from hers. "Not fucking happening," he snarled through gritted teeth, those voltaic eyes lighting Danika's face.

Her attention darted between the wolves as if she sought an ally. "I'm owed retribution."

I peered around my wolfy ward's shoulder. "She was suffering, Danika. She needed to die," I repeated. "She asked for it."

Danika's nostrils flared, those sharp nails catching the light as her fingers curled around the air like she was envisioning tearing out my throat.

The boom of stone grinding over stone rumbled through the room as the massive fissure above us spread wider. Joaquin's stare tracked it as the ground trembled. Garnet crumbled to the floor like the tinkling of glass.

My pulse kicked into overdrive, 'cause nothing about it looked stable.

"The place is gonna go!"

Another loud crack resounded directly over Bower's head. A boulder shifted, then fell. He dove, rolling to the side a blink before it crashed down where he'd just been.

"We need to move!" I said, voice rising as I kept my gaze locked above me.

People made for the door, Alistair and the Ambassador hot on their heels. But Cassandra stayed where she was, and so did I, 'cause like the iron fires was I about to leave my—

"You too, banshee!" Joaquin warned.

Danika's glare fixed on me.

Kane half-turned, calling over his shoulder, "Get the hells outta here, Bry." Then, to Cassian, he ordered: "Stay with her."

The new Beta cut right and came my way, arms wide like he expected a fight from my predictable ass—a fight I wasn't about to win.

Crap.

Glowering, I ran. Cassandra's heels clicked over stone as she followed, gliding closely behind. I probably should've feared having her at my back, having betrayed her and all, but for some reason I couldn't explain, no alarm triggered. Maybe I was broken—well, less maybe and more definitely.

Dust fell as we moved, coating our hair before it kissed our shoulders. One of the salt chandeliers shook, listed, then fell. I dove to the side and chanced a glance back.

"Quickly, now," Cassian called.

Cassandra's crimson eyes were fixed on me, but what thoughts lurked in their depths, I had not one clue.

The black-clad guards stood at the ready, knees bent as if they didn't know whether to fight or flee.

"Go!" I said.

The clouds broke and moonlight spilled through the entrance, painting the air while dust scattered through the beams. I burst into the cool night air, Cassandra flitting out behind me, Cassian and the guards hot on our heels.

Another rumble shook the ground, and I stumbled.

I stared at the door, heart pounding in my chest. One boulder collapsed by the entrance, then another.

"*Get your ass outta there right goddamn now*!" I roared across our connection. "*Now!*"

Joaquin exploded outside.

My Alpha appeared in the distance, Danika locked in his grip, her fiery hair snapping wildly as he dragged her behind him. He closed in on the exit. Ten feet. Five. Four.

Kane dove just as the roof caved in.

My heart stopped.

The two of them slammed to the ground a foot beyond the opening. The mine imploded. The tremors buckled my knees, and I crumpled to the ground, followed by everyone else in sight. The mine caved and caved and caved, collapsing on itself until there was nothing left. A plume of dust filled the world, coating my flesh and lungs. I coughed to clear my throat.

Kane's molten stare sought me out and gave me a once-over. Pushing up on his powerful legs, he climbed to his feet, jerking Danika with him. She hissed and tried to step away.

He held her for a long, pulse-rending second, then released his grip, but stayed where he was. "Don't do anything stupid," he warned her.

Her stare raked from my Alpha to me, held, then back again. Her nostrils flared, every line of her shadow-walkery body coiling as she balked at the order. But she'd made her play and lost, so short of losing her throat, she was out of options.

My Alpha rolled his hands in and out of fists as his boned claws retracted. Slowly. As if it took effort.

Unfurling her spine one segment at a time, Danika angled her chin up, preserving what little was left of her dignity as she turned for her car.

Wait, she was leaving? No. She couldn't. We weren't done. We needed her.

Tugging the hem of my thin sweater, I called, "Please, Danika. We did what we needed doing. Isaac set Ivy on that path. He's the one who stole her from you. The one who starved and tortured her. Hate *him* for putting you in this position."

Danika stopped dead, her crimson glare hunting me over her shoulder, and the hatred in that gaze was a poison words could never cure. The wrong ones, anyway.

A moment stood before me. An opportunity to turn the tides in our favor—or make things *infinitely* worse.

We'd planned to do it anyway, *after* we told the Pack, but I had a chance, and the courage…

Maybe if Danika knew the truth, her murderous rage would turn Isaac's way. Maybe it would bring her back onside. Maybe.

Kane must've read the thought on my face, 'cause his spine locked up. He was probably gonna kill me. Take us both out to save himself the trouble. But he'd wanted this. It just wasn't exactly happening in the order we'd discussed, but it would make for the same ultimate outcome.

His jaw worked as his mind worked the problem, and he must've come to the same conclusion I had, because his chest rose and fell with a steadying breath, and then he inclined his head—in agreement? Permission?

I worried my lip between my teeth, the pressure in my chest building and building and building. My heart pounded against my ribs, a kickdrum that just kept kicking. Oh, sage. I was gonna say it. I was gonna say it! *I was gonna say it!*

For the second time that day, I blurted, "*Isaacisachangeling*!"

Everyone froze. Danika's body rotated slowly, turning my way. That black crept back into her eyes, surrounding the crimson.

"Holy shit," Bower said, as Joaquin edged my way and Alistair turned an uncomfortable shade of gray.

Hands curling, her taloned fingers clicking together, Danika smiled, a childlike laugh breaking from her that had my non-existent hackles rising. "Then Isaac must die."

My shoulders sagged. *Thank fucking obsidian—*

She tilted her head. "And so must his son."

The world shifted. My stomach dropped out from beneath me as bile flooded my mouth and seared my tongue. My throat and muscles burned. Iron fires take me.

"Lucas isn't a danger," Joaquin cut in.

Danika's palm settled over her chest, the calm that took her more terrifying than her rage had ever been. "You knew about this?"

Joaquin's head was angled down, and he glared at her from beneath a furrowed brow, his impeccably styled hair falling across his forehead. "I figured it out."

He sure had, after he'd seen Isaac's rippling face during the fight.

Cassandra stared straight ahead.

Danika loosed a low huff before spitting Kane's way. "No doubt *you* knew." She studied the others before she questioned, "Who else was in on this treachery?"

Who else was her enemy? Who else's head would she call for? Her attention tracked to Cassandra.

Nope. Couldn't let that happen.

"This is new to her too," I cut in. Not the "right that minute" kinda new, but new, nonetheless.

Could we kill Danika? Sure. But would that bring Alistair or Cassandra or the entirety of their people onside? Unlikely. Which was the exact opposite of *what I'd been going for*.

"I want his head," the Southern Dowager declared.

I threw my arms in the air. "Lucas isn't the problem, Danika. We need to stop *Isaac*!"

She scoffed and straightened, chin held up like she'd finally found the high ground she'd been scrambling for. "His very *existence* is a problem."

My gaze darted to Kane, then back. We'd known a reaction like this was a possibility, but having it play out before me rivaled any nightmare Isaac had thrown my way.

"My brother is not—"

"What makes you believe I care?"

I shook my head. "You don't have to, but you should give a shit about what your people need."

A snarling hiss tore through the night. "Do not concern yourself with my people."

"Power of obsidian." I rubbed my temple. Hard. "I know you're hurting, Danika, but this isn't about you. It's not about me or Kane or Lucas or anyone else. It's about stopping the freight train Isaac's barreling our way. It's about this human army he's aiming to build. It's about doing the right fucking thing for Cambria. For your people!"

She stilled, voice soft and sharp, hot and cold. Dangerous. "And what of *your* people? Do all of them know?" Her stare tracked the wolves. "Do *they* agree the boy should live?"

"My Pack's well goddamn aware," Joaquin rumbled. "They watched him change with their own eyes. They saw what he did to Victor, and what Victor did to them. They saw how Isaac tortured his son. And they know Lucas. And they're not concerned."

"We've found a workaround." My palm flattened over my stomach. "A way to identify him. Changelings hold their scars—"

Cassandra's brows raised high.

"You think that matters?" Danika said, spreading her palms wide. "You think this is good enough?" She shook her head. Slow. Methodical. "I have a thirst to be slaked, and I crave changeling blood."

Joaquin pinched his brows between his thumb and forefinger. "Shadowed moon, he's just a kid, Danika."

"Lucas isn't a danger," I insisted. "You can scent that truth."

"He's an *abomination*!" She stabbed a taloned finger my way. "And I want his head." She rolled her shoulders. "A kin for a kin. A life for a life."

A threat, unbridled and raw, one Kane wasn't about to let go unanswered. "If you or anyone from your Clan enter my territory, you're fucking dead, Danika. I'll tear your head from your torso and feed it to the earth." Clear. Decisive. Terrifying.

Her incisors lengthened. "Laws are laws, *Alpha*."

"We're the Conclave, for the wraith's sake," I said. "Laws can be changed." Doing so required a unanimous vote, which wasn't looking too likely in that moment, but still, it *was* an option.

She rolled her wrist again. "Give me your brother, and this ends."

My laugh was sardonic. "Hard fucking no."

"Then we will come for him ourselves."

"Make a move on Luke, and I won't just kill *you*." My Alpha advanced a step. "I'll slaughter every one of your walkers. Tear them limb from limb and bleed them dry, then burn the goddamn pieces."

Joaquin inclined his head. "Those rules apply for me as well."

She twitched, nostrils flaring. "Neither I nor any of my people will enter wolf territory, but if ever he steps out …" She let those words hang. "*When* that day comes," she said, ominous, "I *will* have him." A smile split her face, incisors bared, before she gave us her back and made for her car, her movements measured and easy, like all our worlds hadn't just been upended. Climbing in, she drove away, kicking up rocks and dirt as she went.

Alistair's shoulders rose high on his breaths as he rubbed the back of his neck. "He *is* a changeling, Briar," he said, words feeble and eyes wide, talking to me as if I were the reasonable one.

I swallowed hard. "We need to focus on his father." Seven Iron Hells, maybe if I said it enough, one of them would understand.

Bower's phone was out and he was tapping something on the screen.

Alistair dragged a hand over his hair, looking off into nothing as if he was lost—which was not a stretch, considering the circumstance. "Do we take this public?"

I aggressively rubbed my temples, because, iron fires take me, that had been the *entire point of telling them.*

"Yes. We must," Cassandra cut in.

Alistair raised his arms, palms out as if trying to stay us. "Knowing Isaac is out there could incite panic."

"It should." While panic in Cambria wasn't optimal, it would mean our ears were pricked up, our eyes sharp. People would pay attention. Look for that scar. Hunt Isaac. Find him. And we needed every goddamn resource we had. "Whether you tell your people or not, it's happening. Isaac is out there doing sage knows what. The only way this works is if we're all on board. If we're not, he'll just use us against each other, like he always does. He'll keep slipping from skin to skin, territory to territory, to hide. And he. Will. Win."

"Cambria will want Lucas—"

"HE IS NOT HIS FUCKING FATHER!" I gripped my hair so hard, I wrenched back my scalp. Power of obsidian, what would it take for them to understand?

Cassandra's graceful fingers brushed dust from her dress. "Do as you will, Alistair Jones. But whether you wish it or not, before this night's end, word will spread, and Cambria shall know." With that, she clutched her skirt, and made for her car.

No, no, no!

I didn't know what I'd expected—what I'd hoped—but I couldn't stand the idea of her walking away.

"Cassandra, wait," I called, desperate. So damn desperate.

Kane was rigid, bracing as he made to follow. And I got it, I did, but then ...

I shook my head. "*She won't hurt me.*"

And she wouldn't. I'd seen what she could do, what she was capable of, against Isaac. If she was going to hurt me, she could have done it already.

She halted but didn't turn. In the bullshit of preternatural politics, me going to her could've been viewed as weakness or a concession of some wrongdoing—but I *had* done her wrong. And, at the end of the day, I'd been the one to rip open the chasm between us, so it fell on me to bridge it.

One tentative step at a time, I moved closer. Gripping my obsidian tight, I threw a barrier over our conversation and swallowed hard. "I'm sorry I lied."

Her white-blonde hair flitted gracefully on the wind, like it had gotten the memo on her signature moves. Chin lifting, she stared past me.

"You did not lie, Briar Stone. You intentionally excluded."

It was a distinction with a very acute difference. One that had me wincing deeply, since, sage, it sounded so, so much worse.

My nod was slow. "I know," I said, owning it because it was what it was. Because I didn't wanna do that to her—to *anyone*—anymore. "The last thing I wanted was to hurt you."

I'm trying to fix this. Do the right thing. Scent the truth, Cassandra. Please.

She clasped her hands before her. "You took an onus for Ivy's death that was not yours to take."

The words were flat, which meant I had not a clue how to take them. My chest constricted and I scratched my neck. "I did."

Her gaze shifted to me. "Danika will not forgive."

Oh, of that I was certain. While it would've been nice, Danika wasn't a friend. I didn't need her exoneration, just her cooperation. Cassandra, though ...

"But do you?"

Her face was impassive—hurt or considering, I didn't know. Either way, she wasn't eyeing my pounding pulse like an invitation, so I'd take it.

The breeze caught her dress, blowing the gauzy skirt. Her lips parted. She fell still. Eerily so, which, considering her undead nature and older-than-dirt form, said something. Her mouth opened, closed, then opened again. "I must go, Briar Stone."

My tongue was so dry, it was a wonder I didn't spit dust. Clearing my throat again, I inclined my head.

She lingered for one heartbeat. Another. Then, drifting around me, she left.

My Alpha and Joaquin spoke to their people as I stared after Cassandra, the weight of the former's attention heavy on me.

The steady tap of dress shoes drew closer as Bower strode to my side. "I'd hoped they were a myth." He scratched his scalp, expression drawn. "Changelings."

"No, they are very much not."

I'd done what I'd needed to, said what had to be said, and because of it, the Conclave was broken, like moonlight scattered through the trees. And I had not one damn clue how to fix it.

The Ambassador swallowed hard, then set his shoulders and dipped his chin. "Tell me what I need to know."

Chapter Thirteen

To say things had gone sideways at the Conclave meeting was an understatement. Not that I'd expected high-fives, and avoiding war between the shadow-walker Clans had been a must. But the whole "Danika hot for Lucas's blood in her sister's name" thing wasn't exactly optimal.

Swallowing around the sting in my throat, I stared out the truck's back window into the dark night as we sped through the neutral grounds, praying to the Iron Hells no one was following. Yeah, Danika had *said* she wouldn't cross were territory, and my Alpha would've scented a lie to the contrary, but my paranoia game was on point.

"What are we gonna do, Kane?"

He shook his head, hands squeezing the steering wheel until it groaned. His jaw worked, a protective rage simmering in his expression.

Our headlights lit the red line that marked the edge of his Northern boundary before we flew across it. The second we passed that invisible yet wholly real limit, my tension ebbed. Well, some of it, anyway; the guillotine hanging over our heads was way too sharp to ignore.

My gaze landed on my Alpha as I worried at my lip. "I'm sorry, Kane." Leaning forward, I thunked my head in my hands, guilt souring my stomach. "I was afraid Danika going after Cassandra would wipe the Clans off the table, because we need them. We need *everyone* to make this work." Without the Conclave, Isaac would just slip through the cracks. He'd work his plan. Get away. I plunked myself back against the seat.

"No apologies, Bry." He stretched his neck and reached for me, body still coiled with his post-Danika rage. His grip latched around my hip and he dragged me to him. "Shit might've went sideways, but it was the right call. We hedged a bet Danika wouldn't move on me and Joaquin. And she didn't."

It'd been a calculated risk, one that'd paid off—kinda.

The guilt pushed deeper and my body slumped as I stared out the window. "I just wanted to do something. Wanted Cassandra to trust me."

"I know." His hold cinched tighter. "But we gotta be careful, Bry. Danika's not fucking around. If Luke slips, she'll come for him." He cleared his throat, glanced my way, then back to the road. "I gotta get to the Pack." He took a steadying breath and cleared his throat again. "Tonight."

I worried at my lip harder, 'cause, yeah, he did, but his wolf was still on edge. Him going to them that way was a recipe for violence, the bloody kind I'd been trying super hard to avoid. "We can't. Not like this, Kane."

His knuckles whitened, his grip on the wheel locking down. "*You're* not—"

I slashed my head to the side and folded my arms over my chest. "I said not tonight, Big Bad!"

His jaw ground. "If they find out from anyone else, it's trouble, Bry. It's gotta come from me."

"It'll be trouble either way."

"We need to salvage what we can." The "real fucking fast" was silent.

Salvage what we can. Keep anyone on side we could, because the second they found out, hells only knew where they'd fall. Would the ones Isaac had hurt dissent, like Cassian had implied? Would they stand with their Alpha? Against him? He *could* command them if he needed, but then he'd be no better than Ronin.

He was right, I knew it to my bones, but with our list of allies dwindling fast, the reality of what we faced had my chest constricting.

He tugged up his sleeve, exposing the corded muscles along his forearms. "I'll call in the Pack now. Let them have their say."

"They deserve that, Kane." I pressed tighter into him. "But not yet. Not with you like this."

His exhale was ragged and did not one thing to calm his storm. It crackled around him, charging the air as it pricked over my skin.

I needed to slow his tide before it dragged him under. I had several options on the table to help—one in particular that had always worked before. Wildly inappropriate timing or not, I wasn't above doing what needed to be done. And it *needed* to be done.

I shifted to face him. "I think you should fuck me, Kane."

His eyes flashed voltaic.

Settling my palm over his thigh, I skimmed it higher. "Don't be gentle. Take what you need. Just work this out."

He swallowed hard, staring into the night. His eyes drifted out of focus as he talked to the Pack. Then, shaking himself, he clenched his hands around the wheel again.

My fingers curled over him as I waited. And waited. And waited.

I frowned. "Kane?"

He cut the wheel hard, steering us down an isolated dirt road before jerking the truck to one side. Then he threw his door wide open and launched out. His powerful body torqued and he pivoted, looming over me as he stared down beneath those hooded brows. "Get over here."

Heat pooled in my core as I scooched his way.

Gripping my hips, he jerked me to face him and moved between my thighs. His hard cock pressed into my stomach. "I love you, Bry. So goddamn much." He dipped low and nudged my hair aside. His mouth hovered over my throat, canines grazing my flesh as he growled, "Tell me you know."

I moaned and arched my head back, giving him better access. "I know." Because if I knew anything, it was that Kane Slade and the depth of his emotion for me had no quit—and when it came to him, neither did I.

"I love you too." Straightening, I took his face in my hands and brought his eyes to my own. "Tell me you know."

That stare was electric. "I know."

His rough palm landed on my ankle, then glided up, skimming my knee before it grazed my inner thigh. When his knuckle trailed over my thong, he lingered on my clit, and I sucked in a sharp breath.

"Always so wet for me."

I arched my back and offered him a languid smile.

"Mine, Bry." Angling forward, he nuzzled his face against my womb. "Fucking *mine*."

My fingers threaded through his hair. "Yours."

Taking my waist, he flipped me onto my stomach and snapped my skirt up. His calloused palm found my ass and smacked. I yipped, core clenching as liquid heat pooled there. He edged forward, stripping away my thong before his thick thigh nudged my knees apart and the sound of his zipper drawing down filled the night. I panted with a wanton need as he lined up the head of his shaft against my slit and held it there. His breaths were harsh and pushed through his teeth.

Peering at him over my shoulder, I muttered, "Now, Kane."

He cursed, grip digging deep as he thrust inside.

I cried out, head falling forward, then reached back, latching onto his forearms for purchase.

He set a ruthless pace, slamming into me again and again, sinking himself to the hilt.

"Oh, sage."

"Take it all, Bry." His palm grazed up the length of my spine before it knotted in my hair. Pulling, he jerked my head back. "You drive me fucking crazy, woman."

I arched my pelvis higher, taking him deeper as I pushed back, meeting his brutal stride. God, I loved him. Loved his body and his need. Loved being possessed by him. I loved him with everything I had.

A sheen of sweat slicked my skin, exposed parts sticking to the leather of the seat. He pistoned in and out, his body cracking against mine as he grazed every corner of my soul, hitting my g-spot and every desperate nerve.

My climax rocketed to the forefront. "*Kane!*"

A growl tore from the recessed chambers of his chest before he slowed.

Wait. *No!*

I whimpered. "What're you doing? Don't stop."

He couldn't. I needed it. Needed *him*.

A low laugh broke from him, rumbling through his chest. "You come when I tell you to come," he snarled, that palm coming down to kiss my ass with another smack before he punctuated his next words with a steady barrage of thrusts. "You're reckless and stubborn, and temperamental, and the most beautiful, perfect goddamn thing I've ever fucking seen."

My face heated and I turned to look at him, but his hand at my hair latched tight, holding me in place as he drove forward. My body bucked, a riot of pleasure searing my veins.

"More. Fucking hells, more!"

He drove forward again, hips slamming against mine. His breathing grew harsh, his movements wild and feverish.

My core clenched. "I'm close."

"Come for me, Bry. Now," he ordered, and the words were my undoing.

I screamed, nails boring into him while he punished me with his cock.

A gruff series of grunts tore from his throat as he buried himself deep. "Fuck!" he snarled, then roared as he surged forward and came. He kept surging, every muscle of his torso and forearms tensing as he filled me with his seed.

He stayed that way, chest heaving, until he caught his breath. Slipping out, he flipped me onto my back. I fell limp, languid and spent as my arms splayed above my head.

Fixing himself, he refastened his jeans, then leaned forward, elbows coming to rest by my head as he hovered over me. Those silver topaz eyes skimmed my face, taking me in. Tilting his head to the side, he raked his canines over the heart-shaped tattoo on the inside of my wrist. "We did what we needed to"—he chucked his chin toward my stomach—"but we can't take chances like that again."

I understood, I really did. Problem was…

"I get where you're coming from." My fingers dove into his sex-mussed and tousled hair. "But this is about more than just us now, which is exactly why it matters." My palm rested along his jaw, thumb trailing an easy line over his bottom lip. "I don't want our child coming into a world where Isaac and whatever this stuff with Zahara is exist."

He closed his eyes and let loose a ragged exhale. Sliding down my body, he nuzzled his face against my lower abdomen. "I can't lose this, Bry." He pressed his hot mouth over the exposed flesh there. "Us."

Us. The baby. He couldn't lose the baby. Our family. And neither could I. We'd lost so much already, and the toll of that was etched in the lines around his eyes. In the way he barely slept. In his need to keep me always within reach. Not that the last one was an issue. Having had Kane ripped from me twice was bad enough; I couldn't live through that again. But the raging fire in my chest compelled me to act. To protect. I wouldn't fail Lucas. And I wouldn't fail our child.

The dark cloud in his expression slid back in as Kane hovered over me for several long seconds. There was something in that gaze I tried to grasp, but he shuttered it before I could manage. He rose, then slid my thong back into place, fixing my skirt before he gripped me under the arms and settled me in my seat. Stepping away, he withdrew his phone, punched a text, then stared down at it while he waited for a response. And one must've come, 'cause he inclined his head and climbed back in, the truck dipping under his weight as he moved in beside me.

My brows dropped low. "Something you care to share, Big Bad?" I asked, wiggling his way before I leaned my head on his shoulder, offering him every comfort I could, because our night wasn't even close to done.

"It's time," he said, then fell deathly quiet while he stared into the dim, body cording like rope as he braced.

My stomach quivered, and my voice sounded shaky as I said, "Okay."

His attention tracked to the rear-view mirror as if he looked for someone. I glanced back. After a minute, a vehicle closed in. Kane exhaled and put the truck into drive, then pulled back onto the main road, and headed away. The *wrong* way, with that mystery vehicle in tow.

I frowned deeply as he veered us south. "Where are we going?"

"This way."

"Shockingly, I'd already gathered that much," I deadpanned.

Crickets.

I tensed, every hair on my body standing on end. Sitting straighter, I angled to face him. "Where are we going, Kane?"

Nothing.

Something took root in the depths of my stomach, because the edge in my Alpha's expression didn't sit right with me.

When he neglected to answer, I pushed harder. "Where. Are. We. *Going*. Kane?"

He cleared his throat. "South."

"Yes. Now, *why* are we going south?"

"Because I'm not taking you to see the Pack."

I drew back, an ominous feeling constricting my lungs. "What the iron fires are you talking about?"

"I can't take you with me, Bry." His chest rose on an inhale before his stare met mine. Hard. Determined. "You're going to Joaquin's."

Chapter Fourteen

You're going to Joaquin's.

Kane's words ricocheted around my mind again and again and again. Which meant they took a second to sink in.

Going to Joaquin's, where the Southern Alpha's Pack already knew our truth. Where I'd be safe. And where *my* Alpha wouldn't be.

The shake of my head was violent. "No, the Iron Hells I am not, Kane!" I crossed my arms over my chest like the petulant mate I was. "I'm going with *you*."

His silence reigned, cutting my soul to the quick.

I sat straighter, turning to face him, and tensed so hard my bones ached. "I'm. Going. With. You. Kane."

"No, Bry," he said, moonlight catching his profile. "Word spreads fast in Cambria. By the time I see the Pack, they could already know, so I've got no clue what I'm walking into. Once this goes down, I can't guarantee my territory's gonna be safe. I need you and Luke outta there."

The guilt that twisted my chest hurt. Whether he'd agreed to it or not, what had happened with the Conclave had been down to my ludicrous plan. Which meant I'd made this mess. Had thrown him neck-deep into the worst kinda trouble—so it was on me to help. To do *something*.

I stabbed a hand back the way we'd come. "Turn the truck around."

"Can't do that."

"You can and you will."

He'd goddamn better!

He didn't, and the next twenty minutes dragged as I stared into the night, the broken lines on the road flicking past like a staccato tickertape, our followers' headlights bouncing in my side-view mirror as they moved.

Eventually, he steered us into Joaquin's driveway. His new-to-him, two-story, red-brick-exterior home had a black door and shutters and blended against the shadows of the towering evergreens surrounding his property.

The Southern Alpha stood on his crisp white porch—one that flawlessly matched the thin trim of the windows. His hands were linked before him while he waited, his hazel stare lifting to me.

The tag-along vehicle pulled in and parked beside us, Theo and Lucas inside.

Kane popped his door open and climbed out, and Joaquin closed in. I stayed where I was, the sound of my panicked breathing drowning out the world and their voices as they spoke. The Southern Alpha's hand clamped over Kane's shoulder hard, and he inclined his head.

Pivoting, Kane turned my way and reached for me.

I scampered away. "No!" He couldn't leave me behind. He fucking couldn't. Not for this. I needed to go with. Help him. Something!

"I'm sorry, Bry." He leaned in, his hands landing beside my hips. "You can't be there."

My heart drummed, and my voice was barely a whimper as I said, "No."

"You being there puts him at risk, banshee," Joaquin added, tone easy.

Because my presence made Kane vulnerable. But I was desperate. Being separated from him, and knowing what he was potentially walking into, seared a terror straight to my soul.

"Just take me with you." Tears welled in my eyes, forlorn and burning. "I'll be quiet, Kane. I won't say anything. You won't know I'm there. No one will."

He huffed a sad laugh. "Liar." His knuckle hooked under my chin, and he pulled my gaze to his. "You'll be a target, Bry.

Something they can use against me. My focus'll be split." His stare dropped to my abdomen, and he shook his head. "I can't take that chance."

I hated that he was right, because it stripped me of any choice. I threw myself against him, my fingers clutching his shirt. His powerful arms hooked around me, crushing me to him as he lifted and aimed us away. I pressed my face into his neck, breathing in that wilderness and musk scent. Embedding it, because it was a part of me.

His boots thumped up the porch stairs, his breathing rough as he settled me on my feet. The side of my fist hit his chest, but it was weak. More anguish than anger, because I was scared. So goddamn scared. His hands cupped my face, wrapping around to my hair before he leaned down.

I threw my arms around him, tears breaking free as my mouth crashed with his. The kiss was warm and pained and everything I couldn't say.

He pulled back, chest heaving, those eyes tracking my face like he was memorizing it. His calloused thumb grazed my bottom lip. "I *will* see you again," he said.

And he would, one way or another.

More tears fell, blurring my vision and stealing him away. He pressed a rough kiss to my forehead, then stepped back and let me go.

No!

I blinked my eyes clear and swayed, 'cause he was my everything, and the sight of his retreating back, the idea of him facing that Pack alone … the sheer panic of it made me dizzy. Joaquin's hands shot out, taking my shoulders as he held me steady.

Theo winced, then edged to my other side.

I clutched my obsidian like it could give me strength. It didn't work, and my heart guttered.

Lucas swallowed hard, a guilt and fear buried in those violet eyes that mirrored my own as he looked at my Alpha. "Take me with you."

Every eye whipped to him in unison. Kane stopped dead, and a soft whimper escaped me.

"I can explain myself," Lucas said. "Show them the tattoo."

"No, Luke. You being there could set the Pack off." My Alpha shook his head. "I gotta do this one alone." He clenched his fists, released, then clenched them again. Pivoting, he closed in on the truck, each step away an agony that clawed at my soul.

My brother's shoulders fell.

I trembled, a sob ripping from my chest, because Kane was going to face the horde, and he was going to face them alone.

"Kane," I said. "Come back to me."

His bloodshot stare met mine, strained and hollow. He made no promises, and said no more, just climbed into the truck, put it in gear and left. He didn't look back.

I crumbled, legs buckling beneath me. Joaquin moved in behind me, his arm locking around my waist. Tears streaked my face, their warm rivulets staining my cheeks as I stared after my Alpha.

"Deep breaths, banshee," Joaquin said.

Lucas and Theo stepped inside, heads hung as they moved through the foyer.

My head fell back against the Southern Alpha as I muttered, "I should be there."

"No. You shouldn't."

He was right. I knew it to my core, but it didn't stop the hitch in my voice when I said, "He's walking in there alone, Joaquin."

His grip tightened like he was trying to hold me together, because I was coming undone. When he spoke, his voice was level. Not placating, but not cruel. "Do you really think you could help him?"

I swiped at my tears. Not even close. Even against his weakest wolf. I might get in a hit or two, the way I had with Amber before, but in the end, even she had still gotten the upper hand.

He rested his cheek against my hair. "He's not alone, banshee. Cassian's with him."

I wrapped my arms around myself, fighting not to cradle my womb. We'd fought so hard for every step we'd taken.

Every*thing* we had. And there we stood, at the brink, awaiting a fate that may no longer be in our hands. "That's not enough." I hiccupped a sob. "You could be there!"

"No." He shook his head. "I couldn't." The wind whipped his jet-black hair as he turned me to face him. "Me being at his side makes it look like he needs back-up."

"He *does* need back-up!" I hugged myself tighter. "He's facing the Pack alone."

My Alpha, standing against a legion of weres several thousand strong. Wraith take me.

"He has to go in alone. It weakens him to enter that space with anyone else, *especially* another Alpha."

Because he needed to look confident. Like he was strong. Like he stood by his decisions. Like he was ready to take them on if they disagreed. And if things went sideways, he just goddamn might have to.

Ridiculous wolfy fucking politics.

Ezra stuck his head outside, his smile soft when it landed on Joaquin. "Why don't you two come inside?"

The Alpha nodded. I looked out at the empty road, my heart stuttering a weak beat before I turned and headed in.

The place was nice, all dark-stained hardwoods, linen-colored walls, and arched ceilings. It was warm. Inviting. And it suited him.

Slipping off my shoes, I padded down the hall toward the living room in the distance, then set myself onto the plush brown leather couch there. Soft lamplight lit the space, and I stared out into the dark of the woods beyond.

I was tired. So dog tired, my emotions spiraling into the cavern that had carved itself out in the middle of my heart. But tired or not, I couldn't sleep. My eyes refused to close. I got the logic, why my Alpha needed to do things like he had, but it didn't stop the race of my pulse or the pain in my chest. And it didn't stop the terror.

Ezra's expression matched the gentleness of his voice as he asked, "Can I get you something to eat, Briar?"

I shook my head.

"She'd like some food," Joaquin cut in.

The side-eye I lobbed his way was on point.

"Kane said to feed you."

My sigh was low. Burrowing deeper into my seat, I tucked my legs to my chest and grabbed the neatly folded beige throw from the back of the couch, pulled it around me.

"Hey," Theo said, plunking himself down in the chair to my left.

I set my chin on my knees. "What are *you* doing here?"

"I feel so welcome," he taunted, surprisingly easy, then added, "I'm here to distract you." He nudged my elbow and waited, as if I was supposed to respond, but my heart was heavy, and so was my tongue, which meant nothing came out.

I stared out the window as the moon climbed high, casting long shadows across the yard. I itched to brush our bond, reach for Kane. But the idea of distracting him, even for that moment, meant I couldn't risk it. My palm landed over my abdomen. Risk us.

Theo exchanged a look with Joaquin. "Kane's done good with the Pack, Briar. It's calm since he's been around. Last thing anyone's gonna want is a shift in power. They're loyal to him. He's gonna be alright."

I might've believed them, but Cassian's words just kept ringing in my mind. Most of the Pack were good, but not all. It fed the dread that coursed slow and cold in my veins.

Lucas was sitting across the room, his jaw tight as he flexed his hands in and out of fists. In and out.

Gripping my obsidian, I shielded the conversation from him, because the last thing he needed was to join me in my fear.

"Is that why Kane dropped me here? Because he thought it'd go smoothly? That everything would be alright?" My words were low, soft. Matter of fact. The mirror of the sadness crushing my soul.

The growl that broke from my brother's chest was wolfish as it rumbled through the room. "Stop doing that!" His expression darkened. "Stop blocking me out like you're protecting me."

Everyone stared at him, wide-eyed.

I released my ring. "Lucas—"

"No." He slashed his head through the air. "You don't get to pretend this isn't about me. That it doesn't *affect* me."

"It's not about you, not really."

"Yeah, boss," Theo cut in. "You're just the face of the problem, not the problem itself."

The Southern Alpha inclined his head. "There's a history here you had no part in. The Packs know you. They'll be pissed they were left out of the loop, but they'll see reason," he said, sounding like he was trying to convince himself as well as us.

But would they? They were wolves. Brash, temperamental, politically volatile and easily agitated. And Kane had gone alone. Walked into that perilous den all fucking *alone*.

I didn't realize I'd spoken those last words aloud until my brother let out a sardonic laugh.

"Sucks, doesn't it? Being left behind." He stared down at his feet, shoulders slumped, voice flat. "Being told you'd be more trouble if you're there?"

Silence dropped like a guillotine. My throat stung.

"You're not the only ones my father hurt." His exhale was weary. "I wanna help." He tracked a palm over his tattoo. "Do something useful."

Shadow and sage. But what the iron fires could I say? Because, hate it though I might, he wasn't wrong.

Theo loosely flexed his hands, one at a time, again and again, then dusted them on his jeans, eyed my brother, and stood. "Get up."

Lucas cocked his head and pursed his lips.

Dancing lightly on his feet, Theo prodded, "I said get the hells up, pup."

The hint of a smile tugged at my brother's expression before he rose.

"Come on." Theo raised his fists. "Show me whatcha got."

My brother's stare narrowed.

"You wanted to do something useful." Theo waved him on. "So, let's do it then."

Slowly, Lucas's spine straightened. Inclining his head, he set his position, feet shifting as he angled for a shot and lunged, throwing a punch at Theo's face.

Theo leaned to the side, dodging. "Keep your elbows tight to your sides," he said, then jabbed an open palm over my brother's left ribs. "Protect your flank."

Lucas grunted and shuffled back, repositioning his lean arms as Theo had directed.

Watching them, an idea tweaked, and I tugged out my phone. Pulling up Marisol's information, I punched a text.

Me: You free tomorrow morning for a lesson?

The little dots bounced as she typed her reply. And bounced. And bounced.

Marisol: I am. What time?

I fired off my reply as Ezra arrived, a plate full of … *something* in hand. He extended it my way.

"Take it, banshee," Joaquin ordered, his words gentler than the silent "Or I'll make you" I could read in his arched brows.

Rolling my eyes, I shifted, setting the food in my lap before I plucked up a piece and robotically ate, not tasting anything. When I was finished, I set my head against the cushion and closed my eyes. The food sat heavy in my stomach, weighing me down.

I didn't know how much time had passed, but eventually, the exhaustion kicked in. My heart slowed, limbs going limp as the world faded to black, and I faded with it.

***

Something warm brushed my chest … from the inside. It brushed again and again. Familiar.

Jolting awake, my eyes cracked open.

Rain tapped against the window, and the sky was lightening over the dripping trees.

I lay on my side, stretched out on Joaquin's couch, the blanket tugged high. Across the room, Lucas squared off against the

Southern Alpha, both covered in sweat, hair matted to their foreheads, shirts clinging to their chests. My brother's movements might've weakened, but not the determination in those violet eyes.

Ezra slept, curled into the loveseat, while Theo sat back, feet propped on the coffee table, his bloodshot eyes looking dog tired as he scarfed down a bowl of cereal.

The weres stiffened, heads snapping to the front of the house. The crunch of thick-treaded tires over asphalt was faint, but drawing closer.

Theo chucked his bowl aside and bolted, a panting Lucas nipping at his heels. Joaquin wiped the sweat from his brow and eyed me before he and a groggy Ezra followed.

I rose, my body stiff, joints aching and movements slow, like I was moving through a fog. Mechanically, I folded the blanket, laid it back into place, then followed the others. When I reached the entrance, my heart was sluggish, and although I'd slept, I was tired. My adrenaline had run dry, a well that had been tapped too deep and drained. Hope flared, but my body couldn't respond, because physically, between my child and my fear, I had nothing left.

I stopped just inside the door as Kane stepped from the truck. Relief had me sagging against the doorframe. Dark hollows stained the undersides of his eyes. His arms were loose by his sides, but the creases lining his expression and the tense set of his shoulders told another story.

Lucas ran, launching himself at my Alpha. The two collided with a thunk. Kane looked spent, like he could barely hold on. His dull, silver topaz eyes lifted over my brother's shoulder and hunted mine. The two broke apart and Kane loped forward.

Joaquin and Theo met him by the porch.

"How'd it go?" Theo asked.

"It went."

"Any challenges?"

Kane's fists flexed by his sides and he inclined his head. "A few." He scrubbed a hand over his jaw and told them, "Gimme a sec." His steps thumped heavily as he swallowed the distance between us in six easy strides. He stopped less than a foot away. "Bry."

I stared up at him through my lashes, praying to the wraith that my eyes said what my body could not.

Reaching out, he pulled me to his chest. His arms bracketed around me, his chin resting against my hair. My palms landed over his stomach but were too heavy to go further.

He tensed, then pulled back to see me better.

"What happened?" Joaquin asked.

Kane cleared his throat, his eyes trained on mine as if trying to gauge me. Read me. Figure me out. I knew my response was off. And I wanted to say something, *anything*, but my body wouldn't comply.

"Three upper-level wolves challenged," he said. "The others were pissed but listened."

Joaquin folded his arms over his chest. "They alright?"

Kane inclined his head. "They were submissions." His palm engulfed my cheek before he tracked a thumb over my claiming mark, like he wanted a reaction. But nothing came, because I had nothing to give.

He brushed our connection, but I was too lost to respond. His body grew taut, and I wanted to ease that strain, but it had all been too much, which meant I had no idea how.

Theo set a shoulder against the brick façade. "How'd things end?"

"Tensely." Kane's touch flexed over me. "The energy's off, but it wasn't a bloodbath, so it's a start." His thumb grazed my lip next. "Luke should be good once stuff cools down."

If things cooled down. I wasn't about to drop my guard. Not that I knew how. Not anymore.

Ezra set a shoulder against Joaquin, the weres watching me like glass that was ready to shatter.

Kane's chest rose as he inhaled and pressed his forehead to mine, his words low as he asked, "What can I do, Bry?"

I collapsed into him. "Just take me home."

Bending, he hooked one arm behind my knees, the other my back, and lifted, then took up my shoes and headed for the truck.

"Follow with Luke?" he asked Theo.

At least, I assumed it was Theo, seeing as my face was buried in his chest.

"We'll follow," Theo replied.

Kane's heavy steps carried us away, and his door creaked open before he settled me into the truck. He held the door, watching me for several painfully long seconds before he turned to Joaquin. "Thank you."

Joaquin's nod was sharp. "Let me know if you need anything else."

"I will." Kane slid into his seat, setting himself behind the wheel. The loud rumble of the engine ricocheted in the void between us. His broad shoulder pressed into mine, his warm hand resting on my thigh. "Talk to me, Bry."

I leaned into him, giving him my weight as I asked, "You're alright?"

"I'm alright." He eyed me, then rolled his grip around the steering wheel. "Are you?"

Hugging myself, I stroked my upper arms. "I don't know."

Tension pulsed off him in waves, and when I didn't elaborate, he gripped the wheel tighter. Shifting into gear, he eased us out of the driveway. The hum of the tires filled the void, his stare tracking back to me over and over. My palm traced a slow circle over my lower abdomen as I sank further into him and closed my eyes.

What felt like an age later, we cut down our driveway and he shut off the engine.

The fear for him, for Lucas, for our child; the loss, the desperation, the chaos of my body; and the helplessness, the weight of it all bore down on me, making it hard to breathe. To think.

Kane slid from the vehicle, then carried me with him as he moved inside. He stopped at the landing. "Can I get you anything?"

I shook my head. "I'm just tired."

He watched me for one beat. Two. Aiming for the stairs, he headed straight for our room. Clearing his throat, he set me on the edge of the bed. Crossing to the dresser, he grabbed a set of my night clothes, then took a knee, his hulking form less than a foot away. Slowly, tenderly, he tugged my dress from my body and helped me to change.

"You're scaring me, Bry." He dragged a hand over his hair and swallowed hard, his next words a plea. "Say something."

"I'm sorry."

"Don't be sorry." He set his face to mine, his stubble grazing my flesh as he nudged my cheek. "Just talk to me."

I breathed him in. "It's just … everything." It was all I could manage, and it must've been enough, because he inclined his head.

My finger brushed his wrist. "Stay with me."

"Always."

Lifting the comforter, he lowered me down, then stayed where he was for several heartbeats before he rose and flicked off the light. The rustle of his clothes sounded as they hit the floor, and then I heard the steady pound of his feet closing in on the bed. It dipped with his weight when he set himself down behind me, then rolled me toward him.

I burrowed deep, my gaze skimming his chest and the new lines of scars there. Two sets of claws that had my stomach twisting.

Those last hours had been some of the longest of my life—which, considering the trainwreck of my existence to date, said something. That exhaustion had set into my weak and weary bones, making me brittle. Broken.

My heart, my body, my soul; it was like they'd punched their clocks. I didn't think I had a limit, but as it turned out, that was the colossal kinda wrong.

Sage, I was drained to the cusp of empty. My eyes and limbs were heavy. But sleep refused to come.

Kane's voice was a low rumble that carried through the dark as he said, "Tell me you're good, Bry."

"I will be, Kane."

I just needed to sleep. Maybe then I'd reset. Replenish what had been drained and kickstart my emotional tempest.

I hoped.

Chapter Fifteen

I stood, hands clasped before me in the warm, dry lobby of Loose Ends, Marisol's other business for second chances, or last ones. Give her an image of the person you wanted to see, and she'd create the illusion, show them to you. From there, you said what you needed. A confession, an apology, a profession of love, a goodbye … it was a one-stop shop for emotional relief.

The illusions couldn't talk back—weren't capable of noise at all, seeing as they weren't actually real—but that wasn't the point. The point was getting whatever unfortunate burden you carried off your chest. It was kinda genius, and utterly heart-wrenching at the same time.

The place was on the north-central border of the neutral grounds, surrounded by the higher-end human hotels for our non-married overnighters—hotels that stood desolately empty.

My finger traced my new Coven Leader obsidian. One of two I'd collected that morning: mine and, as our newly minted Second, Marisol's.

A series of ten rooms stretched down the hall to my right, each done in different themes to fit whatever vibe the person required. Bright and childlike, dark and sinister, neutral and calm. The floors were checkerboard, the walls a deep plum. The illusion of a soft mist dusted the ground, skirting my feet before climbing the bottoms of the walls.

Kane loomed across the space, leaning against the counter, arms crossed over his chest, his attention roving between concern for me and my still-flat emotions, and checking in on the

Pack. Things had been restless with them, but no more challenges had cropped up yet, so there was that. Cassian had stayed with Lucas, who'd opted to hang back in favor of a day with Hannah.

My Alpha was tense, what with all that had happened the night before. But there was nothing for him to do, I just needed to find my feet again. And I needed *something* to help me do it, to lift that emotional fog, but I didn't have the first clue what that was.

Theo occupied one of the wildly colorful, ocean-blue waiting-room chairs, his eyes bouncing between his watch and the Tudor-style entrance every five seconds, because Whitney's agreeing to meet him on her lunchbreak from the RC was the only reason his wolfy ass had tagged along.

"She said she was coming," I told him. "Calm down."

He scoffed. "I *am* calm." Adjusting the light-gray T-shirt he wore, he set an ankle over his opposite knee, then lowered it.

"Clearly," I deadpanned.

Marisol emerged from the office to our left, clicking the frosted glass door shut behind her.

I flicked my nail on repeat, the *tick, tick, tick* sound carrying through the room.

"Okay," she said, steepling her fingers beneath her nose. "What do you know?"

The shake of my head was dismal.

"Alright, then." She gestured my way. "Let me see what you can do."

"Prepare to be underwhelmed," Theo mumbled.

Kane huffed.

My frown was deep. Gripping my obsidian, I found my power. The new ring was so much stronger. I pulled, and pulled, and pulled. My face scrunched as I held my breath and pulled harder, my strength roiling through me—before butting up against that mental wall.

Theo's face brightened, and he thrust a stabby hand toward my forehead. "Ooh, I've never seen *that* vein before!"

"Gah," I said, releasing my breath as my shoulders sagged.

Marisol wandered around me, her gaze narrowed, inspecting me like I was a problem to solve. "Hmm." She stopped. "When you were trained on your Aura, what did they tell you?"

I considered this, then said, "How to grip my power and then push it through my vision into the sight."

She inclined her head. "We grip the power too."

I cocked a brow. "But ...?"

"But we push it in a ... different way." She tucked several of her white-gray hairs behind an ear.

There was a click-creak as the front entrance opened. Whitney poked her head inside and Theo shot to his feet, grinning ear to ear at the sight of her.

"Hey!" she said, and everyone offered their greetings. She exhaled a flustered breath and stripped off her coat. "Sorry I'm late. Things are a bit nutty at the RC since the fire."

Theo took her coat. "Saved you a seat," he said, waving an arm at the six available options.

Her laugh was bright as she settled into one and he retook his own. The two leaned closer together, falling into quiet conversation while Marisol refocused her sights on me.

"How do you pull?" she asked me.

I rocked on my heels. "From my heart?" I said, the words more a question.

She smiled. "Of course. Ours just requires ..." Her eyes pinched as she sought the word. "Another layer."

Okay. Interesting. "A layer of what?"

"Sensation." She grabbed a stool from behind the front desk and dragged it over. "What were you doing the first time you presented?"

My brows knitted tight. "Presented?"

Her withered smile was amused. Raising her hand, she wiggled her fingers. I watched, mesmerized, as a cascade of particles rose from her palm, coalescing into a raven that swooped and dove, circling her arm before it faded, one falling feather at a time, into nothing. "When your illusion appeared."

Kane shifted, adjusting his broad shoulders like they ached—which wouldn't be a shock, seeing as his muscles were so taut, they looked as if they'd tear themselves from the bones.

I bit my lip.

"What were you feeling?" Marisol pushed, then added, "Our first presentations are often physical manifestations of an emotion. Humor, desperation, rage."

I pursed my lips. The day I'd manifested—in that moment—I'd been lost in hate for my stepfather. In a need to shield my child and bring them into a world that knew safety. A need to protect.

My hand flattened, itching to cover my womb, to shelter. My gaze flicked to Kane. "I was feeling passionate."

Her chin dipped. "Good. Now, pull from your power, but try to find that feeling. Recreate it. This time, lead it toward your skin."

Protective rage came as naturally as breathing to me, but the feeling from before had been different. Like some hidden piece of me had finally moved into place. Something powerful and possessive; something vigilant, silent, and strong. It was deeper. Maternal.

My heartrate quickened, my pulse thrashing in my ears. I sought that power, then guided it. My skin pricked painfully. Not the agony from before, but still of the un-fun variety.

I winced, fingers furling and unfurling as that stinging sensation crested my hands, and arms, running over my chest and legs, then up to the tip of my scalp. "Why does it hurt?"

Her kitten heels clicked as she moved around me again, hand stroking her jaw. "Because the power is forced through your flesh."

Well, that imagery was … weird.

"Why doesn't it hurt you?"

"Because she doesn't whine like you," Theo cut in.

I offered him a decidedly rude gesture.

Whitney bit her lip to hide her laugh as she shushed him.

He grabbed her wrist and tugged her into his lap.

Praising the wraith and the Seven Iron Hells themselves, I said, "Sweet sage, *finally*!"

Whitney smiled, a deep pink staining her cheeks. Theo's arms wrapped loosely around her waist, like he was giving her the option to move away if she wanted. Instead, she kicked her legs, sliding deeper into his embrace. He set his chin over her shoulder, his expression one I'd never seen on him before: calm.

Gripping my obsidian tighter, I concentrated, seeking out the emotion. It didn't take long. "Okay, I've got it."

Marisol inclined her head. "Now, hold that feeling, and think about what you'd like to see."

It had been fire the first time. Might as well try that again. I thought about heat. My skin pricked again, and a flame shivered across me, then started to sputter.

"That's it, Bry," Kane said, his words low. Encouraging.

The tiredness from the night before started to ebb back in. It wasn't as consuming, but it was enough that my chest tightened. My concentration faltered, and the illusion fell.

"What happened?" Marisol asked.

Looking at her, I lifted my chin. "I got distracted."

"Try it again," Marisol said, "but this time, block out the world. Everyone. Every thought. Every*thing*. It's only you and your power." She tapped her chin. "New students often find it easier to conjure when they select an image that means something to them. Something that has relevance or was important somehow."

My attention flicked to Theo and away, an idea taking me. If I was lucky, there was a small gift I could offer, because he'd said he wanted to see her again …

Shaking out my shoulders, I fixed my gaze on the wall, homing in on a singular spot while I forced everything else from my mind. I pulled at that strength, guided it out. Heat pricked my skin, but I pushed through the pain until it faded, faded to nothing. Small particles drifted from my hands and arms, my chest and face. They floated forward, forming into an image.

A powerful one that was easy to hold. Sable eyes, dirty blonde hair, and warm beige skin. A beautiful face.

Naomi.

Theo stilled. He rose, lifting Whitney with him, then set her down and advanced. He stopped before the image, staring at his sister, taking in her every feature.

Whitney slid to his side, tears brimming in her eyes as she threaded her fingers with his, then set her head on his shoulder. His grip was tight, as if her hand alone kept him tethered.

Kane's arms fell loose at his sides as he looked at Naomi, some unfathomable emotion in that silver topaz stare.

My power waned. The image faded, then vanished altogether.

Theo turned my way. His breath hitched, red rimming his eyes as they screamed their thanks. A lone tear streaked his cheek, but it wasn't sadness that drove it, because those strained lines around his gaze had ebbed.

Marisol inclined her head, her smile a less-than-balanced mix of excited and proud. Then she linked her weathered hands together and instructed, "Again."

***

The house was quiet, the antithesis of the rapid-fire thoughts careening around my skull. Between everything that had happened with Kane and the Pack, and the thought of Mason's dirge at the Great Hall the next night, I couldn't shut down my mind.

Things with my emotions were still … I didn't even know. Off. They were off. I sighed, staring down at my plate, hungry, but not wanting to eat.

I stabbed my egg, and it slipped aside. I stabbed it again, then lifted it toward my mouth. Slithering from my fork, it dropped to the plate with a slap. I frowned, then proceeded to chase its elusive ass until I gave up and grabbed it between my fingers.

I swallowed it down, hoping it would taste like victory. Instead, I got a healthy dose of lukewarm sadness.

My phone pinged and I eyed the screen. A text from Lisa popped up: a screenshot of an article with the headline "Largest Protests Yet as Five Are Killed in Wave of Overnight Attacks Along Border". My stomach twisted as I scrolled down and scanned the story. Reports of people with red or glowing eyes ripping their victims to shreds alongside a map of Ithica that highlighted other regions who'd suffered similar issues. All were clustered on the human side of their western border—the one "shielding" them from Cambria.

Ithica's government had given a statement indicating there had been no breaches, which only fueled the wave of Ithican anti-government sentiments.

"You're protecting them!" one masked woman was quoted as saying.

Them. *Us*.

What the hells? If Cambria wanted Ithica, if we'd actually moved on them, the death tolls would've been a shit ton higher. Painfully so. And there was something off about the descriptions of the attacks. Something not quite … preternatural. And there was only one answer for that.

Clicking Bower's name, I punched out a message.

Me: *It's Zahara.*

The little dots appeared before his message came through.

Bower: *I'm gonna require a full sentence if you intend me to follow.*

Me: *The attacks at the border. It has to be her. She's testing the serums.*

Bower: *Why there?*

Fair question—but the answer didn't take long to sniff out, because it'd already started.

Me: *So your people blame us.*

A pause, then:

Bower: *I'll get back to you.*

My mouth pursed, 'cause the *who* made sense, but the why … What was her endgame? The Ithican government had made their position on us clear. Yeah, there were protests, but it wasn't like the sentiment was unanimous. Unless she pushed it that way, swayed public opinion. Turned them on us. But, again, to what end?

What the iron fires was she playing at? Why did she want to make it look like *we'd* crossed over? Attacked the humans for some reason? What possible reason would we have for doing that? What would she gain from it other than war?

Fucking Zahara.

I let out a heavy exhale. This was my fault. I might not have made the serums, but I'd been there with Isaac when he'd peddled them. Obsidian, if I'd just pushed for more information. Not that Zahara'd been much of a sharer, but still, maybe I could've gotten *something*.

Shoving my phone aside, I sauntered to the sink, washed my dishes, then put them away.

The steady thump of heavy footfalls entered the kitchen. My heart thrummed and I turned, my gaze landing on Kane. He stood, shoulder propped against the wall as he watched me, the hollows under his eyes dark.

"Come somewhere with me?" he asked, his words a low rumble. He sounded like he didn't know if I'd agree.

And the thought of that broke my heart.

Wiping the dampness that clung to my palms, I nodded. "Anywhere."

His Adam's apple dipped as he closed in and extended a hand. I took it and his hold flexed over mine as he steered me out the back door and across the yard … toward a shed.

My face twisted, because what the Iron Hells?

"Where did that come from?"

"I had it delivered earlier." Stopping before it, he let me go, then pulled a key from his pocket and unlatched the thick padlock on the double doors. His silver topaz eyes speared mine before he tipped his head toward the shed. "Go on."

My eyes narrowed as I held his gaze for one moment. Two. Then, palm settling against the wood, I pushed, the hinges quietly creaking when the doors swung open. The light from outside spilled in, flooding the dim and painting the newly laid floorboards. I froze, my heart stopping in my chest. My hands shot to my mouth and I took a single step forward, then another.

My lips parted and I sucked in a soft breath. Lowering my arms, I trailed my fingers over the head of the white convertible crib, the one I'd wanted so we'd have something to grow with the baby as they grew—presumably fast, seeing as it was Kane's. Along the back wall stood the matching dresser and changing table. Baskets, blankets, and sheets sat neatly piled in the corner. Everything. It was all there. My entire list of dream items.

"You found my magazine."

A tentative smile tugged at his mouth. "You stuffed it in the office desk and scratched hearts around everything you wanted."

Subtlety. My most understated quality.

Kane strode to the center of the space, pulled the string to turn on the light along the ceiling, then sealed us inside. He crossed his arms and watched me, the sinewed fibers of his forearms flexing.

The hollow, poisonous sorrow that had festered inside my soul wilted and waned, until it faded to nothing and released me from its grasp. My body sagged, and I turned to my Alpha, voice scarcely above a whisper as I murmured, "Kane."

Some of his rigidity ebbed, but not all. Not even close.

Weaving between the furniture, my pulse kicked up as, one at a time, I took up those soft, plush toys, hugging them to my chest. A cauldron, a black peaked hat and a red-eyed bat. Setting them aside, I fought a smile as I plucked up a mobile that had multiple waxing and waning moons … and a howling wolf.

I arched a brow in question.

His mouth tugged at the corners again, and he lifted a shoulder in a half-shrug.

Turning in awe, I asked, "When did you do all this?"

Sage, when had he even had time?

Thumping the wall with the side of his fist, he said, "Here and there."

I shook my head and rubbed the corner of the soft comforter between my thumb and forefinger. "You put all this together yourself?"

He dipped his chin in a nod.

"Where did you even keep it?"

"In the cellar."

I blinked rapidly, still trying to get the math to work. "When?"

Another uptick of his mouth. "You sleep pretty sound now."

I slipped my lips around my teeth, biting down to hold back my laugh at the image that thought conjured. Of my hulking wolf tip-toeing his unequivocally imposing ass from our room in the dead of night so he didn't wake me.

But still, he'd accumulated it all, got it all ready. For me.

"It's not everything," he said. "There's still some stuff I figured you'd want to be there for."

Because he knew me. Knew I'd want to buy those first cloth diapers, and the clothes. The teeniest of boots, or itty-bitty jackets.

He moved before me, his touch grazing my cheek as he brushed my hair back from my face. "I planned on doing this later, but I know everything's hitting you, Bry. I just wanted to give you something. To try and help."

My stomach fluttered, a wild and completely untempered excitement flitting to life in its depths. This was a gesture. The super-grand kind from movies that made the love interest swoon. And, iron fires, I was swooning. My body warmed, my gaze softening as it held his. I let my smile break free before I squealed and launched myself at him.

He caught me, hands hooking under my thighs before he wrapped them around his waist and bracketed me in his hold. A shudder ran through him, followed by a jagged exhale as his body folded over mine, practically engulfing me.

Nuzzling my face into his throat, I threw my arms around his neck and squished myself tighter against him, the hard planes of his body flush with the soft curves of mine. My emotions reset, crashing back in, a tidal wave on dry sand. Happy. I was so damn happy. Peeking past him, my gaze flitted from one thing to the next, and I wiggle-thrashed against him.

His laugh was heavy, rumbling through his chest to mine. The strain eased from his jaw, his back, and arms. "I know you wanna celebrate the baby, Bry. And I hate that I can't give that to you yet."

I leaned back to better see him, tone softening as I said, "This is enough, Kane."

Those thick fingers plunged into my hair. "For now."

My gaze lit on the crib. Clutching my new obsidian, I sought that emotion and reached for my power. My skin pricked as the particles rose, then coalesced inside. A silver-eyed babe lay there, swaddled as they blinked up at us.

Kane's chest hitched.

Happy tears pricked the backs of my eyes, blurring my sight. They trickled free, their warm rivulets staining my cheeks before I released my ring and ducked my head, swiping them across his shirt.

There was that laugh again. It sated my soul. Untangled that knotted weave of emotions and exhaustion that had tied me down. Held me prisoner against myself.

Pointing, I commanded him, "Take me for a tour, Big Bad!"

He smirked as he gave my ass a tap, then shifted my weight to one hip, freeing an arm. Pointing, he indicated a rectangular, stainless-steel contraption. "That's the trash."

My brow furrowed at the series of sensors and other bits that lined the base and lid. "It looks very high-techy."

He waved a palm over the top, and it made a whirring sound as the lid lifted. Inside were several layers of … something. Not quite a vault, but not far off.

"You afraid someone's gonna try and steal something in there?"

He tapped a pedal with his foot and the lid lowered back into place, making a *zzt* sound as it sealed itself. "It's scent-containing," he said.

Ah, indeed. Because no doubt his preternatural sniffer would find a dirty diaper the unpleasant kind of difficult.

A Persian rug stood on its side, rolled up and leaned against the wall. Steering us to the corner, he aimed for the plush rocking chair there. All the colors flowed, whites, ivories, tans, and varying shades of brown all complementing one another. Exactly as I'd planned but better than I ever could've imagined.

Holding me tight, he lowered us down, and the plush glider chair slid back and forth in a hypnotic flow. Back. Forth. Back. Forth.

My attention snagged on an oddly shaped pillow off to the side. I plucked it up, twisting it in the air as I inspected it. "What's this?"

He slipped it from my grasp and tucked it under his side and elbow. "I read holding the baby for long stretches can be hard on the shoulder." He lowered his arm onto it. "This is supposed to help."

I didn't know if it was possible to love him more. My heart swelled, thumping happily against my ribs as if trying to break free. To get to him.

My mouth crashed against his, kissing him hard. He groaned, his tongue pushing past my lips and exploring my own.

I squeaked, hands twisting into the collar of his hooded shirt before I pulled back. "We're having a *baby*."

Tucking a strand of hair back from my face, he smiled. A deep one that reached his silver topaz eyes and transformed his face. "We're having a baby."

Trailing a finger down the column of his neck, I purred. "Your baby."

A resonant growl rolled through his throat. "*Mine*."

My overprotective, wildly possessive, and wholly selfless wolf. Angling into him, I set my forehead to his temple. "Thank you, Kane."

"You don't need to thank me, Bry."

"No, I do." My fingers curled into his shirt. "I needed this. And you knew I did." Because he always knew what I needed. And he always did what needed to be done.

"Yeah." He nudged me with his jaw, his rough stubble grazing my skin. "I did."

I bit my lip, hiding my smile, and teased, "You're right. It's the least you could do."

His voice was a rough rasp against me as he said, "It is, considering you're literally making our baby."

My mouth dropped open, palm landing on my chest. "Finally, you acknowledge it."

He grinned, and the snort that broke from me came from somewhere deep and needed.

His warm palm flattened, sliding forward onto my hip. "It's all together, but I didn't make it pretty. Thought you'd wanna do that part."

And I did, 'cause barking orders to Kane Slade while I sat back, sizing up him and the room, sounded the best kind of glorious to me.

"I build the house, Bry." He shifted, his smile hungry and hot and humble. "You make it a home."

Sage, the way I loved him. Each time I thought we'd reached our peak, he climbed us higher. I sighed, my core clenching. "If I wasn't already pregnant, that might've done it."

Chapter Sixteen

The next evening, I stood, eyeing myself in the new, floor-to-ceiling mirror tucked into the corner of my bedroom with Kane. My gaze twigged on the copy of *Ancient Histories* where it sat on my bedside table, and I wished again that I understood. That the passages held some meaning.

I glanced back at myself and sighed. My belly didn't poke out yet, not really, but if I looked hard enough, I swore I could see something there. Frowning, I tried to decide if the black dress I'd picked out for Mason's dirge hugged my curves a little too much. I settled a palm over my lower abdomen as Kane closed in, chest pressing against my back as he loomed close behind me.

"I look pregnant." And I loved it, but considering our circumstances, it wasn't what one might call convenient.

His deep voice was a rumble that rolled over my skin. "You look fucking perfect."

I bit my lip. "You're just saying that so you can get in my pants later."

A smirk tugged the corner of his mouth, that rumble deepening. "You're not wearing pants." His palms slid from my hips before he started tugging the hem of my dress higher. I shimmied against him, and he kept tugging and tugging until the scarlet shade of my lacey thong peeked out.

He stiffened, his eyes drifting out of focus. He was gone for one second. Two. An eternity ticked by before he came back.

"Fuck!" Snapping my dress down, he grabbed me by the arm, exploding from the room preternaturally fast before he roared so loudly the damn rafters shook. "LUCAS!"

I blinked hard, trying to keep up. "Kane?"

My brother's door cracked open, his face gaunt, expression desolate. His eyes were bleary, like he'd just woken, and he must've read the barely tempered panic in my gaze, because he straightened. "What's wrong?"

"Trouble's inbound," Kane answered. "Time to go."

Lucas snapped into the hall. "What kind of trouble?"

Kane aimed us down the stairs. "They're coming."

I stared up at him, adrenaline kicking into overdrive. "*Who's* coming?"

He released me, and the car keys clanked as he snatched them from the side table by the entrance. "Some of the Pack."

"How many?" my brother asked, his tone dark.

"A dozen."

My stomach dropped. *A dozen*. Shadow and sage.

Kane's stare was molten. "It's a challenge."

My lungs seized, refusing to work. A challenge? We'd known the Pack might feel this way, but, iron fires, I'd hoped they'd see reason. See Kane for who he was.

I cleared my throat. "Who is it?"

"Priya's boyfriend."

I jolted to a stop. "Her *boyfriend*?" My mind was shock-addled, caught in a slow-motion moment, which meant it took a second for those words to hit their mark.

Kane threw open the front door, then stood, filling the frame as his electric stare blazed across the dark of the night. Waiting.

"How do you know?"

"Cassian. He caught word." He rolled his shoulders. "He's inbound."

Knowing Cassian was coming might've eased the metaphorical claw from my throat—if a gang of vengeance-hungry weres hadn't also been bearing down on us as we spoke.

Kane whipped his chin outside. "Take Luke. Both of you fly the hells outta here."

Lucas planted his feet, his violet gaze hardening. "I can do something, Kane. I can help you."

My Alpha shook his head. "The challenge is supposed to distract me. Keep me occupied, so they can get to you"—he turned my way—"and your sister."

A diversion. A way to block my Alpha so they could slip past while he was busy and slaughter my brother. My blood turned to fire, 'cause like the wraith would I ever let that happen. I opened my mouth to say as much, but Kane grabbed my shoulder and dragged me onto the porch.

"She can go," Lucas said. "But I'm staying."

"Luke—"

"No!" My brother balled his fist and slammed it against his chest. "I'm fucking staying!"

My lungs tightened, my heart thrashing in my ears. I wanted to give him that, because he had earned it. He'd earned a right to fight for the things he loved and the things he'd lost, because he'd lost everything and more in the name of his father. But while with some battles, standing to fight was the only choice, for others, you ran. My Alpha had no option, as a challenge issued must be answered, but us sticking around was a problem with a capital P.

Kane's body tensed. "I need you with her, Luke."

My brother slashed his head to the side. "You're just getting rid of me again."

We needed him to listen, and we didn't have time to hash things out. If I wanted Lucas onside, I was gonna need something to jar him. And I had exactly that …

"Lucas," I said, desperate. "I'm pregnant!"

Kane inhaled deeply.

Lucas's eyes flew wide, his body straining. "What?"

"That's why I need you, Luke." My Alpha's heavy hand thumped onto my brother's shoulder. "I can't send her out alone. I fucking can't."

My brother's chest expanded, his shoulders pulling back. His head dipped in a sharp nod. He was ready.

Kane's grip flexed over Lucas before he released him, then pivoted, shoving the keys at my chest. "Get to Joaquin's."

'Cause Kane's rogue wolves wouldn't cross another Alpha's territory, least of all after blood. Wraith take me, I hoped.

"I will," I breathed.

Grabbing my collar, he pulled me in and pressed a rough kiss to my lips. To Lucas, he said, "Keep her safe."

My brother took my wrist and vowed, "I will."

The roar of fast-moving engines closed in, headlights slicing through the dim, painting the road and trees before they screeched a hard right into our driveway.

Bile rose up my throat, coating my tongue with its burn. Iron Hells take me.

Kane stalked forward. He descended the steps, those powerful legs carrying him slow and easy. His arms hung loose by his sides, his stare tracking across the four vehicles that had pulled up. Electric eyes stared out at us, the malevolence there kissing the air with its stannic scent.

Car doors whipped open, and twelve weres stepped out.

Lucas's hold locked tight around me.

A red-haired wolf at the front eyed my Alpha, and the acid in his gaze was more potent than any shadow-walker venom.

Kane rolled his shoulders, then squared up to the guy as he warned, "You don't want this, Nathan."

Nathan reached into his coat, and the light glinted off something metallic as he pulled whatever the hells it was free.

A dagger. Big, jagged, and iron.

Sweet sage, no.

Kane's boned claws extended, followed by his canines.

Three other weres pulled their blades, mouths open, practically salivating as their attention stalked from me to my brother.

My breath seized.

"*Get to the car, Bry,*" Kane rumbled across our bond.

I nudged Lucas, tipping my head toward the vehicle. He edged to the side, slowly.

Nathan's stare snapped to us before he waved his dagger our way. "The fuck do you think you're goin'?"

Kane's power tore through the night, pushing everyone back. "Eyes on me, asshole."

Another vehicle careened into the yard, Cassian behind the wheel. He threw himself out, his blazing stare wild as he closed in.

My heart stutter-stepped for several ridiculously long beats as the Beta circled the mob and edged to Kane's side.

"No weapons at a challenge, boys," Cassian said. "It's your own power, or nothing."

"Rules? You want us to follow the fuckin' rules?" Nathan hissed.

"If you plan to take his seat, I do."

Take Kane's seat.

The bile climbed higher.

Lucas edged aside again, dragging me with him. Ducking down, he grabbed one of the leftover pieces of lumber on the porch and held it by his side, at the ready.

"Oh, we'll get to his seat," Nathan said, spit flying from his lips. His expression was wide and wild, like he'd been on a bender for days. A bad, V-fueled one that had stripped his senses. He aimed the dagger Kane's way. "You knew what Isaac was before Priya was gutted. Before he hacked her to fuckin' pieces. Before he stole her from me."

Kane inclined his head. "I did."

"You don't think Kane would have gutted Isaac years ago if he'd known what he was capable of?" Cassian cut in. "Kane lost his own damn mate because of him."

"He didn't lose her." Nathan wagged the weapon my way. "She's standing right there. But Priya's not. She's dead and rottin' in the ground. I'll never get her back. I think it's only fair I repay the favor."

His friends crouched, salivating at the prospect of violence.

Lucas pulled me down onto the yard.

Nathan grinned, his face sinister. Dark. "Consider this an official challenge, *Alpha*."

Kane inclined his head. "Accepted," he said, then erupted forward. Their bodies clashed, a heavy crack filling the night.

The others pounced. Cassian lunged, grabbing one by the throat. Chaos descended.

The two to our left cut our way, weaving their own weapons toward us. A promise.

I gripped my obsidian and pulled. Lucas released me, raising the piece of lumber like a bat.

The gold-haired wolf to my right drove forward. Fast. Lucas advanced, planted his feet, reared back and swung hard, catching him in the shoulder. Bones cracked. The guy howled and dropped.

I blinked hard as the limp were's multi-chain-wearing buddy lunged my way. Kane's power roared through me, and my fist snapped out, colliding with his jaw. He grunted, chains clanking as he staggered back.

Through the madness, my gaze found my Alpha's.

His jaw was clenched, a deep gash cleaved across his forearm, another over his chest, both hissing from the iron. Nathan reared, dagger held high. Two other wolves dodged around him, waiting for their shot. My heart stopped.

Kane's muscles were corded, straining against their onslaught. He roared at me, "NOW!"

But my feet were rooted. I couldn't leave him. Couldn't—

Lucas shoved me toward the car. "Run, Briar!"

I stumbled, my brain kickstarting as I fled.

The gold-haired wolf clambered to his feet. Or at least, he tried to, but Lucas let loose on him, swinging over and over, snapping his ribs, then his leg, before he sank the wood into his skull.

That chain-wearing wolf beat his feet my way, maw sitting at an angle. I reached for the car. He slammed into me from behind, crushing me against the door. I swung back, elbow connecting with his head. He grunted. Twisting, I faced him, shoving at his chest to keep him at bay. He leaned in, teeth snapping as he went for my throat. I shoved harder, but the guy was fast. I cried out, fighting for leverage.

Those teeth inched closer. Closer. They grazed my neck.

Lucas appeared at his back, blood coating his shirt and dripping from his brow and chin. He swung the lumber. A loud thunk carried through the night, followed by a chunk of the were's scalp before he dropped beside the limp-as-hells body of his very broken friend.

Holy shit!

It wasn't like it would kill him, but it sure as sage would slow him down.

Lucas grabbed something metal and chucked it into the vehicle. "Inside," he ordered.

My chest heaved as we dove in.

Outside, Kane roared, those boned claws sinking deep into Nathan's side. Kane's face and shirt were blood-soaked, a feral glare in his molten eyes, one with a singular focus. Kill.

No submissions. No setting the terms. Only death.

Power of obsidian.

The chain-wearing wolf stirred. Shaking his head, he crushed his eyes closed like he fought off the worst headache of his life.

The car engine revved to life. I popped it into gear. The were shoved up onto his arms, then clambered to his feet, eyes ablaze as he shifted into our path. Crouching, he readied himself to lunge. I hit the gas.

His eyes flashed—whether it was the headlights reflecting or his wolfy nature, I had no clue. I dropped my foot harder. His gaze widened a second before the car hit him, his face colliding with the hood. I kept going, and the car jumped, an obnoxious thump following as he slipped under the tire.

I cut the wheel hard, slicing us through the yard and around the other vehicles. Rocks and dirt kicked up, arcing wide as the back of the car swung around. A second later, I hit the end of the driveway, then the road.

Lucas's hand gripped the door so tightly his knuckles went white. He asked, "You're alright?"

"Yeah," I said, through a gasp. "You?"

A sharp nod.

Tearing out my phone, I tossed it my brother's way. "Call Joaquin, let him know we're crossing." I dragged my hair back from my face. "And keep a lookout."

His thumbs tapped, bringing up my contacts before he punched call and put it on speaker. "On it."

Slamming my foot to the floor, I beelined for the road to the Southern Alpha's territory. The closer we got, the more a knot twisted in my gut: fear for Kane, yes, but something else, too … something I couldn't peg.

"Banshee," Joaquin drawled.

"It's Luke," my brother said. "Some of the Pack came for Kane."

Silence, then: "Shadowed fucking moon, don't tell me—"

"He's handling them."

A heavy, only partially relieved exhale.

Lucas's stare met mine. "Briar and I are headed your way."

Joaquin's voice darkened. "Where are you?"

The houses grew thicker, closer to the road as the street to his territory loomed ahead.

"We're about twenty minutes out," I answered.

There was a rustling, like he was on the move. "I'll meet you."

From the right, an SUV pulled out in front of us.

"Shit!" I veered a hard left. Tires screeching, the ass end of the car flew wide. The back wheels caught on the gravel shoulder before I righted us with a snap. Lucas slammed into his door, and he grunted.

The SUV cut a circle, giving chase.

"Briar?" Joaquin said.

"We're still here," I panted.

Lucas whipped around, eyes fixed on the back window. "They're following."

My gaze flicked to the rear-view. Wraith take me. I dropped my foot to the floor. "Who?"

His stare narrowed as he strained to see. "Weres. I think."

"Tell me where you're headed, banshee," Joaquin demanded, words tight.

Another side street appeared, and a car came flying straight toward us. Fast. Too fast.

I tensed. "HOLD ON, LUCAS!"

The car slammed into our rear quarter, knocking us around. Metal thunked and screeched. I hit the brakes, tires shrieking over the pavement as we spun one full circle. Two. We jolted to a stop, crossways on the road.

"BANSHEE!" Joaquin roared.

Gasping, I shook myself. The second car sat about fifty feet back, smoke rising from its crumpled hood, while the SUV maneuvered slowly around it and the debris in its wake.

And I thanked sage and the Iron Hells themselves that our vehicle still ran as I shifted into gear and hit the gas again.

My brows lowered, 'cause there was no chance any of this was coincidence. No. It was coordinated. *It was fucking coordinated!*

"They're funneling us, Joaquin."

"To where?"

There was only one place that was a problem for Lucas. And I suddenly had no doubt who'd be waiting for us when we reached it.

Lucas must've come to the same conclusion, but his voice was level as he answered, "The neutral grounds."

Out of wolf territory. Unprotected. Deadly.

Danika.

Joaquin snarled, then cursed. His own engine roared across the speaker.

"What do we do, Briar?" Lucas asked.

Heart pounding in my ears, my eyes darted around like a solution might present itself. My mind whirled, ticking through the options, which were less than slim. But there was one name, one face that shot to the forefront of my mind. Sure, she hadn't forgiven me, but she'd known about Lucas, and heedless of her past, she hadn't moved against him. That *had* to mean something. Maybe there was some sliver of her darkened heart that still cared for me. Perhaps, no matter how much I'd hurt her, she didn't want to return the favor.

I'd seen what she was capable of, the extent of the predator that lay beneath the surface. It was well within her power to tear my brother to shreds so small we'd never find the pieces. But again, she *hadn't*. And she hadn't spoken a word of our betrayal.

Because maybe, just maybe, she didn't actually hate me. Power of obsidian, I hoped she didn't. 'Cause with what I was about to do, it might tip her over the edge.

Either way, I prayed to the wraith she would help, because she was our only chance.

I hated that I was bringing this to her door, that I was about to force her into a position where she had to choose, that I was about to ask for more when I'd already taken so much. But I was out of options.

This wasn't about pride or any of the preternatural bullshit. It was about Lucas. About my child.

"I've got something," I said, letting the words hang.

My brother's gaze met mine.

"Tell me where," the Southern Alpha demanded.

I pointed us west, to Northern shadow-walker territory, and told him, "Cassandra's."

Chapter Seventeen

Sweat slicked my spine as we flew through the neutral grounds. I leaned heavily on the horn to chase people from our path. Buildings whipped by, a blur against our speed.

"Where are you now?" Joaquin demanded over the phone.

"Almost at Cassandra's territory," I said. Then, to my brother, "I don't know how this is gonna go, Lucas, so we need to be ready to run." The trailing SUV's headlights blinded me against the dark of night as it advanced, charging up against our bumper. "You can't be panicked. If you reek of fear, it could trigger her walkers." And if Cassandra's entire Clan got struck by that predatory thirst ... Iron fires take me. Death came at us from every angle, like some big, bloody death sandwich.

Even under the inky sky, I could see that Lucas's violet eyes were hard. "I'm not afraid."

And he wasn't. Obsidian, he wasn't.

I exploded across Cassandra's boundary, crimson eyes following our chaotic progress.

The Southern Alpha's voice was a low warning when he said across the speaker, "The venom line, Briar."

The venom line that meant we couldn't cross into her home without an invite. An invite I'd already received, but one my brother had unequivocally not. An invite I prayed she offered.

"I know, Joaquin, but we're outta options." I swerved around a median. Close. We were so close. "I've gotta go. She needs a heads-up."

"Fuck!" Joaquin snarled. "I'm coming." He disconnected.

"Call her," I told my brother. Then added, "Let me talk."

Lucas punched in Cassandra's number. It rang, and rang, and fucking rang. He hung up, then dialled again. And again, nothing. When the voicemail kicked in, I prayed to the wraith and all things holy before I left my message.

"Cassandra, please," I said, my gaze darting to the rear-view. "Lucas and I are headed your way now. I need your help. I know I lied, and after what you did for me, I've got no right to ask for anything else. But he's the only blood I have left." My next words were a broken, desperate plea. "Sage, please, Cassandra."

Her luxurious cluster of massive, thirty-floor high-rise dens loomed in the distance, their windows blacked out. I turned onto the pale brick road that led to it.

Streetlights caught on the white stone that lined the façade, and the silver and black accents along the balconies and the corners of the buildings. It was a beacon in the dark—one I aimed straight for.

Cassandra's Clan sigil, a waning moon overlaid by a string of smaller stars—the symbol of night—loomed high above. No guards hovered out front. And there was not a preternatural soul in sight.

My grip on the wheel was painful. The leather groaned under my hands as I worked to steady their shake.

Be there, Cassandra. Please!

I closed in fast. When I was forty feet out, I locked up the brakes. Our bodies lurched forward as the tires screeched, careening up to the entrance before we jerked to a halt fifteen paces away.

Bursting out of the car, I roared, "Run!"

The SUV slammed to a stop at our car's ass end, penning the vehicle in.

Lucas and I bolted for the building. Ten feet and closing. Nine. Eight.

There was the clunk of doors opening, followed by the pound of feet giving chase.

Please, Cassandra. Please. Please. Please!

The front entrance flew wide. The Northern Dowager stood, lit by the chandeliers within. She loomed, crimson suit matching those crimson eyes, which were feral as they drifted from the chaos on her doorstep to me.

My lungs seized.

She waved a delicate hand. “Get inside.”

The hot breath of the were at my back kissed my neck. My chest constricted and I shoved Lucas across the venom line. He tumbled forward as the wolf’s claws raked along my scalp and locked around my hair.

I cried out as my momentum brought me up short, legs shooting upward before I was slammed to the ground.

“BRIAR!” Lucas roared, agony lacing the word, before the door sealed shut, cutting me off from him and the Northern Dowager.

I reached for Kane’s power. It surged through me, rolling across the night. The lackey’s grip slipped. Drawing my leg back, I kicked, heel catching him hard in the gut. Real hard. A hollow thunk echoed through the area. He buckled, his face turning blue as he struggled for breath.

The lackey dropped to a knee, hands clutching his stomach, but his fatal stare stayed trained on me.

I clambered up and bolted for the building.

Another vehicle appeared, roaring toward us, Danika behind the wheel. The tires cut hard, aiming for the entrance, forcing me away from it.

Cursing, I lunged to the side, right toward that fucking were.

The wolf grinned as he reached for me.

I threw my fist, my Alpha’s strength coursing through me, and caught him in the chest. He grunted and flew back several feet before falling onto his ass.

The soft thunk of a car door carried from behind me as Danika stepped out, followed by several of her walkers, all fanning wide.

I was surrounded.

Dead. I was good and goddamn dead.

The vamps moved as one, a female grabbing my left arm, a male my right. Kicking my legs from behind, they shoved me to my knees.

"Do not touch her," Danika snarled, eyes flaring wide as she approached. "That honor is *miiiiine*." A malevolent grin split her expression, peeling her lips back from her teeth. Her nostrils flared. "It would seem some of your Alpha's Pack weren't fond of his choices."

My laugh was so acidic, it was a wonder it didn't burn. "And it seems you decided to capitalize, *Dowager*."

Taking a handful of my hair, she snapped my head back. Her incisors lengthened, and her taloned fingers punctured my arm.

I swallowed hard. *I love you, Kane*.

The door to Cassandra's den crashed open, steel buckling under the force. A deafening the-painful-kind-of-death-is-coming roar tore through the world as Cassandra flew into the night, moving so preternaturally fast, I could scarcely track her.

Her rage scented hot and bitter as it stung my airways.

She latched onto Danika's car, launching it aside to clear her path. It smashed into the were's SUV, and both vehicles flipped end over end, sending glass and metal careening through the dim.

Black lines crept across Cassandra's face as she faced off with Danika. "YOU DARE CROSS MY TERRITORY TO SHED BLOOD WITHOUT INVITATION!"

Danika stabbed a finger toward my neck, pressing it tight against my flesh. "Her kin is a changeling!"

"And you believe that grants you charter to come to *my* lands? To do as you please?"

"We have rules!"

"Yes, and I too have rules, Danika Trevino. Rules I demand be obeyed within my borders." Cassandra glided closer, her ethereal grace haunting as those dark veins continued to crawl further and further across her flesh. "Rules you have broken."

"I deserve vengeance."

Something warm brushed my bond before Kane's voice reached me: "*I'm alright, Bry. I'm coming. I'm fucking coming.*"

I wanted to answer, but the scene before me was too perilous to ignore.

Cassandra's head canted, the owl-like angle sharp. "If you harm Briar Stone, I will remove your fucking head."

I swallowed hard. The chasm between them made the air thick with threat and malice, with a hunger for violence that could only be slaked with blood.

Danika tipped her chin behind Cassandra, to where Lucas stood in the den's entrance. "You either give me the brother, or I *will* take her." Her taloned finger traveled along the column of my throat, and I used every ounce of strength I had not to flinch. "She took my family; it is justice."

She was blinded by pain. Untethered. Unreachable. And it was about to cost me everything.

Cassandra straightened. "You are wrong, Danika Trevino."

My eyes widened. I'd taken the heat, claimed Ivy's death as *my* doing to protect Cassandra, to prevent a war. And if she went and debunked that truth to save me in return … Shadow and sage. *Don't do it, Cassandra. Don't fucking do it!* I gave the Northern Dowager a subtle and wildly vehement shake of my head.

"She confessed it herself!" Danika snarled through her teeth. There was a wildness there—one that reminded me painfully of Ivy.

"It was not Briar Stone who ended your sister," Cassandra angled closer, eyes turning a pitted shade of black so deep, it stole the light. "It was me."

Danika's finger stopped, voice going whisper soft. "What did you say?"

"You heard me." Cassandra arched a challenging brow. "You need only scent the truth."

The Southern Dowager jerked my head back, forcing me to look up at her as terror seared my soul and my heart thrashed wildly in my ears. "Then I will take her from *you*."

An engine rumbled in the distance.

Joaquin's G-class surged up and he jumped out. His chest heaved, his hands in fists at his sides. His blazing hazel stare met mine and held, terror and rage and a hundred other things buried there.

"Let her go, Danika," Joaquin warned, taking a slow step right.

"Or you'll *what*?" Danika purred, her smile filled with malevolence and pride.

"Your death is already promised," he said, then tipped his head toward her people, "but theirs isn't." The "yet" was silent. Deathly so. And Iron Hells, he looked broad and dangerous and every bit the Alpha he'd become.

Danika dragged me back a step, like I was a toy she had no intention of sharing. "She and her wolf lied to us." She stabbed a hand toward Lucas. "Protected him." Her teeth bared. "SOMEONE MUST SUFFER!" Her talon punctured my flesh, and I winced as warm rivulets trickled down my skin.

My Alpha brushed our connection again.

Joaquin edged ahead, closing the space between them by another foot. Owning it. But he wouldn't get to me. Not in time.

Lucas's stare narrowed. He shook his head. His skin rippled.

Heart stopping, I silently screamed, *NO!*

His body morphed, bones growing long and lean. Emaciated. His jaw reshaped, turning delicate, and his eyes became a matching crimson to the walkers who bore down on us. His hair lengthened, taking on a fire-kissed shade of red. The same red as Danika's—or Ivy's.

Iron Hells take me. What was he doing? What was he *doing*?

He stepped forward, crossing the venom line to come outside. My stomach torqued. *No. No. No!*

Every eye in the vicinity snapped toward my brother. No, not my brother. *Ivy*. Because head-to-toe, that's who he was, save the back of his neck, that tattoo. The one that followed him in whatever form.

Danika froze, going so still, she could've been stone.

Joaquin let out a low exhale. "Shadowed moon."

"Let Briar go," Lucas said, in Ivy's voice.

The Southern Dowager's lone word quavered as she said, "Sister?"

"Let her go, Danika," he repeated.

Danika's talons retreated a hair, then hesitated. Lucas advanced another steady step. Danika blinked like she could clear her sight, like what she saw wasn't real. And it wasn't, but iron fires, it still was.

"Let her go," he said again, words soft.

Danika's breath hitched and her hand fell.

Ivy-faced-Lucas stepped closer, slender fingers wrapping around my wrist. "Give her to me."

Her mouth opened, then closed, those eyes transfixed on her sister. She studied every line of that face, every fleck of those eyes, the strands of that hair.

Danika's eyes crushed closed. When they reopened, she ordered her people, "Release her."

They stared, slack-jawed, but did as she said.

Slowly, Lucas drew me toward him. My body ached as I shifted to my feet, moving cautiously to keep my muscles from jerking. I couldn't risk startling her. My brother kept pulling until he had maneuvered me behind him.

Joaquin's shoulders lowered with an exhale.

"You're not her," Danika uttered, but her voice was weak.

A breeze cut through the night, blowing that fiery red hair around Lucas's Ivy-masked face. "I'm what you need."

I held my breath, trying to fight the rising fear, 'cause sage only knew what she'd do next.

Danika padded closer, one step, then another. She reached out, her hand trembling.

Trembling? Shadow walkers could *tremble*?

Lucas stayed stock-still, his expression flat, giving nothing away. Danika's talons grazed his cheek, followed by her fingertips. She shuddered before her palm settled over the skin there.

"I've missed you." Her head hung as a howling sob broke from her throat, then another. Lucas leaned into her touch, his hand flattening over hers.

Cassandra glided to my side. Joaquin's body was hard as he, too, began edging over to join us.

Danika's eyes glistened, their whites tinging with red before a bloodied tear slipped down her cheek. As much as I hated her, my heart still broke for her. I knew what it was like to have everything taken. Losing someone was horrific, but having them stolen from you at the hands of another—*especially* someone like Isaac, who reveled in making you watch, making you suffer—that was another level of agony entirely.

Danika's knees buckled, and she collapsed into her sister's chest—*Lucas's* chest. He caught her, cradling the back of her neck and murmuring softly against her hair.

"I'm sorry. I'm so sorry." She sobbed, tears staining her skin before they coated my brother's shirt. "I didn't know. I thought you were gone. It's my fault. *It's my fault!*"

"Shhh," Lucas soothed. "You didn't know Isaac had taken me. If you had, you'd have come."

"I would," she said. "I'm sorry. I could've helped."

"No," he soothed, "you couldn't. I was lost. The Madness had taken me by the end."

Danika crumpled at the words. Not just at their horror, but at the truth she could scent in them. I stood in awe of my brother. Of his strength, his gentleness, and how unendingly smart and brave he was. So goddamn brave. Any trace of Isaac had ended with his blood. My brother was his own man.

"He was too strong, sister. For all of us."

Joaquin advanced another step.

Something brushed my hand, and I glanced to my side. Cassandra's fingers curved around my own. My throat tightened as the weight I'd been carrying, the crushing guilt of hurting her, faded away. She'd helped. She'd been ready to tear and claw and shred everything in her path … for me. She was a friend I didn't deserve.

Tears stung the backs of my eyes. "Thank you." My breath hitched in my chest, and I slumped against her, setting my head on her shoulder.

"We need you, sister," Lucas-Ivy said. "We can't stop Isaac without you." He brushed several loose strands of hair from her face.

Sweet sage.

Danika's attention fell to the edge of the tattoo twisting along the side of his neck. Her talon trailed it, her expression hardening. It was like the reality of the situation, of what—of *who*—stood before her, of my brother's existence, had suddenly struck.

Her stare morphed, eyes blackening as her lips peeled back, expression turning savage.

My chest seized, heart stopping.

Joaquin exploded forward, boned claws tearing from his fists so fast, his skin shredded. Danika's eyes flew wide, a rabid snarl tearing from her as her incisors extended, mouth snapping for Lucas's throat. He tried to dodge her, but too quick, she snapped out, latching him in place.

Time slowed as Danika's fangs closed in on my brother. Four inches. Three.

My mouth opened to scream, but I couldn't breathe. Couldn't think. Couldn't move. The Southern Alpha's fist flew, fast. So unimaginably fast.

Two inches.

Nonononon*o*! My legs went weak. I couldn't lose Lucas. *I couldn't fucking lose him!*

One.

Joaquin's claws struck home, sinking deep into Danika's face. She jolted.

Her arm dropped, falling limp at her side. Lucas staggered back. Danika jerked, then jerked again. Blood streamed down her head, pouring from her mouth and chin, filling the air with that dense copper scent. Her body fell slack. Joaquin ripped his claws free.

She collapsed, landing face first on the ground. Hard. Dead.

My breath exploded from me, my body sagging as the vamps who'd held me raised their hands in surrender.

"We were under orders," the female said.

"Leave now," Cassandra told them, a soft lilt in her voice like death's whisper. "Sort your new ruler. And pray they get your people in line."

They exchanged panicked looks, then fled. The were who had followed us there stepped to the side as if to flee.

Joaquin's stare flashed. "Not you."

My Alpha's truck roared as it slammed to a stop. He launched himself out, molten eyes raking me up and down. He closed in fast, crashing against me as he bracketed me in his hold.

The Southern Alpha offered the nervous-looking were an ominous smile as he tipped his head Kane's way and said, "You're his problem now."

Kane's hand traced a long, easy line up, then back down my spine. Up. Down. Up. Down.

My heart stuttered a beat, legs shaking with relief as my gaze lingered on Danika's corpse. "What happens now?"

Cassandra followed my line of sight. "The Blood War ensues."

Kane, Joaquin, and Lucas stiffened, the latter swallowing hard. While this was particularly troubling information, I was glad I wasn't the only one not in the know. Not that we would be, seeing as there hadn't been a power shift in the Clans in recent—or, I was fairly confident, *recorded*—history.

My mouth opened, closed, then opened again. Nothing about that sounded good. "Blood war?"

"The next oldest of our line succeeds us, and any who wish to may challenge that succession. But most"—Cassandra rolled her wrist and finished—"are reticent."

The door to her building opened and several of her people moved in, surrounding Danika's body.

Brow falling low, I asked, "Why reticent?"

"Because, Briar Stone," she said, her voice softening, "each challenge is to the death."

My eyes grew wide. Well, that was … troubling.

Kane shifted, rolling his shoulders. "How do you know when it's done? When a ruler has been determined?"

Her crimson gaze drifted to him. "The position is not declared held until such time as the challenges have ceased."

I balked. "And what if they never stop? It could go on forever."

She inclined her head, her smile sheer predator as she said, "It could, Briar Stone. So, I suggest it is good that we live a long life."

Chapter Eighteen

Within hours, the calls had been put out to the Conclave. Well, what existed of it. Leadership of Danika's Clan, Cassandra had informed me, would take some time to sort. Alistair and the rest of us implemented blockades at our borders, our people running checks for Isaac. For his scar.

Finally, finally, *finally*, the Conclave were united.

The Coven had proceeded with Mason's dirge in my absence, and my heart broke at missing it. But my ache for Mason's justice was somewhat mollified after I'd sent my decree to the Coven: Drop everything, scour every goddamn corner of our territory until Isaac was found. There was no other priority.

Isaac was cornered—which, knowing him, wasn't good—but with preternatural ground crews hunting him, he wouldn't be a problem for long.

I had Cassandra back, and Lucas was free. We weren't out of the woods yet, and I wasn't ready to totally let my guard down, but with our list of allies, an attack on Lucas would be a death sentence. I'd known the weight of my brother's secret had been crushing but, iron fires, my feeble heart could beat again.

The next evening, Kane stepped up to the glass entrance of the aptly named Coffee House in the swanky-as-hells Canal District, then opened the door wide. A tinkling bell chimed, the antithesis of his hulking presence as he loomed in the entrance, scanning every face inside before his palm flexed over the small of my back as he guided me in.

The cafe was ritzy as gothic-chic got. Ruby chandeliers dotted the black tin ceiling, while curlicue designs trailed its concave and convex metal. Dark-stained hickory shelves lined the walls, filled with glass wolves in varying poses. Howling, playing, fighting. The place was stunning, and the uber kind of convenient, seeing as Cassian's mate ran it, which meant it was trusted. Anyone prepping our dinner, tasked with feeding our family and the most elite of Cambria's beasties, needed to be of the "unlikely to feed us liquid iron" variety.

Plus, my Alpha swore it was the best-rated spot in town—for the wolves. And considering my wolf had chosen me, it was clear he had impeccable taste.

The place was bustling. Black mahogany tables sat scattered around the off-shoot rooms. Dishes clanked. Weres ate, the scents of their food sweet and rich, making my damn mouth water.

Kane smirked, his voice a low drawl when he asked, "Hungry, Bry?"

I smiled and shimmied my shoulders. "Always."

The wolves watched us. Well, they watched Kane. Their curiously cocked heads and raised brows made it clear that the warm and quiet side of their Alpha was one they'd rarely seen … if ever. Not that he was cruel. More that, with them, his don't-fuck-with-me power needed to be locked in place. And it still was, but it had softened. For me. Only me.

Cassian waved us in and gestured to a table at the head of the room. One that would give my Alpha a clear sight of everything and everyone. I was just about to take my place when the keening crystal bell over the door dinged again.

Cassandra glided inside, her crimson gaze drifting our way. Every wolf in the place went still, which was not exactly a shock. Probably wasn't every day the vamp queen herself graced them with her presence. But if it bothered her, she didn't let on. Besides, it's not like they were a threat; next to Kane, she was the deadliest thing in that city.

"Cassandra!" I beamed, arms wide as I closed in, wrapping her in a hug.

Her cold-skinned palms settled against the bared flesh from a keyhole loop at my back. "Briar Stone." She drew away, her attention sliding between me and my Alpha. "You said it was important."

"Yes." I cleared my throat and straightened my babydoll-style dress. We settled ourselves down and I set my forearms on the edge of the table, then linked my hands. "I, um, have something I wanted to ask you."

Her head tilted in that bird-like way as she inspected me. Not like she used to—like I was a bug. More like I was a curiosity. An intrigue. Doubtless my excitement had my heart rate up, singing to her. And I thanked the wraith she was a well-tempered walker with a fondness for, well, me.

Lifting my chin, I smiled. "Kane and I are getting married."

Kane's phone buzzed with a call before he eyed the screen and sent it to voicemail. That silver gaze hunted me, his muscles cording as his thumbs worked, typing a response … I presumed.

Cassandra inclined her head, pointer finger unfurling one segment at a time as she fluidly gestured toward that sparkliest of rocks on my ring finger. "I had deduced as much."

Right. I beamed. "So, wanna be my bridesmaid?"

The Dowager blinked, going preternaturally still. Stiller than usual, which was impressive considering she hovered just above corpse level on a good day. "You ask *me* to be a bridesmaid?" she repeated, as if the words were foreign. Or didn't compute.

Kane's stare shifted to mine. My smile was stiff, and I inclined my head. He angled the phone away, body shielding it as he continued to type.

A bitter tang coated my tongue before I forced it away and returned my attention to Cassandra. "Yes, you." I threaded my hand with hers, feeling the bizarre need to clarify. "At our wedding."

Her crimson gaze softened, and I swore her lip quivered. "You wish me to stand with you on such a day?"

My throat tightened. "You're my friend, Cassandra. Power of obsidian, *more* than a friend. You're … family." The second the word left my tongue, I knew it was true, because she'd stood *with* me through the darkest time of my life. She'd killed

Ivy, one of her own people, to tear me from Isaac's grasp, and she'd risked herself against Danika to shield my changeling brother. She had my loyalty, and every goddamn ounce of love I could give.

Her eyes grew distant, her grip cinching around mine as if she was tethering herself. "You honor me."

No. She honored *me*.

I shimmied my chair closer and swung our clasped hands, school-girl style. "So, can I take that as a yes?"

Her lips lifted in a full—iron fires take me—smile, exposing her beautifully bitey incisors. It completely transformed her face, making her look so … human. "That is a yes, Briar Stone." Spine straightening all militant-like, she set her chin and inquired, "What are my duties?"

I bit back a laugh. So very formal. So very Cassandra. "Help me find a dress. Book flowers. That kinda thing."

My Alpha slid his phone away before he rolled his shoulders, then rolled them again. My gaze met his as I pressed into his side. He exhaled and stilled.

Popping open my purse, I pulled out the planner I'd bought her as a gift, a thank you. It tumbled free, and along with it, the copy of *Ancient Histories*.

The Dowager stiffened, tone going deathly soft as she inquired, "Where did you get this?"

Her eyes were fixed on the tattered journal. "I—" I blinked. "Mason found it at the RC."

Shifting, my Alpha's stare narrowed on her. "You recognize it?"

"Yes, Kane Slade. It was once mine."

My heart thrummed in my chest. Hers. Of course. How the iron fires had I not connected those ridiculously obvious dots? Hers. It was *hers*!

Grabbing the book, I flipped it open to the well-worn page I'd stared at for countless nights, then jabbed a finger at that elusive passage.

Her crimson gaze scanned those pages. *Her* writing. *Her* words. *Her* account.

Changelings are made of the Deep. Of the Dark. Fear is what they know. It is why and what they are. Broken things that seek the chaos. When the call to the wraith comes, they die in the light and return.

"So, yeah, um …" I cleared my throat and said, "What the hells does this mean?"

"It means, Briar Stone, that the fading of a changeling's life calls to the wraith."

I scrubbed my chin, because that answer helped me not one bit.

"Changelings of the Deep do not die in the Iron Hells, because they are born of it. Their deaths must happen in the light." Her graceful fingers rolled, gesturing around us. "Here, on this plane."

I leaned forward, attention rapt. "And then what happens?"

She smiled, all secrets and teeth and predator, and said, "Then they pay for their sins."

Worrying at my lip, I stared down at my hands, bile searing my stomach. "Would that happen to Lucas?"

The shake of her head was slow. "I do not believe so." At the narrowing of my gaze, she added, "Your brother is not *born* of the Iron Hells, Briar Stone."

Sage, please, let that distinction be enough. Let it be true. Taking the book, I settled a palm over it, praying it was real, because a girl could dream.

Cassandra's long, graceful finger traced the planner as if eager to get back to the subject at hand.

I snickered, then slid it her way. "I sensed you'd like to keep track of things."

She stared down at it, her expression … softening. "You sensed correctly, Briar Stone." Her gaze lifted. "What is the wedding date?"

I plastered a wincing smile on my face, crossing my fingers that she didn't already have plans. Like a manicure, or a Hunt. "We settled on August next year. It's a ways out, so we've definitely got lots of—"

A sound like the tinkling of bells rang out when she laughed. "The making of such a dress requires time."

Kane's head drew back, and he blinked before he said across our bond, "*Did she just …*"

"*Laugh? Yeah,*" I replied proudly. "*She does that for me.*"

Every wolfish eye in the place was on us. Watching. Listening. But I didn't care.

Cassandra's brows lowered. "This does not give us much time."

My head drew back. Not much time? A year wasn't much time?

"If you wish it to be ready, we must make haste, Briar Stone."

My Alpha inclined his head. "Let's go, then."

I whipped around to face him. "You're not coming." The shake of my head was almost violent. He'd had his oversized paws in everything else, but I put my foot down at him seeing the dress.

His eyes flashed, body coiling. "Isaac's still out there, Bry. Like the shadowed moon I'm leaving your side."

I slammed my hands over my hips. "I told you I wanted to do this right, Kane." Jabbing his pec with a finger, I punctuated my words as I said, "Which includes you not seeing the dress."

He stretched his neck, looking set to hog-tie me and throw me over his shoulder—which, knowing my Alpha, was a definite possibility. "We're not separating," he said through his aggressively ground teeth.

"We'll only be apart for a few hours."

A rough growl rumbled through the recesses of his chest. "It's not safe, Bry. I haven't had time to sweep or surveil the shop."

I opened my mouth to protest.

His jaw flicked as he clenched it. "I won't leave you vulnerable."

Cassandra raised a graceful hand. "Your wolf is right, Briar Stone. It is not safe." Her delicate fingertips steepled, those blood-tinged eyes finding my Alpha. "If I may offer a solution."

He clenched his fists, his sinewed forearms cording. He inclined his head. Every ounce of his restraint was on full display.

"I will take her to acquire the dress, Kane Slade." The soft lilt of Cassandra's voice vanished, that most apex of predators coming to play as she vowed, "And I will not leave her side."

A truth. One he could scent.

His throat dipped as he swallowed hard. He hated it, and I got it. I did too. We'd been through a lot. Too much. But still …

"I don't wanna half-ass this, Kane." I settled my palm against his rigid stomach. "It's either whole ass or bust."

He shook his head and, in a move fit for Joaquin, stared at the ceiling like he was looking for patience. Saying no, rejecting Cassandra's offer, would be a preternatural insult of the highest order, because a no implied he didn't think her capable of keeping me safe. That she herself wasn't able or secure. That her own people were at risk under her rule. That he didn't trust her. But I did, with my life—*and* the life of my child.

Implicitly.

He must've seen that in my expression, because he stretched his neck again, his stare locking with Cassandra's, and then he inclined his head. "Fine. She's your pain in the ass for now."

Squeaking, I offered Cassandra a high-five. She stared at it, perplexed, so I settled for awkwardly patting her shoulder instead.

Kane scrubbed a hand over his face.

"Where is the wedding venue?" Cassandra asked.

I turned to my wolfy lover, because we hadn't quite gotten there yet, and I kinda wanted to know as well.

"Your call, Bry," he said.

My mouth dropped open, then closed, then opened again as I considered. But nothing came, 'cause at the end of the day, it didn't matter where we got married. Not to me. But Kane, he'd want somewhere he could secure. Somewhere he could make sure was safe.

I nudged his arm. "You pick, Big Bad."

His smile reached his hungry eyes. "You sure?"

As long as he was there, that was all I needed. I nodded. "I'm sure." I high-pitch happy-hummed, then checked the time. This momma was hungry, so we ordered, ate, and before long, I looked at Cassandra. "We should go."

My Alpha jerked me to his chest, his arms banding around me before he set his mouth to mine. When he pulled back, he up-ticked his chin. "Where's the shop?"

Worrying my lip, I turned to the Dowager. "Got any suggestions?"

"Indeed, I do."

Less than two minutes later, my heart was thrumming wildly as I climbed into the passenger seat of Cassandra's car. The bright gray light from the moon painted the city as she pulled away. My wolf loomed on the sidewalk, stretching his neck again and again as he watched us go.

I sighed, then grabbed my phone and fired an excited and very necessary text Lisa's way.

Me: *You still in Cambria, tavern wench?*

Her: *Yeah. Why? What's up?*

Me: *Get your sweet ass to Crimson Brides. We've got a dress to pick.*

***

It turned out Crimson Brides was only a few blocks from Cassian's cafe, which was exactly where my Alpha stayed so he could be close. Unsurprisingly, being run by a vamp, the dress shop was only open at night.

Cassandra and I waited until Lisa arrived a short while later, then headed in together.

The place was a wash of red. Walls, counter, glass shelves, hangers, waiting-room chairs. I swore, I could hear a heart beating … maybe my own. Regardless, if red had a scent, that shop was it.

An ebony-skinned walker hovered behind the counter across the room. She gave a slight bow to her Dowager. "The store is yours," she said, then vanished into the back.

I strode deeper inside and spun in a tight circle, looking for the one thing I couldn't find. The only thing I needed. "Um, Cassandra. You know we're here for dresses, correct?"

Lisa ducked her head to hide her laugh.

A smile tugged at the corner of the Dowager's lips. "They are this way, Briar Stone. Follow me." Gliding forward, she advanced down the hall to our right.

The further we went, the more normal the place got. The ceilings climbed at least fifteen feet high, lined along the upper edges by ornate white wood and hand-carved leafy crown molding. The baseboards were thick, the walls no longer red, but a glacial green color. It was bright and inviting, the shade caught somewhere between a winterscape and a vibrant sea.

"How's Rosa?" I asked Lis, referring to her long-time human girlfriend.

"Good. Itching to be at your wedding."

I snickered. "Fingers crossed she won't need Bower's clearance by then."

She pursed her lips. "Fingers crossed."

Closing in on a set of double doors, Cassandra pushed them open, and my jaw dropped at what stood on the other side.

Reaching out, Lisa snapped my mouth shut.

Dresses. So. Many. Dresses. There had to be hundreds, organized by style, age, or … era. Victorian and modern. Corsets and sequins. Varying shades of colors, ranging from traditional to very, very not. Everything. Anything.

"I suspect white is what you seek," Cassandra said, with the arch of that delicate blonde brow.

My heart fluttered. "You suspect right." I practically floated behind her, arms and legs light as we aimed for the head of the room.

Cassandra swept her hands wide. "Choose what you will, Briar Stone."

I happy-danced my way through the aisles, twirling as I went. "Grab whatever you want me to try, ladies," I told them, 'cause I wanted it to be a group experience.

Lisa shrieked and, needing no further encouragement, darted off, fading into the racks.

"Your human seems excited," Cassandra noted.

I wheezed a laugh. "Brace yourself."

We split off, each pulling our own stacks. The Dowager's choices were heavy with frill and lace, while Lisa's were … questionable. I held up one in particular that would better be described as strings rather than a dress.

My head cocked, trying to decipher which side was up. "Do you even know me?"

She scoffed. "I know your wolf."

Cassandra grazed a long finger over one of the countless buckles surrounding what I *thought* was the pelvic region. "I fear Kane Slade may slaughter any guest who dared see her in this."

As it turned out, Cassandra knew my wolf too.

I organized the dresses we'd selected, arranging them from "what the hells were they thinking?" to "the perfection selection", which, unsurprisingly, consisted mostly of my picks. Plucking one at random, I side-eyed Lis. "Anything new with the protests? Any more articles or—"

She shoved a finger over my mouth. "No. Not tonight, chickie. Isaac, Zahara, all their bullshit, that doesn't touch this." She took my shoulders and gave me a gentle shake. "Tonight, you revel in being the sexiest bitch this side of Ithica!"

I snorted. "You mean *including* Ithica."

She smirked. "I said what I said."

Cassandra's gaze flitted between us, intrigued and oddly warm. "She is correct, Briar Stone. This time has been scheduled for fun. Let us have it."

Scheduled fun. I grinned, then let the world go and did as my sweet ass was told.

I tried on dress after dress, the Dowager joining me in the changing room for each one because she apparently took the "not leaving my side" part of that vow to my Alpha entirely too literally.

My arms grew weak, and I thanked sage my vamp queen was there to save me when I got trapped as I slid into the third-to-last dress. As it settled around me, my heart stopped, and tears seared my gaze.

"It got quiet in there," Lisa called through the door. "Why'd it get quiet in there?"

My voice wobbled when I said, "Get in here."

She peeked around the door before barreling in completely, hands flying to her mouth. "Chickie! You're *beautiful*."

"I know!" I rapid-clapped as I bounced in place. "Strap me in. Strap me in!"

She stepped behind me, taking the ties and working her way up as she tugged them tighter around my ribs. And tighter. And tighter.

I grunted as I found her eyes in the mirror. "I gotta breathe, Lis."

Her gaze was red-rimmed and shimmering with tears. She hiccupped a soft, happy sob, swiping the moisture under her eyes. "Beauty is pain."

"Yes, but perhaps not death," Cassandra noted.

I offered Lis a "what the vamp queen said" expression.

She rolled her eyes and smirked, but loosened the ties.

Spinning, I took in the sweetheart neckline that trailed the upper curve of my breasts, and the corset back that weaved gracefully along my spine. The skirts flared out, flowing layer upon layer, topped with a cascade of intricate lace that was entwined with flowers and lined with beadwork and pearls.

It was heavy, the expensive kind of gown made from quality material with a price tag to match. But it was mine.

I smiled. "This is the one."

Cassandra inclined her head. "I suspect Kane Slade shall fall to his knees."

Lisa nodded, fanning her face before offering me a "what the vamp queen said" expression of her own.

My face warmed.

The Dowager summoned the shop's walkery owner, who expertly took my measurements, jotted them down, then headed off to log the order.

Checking her watch, Lisa flinched. "Shit. I'm on curfew. I've gotta get back to the border."

"Call me," I said. Not a request.

"I will." Pressing a kiss to my cheek, she offered Cassandra a wave, then left.

The Dowager slipped several fallen hairs over my shoulder. "She is a good friend, Briar Stone."

"The bestest." I offered her a grin. "I try and collect good people."

A graceful nod. "I have noticed."

Unfastening the gown, I snapped several pictures before we hung it back up and headed to the front of the store, where Cassandra's walker waited. I reached into my dress pocket, pulling out Kane's fancy-schmancy black card to pay.

"That isn't necessary," the vamp owner said. "My lady has taken care of it."

My brows shot high before I balked. "Cassandra!"

"It is my gift, Briar Stone."

My mouth dropped. There were gifts, and then there were people like her. I closed in on her, my arms banding her waist. While no heartbeat sounded inside her chest, I knew it was there, because she was too good to be without one.

My phone buzzed in my pocket. Pulling back, I checked it. The words "Unknown Caller" lit the screen. I considered ignoring it, strongly, but seeing as I was Coven Leader, it didn't really feel like an option. Not a leaderly one, anyway.

I answered. "Hello?"

"He doesn't want you," the voice hissed at the other end of the line. It was familiar, but not. Like it had changed. Like *she* had.

Cassandra's head rotated, slow and predatory, as her crimson gaze glided my way.

My spine locked straight. "Amber?"

"He. Doesn't. Want. You," she gritted out.

I wheeled around, heading for the window. Scanning the night, I pulled on my obsidian and breathed deep, seeking that Amber scent. But nothing was there.

Cassandra waved away her vamp to give us privacy.

Keeping my cool was likely for the best, but Amber had a knack for stabbing all my wrong buttons, which meant that option had been wiped from the table.

"Funny," I said, my voice taunting with a side of feral. "His mark seems to be on my neck, and his ring on my finger."

"He's marrying you because he has to." There was a savage smile in her voice when she added, "He told me himself." A thunk sounded over the line, like a vehicle door closing. "Maybe I'll come watch, enjoy the show."

My throat tightened, because she'd said it with the kind of confidence that only came from truth.

I rubbed the center of my forehead to push back the headache that rolled in. "And why would he say that?"

"Because you tricked him."

The twist of my face was so sharp, it hurt. "I tricked him into loving me?"

"You tricked him by spreading your legs. By stealing his seed. By telling him you're pregnant."

The world stopped. I couldn't breathe. Was that a question? Or a statement? Because other than me, there were only two people who knew that truth—and neither would tell.

They *wouldn't*.

My legs grew weak, then buckled. I gripped the edge of the counter, but it wasn't enough, and it slipped from my grasp. I fell. Cassandra shot forward, that preternatural speed making her difficult to track as her arms dove under me, cradling my fall before she settled me into one of those red waiting-room chairs.

I stared into the distance, praying to the Iron Hells and the wraith herself to control the quaver in my voice when I muttered, "It's not true." Because, wraith take me, if she'd shared that with Isaac …

Cassandra's stare intensified as she very clearly scented my lie.

"It has to be," Amber snarked. "It's the only thing that makes sense."

The way she'd said it—sage—it sounded less a fact, more a conclusion. I prayed, anyway. My heart shuddered. Clearing my throat, I feigned a confidence I didn't have when I forced my next words through my teeth. "Did Kane tell you that, too?" That I'd lied, and tricked him. That I was carrying his child.

"No. He didn't have to. I'm not stupid." She laughed, a high, animalistic cry carrying through the line. "He's just saving face with you. Making a power move for the Pack. Eventually, he'll have us both."

My gaze flicked to Cassandra's narrowed expression, then away. "*What*?"

"And when he marks me, he won't need you anymore. We'll raise your pup without you. Ours."

Cassandra's expression darkened.

Every feral, possessive instinct in me had my hackles rising, but I kept my mouth shut, 'cause like hells was I about to confirm any of Amber's suspicions.

"You can't kill me without killing him." This was something she should've known, but she was a lone wolf, and not exactly right in the head, so a quick refresher couldn't hurt.

"Once I'm also his claimed, I can," she purred. "He'll be tethered to us both. Your death won't matter."

What the actual goddamn sage?

"He'll kill you if you try." And he would. He'd rip her limb from limb. Slowly.

"No, witch-whore, he won't." The smile in her voice was just as broken as she was. "You don't understand, Briar. He takes care of me."

I blinked. She'd lost it if she believed that. She'd actually fucking lost it. Still, I was nothing if not hostile. "Takes care of you, how?"

A laugh, high-pitched like a yowling-yip. "You think I'd tell *you*?"

"Pfft," I said. "You'd better, because I won't believe you otherwise."

She snarled. "He sends money. Has offered me a beautiful roof, but I cannot take it. Too many eyes are watching."

A roof? Somewhere to *live*? Is that what she meant? I'd known lone wolves lost their tether, but she'd gone next level believing that. I dragged a hand through my hair. "Why the Iron Hells are you calling, Amber?"

"Isaac has something you want." She laughed to herself. "Well, maybe not something *you* want."

An invisible talon gripped my spine. "What does he have?"

Over the line, there was a *boom*. A man yelled. He sounded older, his voice unfamiliar. The yell was followed by a feminine scream. I tried to place it, but it was muffled, which meant nothing twigged.

"You'll see," she said, ominous.

The call ended.

My eyes opened wide, panic gripping my chest and making it hard to breathe.

"*Kane!*" I said across our bond.

His response was instant.

"*Bry?*" His tone was hard. Ready.

"*Is the Pack alright?*" I quavered, hands trembling as I fired off message after message to everyone, checking in. Joaquin, Lisa, Lucas, Theo—even Bower, for the hells' sake.

"*What?*"

"*Just answer me.*"

He went silent for one second. Two. "*They're good. What's going on?*"

"*I'll tell you when you get here.*" 'Cause I had not one doubt he was already en route.

"*I'm coming.*"

My phone pinged rapid-fire as everyone's messages flooded in. But they were all there. Fine and accounted for. I sank deeper into my chair, trying to focus on something. Anything. Because everyone was okay. Had Amber been messing with me? Maybe.

With her, it wasn't off the table. All the same, she'd said some things I just couldn't shake.

Cassandra was so rigid when she lowered herself down next to me, it was a wonder she didn't creak. "Are you alright, Briar Stone?"

There was no point in holding back; she'd heard everything anyway. Not that I'd tried to hide it, 'cause she was a friend, and on that front, I'd already learned my lesson. Voice low and matter of fact, I said, "Kane talked to her."

"Kane Slade is loyal to you," she said before her tone darkened, turning blacker than a moonless night. "If he tried to betray you, Briar Stone, I would skin him myself."

A small, sad bark of laughter broke from me.

"The things she said, Cassandra." My hand trembled wildly as I settled it over my stomach. Slowly, my gaze lifted to hers. "That I'm pregnant."

Her expression gentled, that cool-skinned hand resting delicately over mine. "She did not know, Briar Stone. She guessed." The shake of her head was slow. "But I did not have to guess."

I swallowed hard. "You knew?"

"You are changed. Braver in some ways, more tempered in others. And there is a light in your eyes that had once been extinguished. A light your wolf shares."

I sniffed. "That's a big leap."

"Is it?" she challenged. "He was protective of you before, but now ..." She gave a slow, fluid shake of her head. "His pulse quickens when you stray too far. His eyes darken on everyone. I am certain these hours apart have been hard on him." Her crimson gaze hooded. "But those truths aside, I can scent it on you."

My heart slammed against my ribs, blood going cold. Shadow and sage. Kane had said the wolves couldn't scent it, but if *she* could, then—

"Fear not, Briar Stone. I am the only one."

The shake of my head was wild. "You can't know that, Cassandra."

"Yes, I can," she said with an unwavering confidence. Shifting, she faced me squarely. "I am very old. It has taken an age for me to distinguish the difference. Many mortal lifetimes. It is faint, barely traceable, but it is there."

Many mortal lifetimes. *Many!* Iron fires. If she could smell that I was pregnant … could she tell what it was? A little boy? A girl? Did I want to hear?

I twisted the sleeve of my top. "When did you know?"

Her gaze shadowed. "The first day you came to my den."

My brows rose, my head snapping back. At that point, I could've only been pregnant for days, at most.

And she'd kept my secret, even when she was mad at me. My heart clenched, because she'd still considered me, cared enough to protect me, even then.

"I thought you'd never speak to me again," I said.

Her smile was small. "I was hurt, Briar Stone. But never angry. We all keep secrets to shield the ones we hold dear. It is who we decide to entrust with those secrets that matters."

My throat hitched. "I just … got so used to hiding it, at some point it kind of felt impossible to say anything. And I knew you had your own past with the changeling who killed your father, and I thought—"

"You thought I would see him in your Lucas."

My head hung, the guilt at that judgment coating my tongue with its sour sting.

"I understand how you reached your conclusion. But know this, Briar Stone. I would never harm you or anyone that would matter to you." Her cool fingers wrapped over mine. "For if you love him, I already know the measure of his character."

Cassandra and I had started out with a bizarre truce before she'd slowly grown on me. Like a fungus. She was a chaos of layers, deadly and powerful, day and night, beautiful and sweet. At every turn, she surprised me. But something in the corner of my tiny mind told me she'd formed those layers as a shield—a shield that didn't lower for just anyone, but did for me.

"My kind live long. Our hurts run deep and take time to settle. I would have come back to you eventually."

Considering her concept of time, I wasn't exactly sure what her definition of "eventually" was, but it was the thought that counted.

A coy smile stole across my lips. "You just couldn't stay away."

The low rumble of Kane's truck closed in before its headlights cut through the shop as it pulled up outside.

"Indeed, Briar Stone." She took my elbow, guiding me to my feet and mirroring my expression. "You are an oddly enjoyable creature."

Chapter Nineteen

My eyes were heavy and my body completely drained as I crossed our home's threshold a short while later. The second I did, my Alpha edged in behind me, crushing tight to my back. His palm grazed over my hip before moving forward to settle against my lower abdomen.

I hadn't spoken on the drive home, a fact that'd driven my were nearly wolfy. But I'd needed a minute to sort my erratic emotions. Get control so I didn't sweep him into my torrent.

His power brushed mine across our bond. "You're restless, Bry."

I wiggled tighter into him. "Keeping tabs on me, Alpha?"

"Always," he said through a growl.

And I loved it. Loved the possession and the want. Loved his bold and unapologetic need for me. Loved the way his desperation warred mine for dominance. My nails grazed my claiming mark, body heating as my thighs clenched.

"Bry," he warned.

I bit my lip. Hard. "Hmm?"

"Keep that up and I'm gonna do something about it."

The arch of my brow was coy. "Then do something about it, Big Bad."

He inhaled rough and steady, then rumbled, "Talk first, fuck later."

I let out a small laugh. There went that heat again.

"You good?" he pushed, his words tight, as if he anticipated … something.

My sigh was slow and long. "Amber called me."

He tensed, his body going rigid behind me—but not in the fun kinda way. A pause, and his next words were forced through his teeth. "And?"

I half-turned, peering up at him over my shoulder. "I hate her so goddamn much."

His expression was even, the thoughts in his gaze shuttered, totally unreadable. He traced one of his square knuckles along my jaw, then, setting his mouth to mine, he kissed me bruisingly deep.

His calloused hands took my hips, turning me to face him. His warm palm flattened against the small of my back before it tracked lower to grip my ass. Hard.

I moaned, hiking my leg over him. Rolling my hips, I ground my core against the thick length of his cock. Breaking the kiss, I sucked in a steadying breath, then pressed lightly at his chest. My gaze met his. Water on steel.

"This plan you're working," I said. "I hope you know what you're doing."

***

I sat at the kitchen table the next morning, drowning myself in coffee while I tried to clear the bleariness from my eyes. My Alpha stood down on our dock, a thick, hooded shirt stretched over those broad shoulders as he held his phone to his ear. His silver stare was tense, and trained toward the house, watching.

I itched to reach for his power, to hear what he was saying. I might've pushed it, too, if his over-perceptive wolfy ass wouldn't have felt me do it.

There was a thumping from the front of the house, and I tipped back, peering that way. Lucas paced the front porch, the sun lighting his profile as his hands tore through his hair. His bony feet pounded, back and forth. Back and forth. Sweat stained the collar of his shirt and lined his temples.

My eyes narrowed. Pushing to my feet, I headed that way and swung the front door wide. "What's going on, Lucas?"

Tearing his phone from his pocket, he tried to make a call. "I can't reach Hannah." He cursed.

I frowned.

He rubbed the center of his chest like it physically hurt, his tone forced as if he was trying to stay calm. "I got a weird message from her last night. I didn't get it until I woke up, but she sounded—I don't know. But something's not right. I've tried calling a ton but she's not answering."

A pit formed in the depths of my chest. "Then let's go," I said, because the nagging feeling at the back of my mind refused to settle.

The steady thump of my Alpha's feet sounded as he closed in. The keys clanked as he grabbed them from the table by the door, then stalked outside and aimed for the truck. "Come on, Luke."

My brother's head snapped his way.

"I just tried to reach her wolf. She's not answering," Kane said. The one guarding her. A wolf that should've been very, very reachable. He popped the driver's side open, then sank inside. "And we don't take chances."

The pit in my gut sank deeper, and the seizing of my lungs was absolute.

Lucas bolted to the truck and I followed. Sliding it into gear, Kane veered us outta there.

The tires hummed on the road, my brother's legs bouncing rapidly. His elbow rested on the edge of his window, and his breathing was slow. Not relaxed, more like he was forcing it. His muscles were corded, his pulse pounding against his neck.

Time ticked by good and slow as we crossed into the Southern Coven territory, through the winding streets named for their circuitous shapes. My Alpha cut us onto Lily Lane, a bright, well-to-do road where the houses had big yards and space to grow.

Rounding the corner, Hannah's gray-stone, two-story, three-car-garage house came into view. Her grandfather's tan-colored SUV was parked in the driveway. The place looked quiet. Normal.

That nagging in the back of my mind kicked off again. It hummed along my nerves, spurring my worn senses to life as it set my teeth on edge.

My Alpha's grip was white where his hands were locked around the wheel, tendons straining under his skin.

"*Something's off,*" I said across our wolfy bond.

He inclined his head, pulled into the driveway, and parked, his attention honed, that silence an answer of its own.

Lucas barreled out, rushing for the front door, and thumped his fist against it so hard, the panes of the front windows rattled. Closing in, I gripped my obsidian and drew on Kane's power to push my hearing.

The drip of a tap. Wind rustling through an open window, and the hum of appliances. And something else ... a gurgling sound, followed by a barely audible, uneven bumping.

Lucas knocked again, then set his hands against the glass, cupping them to shield out the sun as he peered inside. He went rigid. "No!" His hand shot to the door handle, and he twisted. Locked. He reared back and planted his foot in the center of the door.

I tried to peer past him, to no avail. "Lucas?"

He kicked the door again. It rattled, but didn't budge.

"I've got it, Luke," Kane told him, maneuvering into position.

My brother's violet eyes were blown and wild, his chest heaving as he stepped back, and my stomach torqued as Amber's vague-as-hells warning the night before rang through my head.

Kane set a dense shoulder against the door, then shoved. The metal buckled and bent. Finally giving way, it swung wide, the frame splintering. Straightening to that full, intimidating height, Kane filled the entrance, his arms hung tense by his sides. He advanced.

Lucas ran past him. Well, he tried to, but my Alpha latched onto his arm and hauled my brother behind him.

"HANNAH!" Lucas roared, struggling against Kane. "HANNAH!"

Silence.

Straight ahead, the kitchen table was overturned, dishes smashed, food scattered. A black pool of dried blood sat cracked across the floor, a brutalized and gutted body next to it. Female. Were. The one assigned for Hannah's protection.

Kane cursed.

My heart constricted as my mouth ran dry and I scented the air. But there was nothing. Literally nothing.

"Wolfsbane," my Alpha said, then half-turned to eye my brother over his shoulder. "Which room is Hannah's?"

"Last one on the right," Lucas answered, his voice strained. He vibrated, skin pale. He swallowed hard, looking ready to heave his guts. And I wasn't far behind.

Kane hung a left and edged deeper into the house, arm extended to pen Lucas at his back but letting him follow.

Streaks of blood painted the floor as if someone had been dragged or crawled. We moved slowly, room by room, until we hit the end of the hall. The door creaked when my Alpha nudged it open. Photos were knocked from walls, their glass shattered. Clothes were scattered across the room, and the drywall was buckled like there'd been a struggle.

My heart drummed in my ears, drowning out the silence.

Kane crossed the threshold, and I held my breath, praying to the Iron Hells.

Let her be alright. Let her be alright. Let her be alright!

Lucas couldn't handle anything else. He needed that girl because he loved her, and he loved her deep and the irrevocable kind of hard.

Please, sage, just let her be alright!

Hannah's bed was flipped, indigo blankets tossed aside, the window wide. A breeze blew, flicking her pale lilac curtains. A jewelry box and makeup lay strewn across the hardwood floor. Her dresser mirror was broken. Blood was everywhere, coating everything.

Kane tensed, his stare going voltaic.

I followed his line of sight. A body sat in the corner. An older man, white hair, skin ashen and pale. Hannah's grandfather.

Claw marks were carved across his forearms and hands, like he'd put up a fight before they'd cleaved his torso wide. His chest shuddered on an inhale, head lolling to the side. His eyes fluttered, unfocused and unseeing. Not dead.

My stomach hardened.

Lucas flew past my Alpha.

"Saul," he said, and the sheer terror in his gaze at the sight of the old man near cleaved me in two.

My head whipped to my Alpha. "Kane!"

He was already on the move, biting into his flesh as he took a knee at Saul's side. Opening the old man's mouth, my Alpha dropped several rivulets of blood onto his tongue, then waited.

Saul gasped and sucked in a sharp breath. The near-lifeless gray of his skin slowly darkened, giving his sepia tone some color. Those gashes stitched, thread by thread, pulling together. He shifted, eyes creasing as he rolled to his side. Moaning, he peered up at us, blinking hard like he was trying to orient himself.

"Where's Hannah, Saul?" Lucas wheeled around, his stare jumping from one corner to the next. "Where the hells is she?"

Her grandfather shook his head, eyes glassy with tears, his voice weak when he answered, "I couldn't stop Amber. I couldn't stop her!"

Bile kissed the back of my throat, because we'd had her guarded for exactly this goddamn reason. But Amber's lone wolf had come out to play. My gaze lit on the ivory night table, which held a phone in a glittery purple case with a rhinestone strap hanging off its end—and two notes.

I closed in, snatching up the first paper. It was covered with a militant scrawl.

Briar,

I've learned your cooperation is required to complete my additional serums. In the spirit of self-interest, I strongly recommend you comply, lest I be forced to take further action.

—Zahara.

I cursed, handed the note to my Alpha, then took up the second. The writing was barely legible, like it had been written by a child. A young one who'd just learned.

"*Call me*," it said, with a number listed beneath. Simple. Terrifying.

"The phone," Lucas cut in. "It's Hannah's." He stared down at it, forearms flexing. "She'd never go anywhere without it."

No. Not by choice.

Kane stalked to my side, his heat grazing my flesh, steadying my breaths.

Every fiber of my being knew who would answer. The same person who'd spent their life torturing us. The same person who'd enjoyed it. And the only one who'd benefit.

Hand trembling, I punched in the number. It rang once. Twice.

"Briiiiiiiiiar," crooned my stepfather's cold, hauntingly familiar voice.

My blood heated, turning to fire. "Fuck off, Isaac."

His bark of laughter was caught in the borderlands between drunken glee and sheer goddamn madness. "That's no way to talk to family."

"Good thing you're not, then."

Lucas lunged for the phone. "Where the fuck is Hannah?"

Saul winced and shifted, the whites of his eyes wide. He was just as desperate for an answer as my brother.

Isaac tsked. "Business first, son."

"I'm not your goddamn son. If you hurt her—"

"You'll do what?" Isaac taunted, with the confidence of a man who recognized his advantage. Then his voice darkened. "I need those supplies, Briar."

My laugh was caustic. "I'm sure you do." My fingers curled, and I pictured closing them over his throat. "You won't get far with her. You've been outed, Isaac. All the beasts in Cambria know what you are now, and they're coming for you."

A pause, calculating as ever. "Call off the searches," he snarled, "or she dies."

Kane's stare flashed as Lucas tensed and a small, choked sound broke from Saul.

My lungs seized, 'cause that was a problem with a capital P. I wasn't about to risk Hannah, but still …

"I can't command the Conclave, Isaac." I swallowed around the lump in my throat. "Give us Hannah, turn yourself in, and *maybe* you'll be spared."

His laugh was caustic. "Let's not lie to each other, Briar."

The answer was shit, but at least it had confirmed one thing; he wouldn't need me to call off the dogs if he wasn't still in Cambria. This was why that deal of his with Zahara mattered so much, because there was only one thing he'd be desperate for: the one thing he didn't have. Safety. Sanctuary. Somewhere he didn't need to lurk in the shadows to keep his head from being cleaved from his wretched goddamn neck. But Isaac was as predictable as predictable got. He wouldn't be wasting his time dealing with me if he'd locked things down with her.

This was Isaac's version of panicking, and it looked fucking good on him.

My eyes narrowed as the reality of that truth struck. The offer of sanctuary against us was a powerful one, and something Zahara would only be able to grant if she was a powerful person … or intended to become one.

"Who is Zahara, Isaac?"

Lucas's glare snapped my way.

Trust me, I mouthed.

"You liked her little letter, did you?"

"Who the hells is she?" I snarled.

"Briar, dear. I'm not about to give up my leverage. I thought we knew each other better than that." A feminine whimper carried across the line. "My list of allies has grown thin. And I require Zahara as much as you require my mercy."

"That's what you call them?" I said through a dark laugh. "*Allies?*"

"When the time comes, I will have exactly what I need." There was an air to the words. A confidence that had the hairs on the back of my neck standing on end.

Kane edged closer, looming over me. Waiting, 'cause no doubt he sensed it too, that encroaching … something.

Saul pushed himself up, knees weak, and made for the bed, breathless as he set himself down at its edge.

As much as I wanted him to be, Isaac wasn't stupid. If being under his thumb had taught me anything, it was that he *kept* his leverage. As long as he needed something from us, he also needed Hannah and Zahara. The only kink in that armor was Amber and her decidedly unstable ass. The same one that had cleaved Mason's head from his body in a fit of rage.

My Alpha's jaw worked, some thought building behind those silver topaz eyes—but, as per usual, I couldn't decipher what.

"*What's going on, Kane?*" I asked across our bond.

The shake of his head was short. Not curt, just … distracted.

My brow lowered before I locked my sights back on the phone. "Give me Hannah."

"Bring me the equipment," Isaac countered.

"Bring. Me. Hannah," I snarled.

A bored sigh. "You need not worry, Briar. She's safe with me."

The laugh I gave then was dark and dripping with acid. "No one's safe with you, Isaac." I dragged in a breath, forcing myself to be calm, because losing myself with him would only cost her.

My gaze slid Lucas's way. Sage, he was just so still, but it was not the stillness of inaction; it was the calm before a gathering storm. And the dark promise in those violet eyes was a terrifying thing—something I'd seen before in Kane and Cassandra. Something that spoke of an unstoppable violence.

"You don't understand, Briar," Isaac said. "This isn't a barter."

No. It wasn't. Not for him—which meant we needed to move, and we needed to move fast.

"I'm not bringing you shit unless I know she's alive."

"Please," Saul pleaded. "*Please.*"

Isaac's tone hardened. "You will give me what I need, Briar, or you won't like what happens next."

A low, guttural sound tore from Kane's throat and he reached for the phone. I darted back, my hand shooting up to block him. His jaw ground, his skin creaking with the clench of his fists.

"Show her to me, Isaac," Lucas said, his tone low, revealing every bit of the man he would become.

Isaac huffed. There was a shuffling sound. Several seconds passed. "Smile, dear. We wouldn't want them to think you're scared, now, would we?" he taunted.

The soft cries that carried over the line clawed at my soul.

Lucas's jaw clenched, nostrils flaring. His fists balled by his sides.

A text flashed up on the phone's screen with an attached photo.

Hannah.

Her hair was disheveled, her hands and feet bound to the chair she occupied. Tears streaked her face, and blood stained her pale pink shirt, but no cuts marred her skin. It wasn't *her* blood.

It was the blood of Kane's were, and her grandfather.

I turned the phone screen toward Saul. He collapsed forward, head in his hands, shoulders hitching with sobs.

"There," Isaac crooned, as if he'd done us some magnanimous favor. "Now, do we have a deal?"

Gaze locking with Kane's, I muttered, "We have a deal."

His voice was bright. "Wonderful. I will send instructions for where Lucas is to deliver them."

My mouth opened at that asinine suggestion.

"Why Lucas?" I demanded.

"Because right now, Briar, he's incentivized to do what he's told."

My brother's eyes closed slowly. Methodically. When they reopened, he was staring straight ahead, his attention fixed on something beyond my sight. A target. His father.

Hannah couldn't die. Lucas couldn't lose her.

This needed to fucking end.

Lucas extended his hand, pulling the phone from my grasp, his hard eyes landing on Hannah's grandfather as he said, "I'm coming for you, Hannah. It's gonna be alright." Then: "And, Isaac ..." The shadow in his voice was darker than any hovel in the Deep of the Iron Hells. "Be ready."

Chapter Twenty

I sat on the basement stairs later that evening, staring into the partially finished basement that was Lucas's room. The drywall was up, puttied and primed, ready for the ice-gray paint he'd opted for. His dresser and bed sat off to the side, the black comforter an unmade mess, while a massive, slate-colored rug lined the floor.

Through the above-grade window across the room, the moon climbed high, its silver rays cutting through the dense, incoming clouds, lighting the fallen leaves in patches.

My stepfather's texted instructions for Lucas had eventually come.

Isaac: *You are to go to your old school. Further directions will await you there.*

Directions that'd doubtless take him to fifty other locations first. That message had been followed by another.

Isaac: *Amber will have eyes on you, Lucas. And if she sees any sign you are being followed, Hannah will die.*

We *had* to find her, which was why we'd been out searching all day. My Alpha's attention had been fixed between the hunt and his phone, texting, heading off for bursts of time to take call after call. I'd fought back the bitterness with a tattered stick, one that was ready to snap.

I'd brought in more patrols for my people, as had my Alpha, and every other Conclave leader. But eventually, the exhaustion had kicked in. The hollows beneath Lucas's eyes were so dark, they were almost pits. Theo had actually face-planted a handful of times, and my own feet kept snagging on curbs or rocks or nothing at all. It didn't take long before Kane forced my pregnant, protesting butt outta there, and dragged Lucas and Theo along with us.

Theo leaned against the wall, and my Alpha loomed to my right, arms crossed over his chest while he watched my brother. Protective. So damn protective. But there was something else. Some thought in those silver eyes I couldn't decipher.

"I love her. I can't lose her," Lucas said as he stalked back and forth. Back and forth. His feet thumped heavy against the floor as his chest heaved, wild and seething like a rabid predator.

Sage, I'd never seen him so mad and lost—and not in a "down the V rabbit hole" kinda way. More like he couldn't see. Like his heart had been taken and he now walked through the dark, hunting its beat. Hunting for Hannah.

My palm settled over my throat. He loved her deeply. The way my Alpha loved me and I him. With everything we fucking had. She'd become his tether. And, like Isaac was wont to do, he'd taken her. Isaac took; he goddamn took. He took what wasn't his and used it against whoever benefited him most. Lucas, me, Kane.

Theo kicked off the wall and stepped into Lucas's path. "You won't lose her."

Lucas dragged a hand through his hair. "You don't know that. You know what Isaac's capable of."

We did, and my stepfather sure as shit wasn't above killing someone else to save himself. My mother's death was testament to that.

Theo rolled his shoulders, hands by his sides. "What do we do now?"

Kane stood there, his stare distant, but not in that talking-to-the-Pack way. He was silent. Painfully so.

His stare tracked to me, then away.

My stomach twisted, because of that *something* in his expression. I swallowed around the dryness in my throat. My breath was ragged and desperate. I hated what that something might mean, and itched to make him voice it. To tell me. But Kane Slade did nothing without purpose.

"I need to go." He dragged a hand up the back of his neck and over his hair, its strands sticking out in random directions. Across our bond, he added, *"Got something I need to do."*

My jaw worked, my pulse thrumming in my head. I breathed deep, trying to control my fraying nerves and the bitter tang that coated my tongue. "Where?" I asked, bracing as I rubbed a slow circle over my abdomen.

His gaze dropped there. He swallowed hard, then closed the distance between us, those voltaic eyes conveying a message I prayed I understood before he pressed a soft kiss to my forehead. "Out."

My stomach dropped. I wanted to push for more, but he moved past me, prowling up the stairs and leaving. I stared at his back, lungs tight, making it harder to breathe as he faded. Faded. Faded away.

Theo's head drew back, and my brother's brow dropped low, clearly lost at the exchange.

I waved them off, because like sage was I diving into that conversation.

A *thump, thump, thump* sounded at the front door.

Getting to my feet, I sighed and moved toward it, Theo and Lucas trailing behind.

When I pulled it open, Joaquin sauntered in, unbuttoning the collar on his dress shirt, then tugging it, loosening its hold on his neck.

"Make yourself at home," I taunted, aiming for playful and hitting somewhere below dismal.

Lucas stalked past him and stared out into the night, his body tense and coiled. "I should be out there looking for her."

I rubbed my hands up the backs of my arms. "You've gotta rest, Lucas."

He sliced his head to the side, hair snapping from the movement. "I can't. Not while she's out there with him and fucking Amber."

Theo moved into his line of sight, cutting him off from me. From everything. "You're no good to Hannah weak."

My gaze flicked to him, 'cause that word… Weak. Not drained or exhausted or tired, but *weak*. And I had not one doubt the choice had been intentional, because the *only* thing my brother wanted was strength. He wanted to be what Hannah needed. To be ready if the time came. This was something Theo understood, seeing as it was exactly what he'd wanted himself for Whitney.

The word must've struck home, because Lucas's shoulders dropped as he gave a ragged exhale. "I just …" His stare fell to his feet. "I can't get my head to stop."

Theo grabbed his shoulder and steered him outside. "Come on, boss. Let's burn some of this off and make it stop, then, yeah?"

Lucas's chest heaved, but he didn't argue, and the two disappeared.

Joaquin's eyes followed them until they were gone, then he strode deeper into the house, his dress shoes clicking. He lowered himself into one of our plush living-room chairs, settling in all comfy-like.

My face twisted. "What exactly are you doing here?"

"Guarding."

"Lucas? That's unexpected."

A shake of his head and a twitch of his mouth. "Theo's got him." He aimed a knuckle my way. "I'm with *you*." No apologies or pretenses, not that Joaquin ever really offered those. His confidence was different than Kane's, more subdued. But he didn't do something he didn't agree with, so if he was there …

"Kane told you what he's up to." Not a question.

He offered a slow, lone nod.

A burning sensation broke across my chest, and I rubbed my sternum, trying to dissipate the pain as I set myself down on the couch. Wherever my Alpha was, I prayed to the Iron Hells and the wraith herself it was worth it. "His plan has to work, Joaquin."

He set a foot on the opposite knee and linked his hands over his stomach. "It does."

The knot that twisted in my gut only got tighter and tighter, a heavy pit growing in anticipation.

My phone buzzed. An article from Lisa.

I scanned it: more images of masked faces from that ever-growing Ithican anti-government faction. Signs from parents of sick children calling for change. Cars burned in the background. The police facing off against protestors. In the next image, they clashed. Tear gas was deployed. In the next, the protestors ran. Clothes tattered, covered in dirt. One of them in particular wore a torn balaclava that caught my attention.

Joaquin shifted. "What is it, banshee?"

"I think I might …" My words faded, my eyes focusing on that face. Well, not his face exactly. But those eyes—his familiar and wholly unique, two-toned yellow-brown eyes. The same eyes that had glared death at me and Isaac when we'd met at that shady border crossing not long ago.

Clicking on the picture, my fingers worked frantically as I fired it off to Bower.

Me: *He's one of Zahara's goons.*

His reply came quick.

Bower: *You're sure?*

Me: *I'm sure.*

Me: *Is he familiar?*

Bower: *I'll ask around.*

"Briar?" Joaquin pushed.

"We might have a lead on Zahara."

His brows climbed high.

"Maybe." I worried at my cheek. "I hope." Shifting, I stared out the front window. Theo held his palm up, and my brother launched a punch. The crack it made carried through the night.

Theo inclined his head. "Good. Again."

Lucas threw. Another crack. Theo's eyes narrowed in a wince, and he shook out his hand, then reset.

Rain tapped against the window and soaked Lucas and Theo's shirts. It grew heavier, falling fast and taking the temperature down with it. Their breath steamed the air, hair matting to their faces.

Lucas advanced, throwing another punch. Crack. Again. Crack. Again. Crack. He stumbled, and Theo caught him. My brother's body shook as a sob broke from his throat.

Tears stung the backs of my eyes, and my heart clenched. In a low voice, I said, "We've gotta find her, Joaquin."

His stare was fixed out the window too. He leaned forward and set his elbows on his knees. "We do."

***

Hours passed, the clock reading midnight as I faded in and out of consciousness. The couch was no longer comfortable, but I didn't have the strength to move. Lucas and Theo had kept at their training until my brother had practically collapsed. Eventually, they'd headed to the basement, and the house had gone quiet, so I could only hope he slept.

Joaquin stared down at his phone, eyes soft, and his mouth lifted into something resembling a half-smile while he read whatever it was he was reading.

"How are things with you two?" I asked, tone groggy.

His head came up.

"You and Ezra," I clarified.

He cleared his throat. "Good."

"You like him a lot." Because in the time I'd known Joaquin, he'd never been one for wolves, or people, or anyone.

His thumb tracked a slow line across his device's screen before he tucked it away. "I do."

"He looks good on you, Joaquin." And he did. Yeah, it was still new, but I was glad he had someone, especially down there in another territory, alone. Settling my cheek along the back of the couch, I offered him a small smile. "I'm happy for you."

He dipped his head, then stiffened, stare going molten before it snapped to the back of the house. I opened my mouth to ask what was up, but he set a finger to his lips, then tipped his chin toward my obsidian. An instruction.

I followed his line of sight as I gripped my ring and cocooned our conversation. "Who's out there?"

His hands landed on the armrests, and he rose slowly, as if he was concentrating hard. "Go look."

My throat tightened as I slid from the couch, padding softly to the pitch-dark kitchen. My attention was fixed on the back window, my brows furrowing when my gaze landed on Kane. He stood outside, his body in profile, facing the woods. His hooded shirt and jeans clung to him. His eyes were electric in the rain.

Water sluiced down his face, dripping from his chin. His breaths were even, clouding the air. He rolled his shoulders and straightened his spine, looming at that towering height.

Pivoting, I edged toward the back door.

Joaquin moved to my side. "Easy, banshee. Not yet."

My stare flicked to Kane again, and that ever-present knot twisted in the pit of my stomach.

A figure skulked out from the trees, honeyed eyes blazing and fixed on him. Amber.

I turned to stone, adrenaline kicking into overdrive, because *wraith take me*. Goddamn *Amber!*

Kane stayed perfectly still, didn't move to hunt her down and tear out her stupid throat. He just stood there, one hand linked over the opposite wrist before him, like he was calm. Like he was waiting for her.

The tightening of my lungs made it hard to breathe. Exhaling to try and cool my blood, I brushed my connection with Kane.

Amber's head rolled from side to side, then tilted back, her nostrils flaring as she scented the air. But the rain would've stolen anything it carried. Her lips twitched, then slowly peeled back from her teeth. "Where is the bitch?"

Bitch. Me. Fucking lovely.

"Somewhere else," Kane said.

Somewhere else, as in, not there with him. A technicality, but not a lie.

"She still lives *here*."

"She has to, Amber," he replied, his tone soft before it turned a savage shade of dark. "For now."

I blinked, because, shadow and sage, hearing those words from his mouth opened a hollow in my chest.

Amber waited as if she suspected a trap. Her shoulders were rounded, her spine slumped forward. Not in submission; it was more like her wolf was taking over, pulling her to the ground, like she'd assume all fours at any moment. Her movements were lupine as she took a single step forward. She wore the same clothes as the last time I'd seen her. They sagged from her frame, dirt-covered, sweat-stained, and ripped at the waist, elbow, and knees.

My heart thrummed in my ears, and I couldn't tell if it was uncertainty or rage that drove it. I gripped my obsidian so tight I thought it might crack. I readied myself. I didn't know for what yet, but something was coming.

My jaw locked, lips peeling back from my teeth. Rage. It was definitely rage. My gaze darted to the back door again. I could make it.

Joaquin's heavy hand landed on my shoulder like he was holding me back. And maybe he was.

Swallowing around the bile that crept up my throat, I faced the window and my Alpha where he waited.

Kane's stare raked her up and down. "You look good."

My face twisted. The bile climbed higher.

She ran a hand over the mats in her hair, and my fingers curled, longing to tear them out.

"Did you think about it?" he asked.

Her nod was sharp, but there was no anger in the gesture, more a lack of control. As if her body wasn't necessarily hers anymore.

"Good." His eyes were electric, molten. "I need you, Amber. I can't do this anymore."

She ambled forward another step. "Just you and me."

A slow smile slipped across Kane's expression, the rain rolling from his lips.. "Just you and me."

It was agony to watch. It cut and gouged and set my blood on fire with a murderous fury that burned, burned, *burned* me through.

Amber slinked closer. "And she'll be gone?"

Kane's mouth arced in a sinister grin. "I can kill her myself if I have to." I flinched as he extended a hand, reaching for her. "But I need you first. That's the only way this works."

She watched that hand, covetous as she closed in, slowly, her own arm lifting and retreating, lifting and retreating, before her palm finally settled shakily in his. His thumb trailed an easy line across her wrist. She shuddered, closing the space between them, coming so close, her breasts brushed his chest.

My heart rattled against my ribs. I tried to breathe. Tried and tried and tried, but my lungs refused to work.

Tears pricked the backs of my eyes as a bitter agony sliced my chest and my stomach rolled.

I was gonna be sick.

Joaquin's hold flexed against me, whether in reassurance or to keep me still, I had no clue.

"You're not okay, Amber," Kane said. Raising their clasped hands to his mouth, he pressed a kiss to her fingers. "Let me take care of you."

My knees grew weak and I stumbled, but Joaquin held me steady.

Her call. Her threats.

Her arms raised slowly, locking around his neck.

"Claim me, Kane," she begged. "Please."

Clutching my throat, I held back a scream.

He shook his head, his free hand stroking her cheek before it trailed down her jaw, then her throat. "You're not strong enough to handle it yet."

Her lips twitched, head rolling like she was working to contain herself. She gave a low snarl, and her hands flexed against him again and again before she offered an alternative. "Then kiss me."

His body was stone, the muscles of his throat and arms straining against the skin as, with gradual progress, he inclined his head and moved forward.

That was enough of that, 'cause there was only so much I could take. The fury searing my veins was so potent, I tasted its bitter sting on my tongue. My grip latched over the back door and I tore it open, exploding outside as I released my obsidian. "KANE!"

Two sets of blazing eyes whipped my way as I charged across the yard, barreling toward them. Amber's lips peeled back from her teeth, and a high-pitched keening snarl tore from her chest. Kane shifted, throwing himself in front of her like a shield.

Not protecting me.

Protecting *her*.

My chest imploded.

"JOAQUIN!" Kane roared.

The Southern Alpha closed in, then grabbed me, his arms latching around my waist as he dragged me back.

I kicked my legs high, thrashing against him. "LET ME FUCKING GO!"

"No can do, banshee."

"She needs to die, Kane," Amber seethed, pushing against his back to get to me.

"I know. But I need you first," he said, his voice easy, like he was trying to coax her back to him.

Her arm slid forward, fingers curled around his chest possessively. Her eyes screamed "*Mine!*"

He leaned back, into her.

The sound that broke from me was so shrill, it hurt. It clawed at my throat until my voice hitched and tears streamed down my cheeks.

Kane's eyes narrowed. Barely. Then he gave me his back and faced her again.

"Kane!" I cried.

He didn't reply. Didn't acknowledge I'd spoken, or that I even existed. Instead, he curled his thick hand over hers and brought it to his chest. With his other, he cupped her cheek, bringing her honeyed eyes to his as he asked, "Do you believe me now?"

Her smile was all teeth and savage, her nod sharp. "I don't want her around."

"I know." He smiled. "I'll deal with her."

Joaquin settled my feet on the ground, and I fell limp in his arms.

"Come back to the Pack, Amber," Kane said, setting his forehead to hers. "I don't want you out there on your own. I can't protect you like that. Please. I need you here. With me, where you're stronger. Where we can finish this."

Her chin lifted, lips brushing his, and her eyes sparked with a wild heat that made my skin crawl. "Okay," she rasped. "Take me, Kane."

Looking at them was agony, so I stared past them toward the void of the forest, begging for this to be over.

He inhaled deep, his power cutting across the night. It tore through me, rocking Joaquin to the side, like Kane had opened a door—opened himself to *her*. His strength rushed out, and her spine arched, her head snapping back as she opened herself in turn, accepting. He held her steady, then stiffened as the power retreated, pulling back to him.

Amber sagged, a soft sigh filling the din as she collapsed into him.

Kane held for one breath. Two.

His stare turned molten as he released her and stepped back. She dropped to the ground. His jaw worked, and he crouched down to her level, his face a hair from hers, all pretenses of warmth long fucking gone.

Sweet goddamn sage. Finally!

Joaquin's arms released me, his hazel stare blazing as I stepped from his side and closed in on my Alpha. My palm found his shoulder, and the dominating, possessive, "you're fucked now" smile I offered Amber was so toxic, it was almost poison.

Her expression contorted, a thousand emotions tearing through her eyes as her gaze shifted from Kane to me, then back.

Kane bared his canines, a low, grating growl tearing from his throat before he loosed his Alpha command: "TELL US WHERE ISAAC IS!"

Chapter Twenty-One

Kane's command ripped through the night, echoed off the trees.

Tell us where Isaac is! Tell us where Isaac is!

Amber's spine snapped straight, rain slicing her face as her eyes grew frantic.

My Alpha had been right when he'd told me his plan. I'd hated it. Every call, every gentle word to her, the implementation. My body still trembled from the sight of her fucking paws on him. Because he'd been brutalized enough at her all-too-eager hands.

She grabbed her head now, fingers twisting around her hair as she pulled. "I don't know," she cried, then collapsed to her side. "Why are you doing this?" She swallowed hard. "I thought—" Her gaze darted around, then back to him. "You said you wanted me."

"You fucked me against my will, Amber. Kept me from the only woman that's ever mattered to me. The only goddamn thing I want you for is to find *him*." He rolled his shoulders. "And you *will* help me do it."

She scrambled back a foot, mud slicking her skin, her clothes. Everything. "No. You don't mean that."

His laugh was darker than the Iron Hells. "Yes. I fucking do."

The shake of her head had her matted hair snapping around her face as she spat, "You're just saying it because of her."

His power cracked on the air, pricking as it rolled over my skin, charged with a savage need for violence.

"Hear this, Amber, and hear it fucking well," he said, his words guttural and cold. "I don't want you. I've *never* wanted you. The only reason I said what I said was to get you here."

Her eyes were wild, agony and realization churning in their depths. He didn't love her. He didn't want her. And she was well and truly screwed. Chest heaving, her head snapped around as if she was looking for an escape. "He'll kill me, Kane."

He leaned closer, rain slipping from his chin as his tone dropped to a low, menacing promise. "So will I."

Her fingers dug into the sopping earth. Her stare lit on me.

My palm slid further down my Alpha's chest, mimicking her movements from moments ago. I smiled, all goddamn teeth. "There is no claiming for you, Amber, because Kane *is* mine. And I am his." I pressed tighter into him. "And we don't fucking share."

She bared her teeth. Quicker than I could track, she lunged. My eyes widened as she closed in, jaws unhinging, aiming straight for my throat. Kane shifted, his arm snapping out, a thick hand latching around her neck before he caught her in mid-air. Her momentum sent her legs snapping forward. He lifted her up, then slammed her down. Her back collided with the ground so hard, she sank deep into the muddy earth, imprinting.

Kane released her, then ordered, "*You will not fucking touch us. And you will not fucking run.*" He rose to his full, dominating height, his stare finally finding me. "You alright, Bry?"

My nod was small. I grumbled, "Took you long enough."

The corners of his mouth tugged, but the smile was tight and didn't reach his eyes.

It had been hard when we'd worked the plan through, knowing what was coming. It'd hurt every time he'd taken her calls, knowing they'd talked. Knowing he'd whispered gentle words in her ear. But that hurt wasn't for me, because there wasn't one question, one doubt in my mind that Kane Slade was mine. Instead, it tore my soul to shreds that he had to pay this price after everything she'd done; that he had to face her. Be sweet and play her game to lure her in.

That's why I'd hated the idea. Not for what it did to me, but for what it did to him. Either way, my Alpha had been right: Amber *was* our best chance at finding my stepfather the super kind of fast. We'd needed my reaction to tip Amber over the edge of doubt. To make her believe him fully. To take what he'd offered. To let him pull her back into the Pack so he could command her and get the information we required.

My brows drew together, and I swiped water from my face as my pulse kicked up, because plan or not, with the things Amber had done to him, him having to help her, to be soft and sweet and kind to her, to let her near him—let her *touch* him—that must have left its mark.

Fingers curling into the hood of his shirt, I jerked him closer. "Are you alright?"

His eyes met mine. "I'm good."

I jerked him closer still. "I know we needed to do it, but if you ever suggest a garbage idea like that again, I'll neuter you myself." A broad smile took him then, and my mouth crashed with his, touch roving his chest and shoulders, hands moving over his back and hair and along his jaw, letting him know I was there. Letting him feel it. I released him. "And you're not touching me again until you bleach every inch of your fucking body."

He huffed a low laugh. It was brash, and proud, and so full of love, a liquid heat pooled between my thighs. One I intended to seek recompense for, to ease the torture he'd endured—but first, we had a job to do.

I stalked to Amber's side. Joaquin closed in, my Alpha so tight to my back, his heat pulsed over my flesh.

"Is Hannah alive?" I demanded.

Amber's maw stayed locked. She snarled, water and spit flying from her lips.

"*Answer her questions,*" Kane ordered.

Her nostrils flared. "Yessssss," she said through her painfully clenched teeth.

"Where is she?"

She thrashed like she was fighting each word. "With Isaac!"

My lips pursed. The questions needed to be clear. No room for interpretation. For misdirection. "Do you know how to find him?"

She thrashed. "No."

Joaquin folded his arms over his chest. "How do you help him?"

Those honeyed eyes locked onto Kane's, and she must've seen the unrelenting promise there, because she shuddered, then answered, "I bring him what he needs."

I scowled. "Where?"

"He moves. Always moves."

I frowned, because that answer was unsurprising and problematic in equal measure. "And what does Zahara want?"

More spittle flew as she said, "War."

The twist of my stomach hurt, and bile kissed the back of my throat. "With whom?"

Her lips drew back in a sneer. "*Everyone.*"

My gaze met Kane's, and I swallowed hard.

"Who is Zahara?" my Alpha pushed, forearms pulsing as his fists clenched.

She shook her head, frantic. "I don't know."

I leaned closer, giving her a good goddamn look at the promise of death in my eyes. "How do we find her?"

Panting heavily, she tore at her damp, matted hair and repeated, "I don't *know*!"

The arch of my brow was sharp. "Does Isaac know how to find her?"

She clawed at her face, dragging her nails down her skin. "I. Don't. Know."

Joaquin's eyes narrowed. "Does Isaac know how to *contact* her?"

A distinction with a very important difference.

"Yes," she hissed on an exhale.

Her answers were her advantage. That information was the only thing standing between her and a promised death. So she gripped them with everything she had, giving us only what we asked for, and not a damn thing more.

A boom sounded, and I snapped around, my gaze landing on the house. The back door flew wide as Lucas stormed toward us, Theo at his side, my brother's hard glare on Amber.

Kane's palm landed on the small of my back and flexed against me.

I returned to the issue at hand. "Where does Isaac think you are right now, Amber?"

Amber's voice hitched. "Getting supplies."

"Does he know we've been talking?" said Kane.

She shook her head.

His stare flashed and he commanded, "*Say it out loud!*"

Lucas closed in, stopping at her side.

Her eyes crushed closed. "No! Isaac doesn't know."

Joaquin's finger tapped over his forearm. "How are you supposed to find him again?"

Even against the dark of night, she grew pale as she whimpered, "I need to call him."

I cocked my head. "From your *own* phone?"

Her canines bared again. "Yes."

I took a knee in the cold, wet mud beside her, cringing as I slid a hand into her pocket and pulled her device free. Wiping her screen clean, I eyed her background image. A picture of my Alpha—a newer photo, one surreptitiously taken at the Conclave. I struggled not to crush the thing in my grasp. I glared at her and dropped the phone into her lap. "Call Isaac."

The corner of her jaw twitched.

My Alpha shifted, squaring himself to her, his voice a graveled growl as he commanded, "*Do what she said, Amber. And no games. No tactics. No secret fucking messages. No tipping him off. Make him think you're coming. Find out where he is.*"

She jolted and pushed to her feet, breath breaking from her in staccato pants as she dialed.

It rang once. Twice. Three times.

My throat tightened. *Answer, Isaac. Just fucking answer—*

"Amber," my stepfather said.

Her stare darted around. "I'm ready."

"Good. I followed the patrols, they've moved past already. You shouldn't encounter issues."

Son of a motherfucker! He'd stayed *behind* the patrols? I should've known, because he was a coward through and through. It's what he did. He lied. He hid. He cowered.

Her neck strained as if she was struggling against the words. "Where am I going?"

A shuffle, followed by the static of wind blowing in the background. "Meet me at Lana's."

Wraith take me—my mother's. My hand rose to my chest. He'd gone back *to my mother's*?

Amber inclined her head, hands trembling. "I'm coming."

The call ended.

I worried at my lip, because her meeting him ... she couldn't. I found my Alpha's gaze. "Amber can't go."

Her feral glare snapped my way. "I'm the only one he'll allow anywhere near him without him slaughtering the girl."

Lucas stilled.

Theo chucked his chin in my direction. "What're you thinking, Briar?"

I gestured Amber's way. "Isaac's the only chance she's got for an out. If she goes to him and finds some loophole in Kane's command"—just like I had when under my stepfather's control, and Joaquin had when under Ronin's—"she'll sabotage us."

Lucas reached out, taking a fallen strand of hair from Amber's shirt before he twisted it in his grasp.

The only way we'd get anywhere near Isaac was with her help. I froze, my eyes snapping to meet my brother's.

No ... not her help. Her *face*.

I breathed deeply as an idea hit me, one that came from Lucas and his encounter with Danika. I hated it with every fiber of my withered soul, but if we wanted to get Hannah out alive, it was the only chance we had. "Lucas."

Amber's gaze moved toward my brother, the terror of understanding darkening her expression, 'cause no doubt she saw Isaac as her way out—her only goddamn way. And if my brother took her place ... Her brows slammed down.

Time slowed, the drum of the rain loud as Amber's arm exploded forward, and she reached for Lucas's throat.

My chest constricted as my Alpha's command for her echoed across my mind. *Don't touch us*, he'd said—*before* Lucas showed up, which meant the command hadn't encompassed him.

Kane's roar tore through the night, echoing inside my skull. His boned claws exploded from his hand, but he was behind me. Too far. He wouldn't reach her. Not in time.

Amber had stripped Kane of things, of pieces that he'd never get back. She'd tortured him for far, far too long. She'd already taken Mason. I wasn't about to let her take my brother too, nor to have Lucas's death rest on my Alpha's shoulders. Kane protected, time and time again. It was what he did. Always.

And it was my turn to repay the favor.

Her canines were extended, her hand open as she closed in on Lucas's neck.

Fingers curling over my obsidian, I ripped my Alpha's power to me, and swung, moving preternaturally hard and fast. My hit landed, obliterating Amber's airway. Her hands flew to her throat as she gasped for air and dropped to her knees.

"You don't ever touch my fucking family," I snarled. My own hands closed over hers, locking them in place as my grip cinched tight, crushing and crushing. "But you were right about one thing." My gaze dropped to my abdomen. To my child.

Her face twisted in agony, and the sight of it made my blood sing.

"You'll never take him. You'll never take our child. And you'll never take another fucking breath." Muscle and tendon tore, sinew snapped, and bone fractured, grinding to dust. Her eyes bulged, turning red as the blood vessels broke, and a single tear slithered down her cheek. I kept drawing that power, my body straining to contain it as she struggled to break free, but she could never contend with my Alpha's strength.

The cry that broke from me was ragged and raw, filled with the savagery of vengeance. I jerked my arm upward, flesh tearing as I cleaved her head from her fucking shoulders.

Her arms slumped by her sides. Her body collapsed with a sickening smack, landing chest down.

Her warm blood slithered over my hands, pooling in a macabre river at my feet as it mixed with the rain and mud. *Drip. Drip. Drip.*

Joaquin cursed.

"Holy hells," Theo breathed.

Four sets of eyes tracked to me.

My chest rose and fell as I released my grip. Her head dropped, rolling aside before it stopped, her vacant, deader-than-dead eyes staring skyward.

Kane's claws retracted. He advanced a step, his tone easy as he said, "Bry?"

I inclined my head, silent message clear. *I'm alright.* Then, straightening, I drew back my shoulders as I took control. "We call Bower and the others. We move now." My stare met his before it tracked across Joaquin, and Theo, then landed on my brother. "You get to Hannah. We'll handle the rest. Isaac dies tonight."

Theo blinked, then blinked again. "I'm really liking that plan, Briar—but, like … holy shit, you're *pregnant*?"

Chapter Twenty-Two

The rain had faded to a barely-there mist, but only an hour had passed, and the night was still dark—the leech-the-light-from-your-soul kind of dark. It dulled the lights of the buildings and set an ominous tone. The hum of the truck tires was low as Kane drove. Theo, Joaquin, and Lucas tight on our tail.

My Alpha's stare kept tracking my way. "How're you doing, Bry?"

We'd changed into dry clothes as we'd set out our plan, made every call. We had every resource and reinforcement we could muster en route. Fast. We just had to hope it worked.

I inclined my head. "I'm ready." And I was. But I wasn't the only factor at play. I worried my cheek between my teeth. I didn't regret Amber's death. Not even close. Just the loss of her usefulness. Separating Amber's head from her body meant this was our only plan. Our only shot at finding Isaac. If this went south, if the plan fell through, if he slipped through our fingers this time, we were out of options. "This has to work, Kane."

The weight of that reality pressed in, heavy and crushing as my gaze followed the terrain. The drive was so damn familiar, and everything about it chilled my bones. There were no good memories left. All it conjured was my brother's suffering, my mother's, and my father's. I hated the place. Wanted it razed to the damn ground—under it.

He veered the truck to the side of the road, gravel crunching underneath us as he brought it to a stop.

“It was either her or Luke. You did what needed doing.” He smiled. “She was dead either way, Bry, ’cause if you hadn’t killed her, I would have.”

Shifting the truck into park, he climbed out, standing at the driver’s door. His heavy palms landed on the seat against my hips, and he dragged me closer. Nudging my knees apart, he stepped between my thighs.

“I love you, woman. You’re it for me.” The back of his hand grazed my abdomen. “I’ve got everything I need in this world, right fucking here. And I’m not losing it.” He set his forehead to mine and growled, “*Ever*.”

I sighed against him, greedy for those words and everything he offered. A heavy fluttering whooshed through my lower abdomen. My body locked, pulse thrashing in my ears. Head snapping up, my eyes were wide on his.

He went rigid. “What’s wrong?”

Was it even possible? It was still so early, but then, I *was* carrying a wolf. My voice was high and bright and so damn desperate as I said, “Did you feel that?”

His brows furrowed. “Feel wh—”

I grabbed his hand, then set my own over it as I flattened it against my stomach. “This.” My heart pounded, aching for that sensation, my words a breathy whisper as I said, “Do you feel them?”

His brows furrowed, eyes locked in concentration while he waited. And waited. My chest tightened.

Come on, little one. Do it again. Please.

There was nothing for one breath. Two. And then, another flutter.

Kane’s eyes closed, breath hitching before his chin and chest rose. His grip tightened around my hips as he dropped to his knees before me, then nudged and nuzzled his face against my abdomen. “Hey, little one.”

Another flutter.

I wrapped my legs around Kane’s back, raking my fingers through his hair. Tears pricked my eyes, this happiness a wild and foreign thing in the depths of our chaos. But if I'd learned anything since Isaac had come along, it was that time was fleeting. And every moment mattered. I'd rip and claw and steal that joy wherever I could, then cling to it with everything I had.

"Our baby," I said.

"*Ours*," he growled, then shot to his feet. Gripping my thighs, he lifted. One hand cradled my ass, the other cupping my face as his mouth crashed with mine. His tongue dove deep as he worked, kissing me with his whole damn body. Gruff grunts tore from his chest, his breaths ragged and hard when he broke from me. "Thank you, Bry." His mouth grazed mine, again and again, slow and easy. "Shadowed moon, thank you."

The crunch of approaching steps had the world rushing back in, dark and cold, along with the reality of what was to come.

Joaquin rounded the truck, those hazel eyes fixed on us as he gave a steady nod. "The others," he said, his words heavy. "They're here."

Chapter Twenty-Three

The air was dense with the sharp scent of fear, and rage, and a violence so cutting, it was a wonder we didn't bleed. A stark contrast to our small moment of peace just minutes ago.

The moon broke through the clouds as we waited at the edge of my mother's property, beyond the trees and out of sight of the house. Kane and Joaquin's wolves surrounded the place, giving it a wide berth, because like hells would my stepfather be flanking us this time.

No scents clung to the air, which was not a shock considering Isaac's obsession with plotting and wolfsbane.

Kane's stare was steady on me. The calm on the horizon of a perilous fucking storm. He was the stillness. Not peaceful, because there was bloodthirsty savagery within him that would put any shadow walker to shame, but it was tempered. Controlled. Ready to be released at the right moment.

Cassandra, Alistair, and Bower waited with us, their brutality thick on the air. The Northern and Southern Covens arrived, trickling in slowly. Well, not all of them. Just the necessaries.

A veritable army against one man. One changeling, who was by far the most treacherous thing there.

The Ambassador held his iron gun at the ready. His eyes found mine. "He was a soldier," he said. "The image you sent."

Was a soldier. My eyes hardened. "Can you find him?"

"He's gone off-grid, but we're looking."

At least it was a lead. Something.

Marisol moved to my side, her weathered hands trembling. Reaching out, I took one in my steady grasp. "Stay with me."

Throwing a barrier around our group, I pulled on every ounce of vengeance I had as I stalked to the middle of the magi, turning so I could meet every eye. "You have your orders. You know what to do. It's now or never. Follow my lead." I dipped my chin. "On my word."

Breaths were taken. Heads inclined.

Facing my brother, I swallowed the fear that tried to break free, because there wasn't room for it. There wasn't room for anything but that unyielding, un-fucking-wavering love. And belief.

"You've got this, Luke," Kane said.

My brother's hand rolled around something in his pocket. His stare was sharp, his focus locked as his face rippled and rolled, transforming. His eyes morphed, taking on Amber's honeyed shade, before dark circles formed under them. His shoulders rounded, his spine curved. His clothes changed, becoming the tattered ones she'd lived in of late. His hair lengthened, then matted, hanging down to cover his tattoo.

My words were low and even as I told him, "Go, get your girl. When the line is clear, Bower will take the shot."

His chest rose on an inhale, his nod sharp. Pivoting on his heel, he left. My heart drummed, pounding violently against my ribs. Pulling on my Alpha's strength, I pushed my hearing and waited.

The slow lope of Lucas's Amber-shaped feet carried as he moved, his attention scanning from side to side. "Isaac?" he called, in *her* voice.

There was silence for several agonizing heartbeats.

Be here, Isaac. Fucking be here!

"Say it." My stepfather's voice rang out.

My gaze darted around, trying to gauge Isaac's location. Kane pointed left, toward the wooded area along the back of the house. His stare went unfocused, the Southern Alpha following suit as they instructed their Packs.

"What?" Lucas said, that mimicked lone-wolf voice now broken.

"Say. The. Word."

My spine locked up.

"*What fucking word?*" I said across my wolfy bond with Kane.

Kane's fists clenched, tendons standing stark against his skin. He shook his head.

Isaac and Amber had had a code? Goddamnit, they'd had a fucking code!

My lungs burned, breaths coming in rapid pants.

Lucas-Amber advanced, then came into view through the dense copse of trees between us. He scratched his arm, then his jaw. "I, uh." Grabbing a matt of hair, he twisted, and twisted, playing up that role. "Shit. What was it again?" he mumbled to himself, voice broken and desperate. "Give me a hint."

Bower shifted left, his eyes searching through the thicket. In a low voice, he murmured, "Show yourself, Isaac."

"Come now, Amber," my stepfather crooned, his words a dark threat. "This is not something you would forget."

I swallowed around the bile searing my throat. If we wanted this to work, Lucas was the only one—the only fucking way!

Isaac stepped from the back of the house, an arm cinched around Hannah's neck, an iron gun of his own digging into her temple. Tears stained her cheeks, and she whimpered as the gun's muzzle sizzled against her skin.

Bower snarled. "I see him, but I don't have a clear shot."

Because Hannah was Isaac's shield. He always had a fucking shield.

Isaac's head rotated like he was looking for something. Or someone. He smiled, all sinister and teeth, then angled his head back and called, "I know you're there, Briar."

My heart seized. *Shit!* We'd been had. We'd been fucking had!

I needed to stall him. Let everything fall into place like we'd planned, then pray like hells it worked.

Kane's body tensed, muscles straining against his skin, because my Alpha was used to ripping and clawing and facing trouble with necessary violence. But this fight wouldn't be won with brute power, something I could see he understood when his blazing gaze met mine. He inclined his head, trust and determination and everything he goddamn had in that expression.

Breathing deep, I steadied. "Let her go, Isaac," I called through those trees. It wouldn't take long before he'd figure out where I was standing, but that didn't matter. Not yet.

His laugh was broken. "I always thought you were smart, Briar. But you really never learn, do you? I thought I'd taught you by now," he goaded, "you never give up your advantage."

My Alpha's jaw ground as my hand latched around my obsidian. I looked at Bower, my eyes hard. "Don't lose him."

Drawing his shoulders back, Bower racked the gun's slide, then inclined his head.

I exhaled good and slow, and drew on my power. It roiled inside me, a tempest that had been building since the second Isaac had stolen my father's face and slipped into our lives. I dove deep, finding that emotion and homing in fast, because it was my tether.

Protect them.

Lucas, Hannah, Kane, Joaquin, Theo, Cassandra, Lisa, my Coven, my child.

Protect them!

A world without Isaac. A world free of that fear.

Protect them!

To the magi, I ordered, "Now!"

The particles rose from my palms, drifting out and coalescing. They twisted and turned, sliding into place like a puzzle, bit by bit, until Hannah stood before me, fully formed, sleeves tugged down over her hands. Sweat slicked my brow and ran down my spine as I moved her.

My Hannah crested the trees, followed by Marisol's, and the illusions of every other magi there as an army of Hannahs approached. Ten. Twenty. Thirty. They marched forward, fanning out wide until Isaac was surrounded. Every corner like a horror house of mirrors, reflecting a terror-stricken Hannah.

"Holy shit," Theo said, words low and caught somewhere between awe and dread.

Amber-faced Lucas hovered at the edge of that crowd. Waiting.

We moved our Hannahs in random patterns and directions, some in front of Isaac, some behind him. His head snapped from side to side, trying to track them. More magi stepped forward, foreheads creased in concentration as they joined in, adding their own Hannahs to the fray. Everywhere I looked, there was a cacophony of her.

Take the bait, Isaac. Take the fucking bait!

"You can't fool me, Briar." Isaac's head snapped to the side. "I know what you're doing."

Maybe he did, but the one and only good thing about my stepfather was his predictability for self-preservation.

Cassandra's dress flitted on the wind, soft and gentle and a complete contrast to the bloodthirst that simmered in her eyes.

"Then you'll know I'm giving you a chance," I called.

Several of the Hannahs veered off. Away. Bower shifted again. Hunting him.

Isaac wasn't about to give up his leverage unless he thought it benefited him, which meant we needed to give him a reason. We needed to out-plot him, give him an incentive to let go.

And so we had: a sea of Hannahs he could slip into. Where he could fade away. Hide.

We were playing him at his own game. Isaac was surrounded, cornered like the rat he was. There was no escape for him, not this time. His death was imminent. This wasn't about his survival, not anymore.

It was about hers.

Isaac's eyes darted around, his face pale. He cursed. Then his jaw clenched, mouth morphing, fading, until finally—*finally*—he took on Hannah's face.

Lucas's Amber-shaped hands flexed by his sides.

Tucking the gun away, Isaac released Hannah. She stumbled forward, tears streaking her face as she heaved out a sob. The illusion-Hannahs kept moving, swarming him and her until they were engulfed. Isaac slipped into their midst, doing what he did best. Hiding.

"Take the shot," Kane said.

Bower's jaw flexed. His gun lowered and raised. Lowered and raised. He cursed, then cursed again. "Which fucking one is he?"

"Look for the scar, Bower Caddel," Cassandra hissed.

My gaze tracked the faces, then dropped to their hands, searching for that scar—but the hands of every Hannah were all tucked into sleeves. My throat tightened. I would've ordered the others to drop their illusions, but with Isaac still armed himself, I was surer than the Iron Hells themselves that he'd go for her.

I needed the *real* Hannah outta there. Fast. I looked at the spot where I'd last seen Amber-Lucas, and a frown creased my expression. "Where the hells is Lucas?"

Kane's body grew taut, his muscles cording. His shoulders rose with each breath. Afraid. He shook his head, followed by Cassandra, Joaquin, and Theo.

My heart dropped, adrenaline spiking as my pulse pounded inside my skull. Sweet sage. We'd lost him. *We'd fucking lost him!*

And we'd lost Isaac too.

I wanted to scream my brother's name. But giving him away wasn't an option.

The sea of Hannahs flowed out, veering into the forest, across the road. Moving away. Luring. Offering escape.

A tear-stained Hannah moved to the periphery of the crowd. She tugged her sleeves down tighter over her hands, eyes snapping around as if looking for help.

Kane seethed beside me, those boned claws extending. His chest heaved as his unfathomable stare hunted the scene. And I got it, 'cause if we wanted Hannah to come out the other side of this, we were only gonna get one shot—which meant we couldn't miss.

I turned to stone, all my focus and will and power and, wraith take me, my goddamn breath, trained on the chaos. Hannah's life hung in the feebly delicate balance, and without knowing where Isaac was, we couldn't move.

The Hannahs moved further and further out. Away. No. No! *No!* We were gonna lose him. He'd get away. *He'd get away!*

Another Hannah caught my eye then, as she moved through the fray, tracking—a predator pursuing its prey. She tipped her head down, her shoulders rounded as she shuffled forward, staring at her feet as if she was scared. She edged out one foot, then another, the ground crunching under her feet as she shadowed the crying Hannah's movements until she loomed at her back.

My heart seized, because illusions were just that—not real—which meant they couldn't make noise.

That tear-stained Hannah froze, then turned.

Cassandra's fingers curled around the air like she pictured them wrapped around a throat—*Isaac's* throat.

My chest seized because, shadow and sage, *who the hells was it*?

The new Hannah squared herself, a steadfast, no-holds-barred determination in her gaze. A gaze that morphed to violet as I watched.

"I warned you not to fuck with her," she said … with my brother's voice.

The crying Hannah's eyes flew wide. Isaac. It was Isaac!

The fear that took him leached the color from his skin, sallowing his face. And, iron fires take me, it looked so damn good on him.

My brother jerked something from his pocket, time slowing as his arm snapped forward. Metal glinted in his grip before he plunged it hard and deep between his father's ribs. Isaac bucked, then grunted. His flesh sizzled. Lucas's face rolled, the long hair shortening, returning to his own mahogany color, his face morphing from Hannah's to his own, filled with savage fury.

"Lucas," Isaac said, his words hoarse and wet. "Son."

"I'm not your son." Lucas's jaw worked. "I'm a fucking Slade."

Beside me, my Alpha's breath hitched, his chest rising with pride.

"I'll take nothing from you," my brother seethed. "You're dead, Isaac. You, your name, and everything you are dies with you."

"I'm in your blood, boy." My stepfather jerked, his voice strained and wet as blood slithered from his lips and down his chin. "You can't change what you are."

Lucas shook his head. "I don't have to, because I'm not you. And I never will be."

Isaac jerked again, his body going rigid as his chest imploded. His face turned red, transforming to his own in a flash. Blood burst from his mouth, misting on the air. His hands shot out, latching onto Lucas's wrist. My brother snarled, then twisted the blade. Skin and bone popped, sounds filling the night before he tore it free.

Isaac's legs buckled. He stumbled forward for one step. Two. He dropped to his knees hard, body jolting as he landed. His gasps carried through the silence, his skin an unforgiving shade of blue.

The weight that had crushed my chest eased. Bower lowered his gun.

I advanced and the Conclave followed, our quiet steps the only sound against the din. My fingers unfurled, sweat beading my temples as I drew back my power. My Hannah faded and faded, until she disappeared altogether. I released my obsidian.

On cue, the other magi let go. Every other Hannah vanished, save one—the *real* one.

My brother's stare locked on his girl. He swallowed hard as he closed in, then pulled her to his chest. She clung to him, tears streaking her dirt-stained cheeks.

The scent of ether filled the air, burning my senses. The ground shook with a violent force. Kane grabbed me. The sky darkened, then darkened some more until it was void of any light. The night split. No … not the night; the fabric of the goddamn world.

Every head snapped around.

The wind turned cold, our breaths frosting it in clouds. Ice crackled as it spread along the road and trees. It coated the house and windows, nipped at my flesh and stiffened my hair.

I spread my stance wide, then took a half-step back. "What the hells is happening?"

Cassandra's incisors lengthened, cresting over her bottom lip. "Now, Briar Stone," she said, a terrifying lilt to her words as they echoed our conversation from before, "Isaac Jenkins pays for his sins."

The wind whipped harder, sending tears streaking from my eyes.

Isaac let out a garbled, gurgled, hissing scream. It was desperation and terror, and it slaked my goddamn thirst.

The night rippled, and a semi-translucent figure appeared against the dimness, growing clearer and clearer. Her hair was so blonde it was almost white. Her black wings flared wide as she stepped through the rift.

The wraith, come from the Iron Hells. Power of obsidian, *she'd come from the Iron Hells!*

Her delicate arms were stretched out, wrists lifted, fingers gracefully held. One long, milky leg was bent, the other extended, toes pointed down. And her eyes—sage, those eyes were a piercing shade of indigo I'd never seen before. There was something about them, like they could strip back my layers, see every corner of my memory and through to my soul. Gauge its worth.

I swallowed hard and fought to hold my ground.

"Shadowed fucking moon," Kane said. His hand linked through mine, an anchor that kept me rooted. And if the tightness of that grip was any indication, I was keeping him rooted, too.

The wraith wore head-to-toe scarlet, the color of fire. Or blood. The dress was stacked layers of lace, fitted to her flawless form. The bottom scraped across the sopping ground as she padded forward, her bare feet scarcely leaving a trail in her wake. Tucking those wings tight to her back, she held my stepfather's stare as she closed in.

"Isaac Jenkins," she said, her voice layered, gentle and hard, soft and shrill, smooth and grating. It rolled through the night, ethereal and haunting. "It's time to come home."

Isaac dragged himself back, blood spurting from his chest in time with the frantic pulse of his heart. He shook his head, his hands trembling and his muscles straining. Even in the darkness, I could see his skin grow pale.

I'd thought I'd seen fear from him before, when he'd faced my Alpha and found himself wanting, but that was nothing compared to the way his eyes bulged now, their whites flaring wide, while a tear snaked down his cheek and his lips quivered, revealing him for the coward he was.

Slowly, she lowered herself to his side.

"No!" he begged. "Please!"

"You should not have run," she said, the words low. It wasn't pity, more like a warning about whatever awaited him in the Deep.

Her delicate fingers extended, caressing his cheek before falling flat against it. Her all-seeing eyes lit up, blazing so bright they painted the damp ground, the clouds and every face there. Raising my arms, I shielded my gaze against the glow, eyes straining as I peered between my fingers, because I couldn't—wouldn't—look away.

A surge of power that made my Alpha's look feeble boomed out. Everyone was knocked back, collapsing to their knees.

The earth split, grass and rock lifting, floating on the air.

Lucas shoved Hannah behind him and edged to the side, moving our way.

The wraith's hand pressed deep, sinking into Isaac's flesh—through it. My stepfather's spine arched, body convulsing as it curved off the ground. Slowly, she withdrew her hand, and Isaac withdrew with her, soul peeling from his body, inch by horrifying inch. His real legs kicked and jerked, eyes rolling back in his head. He grunted and gurgled, arms flailing as he grabbed for that soul, his hands slipping straight through.

"Let this be a warning to any who follow in your path," the wraith declared. "The Iron Hells do not suffer disobedience. You belong to the Deep now, where there is no escape for you."

Stone cracked, the ground rocking under him. The house shifted, then buckled. Glass shattered and trees shook.

I swallowed. Not that I pitied him, because Isaac had earned his end. He'd earned every second of eternity buried in the Deep of the Iron Hells. Every second of what they had planned for him. He deserved it for the havoc he'd wreaked. For every life he'd destroyed.

Kane's body was stone beside me, the muscles of his jaw and neck tense. The eagerness for justice burning in his voltaic eyes was mirrored in Joaquin's, Theo's, Cassandra's.

Everyone's.

Isaac's desperate gaze met mine.

I straightened, rising to my full height, my chin angled high, and I let my own stare spear him through. "All you've *ever* done is take, and take, and take. You took my mother, my father, my child. You took your son's innocence, and you took time. But now, it's your turn to *give*." Give his blood. Give *his* time. And give his fucking life. I leaned closer. "Burn in fucking hells!"

The wraith kept pulling until his soul was torn completely free.

I reached for Lucas, my hand wrapping over his. He held it tightly, his grip painful over my own, but I welcomed it.

Isaac's body shuddered one final time, his eyes fading from black, to gray, until the milky cast of white took them, and he sagged. Dead.

Dead. He was dead. *He was fucking dead!*

A breath left me, tears stinging the backs of my eyes. My gaze fell on Kane. We were safe. Lucas was safe. Our baby was safe.

The wraith lifted Isaac's translucent and pigmented soul high, holding it like it was nothing. Inconsequential. A problem that had been managed.

Her wings spread from her back, flaring wide before they snapped in, out. In, out. Her feet lifted from the ground, and she rose. Moving so fast I couldn't track her, she vanished into the rift in the ground. She was gone.

And so was he.

Chapter Twenty-Five

He was dead. Isaac was *dead*!

The moon weakened as it peeked through the fragmented clouds, illuminating the dying night. It caught on Cassandra's white-blonde hair, my Alpha's silvered gaze, and the muzzle of Bower's gun as he slid it away.

Silence carried. Every face was the same shade of shocked.

"Shadowed fucking moon," Theo said, crushing his eyes closed before he forced them open again, like he couldn't believe what he'd seen. Because the wraith had come, and Isaac was dead.

We were free.

My lungs worked, expanding as my exhales hazed the air. I could breathe.

Hannah clung to my brother and tucked her face against his shoulder, and he whispered in her ear. "It's okay. I've got you." He stroked her hair and closed his eyes. "I've got you."

He had her. She was okay.

Isaac was dead.

Cassandra glided closer. "Well done, Lucas Slade."

My brother's gaze cut to my Alpha's. "Sorry I didn't ask—"

"You didn't need to." Kane cleared his throat and gave a sharp, sure incline of his head. "You're a Slade, Luke. Always have been."

Lucas's chest inflated. He looked down at the knife, then shoved it away.

Theo flicked a hand at it. "Where'd you even get that thing, boss?"

He grinned. "Grabbed it off one of the assholes that attacked Briar and me."

We were gonna have to work on his potty mouth, but that was a bottom-of-the-barrel sorta issue.

My heart thrummed, my shoulders sagging. The fear, the looking over our shoulders, the never knowing … it was gone. Tears seared the backs of my eyes, then broke free. My Alpha turned me to face him, one arm banding my torso, the other cradling my scalp as he crushed me to his chest.

I wept and wept, letting it out. Letting it go. With Isaac.

Hannah's strained gaze took in the carnage. Sad. So endlessly sad. "My grandfather?"

Looking her way, I swiped my tears, mouth lifting in a feeble smile. "He's alive."

A sob burst from her lips. My brother's arms were around her in an instant, pulling her tight to his side.

She clutched his shirt, her tears staining the material. "I need to see him."

"Come on," Theo told her, chucking his chin to the side. "I'll take you."

My Alpha's head dipped in a nod.

"Take Lucas, too," I said, 'cause after what they'd just been through, the last thing I'd do was separate them.

Kane's stare locked on his cousin, then his eyes became unfocused, in that talking-to-the-Pack way.

Theo barked a laugh and offered a salute. "Copy that."

I eyed my Alpha.

"*I told him not to leave them alone*," he rumbled across our bond.

Ducking my head, I hid my smirk, because sage knew high emotion and hormones were a recipe for the teenage kind of trouble.

Hannah swallowed hard. "Thank you," she said, before my brother offered a thanks of his own and the two followed Theo as he led them away.

Cassandra's stare was fixed on my stepfather's corpse, lip lifting in distaste. "I suggest we burn him."

Blood pooled around Isaac's torso, his body pale and sagging. Yes. Burning him was good. Because the idea of burying him, of paying him that decency or having a place on this earth that still belonged to him, a place anyone could visit, made my stomach churn. "Let's do it."

The Dowager's hand flitted through the air as she gestured to several of her Clan. An instruction. They closed in on my stepfather.

But something nagged at the back of my mind. A thought hit and my eyes narrowed, then narrowed further.

"Iron fires," I murmured. "*Wait!*" Disentangling myself from Kane's hold, I scurried toward the body.

My Alpha followed close behind. "Bry?"

Crouching by Isaac's side, I cringed, then cringed again as I tugged his pocket open and reached in, my pulse thrashing in my ears. "Be here. Please, sage, be here!" My hand brushed something cold and metallic. I latched on and tore it free, a smile spreading wide as I stared down at my stepfather's phone. Turning it on, I scanned the contacts—the very limited ones. Me, Lucas, Amber, and another number. One I grinned at widely as I called out, "Bower!"

His chin lifted in question.

"Tell me if you recognize her voice." Putting the phone on speaker, I dialed.

There was a click when the call was accepted, then a voice. *Zahara's* voice. "It's about time you called."

Bower's brows lowered like he was deep in thought. Like he was sorting through his memory, trying to place who it was or like he was having trouble accepting what he was hearing.

I glared down at the screen like it was the woman herself. "Guess I'm not who you're expecting to hear from."

A pause. "Briar Stone," she said, her tone rising as if hearing from me amused her. "Is that you?"

My lips lifted in a snarl. "You've got a good memory."

"You are a memorable woman."

Of that, I was sure. "Kinda looks like you won't be getting that supply you were promised."

A slow inhale, followed by a shuffling sound. "And why would that be?"

My voice was as dark as the night as I answered, "Because Isaac's dead."

A huffed laugh, one full of poison and shadowed promises. "Well then, thank you for letting me know. I suppose I'll just have to make do."

The Ambassador's expression darkened, then darkened more. He tore his device from his coat, thumbs tracking wildly across the screen, the energy pulsing off him bordering on violence.

My fingers curled, nails digging into my palms. "What are you doing, Zahara?"

"What do you mean?"

"The riots, the attacks on your own kind. We know it's you."

"*We?*" she repeated. "And what if it is?"

The lack of a denial, or any sense of her giving a shit, set my teeth on edge. Steeling myself, I demanded, "What the hells are you up to?"

Her voice lowered. Her next words were quiet, but still hard. "Have no fear, Briar. I'm sure you'll find out soon enough."

The line disconnected.

Bower clicked something, then stormed closer, turning his phone to face me. "She look familiar?"

On the screen was an image of a woman. Her hair was different, a deep brown that fell below her shoulders instead of the gray pixie wig she'd worn when I'd met her, but the up-ticked chin and the "I'm fucking untouchable" expression she wore were exactly the same.

Bingo!

An eager thrill chased through my heart and my pulse kicked into overdrive, because we had Zahara. We finally had Zahara. "That's her."

Joaquin's expression hardened. "Good job, banshee."

The Ambassador dragged a hand through his hair and cursed. "I need to go," he said, then, more to himself, "Call Waylon. Get his team ready."

I frowned. "Who's Waylon?"

"One of my men." He lifted his chin. "He's trusted."

Something in my stomach dropped, because what with his strained expression and that reaction … I rose, squaring myself to him. "Who is Zahara, Bower?"

He cursed again, then backpedaled like he was in the bad kind of hurry. His breaths were short and shallow, his answer level as if he was working hard to control himself, and the sound of it made my blood run cold.

"She's a problem."

Adrenaline spiking, I advanced a step and pushed, "What *kind* of problem?"

My breaths, my heart, the entire goddamn world stopped when he answered.

"The former General of the Ithican army kinda problem."

Chapter Twenty-Five

"The *General*, Kane," I said, as I paced back and forth in the living room late the next afternoon. "You know, the one Ithica fired 'cause she wanted to *lob bombs at us over the Phantom*." I raked a hand through my hair. "And now she's sowing discord. Trying to turn the humans against us." Trying to push her agenda, to compel her government to act. Again.

The night before had been everything I'd wanted, but it'd also been well past exhausting … and long. With everything done, my Alpha and I had headed home, then collapsed into bed, staying there until deep into the afternoon. And when I'd finally awoken, my thoughts had jumped to the next problem in our seemingly never-ending line. Bower's words. Zahara.

Lucas was still with Hannah, which meant the house was the deathly kinda quiet, so my words echoed off the walls and around my skull.

My Alpha stood, his shoulder propped against the doorframe, his hooded silvered stare on me. He inclined his head. "They know who she is, Bry. They know what she's doing. Bower's on it. They'll find her and end this."

I stopped, my stare fixed on the floor as my body sagged and I exhaled a heavy breath. He was right. It didn't ease the nagging sense in the back of my mind, but I'd lived with that so long, I wasn't sure it *could* shut off.

Kane kicked off the doorframe and stalked closer, looming over me. His eyes tracked between mine. Calm. So unendingly calm, and always giving exactly what I needed. Him. Always him. With the back of his hand, he stroked slow, soothing lines up and down my lower abdomen.

I bit my lip, my core igniting as my blood pumped through my veins, hot and desperate. Needy, for him.

He arched a hungry brow, but there was something warm there. Deeper. Some thought or idea I couldn't read. Clearing his throat, he took a half-step back. "I don't wanna wait, Bry."

My eyes narrowed, flicked to my abdomen, then back to him. "Pretty sure I can't make the kid any faster, Big Bad."

He huffed a laugh. Rolling his shoulders, he squared himself to me. "I don't wanna wait to get married."

I stared at him through my lashes, grin taunting him as I trailed the tip of my finger down his cheek. "Starting to sound a bit desperate, don't ya think?"

His stare flashed, a smirk deep in his eyes as he lifted his chin. "I'm serious. We put everything on hold because of all the shit with Isaac, but I don't wanna put stuff off anymore. I want you. I want us. Let's just do this." He took my hand. "We can keep it small. Whatever you want. But we move forward, Bry. We live."

My gaze locked with his and, sage, the weight there. He meant it. And no doubt, just like everything he'd done for the baby, he knew I needed it too. Knew I needed something more, something big and bright to look forward to. But still …

"What about Zahara? And everything else—"

"Bower's got it," he repeated. His head dipped. "Whatever you want, whatever you need, tell me. I'll get it done." A vow.

I blinked in rapid succession. Iron fires, I wanted it. But a thousand painfully logical items from a wedding-shaped checklist scrolled across my mind—each and every one of them unticked. "My dress isn't ready, Kane. We don't have the flowers or *anything*. We don't even have *rings*, for sage's sake."

"If you wanna wait for that stuff, we can. But you're all I need." His rough thumb stroked my wrist. "Show me a picture;

I'll grab the rings. Wear whatever you want. Wear a goddamn garbage bag. I don't care. Let's just do this."

My happy tears resurfaced, blurring my vision.

"I've got a venue," he said. "Everything else'll be handled for tomorrow. Just say yes."

The sight of him like that in his low-slung jeans and slate T-shirt, all broad-shouldered and hungry for me in every way—sage, he'd never looked sexier.

Wait … "*Tomorrow*?"

An eager grin took him as he agreed, "Tomorrow."

"I don't know, Kane." I stared down at where he held me. "The timing is just …"

My phone buzzed on the coffee table to my right: an incoming video call. Lisa's name tracked across the screen.

Kane followed my line of sight. "Answer it."

I shook my head. "I'll call her back."

Leaning to the side, he picked up the phone, then held it my way. "Just answer it."

I'd figured our conversation was a *tad* more important, but okay. Frowning at him, I clicked to accept the call. "Hey, you!"

"Hey yourself," she replied, the bustle of traffic and chants from a cacophony of nearby voices loud in the background.

Cocking my head, I settled an elbow on the arm of the couch. "Where the heck are you?"

"City center." Then, for clarity, "Mine, not yours." She angled her phone to show a tall, white-stone building with several rows of thirty-foot-tall pillars and a grand, golden entrance, the sign above reading "*Ithican Parliamentary Hall*". In front loomed a horde of people, fists raised and voices loud.

Swinging the device back, her face filled the screen. "Bower called me in to talk." She moved her eyes tight to the camera. "*Tell* me it's true. Tell me you killed the bastard!"

I grinned down at her. "Lucas took that honor."

Her eyes grew bloodshot, and she sniffed. Pulling back to a respectable face-to-screen distance, her voice sounded desperate as she said, "You promise he's dead?"

"Yeah. I promise, Lis. Isaac's dead." The permanent, rot-in-the-Iron-Hells, make-my-withered-soul-happy, reaping-his-karma kind of dead.

She closed her eyes, tipped her head to the sky and exhaled a freeing breath. "Thank the wraith."

Literally!

Dropping to the couch, I sighed, feeling so damn grateful. My tension ebbed, slowly releasing from my body as my gaze drifted to my Alpha, his words from just moments before flitting across my mind.

Lisa's brow dipped low. "What's up, chickie?"

I pulled back my head. "Who says anything's up?"

Kane huffed a laugh.

Flicking a finger in my general direction, Lis said, "Your face. Always your face."

I offered her my bestest glower.

Waving me off, she pushed. "Seriously. What's up?"

Kane chucked his chin my way. "Tell her, Bry. See what she thinks."

Gasp! My head whipped in his direction, mouth dropping open. That sneaky little mutt!

"That's why you told me to answer!" I said, fighting my smile as a laugh bubbled up in my chest.

"Wait ..." Lisa balked. "Were you *not* going to answer?"

Pulling on my inner Joaquin, I stared at the ceiling for patience. "I was gonna call you back."

"Rude. Just rude." She set a palm to her chest. "Either way, whatever it is, I already know I'm gonna side with your wolf."

My expression contorted. "I haven't even said anything yet."

Lis looked both ways, then started walking fast, cutting through an intersection. "Yes, but you're usually wrong."

My Alpha barked a laugh.

"Such a traitor." Rolling my eyes, I heaved an overly dramatic sigh. "He wants to get married tomorrow."

"You should do it, chickie."

Kane smirked, all victory and pride.

"I'm serious," Lis said. "The stuff we've been through was a lesson. Life's a damn mess. There are no guarantees any of us will even *see* tomorrow. Take the time you've got. Just do it."

I bit my lip, warmth spreading through my chest, because she and my Alpha were right. We'd lost enough time when Isaac was alive. I wasn't about to waste any more. "Think you can get here?"

She made a show of flipping her hair, all sassy-like. "Not even Bower or the border could keep me away."

My sigh was teasing. "Alright!"

Kane stalked my way, his head cocked, his brow arched high. "Is that a yes?"

I laughed. "It's a yes."

Bower … Should we invite—

Voices rang out at Lisa's end, chanting something too faint to hear.

"Sorry," she said, then covered an ear. "It's about to get loud."

A crowd flooded around her, pumping their signs as their chants rose high. "All fam-ilies, deserve the R-C," they called. "All fam-ilies, deserve the R-C!"

My stomach twisted. They moved past, chants slowly fading. "That what I think it is?"

"Yeah," she said, following them with her gaze. "The protests. They're never-ending now."

A *boom* echoed across the line, so loud that the speakers momentarily blared static and crackled. Lisa jolted as she fell to the side, slamming into a car. She grunted. Glass shattered.

Her phone fell. The blue sky above filled the screen, followed a second later by smoke.

"Lis!" I shot to my feet and gripped my own phone tighter, clinging to it as if I was clinging to her. "LIS!"

Kane loomed at my side, his hand taking my waist as he steadied me.

Screams sounded. Sage, so many screams.

A dirt-covered hand descended on her phone, taking it up. It rocked and rolled as whoever it was clambered to their feet. There was a shuffle. Lisa's face appeared.

"I'm alright," she said, with a groan, peering over her shoulder as she dusted herself off and resumed walking.

"Iron fires. Don't scare me like that!" I forced my heart to start beating again. "What the hells happened?"

She pointed the camera toward the protestors who stood around a blazing fire in the center of an intersection, throwing garbage, clothes, anything they could get their hands on into the flames. "Just some overzealous idiot with a Molotov cocktail."

I frowned. "That doesn't sound alright, Lis."

Rounding a corner, she abandoned the chaos, then plucked something that looked suspiciously like glass from her hair as she grumbled, "Next time, Bower's carting his ass to me."

My body sagged. Safe. She was safe.

"So." Setting her back against a brick façade, she drew herself up and shook herself off. Her shoulders hiked as she inhaled deep, and her eyes locked with mine through the screen. "What d'you need me to do?"

My mouth dropped. "Your ass was nearly just blasted to—"

"But it wasn't." She gave a half-shrug. "This is the unfortunate norm here now." Her expression softened, and so did her voice. "Look, chickie, one life. That's what you get. With the shitstorm we live in, the timing's never gonna be right. So just do it. Grab that happiness by the wolfy balls and never let go."

My Alpha looked torn on agreeing with that last bit, and I swore his hand moved to shield his crotch.

"Fine." I tapped the screen with a nail. "Pack a bag and cart your sweet behind to Cambria."

"I will," she promised, then inclined her head. "I'll see you tonight!"

Ending the call, I eyed my Alpha. We might not be able to stop all the rhetoric, but we needed to do something. Approach the Conclave about the RC, make things right, and take that rhetoric—that power to manipulate those Ithican masses—from Zahara's hands. We needed to find a way to make this stop.

***

Three hours later, I stood in our foyer, overnight bag in hand, a sullen wolf with his arms crossed looming before me.

I smiled up at him. "This was your idea, Big Bad."

I'd called Cassandra, filling her in on the updated timeline—which, of course, devolved into me going full traditional mode by not seeing my groom the night before. My Alpha had been sulking ever since, and the sight of it tickled my mated soul.

Kane rolled his shoulders. "If I'd known it'd pan out like this, I'd have had a different plan."

Pushing up on my toes, I pressed my lips to his. Those thick-knuckled hands consumed my waist. Heat pulsed in my chest, spreading lower. Lower. My thighs clenched.

His eyes sparked voltaic. "Keep looking at me like that and you ain't leaving, 'cause I'll tie your ass to the bed."

A soft laugh tumbled free and I nipped his bottom lip. "You wouldn't dare."

An arch of that cocky brow. One of those hands latched over my ass. "Wouldn't I?"

Yes. Yes, he would. That wolf would start a war, raze Cambria and Ithica and the entire damn world for me. To give me what I needed—which absolutely included a good, deep fucking.

My sigh was wistful. I hadn't even left, and I was already pining for him. "I'll miss you too, Kane."

He huffed a laugh that rumbled along my flesh, then tucked several errant strands of hair back from my face. My cheeks warmed and I leaned into his touch. The smirk that took him was nothing short of wolfish. And very, very tactical.

My tongue flicked out, tasting his palm. "I know what you're doing."

His eyes hungered and that smirk deepened. "And what's that?"

"You're trying to trick me into staying." I jabbed his dense chest with a finger. "You're trying to cheat the system."

"No, Bry." His grip latched firmly around my wrist. "I'm working the system."

Working the system, the same as he'd worked it to fight and claw his way through Ronin's order. The same as he'd worked it to get that Binding Vow from Sierra. The same Binding Vow he'd used to bring in Whitney and read me, working Isaac's system to get to me. Every decision, every move he made, revolved around me. I was his world, and he was the moon, circling me.

I bit my lip. "You're working it to your advantage."

"When it comes to you"—his thumb tracked an easy line over my heart tattoo—"always."

There was that heat again. I inhaled an easy breath, because he was all I needed. "You fight dirty."

He jerked me to his chest, his hard cock pressing into my abdomen. "I play dirty, too."

Sweet sage, what he did to me. My gaze flicked to my watch. We *did* have time … Grinning, I threw my arms around his neck, mouth crashing with his.

He grunted, those silver topaz eyes going electric and wild. My movements were sharp, frantic. Greedy. I needed him. Couldn't wait. His hands latched around my hips, his grip hard against the flesh of my ass. He dragged me flush to his body and, as he was wont to do, tried to take control. The languid lines he trailed with his tongue told me he intended to take his time, but I had a thirst to be slaked, and I was on the clock.

Drawing on his power, I shoved him.

He stumbled several lumbering steps, the backs of his legs catching on the couch before he dropped onto it. His brow dipped low as his eyes hooded, and a deep thunder rolled from the depths of his chest.

Taking the hem of my dress, I pulled it over my legs and waist, then freed it from my body, exposing the electric-pink bra and panty set I wore. Tossing the dress to the ground, I told him, "You're going to do what I tell you."

His stare tracked down, lingering on my breasts, then the V of my thighs. His hands clenched into fists as he rolled his shoulders, good and slow. Like it took every ounce of his preternatural control to hold himself back. His cock strained against his jeans as he stretched his neck.

He leaned forward, those calloused hands grazing my knees. Faster than I could blink, he took me airborne before he flipped me onto my back and laid me along the couch.

His gaze turned molten as he closed in, headed south. When he reached my thong, he tucked his thumbs under the sides, then jerked it down, baring me to him. Ducking, he gripped one ankle, hooking the leg over his shoulder, then did the same with the other.

Wraith take me, but the sight of him like that …

I plunged my hands into his hair. He latched onto my thighs, then jerked me closer. His head dipped, and he kissed my stomach, tongue flicking out as he worked his way down. Down. Down. Those eyes held mine as he took a knee.

"You're mine, Bry. After tomorrow, there's no getting rid of me." His tongue trailed along my clit.

I hissed, spine arching off the couch, my heels pressing into his back, encouraging. He gripped my ass, fingers digging deep into that sensitive flesh.

Moaning, I rocked my hips, grinding against him while a riot of pleasure seared through me. My breathing grew heavy. I moaned louder. My body tensed. His tongue worked faster, and one thick finger slid inside, joined a second later by another before he hooked them forward.

"Oh, sage."

"Come for me," he ordered. "Scream my fucking name, Bry."

Power of obsidian, just the words were enough, and they sent me plummeting over that edge. I screamed, then screamed again, screaming his name so loud the whole fucking world would know it.

His head lifted, and the grin he offered was brash and cocky as cocky got.

My fingers curled tighter into his hair as I led him up my body. I nudged his chest. "Sit. Now."

His eyes blazed. With that easy confidence, he shifted back and took his position, leaning into the couch like a king on his throne. His legs splayed wide and loose. He set an arm over the back of the couch, then waited.

Iron fires, what that wolf did to me.

One delicate move at a time, I crawled toward him and climbed into his lap. I straddled him, the draw of his zipper the only sound before I gripped his thick and ready shaft, then freed it.

He sucked a sharp breath through his teeth as he cursed and his head fell back.

Lining him up against my slit, I lowered myself down until he was fully inside me. Then I ordered, "Now, fuck me like you mean it, Kane."

He groaned, one hand skimming from my waist to my breast while the other dragged my bra strap down. Arching, I gave him access, and he took my peaked nipple between his teeth and teased it with his tongue.

His hold locking over my ribs, he slammed into me from below, filling me to completion.

My breaths came in short, shallow pants, and I held on for dear goddamn life. He rocked me against him, working my clit, and hitting my g-spot just right. He filled every corner of me, grazing every wanton nerve. I loved it. Needed it. Never wanted it to stop.

His hips thrust up again and again, pumping into me as he gave me every spectacular inch.

I ground against him, taking him deeper and deeper. His arm bracketed my waist while the other hooked up my spine, his hand locking over the base of my neck as he pistoned into me. His chest heaved and his jaw clenched. The muscles along his neck and shoulders tensed.

My sensitized nerves meant my pleasure from before climbed back high and fast. His teeth latched over my nipple again, sinking in. That bite of pain sent a shot of heat straight to my core. My second orgasm hit hard, and I cried out.

He lapped at my breast before he released it, then snarled, driving into me once. Twice. He came with a growl, flooding me with his seed until his movements slowed. I collapsed against him, body completely spent.

My Alpha rose, his movements lithe as he took me with him and aimed up the stairs for our room.

My face nuzzled into the crook of his neck. "Where do you think you're going?"

He grumbled under his breath, then said, "I'm keeping you."

"You're keeping me for the rest of our unnaturally long lives. But I'm promised to a Dowager tonight. Now put my naked ass down."

He grunted, one foot lifting as he hesitated on the bottom step.

"*Kane*," I said through a laugh.

Giving a rasped growl, he settled me to the floor, then folded his arms over his chest. Gathering my clothes, I redressed and finished packing as I fought not to snicker, because I'd seen many versions of my Alpha before, but sullen had never been one of them. And it tickled my petty heart.

Ready, I took up my clanking keys, closed in, pressed up onto my toes and brushed my lips against his. "I'll see you at the altar."

His stare hardened as he peered down at me. "You'd better."

I gave him a gentle kiss, then left, lingering at the door. "I'll be the one in something white."

His chin dipped in a nod as he smiled, the kind of smile that reached his eyes and transformed his face. He repeated, "You'd better."

My hand twisted over the handle, 'cause the wolf knew what he was doing, and if I didn't leave then, I never would.

"I love you, Bry."

"Love you too." Closing the door behind me, I aimed for the truck. And with each step I took, that nagging sense surrounding Zahara crept back in—but what it was trying to warn me against, I had no clue.

Chapter Twenty-Six

"So," I said, a glass of some potion-infused alcohol in hand as I sat in the parlor of Cassandra's home. It was one of sage knew how many rooms, because her penthouse was massive. "A human, a shadow walker, and a magi walk into a bar."

Lisa snorted and pulled her mascara brush from her lashes, lest she ruin them.

Cassandra sat, spine bone straight as she effortlessly worked an intricate braid through her hair, winding it around her crown. "I do not understand."

"It's a joke," I said through a smirk, as I took in my flawless makeup in the mirror—makeup the vamp queen herself had done. My eyes were blended in layering shades of browns with a smoky effect that straddled the line between stunning and sexy. My cheeks were a soft coral, contours on fucking point, while my lips were full in that "naturally unnatural" kinda way.

Her brow furrowed, considering. "It is not a joke I understand."

"That's 'cause I haven't finished it yet."

"I see. So, it should get better?"

The cackle that broke from Lisa reverberated through the fifteen-foot-high room. The place was lavish: textured ivory walls, gold fixtures, sconces and candelabras, glass tables, antique furniture, and hardwood floors. It was delicate and sturdy, warm and cold in equal measure. And it was very much Cassandra.

I mock-gasped and set a palm to my chest. "Cassandra Ryton, are you sassing me?"

Her lip arced high, exposing the bitiest of incisors. "I would not dream of it, Briar Stone."

Ha!

I'd forwarded Kane my list of wants shortly after I'd left his sullen behind the night before. And I'd done a mediocre-at-best job of keeping my thoughts away from the topic of Zahara, because something kept pushing at the back of my mind, twisting my stomach tighter and tighter. Leaning to the side, I worried at my lip and glanced down at my phone.

Lisa's scowl found me in the mirror. "What are you doing, chickie?"

"Nothing," I said quickly, my voice too high.

Her scowl deepened.

I rolled my eyes. "*Fine.* I just wanna know if Bower got Zahara yet." Or if he had any leads. Or something.

She inclined her head. "I get it. With the protests and the rest of the mess she's stirred up, so do I. But—"

"It's been a day already, Lis. Shouldn't we have heard something?"

"This is a PR nightmare for them. They're probably just figuring that out. If there was something we needed to know, Bower would tell us. Ithica's on it. You did your part. Now let them do theirs." The "and enjoy your damn wedding" was silent.

With that, she checked her own phone.

"Human hypocrite!" I scoffed.

She pointed the device at me like a weapon. "You're waiting for the doomsday clock. I'm waiting for Rosa."

I rolled my eyes harder.

Reaching into her purse, she shook her head and pulled something out. "I still can't believe Isaac's dead. That this mess is almost over."

Not over. Not yet. Not until Zahara's ass was officially handled—which was something I'd be able to check on if someone would just let me *check my phone*!

My gaze flicked to Cassandra, whose silence was notable before she glided from the room.

Lisa closed in, a small box in her hand. Wriggling onto the chaise beside me, she passed it over. "That's for you."

"I gathered as much when you handed it to me," I deadpanned.

Her sigh was taunting. "Why your wolf hitched his wagon to you ..."

Grinning, I flipped my hair. "Because I'm a delight."

She laughed and nudged the box again. "Open it."

Tearing the foil wrapper, I lifted the lid. Inside, a necklace sat nestled in blue velvet. It had a crescent-shaped stone that was white with soft blue and aqua undertones, similar to an opal, but deeper somehow. I trailed a finger along its outer edge. "It's beautiful, Lis."

"I know. That's why I picked it." Her smile softened and she gestured to it. "It's a moonstone," she said, then lifted the matching one from the chain on her neck. "Two halves of a whole."

My throat tightened, tears pricking my eyes.

Her own eyes grew red. "You're not allowed to cry right now. Fix your face."

I snort-sobbed, then fanned myself to keep my makeup in check.

Cassandra approached, her arm held high, a dress hanging from her grasp. No, not just any dress.

My dress.

And it was absolutely, flawlessly beautiful—even more so than I remembered. The sweetheart neckline, the corset back, the flared, layered, and lace skirts whose beads and pearls caught the light. It was perfection.

My tears climbed higher, and my breath hitched. "Cassandra"—my gaze lifted to hers—"how did you . . ."

"As time was short, I presumed the dress you tried on would suffice." She settled the gown over the champagne-colored chaise lounge to her left. "My shadow walker has ensured it was cleaned and tailored to your precise measurements."

My heart clenched as I scurried closer, then threw my arms around her. She crashed against me, cool hands settling over my sides before I drew back, then happy-clapped as I bounced in place. "Help me in! Help me in! Help me in!"

My Dowager smiled.

Lis and Cassandra tugged the heavy dress up, then cinched it around me. It fit like a dream, molding to my curves before falling to the floor in a cascade of wildly expensive layers. My hair fell, half pulled back, several wavy wisps shaping my face while the rest tumbled in loose curls down my shoulders.

Flowers had been delivered earlier that afternoon, courtesy of my wolf. They were a mix of white hydrangeas, viburnum, and roses. Beautiful, and exactly the way I'd instructed. Their sweet, rich scents filled the room.

Lisa's phone buzzed and she peered at it. "Ah! Rosa's crossed the border. You really don't mind me meeting you there?"

I flicked a hand, dismissing her. "Go. Last thing the poor woman needs is an introduction to all of Cambria's preternaturals at once. *Alone*."

She laughed, then gave me a quick peck on the cheek. "You're the best."

I fluttered my lashes. "I really am."

At that, she scurried out, calling over her shoulder, "I'll see you there," before she vanished down the hall.

I approached the heavily tinted, floor-to-ceiling windows. Their coating was some kind of shield-like film. I stared into the Cambrian night, at the neutral grounds' skyline in the distance.

The Dowager followed my gaze. "It guards from the sun."

My head bobbed in a nod. "Do you miss it?" My finger trailed the soft length of her plum-colored velvet curtains. I clarified, "The sun?"

Her attention pushed through the window and beyond, a wistful longing deep in the creases of her expression. "Yes, Briar Stone. I do." The depth of unfathomable loss in that answer tugged at my heart. "It is not just the warmth or the light, but the life it brings. The rainbows that cross the sky, the flowers I will never see bloom, the seas I will never watch glow. I am happy with my decision, with the vengeance I reaped in my father's name, but the cost was high."

I offered a soft smile. "There are beauties in the night."

"There are." A mischievous glint sparked in those crimson eyes. "And the scent of fear is so much more potent."

I shook my head and snickered. "You're such a predator."

"Indeed. And I have had many years to perfect it."

Prodding my cheek with my tongue, I tapped my chin, because I'd wanted that answer for, like, ever. "So, real talk here, Cassandra. How many years are we talking?"

Her crimson gaze slid my way, and she rolled a thin wrist through the air. "I should like you to guess."

"Oh, now *that's* a trap if ever I heard one."

That high, tinkling laugh. "You will not offend."

My mouth twisted. Fine. If she wanted to play, I'd play—especially if it got me that number. I asked, "More or less than five hundred?"

The glint in her crimson eyes was eager. "More."

I swallowed hard. "More or less than seven hundred?"

Her head dipped like she was following her answer. "Less."

Sweet sage on a stick. "Six *hundred*?"

Her smile was wide. "Six hundred and twenty-three."

I stared, my brain stuttering as I tried to absorb that confession.

She smoothed a hand over the delicate braid running along her temple. "This surprises you?"

For a thousand reasons . . .

"Seeing as the world's been fed a different story about how long Cambrians have been around—kinda, yeah."

"Our numbers were fewer back then. It made our existence easier to hide. But some secrets are old, Briar Stone." She leaned in, her voice lowering to a conspirator's whisper, "And I am old along with them."

Good to know. "Well." I peered at her, a slow grin claiming my lips as I rapidly fluttered my lashes. "You haven't aged a day."

Her laugh echoed off the windows, carrying around the space again and again until it surrounded me.

She floated across the room toward an ornate, ivory-and-gold colored vintage dresser, then pulled open a drawer. Removing a small gift bag, she returned to my side. "This is for you."

I eyed her askance, then opened the bag and peeked inside, finding a handful of onesies in all manner of sizes. My heart melted. Sage, they were so tiny. Slipping the first free, my gaze narrowed, head cocking at the words . . .

A bark of laughter burst from my lips, then another and another, until I was keeled over and howling.

One at a time, I held them up to better see. "I Shed", said the first; "Awooo!" was emblazoned on the second. The little butt flap of the third read: "Full Moon Rising!" The fourth said, "De-Clawed", and on and on they went. The "Woof in Training" had ears that stuck up from the hood, little tufts of faux fur sticking from their ends. The last one in particular warmed my itty-bitty heart. "Little Bad".

I cackled, gathering them up as I hugged them to my chest, tears stinging my vision. Iron fires, would I ever stop crying? "I *love* them, Cassandra!"

She dipped her head in pleasure. "I am glad, Briar Stone."

At the thought of my Alpha's face when he saw them, I excitedly wiggled my ass and hugged those little onesies tighter.

Cassandra's body might never experience a child of its own, but that didn't mean that love, that *family*, was out of reach. My eyes stung, my vision blurring. "I can't give you what you've lost," I said, as a tear slithered warm and slow down my cheek. "But I can ask you to share in this."

She stilled.

Something in me clicked into place. Something warm and right. Taking her hand, I settled it over my lower abdomen. "Be the godmother."

A small sound, something akin to a gasp, escaped her. The stiffness in her spine loosened.

Time had hardened her body, stripped away its humanity. But her heart—*that* was human. She was just a woman who cared so deeply, she masked the emotions to survive. To survive Cambria. To survive the political bullshit of the Conclave. To survive herself.

But giving her this gave us both something we desperately needed. Someone who would love my babe. Someone who, through the test of time and our little pup's extended life, would always be there.

Her fingers pressed delicately into my abdomen as if she sought that tiny heartbeat. There was a tension there, though. As if she feared to hope. "What about your human?"

I inclined my head. "I love Lis, and she'll get a title." 'Cause, human or not, she'd end me otherwise. "But she's Ithican. Wraith forbid, but if anything happens to Kane and me, she couldn't keep our child on either side of the border. So, this . . ." I settled my palm over Cassandra's. "This is about more."

An image flashed across my mind, of the night Victor'd died, the first night we'd faced Isaac. When the whites of Cassandra's eyes and the hollows beneath had blackened while lines from shadowed veins tracked over her forehead, through her temples, across her cheeks and jaw. The thought of it still had the hairs on the back of my neck rising. That was the Cassandra Cambria revered—the wild, ravenous carnivore, starved and hunting for her next meal. A hunger she reserved for anyone who crossed her. And anyone who crossed me.

Cassandra's lips parted. "You would have me keep the babe in your stead," she murmured, all trace of the cold predator stripped away. In its place was a woman, warm and wanting. But there was a silent question there, because she was a shadow walker, and our cub was decidedly not.

"Yes. I would have you keep them and protect them against the beasts of this world. They'll always have Pack, but if or when that day comes, they'll need family. Someone who'll outlive us to be there. Someone who'll love them so deeply and powerfully"—I set my forehead to hers—"that they'd raze this fucking world to protect them."

Other than my Alpha and Joaquin, there wasn't anyone in the whole of Cambria I'd feel safer with at my back, or my child's.

Cassandra's chest hitched.

My smile was warm and so full of "I fucking love you" it almost hurt. "You've been a far better friend than I deserve. But that's not all you are. I want a tether. Something that binds you to us and us to you for the rest of eternity. And I want that to be my child."

Cassandra's graceful hand trembled as it drifted, carrying our clasped hands to her heart. Her hold tightened as that predator stalked back in. Her eyes darkened, her chin lifting. "By the night, through the night, and for the night, I take it as my honor, Briar Stone. I will protect this child."

My expression softened. "And love them."

Her gaze turned red, blood tears brimming in the whites of her eyes until a sea of crimson stared back at me. The tears slipped free, followed by a smile so broad, it transformed her face. "And I will love them."

Chapter Twenty-Seven

The drive to Immortal Inc—my Alpha's secured venue—was long. We'd been apart for less than a day, but I already missed him. A lot. It was like a piece of me was absent. I itched to see him again. Couldn't wait to get there.

City lights ticked by as Cassandra's limo wound us through the neutral grounds. The reds and purples and burnt oranges of foliage sat lit by the lampposts. Fallen leaves skittered across the road, lined the sidewalks and the tops of parked cars. The hint of woodsmoke drifted from outside, mixing with my soft vanilla scent. Rich and homey.

The Dowager's crimson stare hunted the night. Vigilant.

As we rounded a corner, my eyes locked on what lay ahead, then widened. Wolves in crisp, black, full-length wool coats lined the road leading to the shop. Kane's wolves. Joaquin's. They formed a veritable tunnel of death, further punctuated by Cassandra's shadow walkers, who flanked them. It was a beautiful show of allegiance, and a coastline of powerful violence. Necessary, considering the guest list.

It should've settled me, eased some of that Zahara-based worry. Instead, something twinged at the back of my throat. A hand pressing in, its invisible fingers slowly sealing over my airway, making it harder and harder to breathe.

We rolled to a stop and Lisa was there, a distinct clunk sounding as she opened the door wide.

Cassandra's attention snapped to me. "Are you well, Briar Stone?"

My brows knitted together. "I don't know, I just . . ."

"You getting cold feet, chickie?" Lisa's head poked inside. "'Cause we can cut and run if you need."

A feeble smile tugged my lips at the mental image of Lisa throwing elbows with the preternatural army surrounding us. But if I said I wanted to run, it wasn't outside the realm of possibility.

I shook my head, because if I was sure of anything in this world, it was my Alpha. But that feeling … "I can't place it. There's just … something."

"I feel it too, Briar Stone." Cassandra said, crimson stare once again fixed out the window.

That shouldn't have made things better, but for some messed-up reason, it did. Because it meant I felt less alone.

Lisa edged aside as the Dowager stepped out, and my brother moved in. My heart clenched at the sight of him and the navy suit fitted to that tall frame. His hair was freshly cut, the longer top strands brushed back, his white dress shirt putting his tattoo on display and making the violet of his eyes pop in contrast.

Tears stung the backs of my eyes, because it wasn't a boy before me. Not anymore. This was a man. Grown and experienced and so damn ready, it made my chest ache.

He offered me a hand.

Adjusting my dress, I placed my palm in his and slipped free, cool air kissing my exposed flesh as my gaze lifted to the building. My eyes widened.

White. The place was top-to-bottom white. Hydrangeas, roses, and every flower in between. It was teeming. Alive. Just the way we liked it.

Lucas took me in, his smile brotherly and warm. Clearing his throat, he pitched his voice low, speaking only for me when he said, "Mom was proud, Briar. Of you"—he tipped his head toward the shop—"and Kane. Of everything. I know she can't be here, but I'm gonna do my best to stand in her place."

My fingers cinched over his wrist, holding tight, because those words struck the chords of my feeble soul.

Two roses sat pinned to his lapel. He followed my line of sight to them. "One for her. One for your father."

I breathed deep, and happy, because it was a piece of them. They were there.

Cassandra glided into place before me, and I pivoted to face forward. To say past-Briar would've been confused at having the Dowager of the Northern shadow-walker Clan as a bridesmaid would've been an understatement. It was definitely an unexpected turn of events, but counting her as a friend was one of the true privileges of my existence.

Lisa handed out the bouquets, then smoothed my dress's front. "We all set?"

I straightened my back, my fingers circling the stems of the flowers as I answered, "I'm set."

She offered me a salacious wink and scurried around in front of the Dowager.

Cassian stood outside the entrance, hands linked before him as he scanned the crowd. When his stare met mine, he inclined his head and offered a smile as he threw the door open.

Soft music carried. I stepped inside.

Leaved vines lined the walls, climbing across the ceiling before meeting in a braided thread at the peak. Briar roses filled every branch, their sweet apple-like scent grazing my senses. The floor was covered in a sheet of soft green moss, while bark-lined logs cut into benches formed the guest seating.

Candles edged the perimeter and lit the aisle, casting a soft, warm, and flickering glow over everything and everyone. How the hells my Alpha had pulled this off, I'd never know. How many people he'd needed, who he'd paid off, and how much money it would've taken …

Shuffling sounded as faces turned my way. Alistair, Hannah, Whitney, Ezra, Marisol, Rosa, a handful of my Alpha's Pack. My eyes scanned the place for Bower, but if he was there, I didn't see him.

Kane towered at the head of the room, back to me, his broad form filling his suit. Joaquin and Theo stood to his right, looking sharp. The Southern Alpha clapped a hand over Kane's shoulder and spoke low in his ear.

Slowly, my Alpha turned. Those silver topaz eyes met mine. His chest hitched, his stare turned glassy and bloodshot.

The way that wolf loved me …

He was a striking mix of beast, brawn, and power in head-to-toe black. And he was the sexiest thing I'd ever seen.

Lucas and I advanced, one step. Two. Three. My heels clicked, each slow step thumping in time with the beat of my pulse.

My gaze held on my Alpha. Him. All I needed was him. Kane Slade was the calm in my storm. But when he needed to be, he *was* that fucking storm.

He watched me, chest expanding as his stare turned hungry. But it was different somehow. That need was still there, but this … this was deeper. Because he wanted me—*all* of me.

The staccato beat of my heart slowed. Evened. Grew steady. And so damn eager.

Lisa and Cassandra took their places.

Lucas's elbow flexed against mine as he leaned closer. "No one will love you like him." My smile was soft as he kissed my cheek.

Kane stepped forward.

"Take care of her," my brother said, and whether it was a threat or a request, I couldn't say.

Kane took my hand and inclined his head. "I will." A vow.

Lucas stepped aside.

My Alpha's stare held. And held. And *held*. "You're perfect," he said, his voice thick as he moved us into position.

My skin heated, a sudden and bizarre shyness overtaking me. My gaze dipped.

His thick knuckle hooked under my chin. "Eyes on me, Bry."

Him. Only him.

He straightened, power rolling off him in waves.

I was already irrevocably connected to him, to his wolf. But marriage, that was a symbolic custom. One that bound us in every other way. And I wanted that for me, for our child. To take his name, to become a family. For it to be official and binding. To tether us together in this world and the next.

The Justice of the Peace, some wolf I'd never met, began, talking about the importance of marriage, but I was lost in Kane. In the depths of that stare. The warmth of his hands. The brush of his power when he reached for me across our bond, and I fought the purr itching to break free.

"*Easy, Bry,*" he silently rumbled.

I bit my lip, a blush burning my cheeks.

The J. P. turned to those gathered. "The couple have requested to speak their own vows."

Kane rolled his shoulders, squaring himself to me. Open. Ready. Giving me everything he damn well had.

"Bry, you're the only thing I've ever wanted. You're the only thing I see. The reason I breathe." His fist closed and lightly thumped his chest. "The reason my heart beats.

"I'm not a selfless man. I'm possessive and hungry and desperate for you. I want everything you've got. Your body, your mind, your heart, and your soul. You're the only thing I need. You've always been it for me. And in this life or the next, you always will be, because my world begins, and my world ends, with *you*." Taking my finger, he slid into place the impossibly stunning platinum band I'd wanted, the series of delicate diamonds that lined its circumference dancing as they caught the candlelight. And the weight of it there, it felt right. Just like him.

My eyes misted, breath catching in my chest. I swallowed hard.

Lisa handed me Kane's ring, a black titanium one with clean lines woven across its outer circumference.

"I was made for loving you, Kane. You. Only you. Everything I have and everything I am is yours. *I* am yours. Forever. Always." A soft smile claimed my lips, and his grip locked tight around my hands. "I've loved you through every second, every breath, and every beat of my heart since the moment we met. You've saved me in every way. Pulled me from the dark and into your light. You're the safety I seek. The warmth I crave. *You* are my home. And in this life, we will either find our way, or we will make one." My gaze caught on something—a word etched on the inner band of his ring.

Hers.

My heart thrummed wildly, eyes blurring as I slid it into place.

Arms banding my waist, Kane jerked me to his chest, his lips crashing with mine. His tongue invaded my mouth, and I yielded to him. Everything. He could take and take, and that well would never run dry because my love for him was endless.

A chorus of whoops and clapping filled the night, interjected by cheers and the piercing ring of a whistle.

My Alpha drew back, a wicked grin taking over his expression as he leaned forward, hooked his arms under my ass and lifted. "No escaping me now."

My cackle was half humor, half taunt. "'Cause that was an option before?"

His grip cinched tighter, his eyes flashing, the arc of his brow a warning and a challenge. "You could try." His grin was all starved beast with an edge of need as he trailed a finger down my satiny waist. "I love this dress." Then, across our bond, he added, "*But I'm gonna love tearing it off you later even more.*"

My arms looped lazily around his neck and I teased, "*What are you waiting for?*"

His brow ticked higher. Settling me to my feet, he reached for the material at my back.

Shadow and sage!

"*That was a joke, Kane Slade.*" I jabbed his pec. "*If you rip one thread on this thing, I will* neuter *you!*"

He barked a laugh, hands lowering to a respectable, guest-appropriate level on my hips.

The place was cleared, with tables set around the perimeter, and a small open space for a dancefloor at the center. Food was served, music started, and the party began.

Lisa and I danced, dragging Rosa with us. Cassandra joined, clapping her hands off-beat as if she had no concept of rhythm while she shuffled robotically from side to side.

Before long, a slow song started, and my Alpha—my *husband*—interrupted us for his turn. His broad palm settled over the small of my back as he pulled me to him, his chest like stone against the soft lines of my front. He started moving, leading as he swayed us to the easy melody.

"This is it, Bry. You and me."

I nuzzled my nose into the hollow of his throat. My sigh was calm and content and just … happy. Yeah, we were still waiting on the Zahara news, but this moment was ours. Surrounded by everyone we loved, and a handful we were forced to tolerate.

His calloused touch grazed the bare skin of my arm before it climbed to the cap of my shoulder, over my collarbone and along my throat to encompass my jaw. He angled my face to his.

Gooseflesh crawled up my spine, prickling over my scalp.

"Mine," I whispered.

Those eyes flared and flashed, the liquid heat burning there almost searing me to the spot. His deep voice rolled over me—through me—as he growled, "*Yours*."

My core tightened as I trailed my tongue along the backs of my teeth. "Does Big Bad like to be owned?"

"By you." His grip bracketed my waist, pinning me in place as he leaned forward, mouth ghosting over mine. "Damn right. And my *wife* is gonna own my cock when I fill her with it tonight."

I stumbled, knees going weak, because sage take me. I clung to him, pressing closer. So close. I couldn't get close enough.

Around us, heads turned, and throats cleared. And in that moment, I thanked the wraith and the damn Iron Hells themselves that my brother's ears weren't preternaturally potent.

Pressing up on my tiptoes, I nipped at Kane's lip.

Theo shook his head, set a hand over my brother's eyes and mouthed, "*There are children here!*"

Lucas swatted him away, then reached for Hannah and led her to the dancefloor. Theo extended an arm Whitney's way. Her smile was shy as she took it. In true Theo fashion, he twirled her, then tugged her close, tucking her into his chest as he moved.

"I can't believe you pulled this off, Kane." I nuzzled into him. "Thank you."

"I'd raze this world for you, woman."

And he would—then he'd raze it again for good measure.

I settled my head against him as the song changed, tempo kicking up, but we stayed where we were. Moving to the beat of his heart. Slow. Easy.

Something buzzed. Loud. Obnoxious. A phone. I frowned, 'cause just rude!

It buzzed again.

Lis held up my purse and mouthed, "*It's yours.*" Her eyes widened. "*Bower.*"

I stilled, that earlier anxiety slithering back in like a snake, coiling around my chest and throat.

Kane stopped us, and Lis closed in. Taking the device, I accepted the call.

"Bower?"

"Run!" he said, that lone word hard, serious, and goddamn terrified.

Kane fell preternaturally still.

Across the room, bodies stiffened. Heads snapped our way. Joaquin, Cassandra …

Lucas eyed the others, his stare sharpening as he pulled Hannah close.

A second buzz sounded from somewhere, followed by another an instant later. Lisa and Rosa peered down at their own phones. Humans. *Only* the humans. And the expressions on those human faces changed quickly from the pinched brows of confusion to stark understanding before they turned slack, pale, and terror-filled.

"It's a government alert for Ithica." Lisa's gaze darted across her screen as she read. "Military are in the streets there. It says, 'Shelter in place. Take cover.'"

The hairs rose on the back of my neck, and the uncontrollable kick of adrenaline surging through me had my mind spinning. "What?"

"The Embassy's got a bunker," Bower roared down the phone. "Get here now, Briar! She's taken the—"

The line went dead.

Run. Run. *Run!*

The word echoed across my mind. A thousand questions followed, careening around my skull. Most important of all, was what were we running from?

An air-raid siren blared outside. My gaze snapped to the window. The Embassy. It was coming from the Embassy!

The thing was loud to the point of deafening, and I cupped my ears. It was a warning that screamed of inbound trouble, but what the Iron Hells that trouble might be ...

Time slowed.

Kane's stare turned voltaic.

There was a boom from outside. Metal shrieked. The ground quaked. My heart stopped. Every head in the room whipped that way.

A rumble shook the floor. I stared down. Another rumble followed, the ground vibrating harder. It rocked the tables, sending forks and glasses flying. Crystal shattered, shards careening in every direction.

I had not one clue what was happening, but every instinct, every fiber of my being, told me that whatever it was, it had to do with Zahara.

Run. We needed to run. We needed to *fucking run*!

"GO! EVERYONE, GO, GO, *GO*!" I called. And under *any* other circumstance, me calling that order might've triggered some preternaturally delicate senses and started a war. But in that moment, it was the catalyst to get feet moving.

My Alpha's hold tightened over my wrist, and he threw the door open. Cassandra closed in, flanking me to my other side. A whistle sounded, followed by a whoosh that grew louder and louder the closer it got. My gaze lifted. Above us. It came from above us. Something blazed, streaking the inky night.

No, not just something. *Many* things.

"What the hells is that?" Theo said.

Kane was rigid, his eyes fixed on the sky. Then those eyes went wide. “Shadowed fucking moon.”

My heart stopped as understanding hit. “GET DOWN—”

The bomb landed, hitting across the street. The flash blinded me as a boom rang out.

An explosion rocked the night, throwing us back before we were consumed by fire, and pain, and blood.

Chapter Twenty-Eight

My eyes cracked open. I lay face down on the floor. Dust coated the air, only clouding more as I breathed. It tasted of chalk and filled my lungs. There was a ringing in my ears, high-pitched and keening, but it faded fast.

Glass and debris were scattered everywhere, the windows and doors gone. I crushed my eyes closed, trying to clear my sight before they reopened.

Bombs. They were dropping *bombs*!

Kane. Lucas. The wedding. My baby.

My hands flew to my stomach and found no wound. Okay. They were okay.

I shot up, or tried to, but something heavy pinned me down. I glanced back. A table.

"I've got you, Bry," my Alpha said, climbing to his feet several paces away. He grunted, then closed in. A second later, the weight was gone. His hand took my elbow and he pulled me up.

Slowly, people got to their feet, and my pulse pounded in my ears as I scanned faces. Lisa and Rosa lingered, shaken, in the corner; Kane's wolves stood scattered throughout; Cassandra's stare was on me as she dusted herself off several paces away. Joaquin looked Ezra over, while Theo hugged a crying Whitney to his chest. Alistair lay unmoving against the far wall, a metal shard puncturing his chest, downed flower petals coating his back. Dead.

The scent of ether filled the air.

Lucas. Where was Lucas?

My brother coughed, and my gaze darted that way. His hand was around Hannah's wrist as he tugged her to her feet. She bled from a few small cuts across her face, but not enough to be fatal.

Theo pulled Whitney with him as he approached us. "It's a goddamn warzone out there."

My gaze met Kane's. I had no clue what was happening or who we could trust, but we were low on options. "The Embassy. We need to get to the Embassy."

The nod of Kane's head was sharp. "LET'S MOVE!"

Joaquin strode ahead of Ezra while Lucas shoved Hannah forward, and the others fell in behind. We barreled outside, the city dark, save for the soft dusting of the moon lighting the carnage around us. My heart stopped at what I saw.

Wolves and shadow walkers lay broken and lifeless, blood and body parts everywhere. Cars were flipped or shredded, stone and debris sat scattered. Buildings imploded.

My chest heaved, adrenaline searing through my veins.

Another bomb dropped. Close. Entirely too close. It impaled the side of No Man's Land before it blew. The pub's wood and brick and steel exploded, tearing through the air as shrapnel flew.

Lisa stopped, hands flying to her mouth as she watched it burn.

"MOVE, LIS!" I tried to turn back, to keep her ass going, but Kane held tight.

"You must not stop, Briar Slade," Cassandra said, a tightness in her voice I'd never heard before.

A piercing whistle carried from above. Close. Too close.

My gaze shot skyward, following the bomb as it descended, aiming for the shops a hundred feet out. It fell. And fell. Kane grabbed me, throwing us to the ground as he shielded my body with his.

It hit.

Everything flashed white. The blast wave struck. We were thrown aside. Away. We tore over jagged ground. A sharp sting pierced my leg. Kane grunted and crushed me harder.

The clink and tap of wreckage falling filled the world for an impossibly long time before it finally stopped.

Kane's jaw ground, and he snarled.

"You okay?" I asked. He didn't answer, and I blinked up at him. His stare was pinched, his muscles strained. Pain. He was in pain. A lot of it. My hands frantically roved his back and came away red and wet.

My stomach hardened. "You're bleeding."

"Don't move, Bry," he ground out.

"Kane!"

"Don't fucking move."

"We have to." Head angling back, I oriented myself. We lay in the middle of the road, about fifty yards from the Embassy. We needed to get there.

A fire burned nearby, black smoke filling the air. My lungs shuddered when I couldn't see the others.

I scrambled out from under Kane and got to my feet. Blood stained his shirt, soaking his jeans. Shards of hissing iron stuck out of his skin. I grabbed his arm and tried to pull him up. He rose, getting halfway there before his steps faltered and he collapsed.

Shit!

I dropped to his side.

"The hells are you doing?" His voice was weaker. There was less gravel to it—and Kane Slade always had room for gravel. This was bad. Very fucking bad.

He pushed up, trying to stand again, then fell, knees hitting the ground with a thud. Blood poured freely and he buckled forward, his hands bracing his fall to stop his face eating the concrete, but barely.

"Kane!" I cried.

His shoulders heaved as he crushed his eyes closed, then forced them open again. "I'm good, Bry." He coughed, then spit a deep, thick swath of red liquid to the side. Wiping his mouth with the back of his arm, he tipped his chin my way. "Keep going."

"Stop talking!" I said, my eyes tracking his wounds. Iron punctured his kidney, and wood his upper chest. I grew dizzy. Wraith take me.

"We don't have time for this, Bry. Get to the Embassy."

My scowl was deep. Stubborn wolf! "If I don't get this shit outta you now, neither of us will make it."

He growled, but must've gauged that truth, because he didn't fight me.

"It's probably gonna hurt. Don't you dare bite me, Big Bad."

A low huff rent from his throat. I wanted it to be laughter, but it was more akin to choking … on blood.

Black lines tracked out from the iron. I swallowed hard, then planted a foot against the ground for leverage. I latched onto the metal, my skin burning as I cried out, and pulled.

It slipped free with ease, but he didn't move. And the black lines didn't recede.

Another whoosh, then a *boom*. The rumble shook. More screams carried. My heart dropped.

My hands trembled as I took hold of the wood.

"It's deep," he said, voice hoarse.

Inclining my head, I gritted my teeth and held tight, trying for all I was worth to steady the frenetic pounding of my pulse. It didn't work.

I pulled. The wood moved an inch. Kane grunted. His thick fingers gouged into the concrete, crunching and grinding it under him as he left deep grooves in his wake. I winced and pulled again. It gave another inch.

Iron fires, it wasn't enough. Twisting my obsidian, I drew on its power, then reached for his strength. I hated to take anything, 'cause sage knew he needed it, but if I didn't get that stupid wood out … No, I wouldn't think it. *Couldn't*.

His power tore through me, and I jerked. The wood ripped free, and I flew back with it, stumbling and tripping onto my ass three feet away.

My Alpha fell limp.

"KANE!" I cried, scrambling back to his side.

The bond between us, that tether to my soul, faded, started slipping. It was like an anchor, dragging me below water.

Dying. He was *dying*. He didn't have strength, which meant he needed mine.

"Take from me, Kane," I ordered, then cried, "*Just fucking take it!*"

His breathing slowed, then slowed more.

If he couldn't take, then I'd sure as hells give. Reaching inside, I gathered what I could before I forced it through our bond. His body jolted, muscles straining as his spine arched and he gasped a breath.

My Alpha's color returned. Slowly, his wounds stitched closed and those black lines receded. My heart began beating again.

He groaned, his body creaking as he rolled his head to the side.

I took his face in my palms, my eyes moving between his own. "You can't scare me like that." My vision blurred until there were two of him. Then four. "We die together, Kane." I pressed my lips to his in a chaste kiss. "But today's not the day."

He steadied himself as he shifted, then sat up, his words hoarse as he said, "Not today."

I followed him to his feet. He held my wrist as my eyes scanned the terrain for faces. More debris littered the road. More bodies. Sage, so many bodies.

We started forward, making for the Embassy.

Brick and stone lay scattered across what was left of the road. Buildings had imploded or split, threatening to fall at any second. Immortal Inc still stood, but sage only knew for how long.

Smoke billowed high on the air, filling my lungs and shortening my line of sight. Blood painted the rubble, stained clothes, and faces … and souls. The air was so thick with the scent of ether, my eyes watered and bile kissed the back of my throat.

Lisa appeared through the falling dust, dirt and blood covering her clothes and face. With one arm around a coughing Rosa, she peered around, her wild gaze searching the melee. When it met mine, her shoulders fell, relief washing her features.

Another whistle sounded, drawing closer. Closer. *Closer.* Entirely too close.

"Shadowed moon," Kane said.

My chest constricted. Wraith take me.

"LIS, GET OUT OF THERE!"

Her head angled to the sky, her eyes going wide before she shoved Rosa aside. She ran, making it all of four paces before she tripped over a jagged chunk of asphalt.

"LISA!" I cried.

My Alpha jerked me to the side, throwing us behind what remained of a battered and broken vehicle.

BOOM.

The vehicle shrieked and rocked, threatening to crush us. Kane shoved his shoulder into it, knees and feet planted as he roared, fighting to hold it back. His body shook from the effort, muscles and veins straining against his skin. Cracks and bangs filled the world as things collided with the vehicle again and again and again. Until it stopped.

I grew dizzy, heart pounding in my ears.

Someone screamed.

Kane's ragged breath exploded from his chest as he shot up and took me with him. My gaze speared the chaos.

Screams and moans carried in the distance.

Rosa sat crumpled, eyes unseeing, hand outstretched toward a body to our right. A body whose leg was missing, side pierced by steel. A pool of red surrounded it. My gaze tracked north toward the sleek black hair that lay sprawled out from a hauntingly pale, blood-soaked face.

My steps lumbered, then faltered.

Lisa.

Her umber eyes stared off to nothing, her pupils hazed with white. Vacant. Dead.

"No." I croaked. "No, no, no, NONONOOOOOO!" I ran for her.

Kane's thick arm banded around my waist, his grip locking tight. He jerked me to him, and pulled my face to his chest, blocking her and everything else from sight. "Don't look, Bry. Don't look."

I thrashed, my blood-and-dirt-stained dress tattered and heavy as I struggled against him, desperate to do something. Sweet sage, *anything*! "Let me go! I can help her. *Letmego!*"

"You can't help her, Bry. It's too late. She's gone."

"NO!" I screamed. It hurt. Iron fires, the pain. It hurt so fucking bad I couldn't breathe, and I gasped, lungs burning as white filled my vision.

My Alpha angled forward, hooking his hands under my thighs and hefting me to his chest before he ran. Away.

No. I couldn't leave her. *I couldn't!*

"Stop!" I hit his chest. "She needs me, Kane. Stop!"

"I'm so sorry," he said, his tone strained.

"NO!" I reached for her. "We can't leave her. *We can't fucking leave her!*"

"There's nothing you can do. She belongs to the wraith now." He held tight. "When this is over, we'll come back for her. I promise, we'll come back."

The wraith. Her soul waited for the wraith.

I jolted with his every stride, my eyes on her. I couldn't look away. I'd never see that smile again. Never hear her voice. Never hug her or laugh or cry together. Never. Never. *Never!*

A silent sob broke from my chest, and I collapsed against him.

Somewhere in the distance, another whoosh sounded out. Kane's eyes snapped up. Something told me I should be scared, but I just … couldn't, because I couldn't think past Lisa. Couldn't see anything but those vacant eyes. Couldn't feel anything but the pain.

That whoosh grew louder. Deafening.

Sweat slicked Kane's temples as he barreled us up to the Embassy's entrance.

BOOM.

The bomb hit, landing right where Lisa lay.

I screamed.

Asphalt and stone flew. The ground shook, rocking us to the side. Kane's free arm shot out, steadying himself against the façade of the building before he tore open the door and careened inside.

My Alpha spoke, whether to me or someone else, I had no clue. Loosening his hold, he lowered me to my feet. My legs were weak. Unsteady.

Bower stood across the room, his face pale as he yelled something and waved us toward him. My Alpha hauled me behind him. My legs were heavy and I stumbled with every step. The lights flickered, the floor shaking beneath me.

Or maybe it was me that shook.

Slowly, sound filtered in: the thump of our footsteps, the heaviness of our breaths.

A loud clunk sounded out.

"In here!" Bower said, body straining as he swung open a thick, vault-style door.

We barreled through it to the stark, white room beyond, and a heavy clang reverberated around the place as he sealed it tight behind us.

"Iron Hells," Joaquin said, face ashen as he closed in, colliding with my Alpha and throwing his arms around him. "I thought you were dead."

Kane's free arm thumped against him, his eyes on me. He cleared his throat. "Not yet."

Joaquin turned my way, gaze bloodshot. "Banshee."

My eyes were bleary as they tracked the room. A cavalcade of guns lined the wall, along with people. Faces I couldn't gauge. "Who else?" I murmured. Who else was missing? Who else was dead? Who else did we lose?

"Pack on both sides," Joaquin answered, then added, "And some of Cassandra's people."

I scrubbed my eyes clear. "Is …" My voice hitched. "Is Lucas—"

"I'm here, Briar." My brother shoved his way toward us through the throng of humans and preternaturals. His face was marred with cuts, his shirt blood-stained and torn. He threw his arms around me. Cassandra closed in, Hannah at her side. Dust and soot streaked their faces and hair.

They were alive.

My eyes narrowed as I turned them on Bower. "Did you know about this?" Fire exploded in my veins before he could answer. My hand latched around his throat, and I drove him back until he collided with the wall, grunting. "DID YOU FUCKING KNOW?"

Silence descended.

Bower's face turned red, but he didn't fight me. Just shook his head, his voice hoarse as he forced it through his airway. "No."

I stared into those royal blue eyes, seeking the lie. My Alpha didn't react. Still, I prayed to find it, to see it, because my blood sang for vengeance, and Bower was a ready target. But the lie wasn't there.

It wasn't fucking there!

I released him with a shove, then pitched to my left, giving the wall my weight.

My Alpha stalked closer, taking his position at my side before he rose to his full, menacing height. He looked at the Ambassador and snarled, "The fuck's going on out there?"

Bower rubbed his throat. "Zahara caught wind we were coming for her. Her militia moved on the government and seized it, then took the army's base." His attention fixed on me. "She's got everything, Briar."

The words filtered in slowly, sinking deep until their meaning struck.

Everything. "The iron weapons," I said. Iron weapons she'd aimed straight at us, intending to wipe Cambria off the fucking map.

She'd wanted to become a weapon. It turned out she'd gotten that wish.

Cassandra's crimson eyes narrowed as she drifted in beside me. Her cold hand reached out, her long fingers threading through mine. She pulled me to her.

My head fell to her shoulder, and I hiccupped a sob, then focused on my breathing. In. Out. In. Out.

Whitney shook wildly, her fine braids vibrating, tears streaking her dust-stained cheeks. Theo's expression creased, his hand shooting out before it closed over hers. He pulled her close and she leaned into him, turning her face into his side.

He cleared his throat and eyed Bower. "How the hells did Zahara take the base?"

It didn't take much to guess that answer.

"The serums," I said, my tone hollow as I stepped back from Cassandra. The fucking *serums*!

She'd already been using them to sow discord, but the second the tables had turned, the second she'd been caught, she'd needed to change the game. And if that was true, there was no chance in the Iron Hells anyone else inside Ithica could contend with her.

I swallowed around the dryness in my throat. "They need our help."

A shadow walker in the corner shook his head. "They're lobbing bombs at us."

My teeth clenched tight. "It's not *them*." Not the humans or the government. No one else. I lifted my head. "It's *her*. And if we don't stop her, no one will."

Cassandra aimed a seething glare at the vamp. He shrank back as she turned to me. "I am with you, Briar Slade."

My gaze found Kane's.

His grip locked around my jaw, his stare boring into mine. When he spoke, his lone word was a promise and a vow and everything I needed. "Always."

Always with me. We lived together; we died together. *Always*.

I took a beat, then a breath, holding onto his musk and wilderness scent. I used it to steady my hands and the staccato rhythm of my heart, because I needed to be ready for what came next.

I pivoted to face Bower. "We need to get across the border."

He rubbed his chin between his thumb and forefinger. "The army base lines it, Briar."

My head cut to the side, 'cause I'd seen those photos back when the threat of Ithica's bombs originally loomed. "Not the entire border."

Kane crossed his arms over his chest, pure Alpha. "What're you thinking, Bry?"

"I think we use her own methods against her."

The dip of his head was slow. "Use her own crossing?"

The one she'd forged to broker her Cambrian deals. "Yes."

"It won't work," Bower cut in. "That gap was sealed."

A low, muted boom shook the building. The walls and floor trembled. Glass clanked. Dust fell. I eyed the ceiling. The bunker held, but for how long?

Clearing my throat, I asked, "Does she know they sealed it? The gap?"

Bower shrugged off his suit coat and chucked it onto the table to his left. "Everyone in Ithica does."

Joaquin rolled his shoulders, picking up what I put down. "Zahara's gonna need every resource she has to hold her advantage right now."

Theo's stare sparked. "So she's less likely to waste any watching the crossing."

Cassandra's head tilted at that inhuman angle. "We cannot know that for certain, Briar Slade."

No, we couldn't, but still …

"It makes sense. She won't waste efforts where they're not needed, because she's only gonna get one shot at taking us out." One kick at her really goddamn stupid can.

Theo stroked a slow, soothing path over Whitney's hair as he looked at Bower. "You said your people sealed the gap. Sealed it how?"

The Ambassador unfastened the top button of his dress shirt. "Concrete."

My Alpha stretched his neck. "We'll get through."

My nod was sharp, my eyes tracking over every face there. "We've all seen the schematics of their base. We know what we're walking into."

Bower's brow arched.

Cassandra tugged her lip, exposing a fang. "Ithica are not the only ones with eyes and spies, Bower Caddel."

Inhaling deeply, I said, "This will be a mess." I stared down at my hands, at the drying blood that coated my palms and caked under my nails. "But we might have a window." I didn't know how brief that window might be, but something was better than nothing.

"How so?" Theo asked.

"Initially, Isaac didn't wanna hand Zahara the keys to the kingdom, so he put in a failsafe. Made the serums short-lasting."

He might've been a piece of shit, but at least he'd had that much sense.

Cassandra leaned closer, her attention piqued. "How short, Briar Stone?"

"A few hours."

"A *few*?" Bower's brows lowered. "What's that mean?"

Exactly? I shook my head. "No clue, but I knew Issac." And, like my stepfather had said … "He wouldn't give away an advantage. So I'd guess shorter. Three hours, likely five tops."

Kane's head snapped to Bower. "When did the trouble start on your side?"

The Ambassador checked his phone. "An hour ago. She was coordinated. Moved fast."

Not shocking for a former fucking General.

Joaquin glanced back, checking on Ezra before he dragged a hand along his jaw. "How much serum do we think she has left?"

In the scheme of her faction's numbers, I had not one clue, which meant my frown was deep when I answered, "Enough."

Bower's head dipped. "She's tactical. Wouldn't move if she didn't think she had the resources to see it through."

No, not with the stakes so high. Like, a-spike-through-her-skull kinda high. Besides, once she'd removed all the major players from the board, it wasn't like she'd be needing those serums anymore.

His attention jumped between the wolves and the Dowager. "If they've got your abilities, will they scent us?"

"The question is not if they will scent us, Bower Caddel," Cassandra said, that soft lilt knowing. "It is whether they will know what it is they are scenting."

He frowned. "You don't think they will?"

"When my kind are changed, it is an assault on the senses. Most become crazed or frantic for a time, overwhelmed by the thirst."

He cleared his throat. "The thirst?"

She inclined her head. "For blood. Any blood. When we are … young, we do not discriminate against the vein. And with a transformation this rapid"—her long fingers rolled the hem of her sleeves toward her elbows—"they will have power, but they will not have control."

He inhaled good and slow. "How long does it take to *get* control?"

Her crimson eyes flashed, that smile all razored teeth—the stuff nightmares were made of—as it caught the light. "That will depend."

Theo's hands rolled into fists. "On what?"

Cassandra's long fingers fanned wide. "On whether they try."

The Ambassador rubbed the back of his neck. "So, what're we walking into?"

"A Hunt, Bower Caddel. You will walk into a Hunt."

Lovely. Just *lovely*.

My stomach rolled, acid searing the back of my throat while I fought with everything I had to keep its contents down.

"Watch for illusions from the magi," I said. "*If* they've figured out how to use them, it'll be their best bet to distract."

Bower eyed my Alpha and Joaquin. "And what do we think with the weres?"

"Wolves are born," Joaquin said, "we're not made. We grow with our change. Adapt over time." He chucked his chin Cassandra's way. "No bloodlust for us, but emotions are heightened."

"They'll probably have a need to establish themselves," Kane said. "Figure out their place in their power structure."

Bower's forehead creased. "Would that mean infighting?"

Joaquin's brow lowered as he thought about his. "Maybe."

"They could see us as invaders," my Alpha said.

Theo folded his arms over his chest. "Invaders that'll need to be dealt with."

Violently.

"Which would trigger that territorial instinct." My Alpha eyed Joaquin, a silent conversation passing between them. "We know what to anticipate with the wolves," he said. "We'll handle them."

"My people will deal with the shadow walkers," Cassandra added.

I gave a slow nod, but kept my mouth shut, 'cause I had a plan all my own—well, for me and Bower, even if he didn't know it yet. And surer than the hells my Alpha wasn't about to like it.

We'd be wading neck-deep into a shit show. The worst kind of bad, because crazed humans with preternatural powers was the crappiest of combinations.

Bower's attention shifted to my Alpha. "What should I tell my people?"

Kane rolled his neck. "To kill them."

"I've got men. We can rally what's left of our army." Bower's tone turned somber. "But Zahara's got powerful artillery behind her. We're gonna need numbers."

"The Pack's inbound," Kane said. What was left of it, anyway.

Joaquin gave a sharp nod. "Mine too."

Cassandra's delicate hand drifted to my shoulder. "I will inform my people."

I wanted to offer my people too, but dragging the magi into this would be like taking words to a gun fight. Literally. They had abilities, and they'd served their purpose, played their role in defeating Isaac, but what lay ahead was a bloodbath of fatal proportions, which meant we needed power, raw and brutal.

My head dipped. "Mine will manage the wounded here." I eyed Bower. "Who's got the ability to shut Zahara down?" To access that base, and override it.

His mouth tugged at the corner. "Me."

A small sob broke from Whitney and Theo's arms slid around her back, then lower to her waist, pressing her to his chest.

"We need to get there before they take the serum again," he said.

Stalking to the right, I snapped one of the guns from the wall, then shoved it at my brother's chest. "I don't know how long this place will hold. If you think it's gonna go, take Hannah, and Whitney and Ezra." Because the Omega wasn't a fighter. His skills would be better served helping Cambria's carnage. "Get them the hells outta here. As far from the city center as you can."

He nodded his head.

My heart pounded in my chest, beating so loud, I could scarcely hear myself think. My stare tracked from Theo, to Cassandra, to Bower, and Joaquin, until it found my Alpha's, holding on to that unyielding strength. I straightened, my spine unfurling one segment at a time.

We might've been backed into a corner, but cornered animals had a propensity to bite. And when you had teeth like Cambrians, it was time to watch the fuck out.

I closed in on the exit. "Let's go."

Chapter Twenty-Nine

Kane cut his battered truck a hard left, aiming for the gap. Ash flew, coating the air, as bomb after bomb was lobbed. The blasts lit the rear-view mirror, smoke and embers billowing as they stained the sky an eerie shade of crimson death.

The calls had been put out: any capable enough, get your asses to the border with us; the rest, move to the periphery of your territory. My magi and Alistair's Second would need to do what they could for the wounded.

I wanted to know all we'd lost. *Who* we'd lost. I wanted names to offer vengeance. But in the end, it didn't matter. Even one was too many.

Lisa. I'd lost Lisa. She was dead. And wraith willing, Zahara would be following soon.

I was quiet. Focused on the pressure building in my chest. How much more could I lose? How much more could I survive? It hurt. It hurt. *It just damn well hurt.*

Kane looked at me from the corner of his eye. His tension rolled off him in waves, raking my skin, rough and grating.

I knew what he wanted, for me to talk, to get everything eating me alive out, but I couldn't give it—not yet. If I opened that floodgate, I'd never get it closed. Swiping the moisture from my cheeks, I shoved everything—my loss, my rage, my motherfucking thirst for Zahara's blood—to the back of my mind, because if this was gonna work, I'd be needing every ounce of wit I had.

My Alpha's palm rested on my leg, clad in the loose-fitting military-style clothes Bower had tossed our way before we left.

But Kane didn't offer any words of comfort. No promises of victory. Because with what we were about to walk into, there was no guarantee we'd walk out.

Cassandra, Theo, Joaquin, the Ambassador, and a handful of others followed tight on our ass. A wildly terrifying sight. We'd opted on multiple vehicles, spreading ourselves out, 'cause if one of those bombs hit, our odds of survival with the group separated were better.

My Alpha punched it. The truck roared into the farm field, skidding to a halt before the wall. Some wolves waited, some shadow walkers. Their stares were a terrifying torrent of heartbreak, fury, and determination. Ready. They were fucking ready.

Kane and I flew from the vehicle, not slowing for the others. When we reached the gap, that towering concrete barrier, at least forty feet high, loomed before us. It was smooth, impossible to climb, and generally a giant-ass problem.

I checked my watch. My chest constricted. Only a couple of hours left for those serums—I hoped.

The rustle of leaves and crunch of earth grew louder as the others closed in. Were after were, followed by shadow walkers. One hundred at least. There was no doubt we were a dangerous collective, but against an iron militia of bullets and bombs …

Cassian stalked forward. "We've got more coming, but the roads are shit. Impassable in places. Buildings are down and blocking the routes."

Kane gave a steady nod before he and Joaquin took the helm and made for the wall, Cassandra and I following tight behind.

"We can't go around, so we go through," my Alpha said, drawing back before he let loose a roar that shook the world and rattled through my skull. At the same time, his square-knuckled fist connected with the concrete. A sharp crack echoed through the night. Dust and rock crumbled. Joaquin's hit landed next, then Cassandra's. Blow after blow landed. Weres and walkers cleared the debris. But it was slow-going. Too slow.

Shadow and sage, we needed to get there. Fast. The pressure in my chest kept building. Fear and fury. It needed a release. Drawing on my obsidian, I pulled that wolfish power and planted a foot. Lisa was gone. There was no wall in the world that could hold back the vengeance I had coming for Zahara.

I charged and screamed, closing in on the center of the concrete before I drew on the tether with Kane and kicked. Hard. A snap echoed through the night, and the wall cleaved, a fissure splitting three feet up the side.

Kane stumbled back, closing his eyes as if fighting to steady himself.

Everyone stopped. Heads turned my way.

I kicked again. Another snap. The fissure climbed higher. I kicked again, then again. And the sounds that broke from me were guttural and so animal, I barely recognized them as my own. I kicked *again*. Something groaned. The wall ruptured. Rock shifted.

My Alpha's eyes flew wide and he roared to the others, "MOVE!"

Everyone scrambled back as the stone cracked. A loud grinding shook the earth, and it tumbled end over end toward us.

Someone latched onto my collar, ripping me away. Kane snapped me to him before he backpedaled, preternaturally fast. The wall crumbled, the sides rolling in as it collapsed, running further and further out like dominoes. Dust plumes filled the air, and I covered my mouth with my arm.

Bower cursed.

Theo stared at the carnage. "That'll do it."

Joaquin gave a nod. "Nice work, banshee."

Slowly, like watching blood dry, the dust fell, and the sky cleared.

Cassandra advanced. "Make a path!"

There was a scuff of feet as everyone moved in. Pieces of debris were thrown aside and piled up until a passage was opened that was wide enough for us to drive through.

Sweat slicked my spine and forehead, my damp hair clinging to my skin. I dragged it back, breath ragged, as I glanced over the border.

Silence fell as every preternaturally honed eye in our patchwork infantry scanned the distance, looking for anything. The wolves scented the air, eyes electric.

Kane's clenched his fists over and over, as if he were picturing wrapping them around someone's throat—tearing it out—before he said, "It's clear."

"Good enough." Bower tipped his head to our cavalcade of vehicles.

"You're with us," I told him, then climbed in, moving to the middle.

He and my Alpha followed, sitting on either side of me.

The crunch of our tires was loud as we crept over the boundary and into Ithica, the truck rocking over the uneven gravel terrain. I didn't know what I'd expected: a change in the air, the colors to be different, a drop off in power. Something. But it just felt … the same.

Bower offered Kane directions as we wove through the ghostly streets of Ithica, past the cookie-cutter houses and pristinely manicured lawns. The trees were trimmed, vines woven into kitschy shapes: a horse, a dog, a bird. The buildings were new, and not made of wood or old broken brick or worn stone. No vines or wildflowers climbed their façades.

The place smelled like cut grass and wood stain. It all just felt so … controlled.

Had Lisa lived there? In a home just like these? A home she'd never return to?

Humans watched wide-eyed and desperate from their windows, peeking through blinds or from between drawn curtains. Prisoners with no chance to win—no chance but us.

We followed the western border, the properties growing sparser and sparser, until high barbed-wire fences began lining the road, joined by signs that read "Military Zone. No Stopping Permitted".

Drawing on my obsidian, I threw a cocoon over our cavalcade, 'cause the last thing we needed was for Zahara's people to hear us coming.

The trees grew denser, a blood moon rimming their branches in a fitting, haunted glow. The crisp scent of pine filled my nostrils. That and the stannic burn of fear. It was heavy, making the air thick, coating my lungs.

"Here's good," Bower said, then pointed right. "The base's about four hundred meters through that thicket."

Kane veered us to the side of the road, then slammed the vehicle into park. Climbing free, he reached inside and led me out. He scented the air, his eyes going a darkened shade of silver.

Bower exited.

My Alpha took my face between his immense, rough hands. "You stay with me."

My chest tightened. "For as long as I can."

His stare flashed, and his eyes searched mine, a barrage of emotions ripping through his expression. Anger. Apprehension. Unease. Fear. Understanding. "You've got something planned."

I did have *something*. Didn't know if it qualified as a plan, but I wasn't about to undersell myself on that front, so I did the next best thing and kept my mouth shut. Let him read into that what he would.

His chest expanded with the depth of his breath. His jaw clenched, muscles there flicking and pulsing. I had not one doubt that he was less than a fan of us separating. But things had reached a critical mass. The we-actually-might-not-survive-this-time sort of critical. And with what we were headed into, splitting our focus, fixed on one another wasn't gonna fly. It was all or nothing.

I faced the others as they formed a shoulder-to-shoulder line. A wall of our own. A seething one, hungry for blood and violence.

Theo and Joaquin fell in at Kane's side, Cassandra at mine.

The Ambassador approached. "My people are waiting just inside the tree line."

"And you are sure we can trust your people, Bower Caddel?" Cassandra questioned.

He inclined his head. "I'm sure."

No one moved to rip out his throat, so it had to be true—or at least, he thought it was.

I looked at our Cambrian horde. Their eyes were angled our way, waiting. I tipped my chin up and gave them my order. "Don't fucking die. Not one of you. We've lost enough. Now it's her turn."

A chorus of grunts followed.

Theo nudged my side. "Great pep talk."

A loud boom reverberated through the forest. It rattled the trees and sent pine needles falling. They tumbled, drifting on the air until they joined the fallen leaves on the earth. Another boom carried. The distant sky over Cambria was lit a blinding white, then enveloped by a mushroom cloud of smoke. A wave of acrid, sulfurous gun powder drifted toward us. A weapon. The really big, bomb-lobbing kind. The same bombs that had torn Lisa apart. Ripped her from me and sent her to the wraith.

The same bombs I'd be ripping from Zahara's power-hungry grasp.

"We ready?" Bower asked.

"Past ready," I said.

He straightened his spine, edged to the lead, and advanced. We followed, the weres' boned claws tearing free.

The wolves stepped up to the fence. The muscles of my Alpha's back and arms tensed and bulged as he cleaved the chain-link apart. Metal shrieked then fell aside, clearing the way. Cutting through, we breached the trees, keeping low.

A sharp wind rolled through the night, whipping my hair. My heart thrummed in my chest, honing my focus. My breaths came short and shallow. The cool night wind kissed my skin, my breath steaming with every exhale.

Howls carried, rolling through the dark. Well, maybe not howls, exactly—more like snarling screams. They echoed across the woods and reverberated around the trees. Haunting.

They were terror-filled; the sounds of people cornered in their minds—or cornered for real.

Sage, it was loud. It pounded against my skull, boring deeper and deeper until it became a part of me, echoing through my memory for eternity.

My chest constricted.

There were so many, their voices layered into a chaotic cacophony as they called into the night, "Help! *Please!*" But who they were, I had no clue.

Lights shone in the distance, some stationary, others moving, joined by the rumble-groan of heavy machinery.

A horde of human soldiers crouched, hidden behind a copse of brush, binoculars out as they searched the distance, all dressed in camouflage. They did a good job of blending in, but the rapid thump of their hearts meant they couldn't hide from us.

I expanded my shield to encompass them.

When our sound reached their ears, their heads whipped our way, followed a second later by their semi-automatic-style iron-bulleted guns.

"Easy," Bower said, hands raised in a directive.

The soldier's chests heaved. Wide eyes met us, the whites standing in stark contrast to the green-and-black paint that coated their faces. Their stares tracked rapidly from the weres to the shadow walkers. They averted their guns, but their hands stayed locked around the triggers. Not that I blamed them.

Bower took a knee next to an older, silver-haired man I guessed was their commander and instructed, "Fill us in, Waylon."

Waylon. The name was familiar. Bower had mentioned it once, after we'd killed Isaac, and he'd first discovered Zahara's identity.

Waylon's hand curled into a loose fist, his index finger extended, and he gestured toward the carnage. "They've got hostages."

I angled my head down, glaring through my brow. "How many?"

"I can't say what's inside, but by our count out here, 'bout fifty-two. Must've grabbed them on their way in, 'cause most are civilians."

"Where are their weaknesses?" Cassandra asked, her voice rich with that soothing lilt, the one I'd only heard her use right before she started stomping skulls or tearing out throats.

The soldiers all eyed her, swallowing hard before they tugged up their neck gear.

"A handful know what they're doing, but most are inexperienced," Waylon noted. "She's ordered them to set up a perimeter, but they don't know how to hold it. They've got holes at three o'clock and ten o'clock." He indicated two points along the tree line boundary.

Joaquin gripped one wrist with his opposite hand. "And their strengths?"

"They're erratic. No control. They just react."

A strength because it made them unpredictable. And that was a real-ass problem.

The soldiers watched us, a mix of gratitude and hesitation in their wary gazes.

Bower took up a pair of binoculars and peered through them. The longer he looked, the more his body tensed. He inhaled slowly, then offered them my way.

Setting them to my face, I scanned the horizon.

A cluster of humans stood bound off to the far right, while a line of soldiers lay propped on their sides by the furthest barracks wall. Their mouths were taped shut, their legs and arms tied behind them.

"Please. Don't do this!" a woman said, her voice faint and containing an odd combination of fear and grit.

A pair of crimson eyes flashed in the distance. Well, sort of crimson. There was something off there. A disconnect. Like something was broken. Their humanity was gone, and not in that "older than dirt like Cassandra" kinda way. It was more like the way Ivy had been, bordering on the Madness.

"Where are the bombs?" I asked.

Waylon pointed straight ahead. "Long-range missiles are there." Then right. "Rocket launchers there."

The warm rain kissed my skin and slithered down my cheeks. It coated the ground, reflecting the light, and shone on every malevolent face in the distance.

My mouth thinned. "And your former General?"

Cassandra's crimson stare sparked.

Waylon adjusted his gun and shook his head. "We haven't had a visual of her."

There was something in the way he said it. Not that she wasn't there, just that she wasn't visible. "What's the most likely location for a command center?"

Waylon indicated a building on the left. "The armory."

Three men prowled outside its entrance, eyes glowing various shades of electric green and blue and gold and completely fucking unhinged.

Weres. Well, the serum version, anyway.

Another cluster huddled in the distance: human, but decidedly not.

I lowered the binoculars, my hands curling into fists so tight my skin creaked. I turned to Bower. "Get me there."

Joaquin and Theo tensed. My Alpha fell still. The deathly kind of still.

The Ambassador cleared his throat. "I'll do what I can."

"How many are armed?" Joaquin asked.

"About twenty-seven that we can see."

Not a bad number, but in the right hands, twenty-seven iron weapons could do a shit ton of damage.

Theo's brow lowered. "Why so few?"

Kane's stare turned molten as he stretched his neck, his voice guttural as he said, "'Cause the serums mean they can't be trusted."

Waylon gave a sharp nod. "They're contained, but barely."

My eyes narrowed, because something just … wasn't right. Was it possible twenty-seven armed militia and a swarm of serum-laden humans had taken the entire Ithican government on their own? Sure. But did I think Zahara was too calculating to attempt to pull off a coup with those kinds of numbers? Abso-fucking-lutely.

Which meant there was something we weren't seeing.

Another soldier moved in, passing Bower two handguns.

The Ambassador racked them before shoving several clips into his pockets. "The weapons need to be handled first."

'Cause if they weren't, we'd be good and dead real damn fast. Everything for naught.

The soldiers raised their own weapons. "We're on it." They moved into position, which was good, 'cause we needed the advantage they offered. The distance they could give us.

I listened as the others talked strategy, but my stare held on the armory, my thoughts on what lie inside, and—wraith willing—who.

Kane's hand latched onto my shirt, his stare intense and wild with the primal need to protect. Always. Sage knew how hard suppressing that instinct for a married, mated Alpha had to be, but when push came to shove, Kane Slade *always* did what needed to be done.

His eyes moved between mine as if he were burning them and every last one of my features into his memory. His chest rose and fell, not steady, untamed.

"Do what you gotta do, Bry," he said. "And do it fucking good."

A brutal smile lifted my lips, more beast than he'd ever be.

His forehead met mine for one second. Two. He pulled back, his expression darkening as he called his own wolf forward. His voice was a low, thundering growl. "I love you."

My fingers knotted in the chest of his hoodie. "I love you too." Pushing up onto my toes, I pressed my lips to his in a kiss. It was warm and brief, and contained everything I wanted to say but couldn't. Releasing him, I tipped my head toward the fight, my voice lowering in a dark vow. "None of her people will be left standing."

"None," he growled.

"Once the firefight starts, our window's gonna be short." Because surer than shit, they'd grab whatever iron projectiles they could get their hands on and aim them our way.

Theo's dark grin sent a shiver down my spine. "Then we'd better move fast."

Stepping back, I moved to Bower's side.

Joaquin's hand locked over my upper arm, his power pulsing off him in harsh waves. He squeezed. "See you on the other side, banshee."

I inclined my head. "One way or another."

He released.

Theo flexed his fists, his blazing glare honed and ready.

Those black lines crawled out from Cassandra's eyes, her words terrifyingly soft as she said, "They know not what comes for them."

My smile was hard. "Let's hope not."

The wind caught on her hair, flitting it around her face. "We end this today, Briar Slade."

I exhaled a steadying breath. "Today."

Her gaze flicked to my lower abdomen, then toward Zahara's horde. Her eyes morphed, growing darker and darker until they held a void so black, it stole the light. The blackness crawled over her eyelids, then down her skin like inky veins. And it made her the most terrifying thing there.

Bower's men called positions, moving ahead, weapons at the ready, eyes on their sights.

The Ambassador raised his gun, then said to me, "Stay behind me."

Kane and Joaquin cut the weres to the left.

The Dowager turned to her people. "We send them to the night."

I advanced.

"Line up your targets. On my word," Bower called to his soldiers. "And do not miss."

His men took aim.

I released my hold on the sound, but not my obsidian.

"FIRE!"

Gunfire rang out, a staccato break of deafening pops. Muzzles sparked; screams sounded. Around the base, blood misted the air. Bodies fell. Serum-tainted eyes turned our way.

"Move. Move. *Move!*" Waylon called.

I ran, my own target in sight as I kept tight to Bower's flank. He pulled the trigger, letting loose shot after shot until he'd emptied all his rounds.

Shrieks carried from our right. Feral. Inbound. Several serum-tainted vamps headed straight for the Ambassador and his men.

He cursed and reached for a new clip while his soldiers swung toward them. The guns fired, but not fast enough. Fangs were extended and flesh was torn as several soldiers were caught.

One of the vamps closed in on Bower.

Like the iron fires was she having him on my watch.

I pulled Kane's power and exploded forward, my fist flying and catching the vamp in the jaw. A loud crack sounded out as her bone snapped, her face now sitting off-balance. She snarled, her crimson stare latching onto me, then my throat. Her head cocked. Her teeth bared. She charged, reaching for me.

The click of Bower reloading filled the night. His arm swung out, the gun's barrel landing on the woman's temple. Her eyes started to widen. He pulled the trigger.

Her head jerked, skull splitting. Blood and brain flew.

She dropped.

Bower's chest heaved, red coating his face. He lowered his head in thanks, then kept moving.

I chanced a glance at the weres and saw Kane's fist driving forward, connecting with a tainted were's chest. It knocked the man back, sternum imploding as he lost his footing, then crumbled to the ground. The stolen glow faded from the man's eyes, until it left altogether. Two more tainted weres moved in. Kane planted his foot into the knee of one. The other pounced.

Joaquin cut across my line of sight, growling as he threw the were he was fighting against a nearby truck. It rocked, metal buckling.

Two human women pushed their hands forward, foreheads streaked with sweat and eyes narrowed. Small flecks rose from their hands, coalescing into people-esque shapes before them. The images were weak, and the women's bodies shook as they struggled to hold their illusions, but they'd picked their side, so they'd earned no mercy.

"Illusionists!" I yelled.

Waylon swung that way, rounds cracking as he took them down.

To my right, Cassandra snarled, incisors extended, as she opened her mouth wide and lunged. Her fangs sank into a red-eyed woman's throat. Twisting her head, the Dowager tore free. The woman staggered as Cassandra spat a decidedly deadly hunk of meat and sinew and flesh onto the ground.

Bodies flew. Bodies broke.

A boom rang out, light filling the area, and a machine rocked as one of the missiles was launched.

Kane and Joaquin threw blow after blow, clearing a path. A path Theo took when he made for the missile launcher and the human controlling it. His grip locked over the scruff of the guy's neck and he tore him back, throwing him to the ground before he impaled him with his claws.

"BRY!" my Alpha roared in warning as a were tore through the ranks.

Foam dripped from the man's mouth, slipping from his chin and staining his shirt. Bower took aim, but the guy's movements were uncoordinated and erratic, too hard to track as he careened our way.

Steeling myself, I exploded forward. His arm drew back, those claws arcing high before they descended on me. I ducked, slipping under his swing. Pivoting on my heel, I drew my Alpha's strength, grasping were-guy's wrist in a bone-crushing grip. As he swung his other arm my way, I grabbed that wrist too.

He snarled.

Jumping, I planted my feet against his chest, and snapped my legs out.

A howling shriek pierced the melee as his shoulders popped, then tore. I held my position, driving my heels into him as I pulled harder, and harder, and harder. His shriek grew louder and my body shook, sweat slicking my spine. At last, his flesh ripped, then gave way completely, and his arms cleaved clear from his body.

I fell, blood spurting from were-guy's torso as he collapsed onto his back.

Bower stepped in, looming over him, then emptied two shots into his chest. The guy kicked. He fired another. Glancing my way, he extended a hand, then hauled me up. "You good?"

Adrenaline coursed through me, making my soul sing with rage. "Real damn good."

He nodded and ran, popping off shots as he wove us past fight after fight, until … "THERE!" he called, pointing to a door thirty feet out, at the head of the armory.

We closed in. Close. We were so damn close. Zahara's time was almost up—

The door swung wide. Humans spilled out. A lot of them. Forty. Fifty. Sixty. Sage, there were so many.

Zahara exited, her gaze assessing as she took in the melee. Her movements were easy. Unfazed. As if she'd anticipated retaliation, and kept her numbers hidden for exactly that purpose.

"Fuck!" Bower barked.

His remaining soldiers called for everyone to take cover, keeping low and crouching behind vehicles and the corners of buildings. I stayed where I was. So did Kane, and Joaquin, and Cassandra, and every other preternatural. Because we didn't fucking run.

We didn't hide from them. They hid from *us*.

My pulse kicked into overdrive as I advanced. "ZAHARA!"

Her head snapped my way, her eyes narrowing as if she was trying to place me.

My mouth lifted in a sinister smile full of deadly promise. "You're in for a world of fucking hurt."

Recognition dawned, and her stare raked down my body before it climbed back up, slow and dripping with condescension. "Looks like you already found it."

My soot-and-blood-soaked. Kane's blood. My own. *Lisa's.*

I advanced a step. "You killed her."

The lift of her brow was a dose of unfeeling bitch with a side of absolute pride. Voice rising, she asked, "Killed whom?"

"Lisa."

She straightened. "That human friend of yours?" Because of course, she'd done her research. "The traitor to her species?"

"Says the woman who's executing a coup against her people."

She tsked. "So quick to judge." She cocked her head. "I recall you helping with this plan."

"Not willingly." Never goddamn willingly.

Her new people waited, their eyes darting between us and the horde of dead and dismembered bodies that littered the ground. Their hands trembled, the sharp and bitter stink of fear coating the air. It stung my airways, sang to my blood.

Fear was good. Fear might stay their hands. Make them reluctant to move, lest they draw our beastly eyes.

"Stand down, Morgana," Bower called.

She cut her eyes to the side. "It's General to you."

"I heard you lost that title," I said, goading her, because I needed her to show her hand. I needed to see what cards she was willing to play—and which she wasn't.

Her laugh was cutting and devoid of humor. "Indeed. And I've decided on an upgrade."

I arched a brow high. "Not sure deposing the government and seating yourself in its place counts."

"Only power counts, Briar." She shrugged. "And those who hold it."

Bower shook his head. "This isn't the way."

Her expression darkened. "Ithica has afforded Cambria too much control. We have allowed their trouble to seep across our borders. Allowed them to slaughter our kind at will. Allowed them to decide which of us deserve their help." She stabbed a hand toward her faction. "And *we* have decided it's time for change. To take that power and privilege into our own hands. Decisions needed to be made." She settled a palm over her chest. "So, I took the burden of making them."

Burden. Like she was some goddamn martyr.

I glared at her. "You woke a beast you should've left sleeping."

Her smile widened, baring teeth. "If I have my way, you'll be sleeping forever." Holding my gaze, she cupped her mouth, amplifying her words. "Your serums," she called. "TAKE THEM!"

Her humans brandished vials, then unstopped them.

I turned to stone.

They drank.

One by one, their bodies locked, the veins along their necks and faces straining against their skin. Eyes flashed; some mutated, roiling until their whites filled with red. It wasn't like the shadow walkers, where the blood they consumed tinged their eyes. It was more like their own blood had seeped through, staining them.

A woman plunged her hands into her hair and screeched. She doubled over, chest pumping rapidly as she gasped for air. The guy beside her roared, head thrown back, mouth hinging wide as his canines split and extended. His eyes turned an electric shade of indigo. There was a *crack, crack, crack* as his hands mangled to form claws, but not like those of our wolves. More like his bones had broken, the fragments tearing through his flesh to form jagged spears.

Iron fires, take me.

The night filled with a cacophony of shrieks and cries. Nausea twisted my throat, cresting along my tongue.

Theo crouched, arms wide as he set his position.

Serum-tinged eyes darted around, wide and wild. They shifted, restless and completely untethered. Their shrieks rang out, followed by snarls and howls.

Nothing happened for one breath. Two.

They attacked.

A roar boomed through the night. Deafening. Unmistakable. Kane.

His boned claws pierced the chest of one of Zahara's people. He lifted his arm, raising the man's writhing, pissing, and spitting body high before he struck out, heaving him away. My Alpha ran, vaulting himself onto a nearby missile launcher.

Those tainted weres descended on him. So many. Too many. Their screams rang out. A severed arm flew, followed by a head. They climbed Kane's back, tore at his arms.

Wraith take me. He couldn't hold them. *He couldn't hold them!*

"JOAQUIN!" I called.

His head snapped my way, those hazel eyes lighting the night.

I jabbed a hand toward my Alpha.

He slammed the pseudo-were he faced to the ground with a sickening thud, then made for Kane. But less than ten steps later, another horde of Zahara's weres descended. Theo moved in to help, biting and ripping and clawing his way through, until they consumed him too.

Cassandra tore one human-walker from her arm, then another from her neck. They climbed her. Two, then four, then eight. She dropped to her knees.

There were too many! Zahara would finish with us, then move on to Cambria. She'd destroy everything. Every*one*. I'd lose them all, my friends. My family. The only things that mattered.

A scream built in my chest. Gunfire sounded. Theirs or ours, I had no clue.

One of the blood-eyed humans exploded toward me. Saliva trailed from her parted mouth, slithering down her chin. She licked her lips, and a high, hissing, and dangerously guttural shriek peeled from her throat.

The Hunt. It was the Hunt. And I was unequivocally on the menu.

I kicked out, planting my foot in the center of her chest. She fell, landing on her back. Scrambling aside, she moved onto all fours, prowling toward me.

Obsidian, that movement, that disconnect in their eyes—it was like Ivy.

"Ivy," I murmured. Something sparked in the back of my mind. Something akin to hope, because if I was right … Ivy's power had been tethered to my stepfather's compulsion, to his control over everyone under his thrall. What if—sage—what-fucking-*if* it was the same for the genetic wolfy link Isaac had used from Naomi to forge Zahara's serums?

Cassandra drifted to my side. "Do what you must, Briar Stone." Her blackened eyes locked on the wannabe vamp. "I will take this one."

My gaze snapped around, seeking my Alpha. When I found him, my soul shattered.

He was down, one knee planted as seven of those tainted weres tore at him, claws ripping his chest and shoulders and sides. They came at him from all angles, impossible to stop.

No … not impossible.

"*Command them*," I told him across our wolfy bond.

Silence.

I prayed he was just too distracted to answer, 'cause the alternative wasn't an option. So I filled him in. "*Isaac used* Naomi *for the serums*." Killed her to steal her genes. To access her power. "*She was your wolf. In your Pack. Under* your *rule. She was tethered to you, Big Bad*." And if that was true …

Again, nothing.

More human-walkers climbed Cassandra. Two, then four, then eight. She dropped to her knees. My heart constricted, terror burning across my soul. "*Please, Kane. Please!*"

A roar filled the night. *His* roar.

"WOLVES!" My Alpha's power broke from him, knocking everyone back, before his brutal, guttural voice ordered, "ON YOUR FUCKING KNEES!"

Time stopped. I held my breath.

Every wolf—theirs and ours—tethered to Kane slammed to the ground.

Some of their faces and bodies strained as they fought that command, but therein lay the problem—for them, at least. They'd picked a power with which they could not contend.

Zahara's head whipped from side to side, her voice frantic. "What did you do?"

I advanced. "You wanted our power." I lifted a shoulder in a shrug. "Well, you get what comes with it."

My Alpha's chest heaved, arms hanging loose by his sides, his silvered stare raking those pseudo-wolves before it snapped to Cassandra, who snarled and clawed at Zahara's walkers. Kane, Joaquin, and the rest of our Cambrian weres closed in to help. Blood and bodies filled the night with that coppery scent. Theirs.

All. Fucking. Theirs.

Zahara staggered, her face contorting as her lips drew up in a snarl. She reached behind her, drew something from her back. A gun.

She aimed, then fired.

A pop sounded, trailed by a high *zzt* as something whizzed past my head. Another followed. Bower roared, shin snapping out from under him as he dropped, his leg a mangled mess.

A sharp sting jolted my arm, then my thigh. The bullets punched straight through. They burned, the pain searing, and I lost my footing and pitched backward. My vision flashed white. I cried out.

I'd been hit.

Black lines and blood trailed from the gaping wounds—wounds that were slow to close. Too slow.

"BRY!" Kane boomed.

Iron fires! I hissed, agony tearing me apart inside as I pushed myself to my feet. Unbidden tears seared the backs of my eyes. But I wouldn't quit. I *couldn't*!

I gripped my obsidian, called on Kane's power, drew back and charged. Zahara sidestepped, but not before my fist connected with her shoulder, knocking her off-balance. Her footing faltered. She stumbled. My momentum carried me forward, past her, so I turned, crying out as I twisted my torso and my elbow flew, colliding with the back of her head.

A strangled sound left her as she collapsed, the gun skittering away as her palms crashed against the asphalt.

Her eyes rolled in and out of focus, trying to track me as I moved. She blinked, then blinked again, before her attention lit on a body just steps away.

I followed her line of sight. A knife lay beside the body. An *iron* knife!

Gasping, she scrambled toward it. I ran, fumbling as I dove for it, but not in time.

Snapping up the knife, she whipped it my way and plunged it deep into my shoulder. I snarled, stumbling back several feet and falling on my ass. A searing pain shot across my veins, running through every corner of my body like liquid fire. Iron Hells, I could barely see past the agony. The world flashed white, fading in and out of focus. The scent of burnt flesh filled the air as my skin hissed and sizzled.

Weak, I reached for the knife, struggling to tear it free. Zahara crawled toward me, palm slamming over the butt of the hilt, shoving it deeper. Her fingers wrapped over mine. She twisted.

I thrashed, breaths short and shallow as the blade ripped and shredded me within. Blood poured from the gaping wound. Too much blood.

"BRY!" Kane snarled, throwing aside the vamp he was fighting. But another moved in.

"I'm glad your Lisa is dead," Zahara slurred, blood dripping from her lips where it spattered against my chest. "I hope you enjoy joining her." Her face contorted and she twisted the knife again.

My vision faded at the edges, along with my consciousness. I couldn't think. I needed to do something. Stop … someone.

"*Banshee!*" A familiar male's dread-tinged voice called from further away.

One I couldn't place.

Then a slender figure with black-lined eyes appeared in the distance. Terrifying and beautiful. Her white-blonde hair wisped on the air as she flew toward us, all grace and brutality.

My eyes narrowed. I knew that face. *How* did I know that face?

Cassandra. My friend. She was coming. But not fast enough.

My eyes closed, but I forced them open again. I couldn't give up. Didn't know why, but there was a reason. Something I needed to fight for. Or someone.

I coughed and gasped, then reached for the knife again. More blood filled my throat. I couldn't pull air. I was drowning. *Drowning*!

Something stirred in my lower abdomen. Something inside me. It was small, and helpless, and mine.

My baby.

My *baby*. A life more than my own. A life I needed to fight for.

But I couldn't do it alone.

I reached across our bond for my Alpha.

"*Take it, Bry!*" Kane ordered. "*Take everything you fucking need!*"

I stilled, my fist closing over my obsidian as I brushed our connection once. Then again. I dove in, latched on with everything I goddamn had, and pulled.

My Alpha stopped dead and collapsed to his knees, throwing back his head, his arms flaring wide as he roared.

A wave of power slammed into me. My spine bucked, limbs going rigid as the power seared through every corner of my body. My soul. A scream tore from my throat, one so raw and full of unimaginable strength, it was barely my own. The sound shrieked across the night as my palms slammed into Zahara's chest. Her weight vanished as she flew into the air.

My blood slowed, and I tore the dagger free. The black lines around my wound's edges receded until the flesh began stitching itself. I coughed, spitting up blood, and sucked in a breath.

But it wasn't enough, so I pulled another and another, each growing successively deeper until the burning in my lungs was sated.

The pound of heavy feet sounded, uneven and spent as Kane lumbered in. Sweat slicked his temples and brow, and his shoulders rose high with each breath. He brushed my hair back from my face, his stare voltaic as it took me in.

Zahara stood, thrashing in Cassandra's unaffected, one-handed grasp.

My gaze snapped to the Dowager's. "You didn't kill her?"

Her head drew back, a decidedly human gesture. "Oh, no, Briar Slade. I would never take such an honor."

That … *that* was why we were friends. Because she knew I needed that retribution. Knew I'd earned it.

I inclined my head. "I've got this."

The Dowager released Zahara with a shove.

Zahara took in the melee of bodies. Her people. Dead. All of them.

Her eyes flared, fear cresting for the briefest of moments before she schooled her expression. Righting herself, she straightened her hair, then angled her chin high as if she was fighting to hold onto a dignity that had long since gone. "You'll regret this."

Slowly, I rose, spine unfurling as I squared myself to her. Angling left, I kept my knees bent, stalking her like the predator I was—the one I'd become because of Isaac. Because of *her*. "No. I won't."

Kane edged in, Joaquin and their Packs following close behind. Cassandra and her shadow walkers glided around my other side, while Waylon and Bower's other soldiers closed out the circle at my back.

My Alpha's hand linked over his opposite wrist as he watched. Blood dripped from his jaw. His stare slid to mine. He inclined his head.

Zahara shrieked and charged. Lifting a leg, I kicked out, planting a foot in her stomach. She came up short, the air leaving her lungs in a rush. She collapsed onto her back. Hard. I dropped a knee to her chest. She jolted under me, head lolling back and forth while her gaze darted around as if she was looking for help, or escape.

But none would come.

My grip wrapped around her throat and locked tight, fingers digging into the flesh along her vertebrae there.

Her face turned red, then blue. Blood vessels broke in her eyes, turning them a macabre shade of slow-death perfection. She kicked and thrashed, her nails tearing through the flesh of my forearms and wrists. My skin was slick with blood and sweat, making it impossible for her to find purchase.

"Stop," a garbled voice called. The scuff of something dragging over the ground drew closer.

My gaze shot in the direction of the voice.

Bower hobbled forward, his back leg bloodied and dragging behind him as he advanced. His men parted to make way. He limped toward me, a makeshift tourniquet tied high on his thigh. "Don't kill her."

I hoped he was joking. He'd goddamn well better be, 'cause if he wasn't, his stupid, shuffling ass was next. I didn't give, holding firm as I snarled through viciously ground teeth, "*Why*?"

Her thrashing slowed. She radiated less power, just desperation and a pathetic will to survive.

"We need to make an example of her," Bower said.

Theo cocked a brow.

"I already am." Let everyone see what happened when they came for us, because Zahara had been right about one thing: it *was* better to be a weapon than to have one.

Her arms made the slow descent to her sides.

Bower moved closer, his hand landing heavily on my shoulder. "If one of *you* kills her, it gives credence to her claims."

Her claims about us. About our brutality. About how little we valued their human lives.

My Alpha cursed, then cursed again.

Joaquin's jaw worked as he edged forward. "He's right," he said, voice hard as if he hated every word. "Kill her, and she's a martyr."

The Ambassador nodded his head. "Don't give her that power, Briar. Spare her, and she *will* be punished." He drew back, an intensity in his voice. "Trust me. Please."

My chest heaved, pulse thrumming in my ears.

My gaze sought Kane's.

"I'm with you, Bry." He rolled his shoulders. "Whatever you decide."

Lisa deserved justice. But more than that, she deserved for her death to mean something. Because she meant something—meant *everything*—to me. If she had to die, then let that death change our worlds. She'd held me together, saved my heart and my soul more than once. If this was what it took to pay that back, I could do that.

For her.

It took every ounce of will I had to unfurl my begrudging fingers, the joints stiff and aching as they released. Zahara gasped, then coughed and sputtered as she struggled to move. Feeble and weak.

I shifted, then rose, towering over her as I glared down.

"Seize her," Bower ordered.

The soldiers descended, flipping Zahara onto her stomach as they bound her hands and feet, then lifted.

I stepped into their path. They stopped.

My fingers latched around her hair, and I forced her face to mine. "Someday, the wraith will call your name. When your time is up and she comes for *you*, her wings will beat in time with your final breaths. And that day will be your beginning. Because on *that* day, you will spend the rest of eternity begging for mercy. And I'll take solace in knowing that mercy will *never* find you.

"You will scream, and you will rot, and you will burn. And no one will come, because in the span of *this* world, you are nothing. You are forgotten. But in the span of theirs ..." I softened my expression and lowered my face to hers, my voice a lethal whisper as it caressed her cheek. "The blood you left in your wake will seep into the Deep. It will follow you down, and you'll drown in it for the rest of for-fucking-*ever*." I released her with a snap.

The soldiers straightened, then dragged her limp and pathetic form away.

Theo sauntered forward, breaking the flesh of his thumb with his canine and holding it Bower's way. "Open wide."

The Ambassador cringed but did as he was told.

My Alpha reached for me, his hand engulfing my own as he crushed it in his grasp. I leaned into him, giving him my weight.

Cassandra's tattered dress flapped in the wind as her cold shoulder grazed my own. "My, my, Briar Stone." Her head canted forward, those sculpted brows high as her crimson gaze settled on me and a proud smirk stole across her lips. "And you claim *I* am terrifying."

A sad, humorless laugh slipped from my chest, because there was still heart-rending work to be done. Ithica was safe in Bower's capable hands, and our own people still needed us. But before we left, there was something else I wanted—*needed*—to address. A boon to offer Ithica in the face of disaster. A gap to be bridged.

Rising to my full height, I scanned what remained of the primary power of the Conclave, 'cause I needed to strike while the resolution iron was still blood-stained and raw.

"The RC," I said, meeting each of their eyes. "I'd like to revisit the concept of eligibility. Figure a way to make the RC available to everyone." If the humans had gotten one thing, one grievance, right, it was that.

Cassandra's gaze roved the dead. "I would agree, Briar Slade."

Joaquin dipped his chin in a nod. "I'm with you, banshee."

My Alpha's mouth lifted at the corners. He looked proud as he inclined his head and pressed a kiss to my temple. "Always, Bry."

I turned to Bower. "Tell your people."

He winced as his bones crunched and knit. "They'll be glad to hear it," he said, words tight. He stepped back, clearing the way for us. "We can sort the details later. Go, help your people. We'll handle this."

"I'll send my wolves to collect Cambria's dead," Kane said. He extended a hand, and the two shook.

"They'll be ready."

Releasing the Ambassador, my Alpha reached for me. His grip locked over mine, a vice keeping me tethered, and I gripped back just as tightly.

"Briar," Bower called, as we began to move away.

I glanced back.

Straightening his shirt, he turned to me. "Thank you."

The return drive to Cambria was somber. Yes, we'd won, and that looming threat was finally gone—but we'd lost so, so much.

As my own device had been destroyed somewhere in the mayhem, I stole my Alpha's phone. My hands trembled, my chest constricting as I sent a message to my brother.

Me: *This is Briar. Tell me you're alive.*

I held my breath as I stared at the screen, waiting. The bubbles popped up, his reply immediate.

Lucas: *Hannah, me, Whitney, Ezra. We're all good. What about Kane? Theo? Joaquin?*

Tears seared my eyes, and I exhaled, ragged and free.

Me: *Alive.*

The deeper into the city center we moved, the more impassable things became. By the time we reached Cambria's neutral grounds, the hardest-hit region, the roads were pockmarked with holes, chunks of stone or wood, and shattered buildings. And bodies. So many bodies.

Dirt-covered magi, weres, and shadow walkers moved about in the darkness, eyes bloodshot, faces tear-streaked as they cleared the rubble and freed the dead.

So much loss, on all sides. We'd all suffered. We'd all paid a cost that could never be recovered. We all had healing to do.

Easing to a stop, slowly, we all climbed out of the truck. The scent of dust was heavy on the air, and the world around us was filled with the sounds of soft sobs, the scuff of feet, and the crunch of things being shifted.

Kane, Joaquin, Cassandra, Theo, and I stood shoulder-to-shoulder, watching our people as we took in the carnage.

Theo's attention raked the disaster. "What the hells do we do now?"

I inhaled deeply. "The only thing we can."

His eyes met mine in question.

Pulling back my hair, I bent down, grabbed a broken board, and set it aside. "We rebuild."

Epilogue

Three Years Later

I stood in the neutral grounds, people buzzing past, talking, laughing. The night sky was dark, the stars above bright. My fingers trailed over my moonstone necklace as I took in the towering bronze memorial. The one carved with name after name of our fallen—and, in honor of our allegiance with Ithica, the names of their fallen as well.

The years had passed, but not a day went by that I didn't think of Lisa. Or Mom, Naomi, Mason, Ivy—all of them. I'd shut it out for a long time, refusing to think. It still hurt, but gradually that hurt had transformed, becoming replaced by memories. Memories that brought smiles.

Things I'd never forget. Things I never wanted to.

The Blood War to replace Danika had been short; after all we'd lost, the shadow walkers had no taste for violence. Both she and Alistair had been replaced with tolerable options. And, as the only capable official left, Bower had taken over the government until things could be stabilized, after which he'd been formally elected. The non-Zahara-affiliated humans had been grateful for our help, and had come out in droves with everything short of torches and pitchforks for her sentencing—which, happily, was a life behind iron bars.

A revamped, open-border policy had followed, one we were still smoothing the kinks out of. But the tensions had faded.

Cambria had rebuilt, and new buildings stood in place of the old. But we'd kept to that natural look. Wood exteriors, lots of plants. It wasn't overgrown yet, not like it had been. But that would come.

My daughter, Naomi, held my hand, holding tight while she swished side to side in her pretty pink dress. The breeze caught on the shoulder-length strands of her vibrant silver hair, a gift from her daddy. But those cobalt eyes—those were all mine.

She tugged me as she stared back toward Immortal Inc. The shop had fared alright in the firefight. Well, it had stayed standing, which, compared to half the city center, was the best we could've asked for.

With No Man's Land an inherited property and Lisa the end of her family line, said land had been handed back to Cambria, and my Alpha and I had bought it, restoring it to its former glory. With Theo's wedding to Whitney approaching, we intended to gift it to the happy couple, 'cause no one could keep the spirit of that place alive, do it justice, like him.

I smiled down at my girl. "Come on, sweetheart."

She squealed, little legs pumping as she feebly dragged me toward the shop. Lampposts lined the road, lighting every face we passed. We climbed the steps, I pushed open the door, and my little wolf toddled forward as we crossed inside.

Ezra's tattoo gun buzzed, the sound filling the shop as he worked an intricate design along a male shadow walker's shoulder. Tucking his long hair behind an ear, he exposed the still-fresh bite from Joaquin's claiming mark.

Lucas sat at the next workstation, eyeing his work on a male were. He'd stopped shadowing Ezra the year before, going solo. His work was intricate to the point of damn near flawless, and he'd slowly become the most requested artist in the place.

He'd filled out more, his shoulders widening and arms thickening. Not Kane thick, but well on his way. Facial hair lined his squarer jaw, most of the youth having left his features. His head lifted, a smile splitting his face when he eyed little Naomi. "Hey, you."

She giggled, feet pitter-pattering as she fast-waddled his way. "Uncle Luke!" she squeaked, his name sounding more like "Wuke".

He ducked to the side, wrapping his free arm around her in a hug.

Our girl had a giant heart. Loved absolutely everyone she met. And I didn't know where the hells she'd gotten it, because her parents certainly didn't.

Lifting Nay to his knee, Lucas set aside the tattoo gun and took up his cloth, wiping down his work. To the were, he said, "What d'you think?"

There were still people who hated what he was, and in a way, I got it. Isaac's actions had left a jagged and lasting scar. Lucas being the one to plunge the dagger into his father's chest had helped, and most of Cambria now accepted him, but not all. Still, between me, my Alpha, Joaquin, and Cassandra, no one was the ten shades of stupid it'd take to do anything about it. There was enough power around him to keep trouble at bay for now.

The leather chair creaked as the twenty-something were stood, back to the full-length mirror on the wall, eyeing my brother's work. "Shit, bro. This is wicked."

"We'll finish the details and add some more color depth in your next session." Lucas's gaze was critical, his eyes narrowing at the corners as he scanned the lines. "Should only take one more sitting."

"Can't wait." The guy lifted his arms and flexed, admiring himself.

Theo sauntered out from the back office, a stack of receipts in one hand, a sandwich that'd sloughed crumbs all over his shirt in the other.

My brother started cleaning his area, and Naomi squiggled from his lap and beelined for Theo—or, more accurately, his meal. The girl was wolf to her core, a little handful always ready to run and play and eat. Sage, so much eating. Between her, Lucas, and my Alpha, it was a wonder we ever had food. And I loved her for it. Loved her for who and what she was, and for the holes in my soul she never even knew she'd filled.

"Please!" Naomi begged, tiny arms stretched skyward.

Theo grinned, hefted her onto the counter, broke off a corner of bread, and handed it over.

The office door stood wide, Kane a king in his chair as he sat behind the desk. Joaquin loomed over his shoulder as they looked at some drafted design schematics, marking things here and there as they spoke. My Alpha's stare lifted, his mouth tugging at the corner when those silver topaz eyes locked with mine. They flashed before he offered me a devastating wink.

My core clenched. I bit my lip.

I sauntered closer, propping a hip against the doorframe. "How're things going with the RC?"

The Conclave still oversaw the Recovery Center, but the accessibility and profit process had been restructured in every damn way. For the sake of transparency, we'd opted to forgo separate wings and labs. Services still came at a cost, but that cost was calculated based on a percentage of the patient's income, which opened the door to all humans and leveled the playing field on pricing. Ten per cent hit everyone the same, but those who made more, paid more.

Making the RC available to more people had meant seeing more patients, which in turn meant more jobs. Hence the extension the weres had volunteered to oversee for the emergency ward.

"Good." Joaquin inclined his head. "Should break ground next week."

That *was* good. Real damn good.

"Theo will take your payment," my brother told his client, who headed that way.

The front entrance swung open as Hannah sauntered in, and the way my brother's face transformed … a bizarre mix of eagerness and calm filled the grin that he wore.

"Did you get them?" he asked her.

She beamed, smile broad, and she wiggled her toes. There was a clank as she brandished a set of shiny silver keys. "Got 'em!"

He clapped, the sound making my ears ring. He closed in on Hannah, fast, arm snapping around her waist as he scooped her off her feet—feet that dangled and kicked as she laughed and buried her face against his cheek.

They'd been scoping apartments for a while. Kane and I had offered them cash for a home. To build something, buy it, whatever they needed—but Lucas's *no* had been swift and hard. He wanted to make his own life. Earn it the way my Alpha and I had earned ours. And there was so much pride in Kane's eyes when he heard that response, because it told us we'd done our jobs. We'd taught my brother to stand on his own two feet, to *make* his way in this world, instead of taking it.

"Which one was it?" I asked.

Lucas set Hannah to the floor and draped an arm lazily around her shoulders.

Her fingers traced a slow line over his abdomen, that pretty smile just for him. "Our top pick."

Theo handed another corner of sandwich to Nay and loosed a low whistle. "That was a sweet place."

They'd been squirreling away savings for months to have a deposit and some "just in case" cash. They'd had their eye on a specific sector of the newly rebuilt neutral grounds. It might not have been far in distance, but it hadn't stopped my selfish ass from pouting about it. I'd kept my mouth good and closed around them, though, partially because my Alpha had made me, but mostly *for* Lucas. He'd faced enough for a thousand lifetimes. He'd had too much happiness stolen. He'd earned as much as he could get.

But alone with Kane, my tears had come, because Lucas leaving was bittersweet. Between him and little Naomi, the house was so loud and full of life. She would miss him, though she'd been appeased when he and Hannah had promised lots of sleepovers. It'd take time to adjust, but my brother wouldn't be far.

I smiled to myself, since it wasn't like the house would be empty for long.

Shift done for the night, Lucas grabbed his coat. "Let's go see it, then."

Hannah beamed, a small blush staining her cheeks. To me, she said, "We'd like to have everyone over next week for dinner."

I smiled. "We'd love that."

The two grinned, said their goodbyes, and left.

Theo set his sandwich aside as he printed off a receipt for the were. Naomi's little eyes darted toward it, followed by her hand as she grabbed the sandwich and took a decidedly big bite.

I turned away to hide my laugh.

My Alpha rose from the desk, and he and Joaquin sauntered out, the latter's eyes blazing as they landed on Ezra. When Naomi spotted her daddy, her little arms reached out for him. He plucked her off the counter, nuzzling his jaw across her cheek. She giggled, ducking her head as if it tickled.

"How're my girls?" his deep voice rumbled.

My hand flicked Naomi's way and I smirked. "Our little beastie is trouble."

His stare fixed on mine. "Just like her momma."

I shimmied my shoulders and grinned, all pride and teeth. Because having a miniature ally with whom to rankle my Alpha was the best kind of fun.

Headlights tracked through the room as Cassandra's vehicle pulled up. Lucas's freshly tattooed were loped out as she glided in, a big, pink-wrapped gift in hand. Gifts. So many gifts. She brought one every time she showed up.

I snorted and shook my head. "You don't need to do that, you know."

The Dowager waved me off with a flick of her delicate wrist. "You have said this before, Briar Slade."

"Yeah, Briar," Theo called. "She doesn't care."

I rolled my eyes.

"Cassy!" Naomi squealed.

Cassandra waved, her long-limbed fingers moving in a graceful but decidedly inhuman way.

Theo closed in and clapped the Dowager on the shoulder. "You'll get the hang of it."

Her gaze dropped slowly to his hand. Lowering his arm, Theo rocked on his heels, looking anywhere but at her.

Kane set down Naomi, those chubby legs kicking fast as she aimed for Cassandra with outstretched hands. Seeing as we'd raised her around every manner of Cambrian beastie, I wasn't sure if our girl's survival instincts were really on point, but it didn't matter. Those beasties loved her like their own. They'd kill for her. Die for her. Maim a bitch as an example. Whatever it took.

Naomi smiled so widely, her little eyes crinkled. "For me?"

"For you," Cassandra replied, passing the gift over.

"Naomi," I chided. "What do you say?"

She ducked her head, that squeaky voice tickling my heart as she said, "Thank you, Aunt Cassy."

My girl tore into the box with her nubby little fingers. Popping the lid, she pulled out … something. Cassandra turned so Naomi was hidden from sight, and the two whispered together for a second.

Kane angled his head away and barked a laugh.

Turning back, Cassandra peeled her lips back from her teeth, instructing Naomi as she said, "Just like this, little one."

Naomi mimicked her, those cobalt eyes twinkling so proud and bright as she bared a plastic set of fake shadow-walker fangs, incisors extending down her chin.

The cackle that broke from me had me keeling over. I laughed so hard, tears blurred my vision, and I gasped for air. Grabbing my phone, I snapped a picture. Iron fires, so many pictures. My girl made up my entire camera roll. Naomi giggling. Naomi on Daddy's shoulders. Naomi on Lucas's lap. Naomi pulling Theo's hair. Naomi howling at the moon.

I offered Cassandra a shake of my head. "You're too much."

"The child wanted to become a shadow walker. What else was I to do?" she countered, as if there was legitimately no other choice.

The weres in the room froze.

I arched a brow. "You're aware saying no is an option."

"You must bite your tongue, Briar Slade." She tapped Nay's fake teethies with the tip of her nail, making Naomi happy-squeak. "Saying no is your job. But I am the fun Aunt Cassandra."

Would I have put Cassandra and fun in the same universe before things had gone down? Hard no. But just like the rest of us, she'd changed. Her bite was not so sharp. She still had it in her, but every day she spent with us was another day her humanity crept closer to her six-hundred-year-old surface. She seemed younger. And I swore to the wraith, that translucent edge to her skin had waned.

Naomi darted across the room, heading for Theo. Latching onto his leg, she sank those plastic chompers into his shin. Theo threw his head back and yipped, then pretended to hobble away, dragging her across the floor with him.

A chorus of giggles ensued, and my heart melted.

I snickered and said across our bond, "*And here you thought your cousin would be the bad influence.*"

My Alpha huffed a laugh.

"Come on, sweetheart," I called to Naomi. "Time to go." Detaching herself from Theo, she scurried our way. Cassandra and I each took a hand, then led Nay outside.

"What do you two have planned?" I asked, heading for the Dowager's SUV: a new-fangled one she'd bought specifically for the safety rating, because having Naomi in anything less simply "would not suffice".

"We are hunting shadow walkers."

I was certain she meant it as play. Almost certain. Kind of.

She settled my girl into the car seat and started fastening her in. It was such a mundane task, but it suited her, and I loved it. Seeing little Naomi so comfortable and completely fearless when she was surrounded by so many baddies showed me that she really was her mother's daughter.

The Dowager's crimson stare flitted my way. "Have you told your wolf yet?"

I smirked, throwing a cocoon over our conversation as my gaze dropped to my stomach. "Caught that, did you?"

Cassandra smiled.

Worrying at my lip, I glanced back to the shop, then again to her. "Can you tell what it is?"

Her smile widened, incisors gleaming in silvered moonlight. "I can. Would you wish to know?"

I bobbed my head, rapid-fire.

"There are two."

My eyes snapped wide as I sucked in a sharp breath. "You take that back!"

Her tinkling laugh carried through the night. "And you will have sons."

"Shadow and sage." My palm settled over my newly forming belly. One with *two* little wolves inside. Boys. So many boys. Little Nay and I would be outnumbered, but we'd manage. Happily.

Reaching into the truck, I pulled out Naomi's pack with all her clothes and handed it over. Not that she needed them; Cassandra had stocked up on supplies of her own. Had literally given the kid her own room. She'd wanted to do more, but I'd put my foot down at the mention of an *entire wing*. There was a fine line between being spoiled and acting it, and a toddler with real estate was a hard line for this momma. Cassandra had relented, but insisted we "revisit the issue in the future".

Kane stepped out, our own bags in hand, black shirt fitting his broad chest and shoulders, showing off the dense muscle below. His sleeves were rolled up his forearms, those low-slung jeans framing his powerful thighs as he moved.

We were headed to Ithica, to that mountainside resort I'd eyed in Lisa's screenshotted articles so long ago. We'd visited a handful of times since, but this would be the first alone. Thermal waters, forest, privacy. It was a dream. My peace. And being there together with him …

"*Keep looking at me like that and I'm gonna do something about it,*" he said over our bond.

Heat pooled between my thighs. "*I certainly hope so.*"

A low, rumbling growl thundered from the deepest recesses of his chest, igniting my heat to fire.

Stepping in, he set a kiss to Naomi's little temple. "You be a good girl for Aunt Cassy, alright?"

Her little fingers twisted in his hair, and she nuzzled his cheek. "Okay, Daddy."

His Adam's apple dipped like he was having trouble letting go—because, of course, he was. He was Kane Slade, and that wolf loved fiercely, with everything he had. And walking away, even for just a few days, was wont to tear at his heart.

He pressed another kiss to her temple, straightened, then cleared his throat, and moved back.

I fought the misting of my eyes as I turned to little Nay. "We'll be home in three days, okay, sweetheart?"

"Okay, Momma," she said, that little lip wobbling.

My chest near cleaved in two. I hesitated.

Cassandra set a palm on my shoulder. "I love you, Briar Slade, but if you are about to change your mind and take this child from me, I will reconsider that sentiment." Her fingers flexed against me. "And start a war."

I hiccupped a sob, then snorted. "I wouldn't dare." Pressing a kiss to Naomi's soft cheek, I turned away, because if my girl saw my tears, it'd only feed her own. "Love you, baby."

"Lah you too, Momma."

I pressed a kiss to the Dowager's cheek too. "Thank you, Cassandra."

"You need not thank me. Time with your precious creature is enough."

"Call me if you need anything."

"I will." At that, she climbed into the vehicle and clicked play on some upbeat kids' song that carried through the open windows. Naomi's high voice sang along, her words out of time and not matching the lyrics at all, but it was as adorable as adorable got—only getting better when Cassandra bobbed her head and sang along too.

The wheels crunched over the asphalt as she steered them away, my little girl's laughter carrying across the night as they left.

Kane's hand landed over the small of my back. "You ready?"

I inclined my head.

That touch slid to my ass as he popped open the passenger-side door. Taking my waist, he lifted, then set me onto the seat. I scooched to the middle and the truck dipped under his weight as he climbed in on the driver's side.

It was so quiet, just the two of us. And while it might've been needed, I already missed our girl.

Kane shifted into gear, then took us outta there, aiming for Ithica. His hand sealed over my bare thigh, then tracked higher, and higher. He kneaded my flesh, eager.

When we reached the border, the lone guard eyed us with a smile, then waved us through, her presence more for posterity than protection. We aimed for the lake district at the base of the human side of the Cortez Mountain range, and pulled up to the two-story cabin.

Logs lined the exterior, a massive wrap-around porch decorating the perimeter. Windows filled the front, all peaks and apex shapes that faced the water, which was glacial, its aqua shade still vibrant under that silvered moon.

It was perfect. No preternatural ears to hide from. Just the quiet, and us.

"I love this place."

He slid the truck into park. "I'm glad, 'cause it's ours now."

My head snapped his way. "*What?*"

A wolfish grin took him. "I talked to Bower. Got it sorted. Only one more document to sign, but"—he pulled the keys from his pocket—"it's ours."

He'd bought it, for me. This was big, for so many reasons. The first Cambrian landowners in Ithica. Our own getaway.

Like the greedy minx I was, I snatched the keys from his grasp and scrambled out, tearing up the steps and through the front door. I bounced on my toes, happy-clapping as I spun in a circle, then clambered up the stairs to the loft and the overlook. The place was open-concept, with barn-board walls, a stone kitchen and fireplace, plush, brown, and ivory-toned furniture, and bronze fixtures. It was a cottage dream.

And it was ours.

Kane edged in behind me, his heat grazing my flesh. Those rough hands landed on my hips, then snaked forward, crushing me to his chest. His cock hardened, digging deliciously into my back. "Your scent's faded, Bry."

"And whose fault is that?" I half-turned, peering at him over my shoulder.

He frowned. "I can't say no."

No, he couldn't say no to Naomi sneaking into bed with us, because Cassandra wasn't the only one Nay had wrapped around her itty-bitty finger. And with every fiber of my withered soul, I loved my big bad being so powerless against the tiny creature we'd made.

I bit my lip, hiding my smile as I set my head against him. "You know the Ithicans can't scent me, right?"

His stare turned molten as he eyed me. "*I* can scent you," he growled. Not angrily. But with that ravenous hunger that never waned.

Years, he'd loved me. Years, I'd been his. And it was never enough. He always wanted me. Wanted more. Needed it. And so did I.

My voice lowered, my tone sultry as I pushed my ass into him. "Then stop talking and do something about it."

"Careful what you wish for." He charged us toward the railing. His knee drove between my thighs, pinning me there, one thick knuckle tracking up and up and up until it grazed the thin, vibrantly pink lace of my thong. Twisting it in his grasp, he tore.

I jolted, my core tightening. "You don't like my clothes?"

"I like them better on the floor. In fucking pieces."

Angling my head, I nudged his cheek with my nose. "Maybe I just shouldn't wear any, then."

His jaw was set, teeth clenched tight. "As long as I'm the only one who sees." Grabbing my dress at the hem, he jerked it over my head and tossed it aside before his mouth crashed with mine. He grunted, one hand in my hair as his tongue dove deep into my mouth. Taking my palms, he set them over the railing. "Hold tight, Bry."

I did, body heating as I waited. And waited. And waited. I eyed him over my shoulder, a scowl crossing my face.

His stare raked up my legs, then held on my ass. "Just enjoying the view."

I pressed back against him.

He huffed out a heated laugh. "So impatient." Setting his shaft against me, he glided it up and down my slit.

I moaned.

He sank deep, driving himself to the hilt. I sucked in a sharp hiss. His shaft filled me to completion, hitting every ravenous nerve as he pushed, then retreated. Pushed, then retreated.

Kane groaned. "You look so fucking good when you take me like this."

I whimpered, desperate for his praise. For his touch. For his release—and mine. We were a match. Push and pull. Bite and lick. Taste and torture.

He rocked again, driving harder and harder. "Fuck," he snarled, then pulled out with a snap. "I wanna watch my wife's face when she comes." Moving preternaturally fast, he spun me, then lifted, setting my backside onto the railing.

I opened for him, and he pushed his slick shaft inside me again.

My head fell back, my mouth open as I gasped for breath. His palm connected with my ass and a crack echoed across the cabin.

I cried out, core clenching. "Oh, sage. More," I begged. Pleaded. Desperate.

His smirk was cocky and proud and filled with sheer wolfish greed as he drew back and smacked again.

I jolted, bucking into him, head falling back as my hair skimmed my spine.

He kneaded that sensitive flesh. "Eyes on me, Bry."

My gaze locked with his. The charge between us sparked, wild and electric and hot. So damn hot. It scorched my soul, burning every part of me it touched.

His hips rocked, going harder and harder.

"Come for me," he ordered.

Power of obsidian. The command and control would never get old. I needed his push, just the same as he needed mine. We gave what we needed. Strong, unyielding, and unbreakable; world-ending love.

My body was his to use, to command. And, iron fires take me, when that orgasm hit, it exploded through me, chasing across my riotous nerves. My soul. My legs locked around him, heels driving into his back, urging him deeper, faster. His cock worked my g-spot as he ground over my clit.

My Alpha came hard, his stare intense as he growled my name through his teeth. He thrust over and over as he spilled inside of me. He slowed, and slowed some more, until he stopped altogether.

I purred and collapsed forward, giving him my weight. His hold banded around me, and he kissed my temple, chin settling over my hair as we caught our breath.

"Mmm," I purred, palms grazing his muscular ass before I gave it an appreciative pat. "Good work, Big Bad."

He huffed a rough, sated laugh.

"Does my scent earn your approval now?"

"It's getting there." He hefted me up, carried me to the large, plush, patio-style lounge chair and settled me back against its pillows. Ranging over me, he hovered in place, taking me in. "You're mine, Bry."

Every day, he said it. And never, not once, did it not land. My fingers and toes tingled, that warm, safe, wanted, and content feeling enveloping me.

"I'm yours, Kane." I trailed my touch along the rough stubble of his jaw, then shoved my extra-blingy wedding ring in his deliciously sexy face. "*Forever*!"

He sucked that finger into his mouth, his tongue doing dangerous things that felt more like a promise before he released it, dropped to his back, and took me with him.

My laugh was smooth and sultry as velvet. I wriggled closer, and his arm cinched around my sides, pinning me to him.

We stared out over the upper balcony as that glacial cerulean water lapped against the shore. The moon stood high and full, its reflection rippling and rolling over the waves. The air hung thick with his musk and wilderness scent and, well, our sex.

I sighed long and heavy. "I'm happy, Kane." So damn happy, and light, and free. We'd lost so much, but we'd come through the other side stronger, and we'd gained *everything* in return.

"Fuck, Bry." His hold locked around me as he pressed a kiss to my lips. "That's all I want. You, little Nay, Luke—you're it for me."

I bit my lip, trying to control the anticipation, because an opening had just presented itself. One I intended to use. "That's *all* you want?"

He drew back to better see me. His stare narrowed, reading between the lines. "You want another one?" He nipped the corner of my jaw, then raked those teeth along my mark.

Arching my spine, I pressed into him again. Closer still. I could never be close enough.

"'Cause I'll give you whatever you want." Those teeth sank deeper. His cock dug into my side. "Any-fucking-thing."

"Is that so?" My brows arced high, smile spreading wide, like a thief stealing across my lips. Iron fires, I loved him. How I'd been so lucky to stumble across his path, I'd never know. But I wasn't about to question it. He was mine, and I was his, and we'd either find our way through this world, or we'd make one … and drag everyone we loved along with us.

Taking that warm, calloused hand, I skimmed it down my collarbone, over my breast and the curve of my waist, to the flat of my stomach, then pressed it over my lower abdomen.

"Well, I might have something to tell you."

The End.

Acknowledgments

As ever, thank you to my husband for supporting me when I slither into my writing cave. For listening to all of my rantings. For believing in me. And for throwing me snacks when I require sustenance and love.

To my parents for never missing an opportunity to tell me you're proud.

To my brother and my sister-in-law for your encouragement and support.

Thank you to my critique partners, Keri, May, Tara, Regina, Justena and Kim. Your insights are invaluable, and your support priceless. I'm so lucky to have such an amazing group of women in my corner.

Thank you to my editor Molly Powell, and my team at Hodderscape, from the spectacular cover designers to the marketing group and everyone in-between, with special mention to Marina and Dominique for all you do. Thank you all for riding this journey with me. Thank you for your eyes, your expertise and your help in making these beautiful books what they are and bringing them to life in a way I could have only ever dreamed.

Thank you to my agent, Helen Lane for believing in me and my stories, for being my sounding board and support. For our shared incessant texts and jokes and laughter and love. Thank you for being a friend.

And finally, to my readers. Briar and Kane's story has occupied my whole heart since I first started dreaming of their world, and I'm so glad I got to share all their angst and pain and love with you. This journey would be nothing without you and your love for these characters. From the bottom of my heart, thank you.

About the author

K.C. Harper grew up on Canada's east coast and spends her time plotting to destroy the happiness of her characters. She's an avid reader, developmental editor, and a full-time human servant to a 4.5 lb teacup chihuahua.

WANT MORE HODDERSCAPE?

JOIN US!

Sign up to our mailing list to get exclusive early sneak peeks and offers:

Follow us on our social channels:

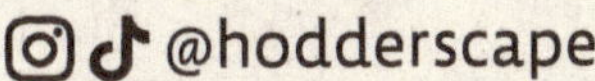

Buy our books, find out more, and discover exclusive content:

www.hodderscape.co.uk